I0672172

Cassavora County

William Stroud

Waldport Press

2
Library of Congress Cataloging-in-Publication Data

Stroud, William Cassavora County / William Stroud p. ;
cm. ISBN-13: 978-0-9820534-1-6 (pbk.: alk. paper) ISBN-10: 0-
9820534-1-X 1. Fiction. 2. Xenophobia. 3. Prejudice. 4. Politics.
5. Humor

Printed and bound in the United States of America

The publisher's policy is to use permanent paper from mills that
operate sustainable forestry policy, and which has been
manufactured from pulp processed using acid free and
elementary chlorine-free practices. Furthermore, the publisher
ensures that the text paper and cover board used have met
acceptable environmental accreditation standards.

For further information on Waldport Press, visit our website:
www.waldportpress.com

Acknowledgements:

A writer never works in a vacuum. And just when the plot and characters are well blended and seem to be coming together, a sudden impulse hits you that all is not well. It's then that you turn to others who are able to stand back and be more objective about your newborn. I imposed on family and friends liberally, to discuss my raw ideas and help me carve them into something imaginative and entertaining. I thank the following people who put up with my pleas to read through rough material and who took the time to offer valuable insights and comments. Ed Rasimus, himself a highly decorated fighter pilot and fine author, read an early copy and urged me to turn the dogs loose. Avril Nero also read the roughest of drafts and provided valuable comments in far reaching areas. Peter Wodarz and Daniel Broudy edited the book and in the nicest of ways held up a literary mirror and let me judge for myself. Bonnie Halle listened to my never-ending babble, read the book, and offered so many helpful insights into the makeup of the characters. Every step of the way, day and night, my wife, Jan, read and corrected and read more carefully than I ever could. With everyone's help the result is a much stronger and coherent story. Without everyone's help, this novel would still be only a flurry of tattered tales.

It may start with duty and love of country, but when bullets streak past your canopy and bombs shred the jungle, it's only you and your buddies that matter. —Jake Morgan, from his unpublished Vietnam novel

Jake lay sprawled across his rumpled bed, a Roman emperor, both eyes glued to the ever-fascinating spectacle of a woman sliding catlike into her clothes. Long legs, cupcake breasts and nipples as hard as burnt rubies sent chills down his belly.

His clothes lay carelessly clumped across the Turkish carpet. Spots of morning sunlight speckled the floor.

He flexed his arms, stretched, focused on the way her body willowed, the curve of her back. So slim, so quietly gentled. Looks deceived.

Cecilia tugged up a slim gray wool skirt, tucked in the white silk blouse, shot him a strong, white-toothed smile, a lock of dark hair blocking out one brown, almond-shaped eye. "I should be back this way soon. I've got your number." She winked. The blood surged. It was a little joke between them. Would she come back? Would he welcome her back? She did. He did. Just a little spark and crackle. Strings of attachment seemed to be twining into rope.

He pictured the hang of her breasts when she rode him, her soft lips melting on his skin, the incredible way she warmed his core.

Cecilia peeled the taupe hose off the back of the chair, toes gracefully narrow, tipped politely red, feet slim and smooth. Pretty toes. One foot stepped into a stocking. Her hands slid up her leg, slowly enough to make an angel wet his gown. Then she smiled again and fastened a garter. No panty hose. Not ever. Cecilia had broken the code. Convenience and lust are blood enemies.

"If your heart is set on jumping into the school board mess, I'll help." She used her modulated, anything-is-possible, evocative PR voice, melting Jake's ears. She could have whispered, "Laundromat" and he'd have set a blood pressure record for his age group.

Everything about her face, her body, her voice dug deep into him, slammed his mind shut to anything but her, made him a voyeur and seducer, a gentleman and rogue, turned him to liquid fire. His whole body stiffened as Cecilia did a two-step stroll that'd have Dracula kicking a hole in his coffin. She picked up her high heels.

"You Chinese are so clever." Jake put his hands behind his head, watched her slide her feet in.

She wagged a finger at him, acknowledging the cliché. "I could talk to the Senator, maybe get you some print coverage, get him to mention your name." Her calves flexed, the stocking shimmered.

"I like it better when you talk dirty." She ignored the comment.

"Running for a backwoods board of education? This county's medieval. All lords and serfs." Her eyebrows arched, "What makes you think you could pull it off, or want to?"

"Don't say anything to anyone," he sighed. They'd wasted precious minutes on the stupid, political discussion last night. They should have stuck to lips and tongues in private places. But, women like Cecilia were apostles of power. More than that, she used her share of it like a scalpel in the hands of a surgeon. Asking her to help would settle the question. She'd dial the right numbers and get things done. He wasn't ready.

At their first wonderful meeting, he'd mentioned he was an unpublished writer. She read his stuff, gobbled it down, soaked it in. A couple of magazine editors asked to see his work. Cecilia could make a rat stick its head in a trap with a smile on its face.

"You might want to think about replacing those curtains." She nodded in the direction of the single window.

"Fornicate the curtains."

"Is that 'man talk' for 'I've got my mind on something else'? Something lighter, less obtrusive." She smiled, blinked seductively.

Nothing wrong with her feminine instincts. "I'm planning a full frontal assault."

She stepped toward him in a sway-hipped glide. "You're not going to make me do those dirty things nobody else would let you do?" She thrust out a hip, gave a little-girl pout and Jake's blood pressure redlined.

"Yeah, those." He pulled her on top of him, then rolled over her. She was so light, so pliable. "Allow me to demonstrate."

"Don't hurt me!"

"Don't worry. I'm old and weak."

"You've never been weak in your life," she laughed.

"But you're going to wrinkle me."

"I'll straighten out the wrinkles. I'll spank the bottom.
I'll make you beg." Her hands were warm silk, her breath a
spring breeze.

She licked his ear lobe and whispered to him. Her breath
was coming faster. He ran his hand slowly up her thigh and
slipped a finger under the leg band of her panties, feeling her
gasp. She was already wet and the thought intoxicated him,
knowing she'd been waiting for him to use her again.

Afterwards, they lay entwined, sated for the moment, the
only inhabitants of dreams and clouds.

"Do you ever miss me?" It was a simple, yet complex
question.

"Yeah."

"I don't mean just the sex?"

"There's more?" She smiled into his neck, slapped his
arm in mock anger, and pulled him closer, her head sliding to
nestle in the crevice of his arm and chest.

It was a nice thing, he and Cecilia. A man had his needs
and so did she. They fit together when they were together.
Lately they'd been fitting together a lot. Much safer than love.
Call it love on a diet. He didn't pine away when she was out of
his life, but he thought about her. Even that surprised him.
Somehow, with Cecilia he'd avoided the usual entanglements, or
maybe she had. Or, maybe loved had smiled and they were
blind.

She'd been working PR for a big Veteran's Day bash, when they met. Not here. Not in Cassavora. The city did things a cash-skinny county couldn't afford. One was a full Veteran's Day slate, with parades, speeches and a party that lasted. Not a bad way for the mayor to make a strong political statement and not a bad way for Cecilia's Senator to tag along. She called it mutual political masturbation.

Jake meandered through the crowd, sheathed in billows of roasting meat, clutching a cup of beer. Cecilia brushed past him between the barbecue pits, giving him a nod and a busy smile, with a deprecating glance at the Hawaiian shirt. She was taller than he would have expected, dark haired, gorgeous and sauntered in the lithe way patented by Asian women. The dress was impeccable, the backless heels a nice fashion counterpoint at a pork eatin', beer swillin' barbecue.

"Maybe you can help me," he'd said.

"With what?"

"I was thinking of cheating on my wife." She gave him the 'must have lost your mind' stare.

"You know me?"

"Cute Chinese chick?" He framed it with his most charming smile.

"Actually, I'm American, Chinese-American."

"Actually, it's my ex-wife."

Against all odds and her better judgment, she found him later, told him she had the weekend off and to wear something more conservative. It hadn't been the love fest he'd planned. She took him to an art gallery. He bought her a crisp, two-olive martini. They ate Italian in a little place he'd never heard of, refreshing his memories of Venice.

Now they met when they could, when she was in town, sometimes out of town. He never asked if she were married. He thought about it.

It wasn't a fling, anymore than tea at the Ritz was fast food. She wore wedge heeled house slippers and Katherine Hepburn silk pajamas, with a body the young Katherine would have killed to have. Victoria's Secret goes to the Ritz. Espresso with amaretto and a twist.

"You know something you never told me?" Cecilia was fully dressed, one hand on the bedroom doorknob.

"I tell you everything."

"Why your wife left?"

"She wanted new curtains. I threw her ass out." He flopped his head on the pillow when the door lightly closed. Silence filled the vacuum. Story of his life. Career behind him. War behind him. Marriage behind him. He let the silence echo, ran a hand through his graying hair. The fabric of his life hung loose and thin. Not the way he liked it. He reached down, patted his gut, and wondered if his old flight suit would still fit.

Cecilia was the young, Ivy League bookmark in the middle of his middle age. Beautiful, smart, sexy. Could he say inscrutable without being stereotypical? Who gave a shit? He covered a yawn, then rolled to capture the sensual floral fragrance of her pillow.

He rolled again and his feet found the floor. The tight weave Turkish rug felt good. His gut tightened. He breathed deep, sighed, ambled toward the kitchen. Writing went best with sex and beer.

Bits of a fighter pilot's doggerel floated past. He sang softly, "Mary Ann Burns was the queen of all the acrobats. She could do tricks that would give a man the shits."

Dishes rattled, steam hissed. He poured coffee from a French press into a handmade pottery cup and clicked on the local radio talk show. "What this school system needs is ---" Everyone wanted changes. Nobody wanted to change. Everyone who'd been to school was an authority, even some who hadn't.

Cecilia salivated when he'd mentioned he might run for the Board of Education. Still, he wished he hadn't brought it up.

He snapped off the radio, his mind still tuned to the sway of her hips. The coffee wasn't the eye-snapping dream killer he'd hoped for. A touch of the mouse blinked his Macintosh open.

The first four emails got the D bomb. A last lonely e-mail stared back. From his ex. "Jake, we still have a few financial details to discuss."

Five years after the divorce and Jill still pinched. She'd leave him eating dog food in an attic. Discuss? Fuck her. Another D bomb.

He opened the folder, Second Novel and jumped back to the 18th Century. Lord Rip Tide and Lady Harriet battled alone on the open, wind blown sea. Somehow, he'd get his heroes safely to the shores of Harriet's lost ancestral estates, no easy feat from the wrong side of the Atlantic.

His first novel, a symphony of his year in Vietnam lay in limbo. Too violent, whined one agent. Too placid, harped another. Rejections bulged his lower desk drawer, hidden like ugly sheep at a redneck orgy.

The second novel had been Cecilia's idea. "Forget about axe grinding and get back to story telling," she'd suggested.

"Vietnam is the only story I know."

"So, you think those other writers were born in the eighteenth century? Pull your life apart and use the parts that fit. It's better than reliving the darkest days. Who knows? Publishers need a lot of manuscripts for the romance crowd. Besides, it'd be fun."

He'd told her to mind her own business and waited to start until she left. She'd been right. It was fun to let his sense of freedom flow across the pages and engage his latent passion for history.

The cell phone rang. "Have you gotten over me yet?" Cecilia purred.

"I get into you, but I never get over you."

"Good answer, fighter pilot man. Now the million dollar question."

"I don't have any diseases."

"A political question."

"I never had sex with that woman."

"From somebody who needs to know."

"Want to be more specific?"

"No."

Jake pictured her breezing on the expressway, cell phone pressed to her ear, dark hair blowing in the wind, politicos hanging on every lusty word. "I told you I haven't decided. But, if I do run, it's just for fun."

"I'll be the first, right? And, by the way, nobody in the history of the world ever got into politics for fun."

"You wanna be the first? Little late for that."

He heard her laugh. "I want to be the first." There was a pause.

"You'll be the first." Christ, she was a bulldog. Maybe she'd sneak in, cart his furniture off to Goodwill, and install new curtains.

"Cecilia?"

"Yes?"

"You studied the whole history of the world?" Politics. Women.

The problem was, Jake didn't know what he wanted. Things usually worked out if you knew. But he wasn't going to bust his brain about it this morning.

A few minutes earlier, across the street, as Cecilia turned the key in the ignition, Thelma Norton clutched her faded pink and white flowered robe and waddled down her concrete driveway. A slight breeze caught the gray, thin strands of her sleep-matted hair. The morning paper, neatly rolled, rested gently near her mailbox. The mailbox hung precariously off its post, a side caved in.

As she adjusted her wire-frame glasses, a bright blue convertible pulled out of Mr. Morgan's driveway. Mr. Morgan didn't own a bright blue convertible and the young, Asian woman with a phone to her ear wasn't Mr. Morgan's wife. The corner of Thelma's mouth twitched. She blinked twice and clicked her tongue, a muted indication of a shallow boat hitting some rocks in the stream.

A woman wasn't coming out of Mr. Morgan's driveway this time of the morning because he'd invited her for coffee and grits. Thelma pursed her dry, colorless lips. She knew what those kinds of women were like. They didn't speak any more English than the Mexicans. Men who should have known better had brought their little Jezebels to this county forty years ago, and the good people of this county chased them off. This was a Christian county, not a place for a bunch of little slant-eyed bar girls who didn't even know how to speak English.

Rumors greased a county's thriller instinct, the dirtier the better, with suspicion of fucking being the most popular. Thelma's dialing finger itched.

2

There's a lot goes on in this county I don't know about. Frankly, I don't care. Behind closed doors is one thing. Out in public is another. —*Sheriff Sam Goddard.*

The same night Jake and Cecilia discussed the origin of the species, a black Camaro eased cat-like down a residential street, glided close to the curb, and purred to a stop in front of a large, two-story, redbrick home. Light from the porch bled down the long, curved sidewalk, with no hope of making it to the car.

Moonless night, the man thought. He squinted up the street. Nothing much to see. He scratched his nose, then his crotch. Most of the heavy homes sat on great expanses of manicured lawn, well back from the road. Insects chirped their cacophonous love calls and a thick, sweet smell of magnolia overcame the scent of the cardboard pine tree hanging on his rearview mirror.

The man peered at the house a few moments, thought about pulling up the gently twisting driveway, but decided not to chance it. She should be giving him a signal. He glanced at the luminous dial on his watch, then gazed back toward the house.

Inside, the woman languished on her couch, eyes closed. A broad-screen TV blared, but she couldn't hear it. Her breathing was heavy, even, just below a snore. When the TV exploded with a salesman promising no down payment, not a dad-burned dime, she blinked, sat up and shot a glance at her watch. Springing to her feet, she quickly used her hands to fluff her dark brown hair. Maybe she wasn't too late. No time to panic. She clicked off the TV on her way to the front door and flicked the porch light off and on. Car, headlights out, angled up the drive. Her high heels clicked on the hardwood stairs, adrenaline surging into private places.

The man stepped out of the car, gave a last glance around, thought of an excuse in case anyone saw him, then hurried to the rear of the house and let himself soundlessly in through the unlocked back door. He was still working on a possible alibi when he entered the house. Even unlocked back doors were not impossible to explain. Tonight she'd better be ready. His long, grueling day demanded a happy ending.

He was a big guy and when she heard the heavy footsteps, she almost giggled out loud, like a young wife who still thought her husband handsome and smart. Only she wasn't young and this wasn't her husband. She donned a white cheerleader's sweater, emblazoned with the outline of a pale blue bullhorn and the letters CCHS. She wriggled into her short, blue and white pleated cheerleading skirt and slipped on blue sneakers over white bobby sox. On the dresser sat a bottle of merlot, uncorked an hour before for its own heavy breathing. Two crystal tulip glasses stood guard, flashing glints of light.

When she heard him outside the door, she picked up a chrome baton with white rubber balls on each end and began to twirl. The dark leather wingback chair sat exactly where it was supposed to. He plopped down, his elbows draped on the thickly padded arms.

Act one. She began her routine, whirling and twirling, jumping, and bending to show off the white cotton panties. She never looked at him, but his eyes never left her. She hummed to herself, mimicking the beat of the drums. For a woman over fifty, she wasn't doing too badly, although endurance might be a problem. Fortunately, a long routine wasn't in the offing.

Her varicosities pulsed unnoticeably in the subdued light, and he ignored the breasts that swung like ripe fruit a nudge away from dropping from the tree. He didn't complain. Perhaps the hips were a little wider; perhaps the Pacific Ocean was too. No problem. A willing woman was a gift from God.

He crooked his finger, motioned for her to come forward. She came. With the baton tossed on the bed, she stood directly in front, legs apart, hands on her hips. His palm crept from inside her knee up to mid-thigh, raising the hem of the skirt. She trembled. He smiled.

"So," he said, "are you ready for practice?"

"Yes, Coach." Was she ready for practice? She was ready to give a hundred and ten percent for a full four quarters and still outrun Man-o-War.

"I can't hear you!"

"Yes, Coach!" she answered the singsong command loud and strong.

"That's better." His hand moved up, touching the elastic around her panties. He began to stroke her thigh. Her breathing stopped.

"Oh, my God," she thought. The forbidden movement enthralled her, caught her in the moment. His hand moved higher. She loved the teasing, and he did it so well. He could get her to the edge, and keep her there, and keep her there until she thought she would scream and cry, just the way she had in high school when she had been Bobby Joe's girl, when they did the four legged monkey for the first time in the boys' locker room. Maybe this was even better.

"Stay here." The man eased himself up from the chair. She stayed where she was, staring at the wall, hardly breathing. He poured a glass of wine. She heard the faint splash in the glass and rustle of his clothes as they plopped to the carpet. She pictured his body, a little thick at the waist maybe, but she'd seen worse. His hair was thinning and there was an ugly appendectomy scar, but who was she to complain. Never had she complained. She knew he'd be naked, except for his athletic socks. He was one of her favorite lovers. Secrets being the banquet of lust, it wasn't something they talked about. A true meeting of the dirty minds.

He grabbed her at the waist and tossed her on the bed, cast her panties aside and wadded her cheerleader skirt up to her waist. He tucked pillows under her bottom, raising her to the proper height.

"Hut!" he barked.

"If only he'd lift my sweater," she thought. "Bobby Joe always liked that best."

"Hut!" he barked again, "Blue, twenty-one."

She loved it when he called an audible. She raised her arms over her head and felt him reach out and grip her wrists as he settled his weight onto her.

There were so many possibilities. Over the years she had learned every move, when to raise her arms, when to raise her legs, when to kiss him on the lips and when to yell go, go go!

"Hut!" came the command and then a steady rhythm, "Hut! Hut! Hut! Hut!"

"Go team!" She squealed.

"Hut!"

"Push 'em back! Push 'em back!" Her voice echoed off the bedroom walls.

"Hut! Hut! Hut!"

"Hike!" she screamed. "Oh, my God! Hike!" And later, when they had sipped some wine and she saw he still needed what he needed, she went to the closet and took out the riding crop. He liked a double feature, and this one starred the queen of the ass kickers. Standing beside his chair, she popped the leather crop against her leg. "You've been a bad boy, fooling around with that young cheerleader! Get on the floor," she hissed. The transition came easily, as if she had an internal, two-position switch marked Sweethang and Cruella's gone batshit. Little crystal beads dotted the man's upper lip and an electric shock raced down his groin. With an unsteady hand, he put the wine glass on the floor beside the chair and slid forward onto his knees. A chillingly deep thrill clinched his spine. He was hard again, but a different kind of hard, weaker, less powerful. The first act only warmed the outer layers. This one bored deep into his guts, slipped him into a time tunnel, where pain was love and love was sex and he didn't need a therapist to tell him it felt gooder and gooder.

"All the way down!" His breath flowed heavy and tapered to a shuddering wheeze. The whip lashed across his bare buttocks, leaving a dark pink stripe.

"Oh, dear God!" He clamped his jaw until the mandible muscles bulged.

"What was that?" She didn't wait for an answer, but bent over, thrust her hand between his legs and pulled at his semi-erection.

"Holy shit," he whined, "not so hard!"

"You like it like this." Her voice had an edge that said she knew what she was talking about. She released her hold and a split second later the crop again came down across his back. This time the tip rounded the edge of his bottom and stung his pendulous nuts like an angry wasp.

"Sweet mother of God!" he whined.

She gripped him again. Harder. The testicles felt like ripe grapes. His eyes bulged, his tongue hung out of his florid face.

The crop swished back down on his ass. "Who's the coach now?"

"You are!" he whimpered.

"Say it!"

"You're the coach!"

"And what are you?" She let her fingers slide lightly up the shaft then gripped his testicles again. His whole body shivered.

"I ... I don't feel too good." He started to urinate, the pale liquid running warmly over her hand.

"What the fuck are you doing?" she shrieked, jerking her hand back. Shock morphed to anger. Her lips went thin, her face rigid. She stole a glance at the light yellow circle staining her splendid, white carpet.

She smiled grimly and took another nut-cracking shot at the exposed testicles. The riding crop down hard, with a nice pop. The man's arms and legs gave out and he dropped to his chest.

3

The thing I like most about our school system is the close-knit community we serve. It's like running a school system for your friends. —
Superintendent Lucinda Whitehall, Remark at a School Board meeting

Cassavora County straddles the middle of the state and Fletcher is its only sizable town. A green and outwardly friendly place, Cassavora lays flat, laced with open stretches of arable land, dotted by lime hued rows of tall, sweet corn and dark green regiments of rough, low bush cotton. A quarter of a mile in any direction, black cows graze on great expanses of emerald fields, bordered by oak and pecan and pine trees. In cotton season, you might find yourself inconvenienced by a huge, glossy green, cotton-picking contraption taking up most of the two-lane road.

It was to the peaceful countryside that Sheriff Sam Goddard escaped each evening. But, sometimes he couldn't escape the job.

At first, the ringing phone was a dim echo in the silent halls of slumber, then an irritating intruder, like a nagging fly buzzing you closer and closer to insanity. Fresh from a full three hours sleep, he threw his arm across the blanket, cleared his throat and lifted the receiver.

"Hello," he rasped, "Who's dead?"

"Sheriff, I just wanted to be the first to tell you. Jake Morgan is running for the Board of Education." The voice on the other end was all too familiar.

"Jesus Christ, John Paul, you woke me up to tell me that?" The words came out in a hoarse croak, shaking off sleep, working up to indignation. "It ain't a riot, or a jail break and nobody's dead?" He cleared his throat.

"Thou shall not take the Lord, thy God's name in vain!"

"Gimme a break, John Paul, I was prayin'. Who in hell is Jake Morgan? And, by the way, thou shalt not wake up a man with a gun in the middle of the night and piss him off!" He was too groggy, tortured to mount an effective deterrent.

The deputy ignored the sarcasm. "He's the former military guy. The former Baptist. The one who's been writing all those letters to the editor."

"Well what ya waitin' for?" A pause.

"Uh, I don't understand, sheriff."

"Git on out there and arrest his ass." The pregnant pause gave birth.

"What for?"

"Impious inside the city limits? Making Deputy John Paul nervous?" Another pause. Not even a breath. "John Paul, how long you been working for me?"

"Three weeks, sheriff."

"Let me give you some advice on making it to four."

"Yes, sir."

"Don't wake me up for crap like this."

"I just wanted you to know."

The sheriff gleaned a little satisfaction as the voice on the other end turned a tad defensive.

Goddard slipped the receiver into its cradle, rolled over and stared at the red, digital numbers on the alarm. Five, three, zero. He wished himself another hour of sleep. His wish went unanswered. Being a light sleeper was a curse, especially if you were a county sheriff. Just when you thought you'd gotten things under control, some idiot would get drunk and ram his car into a telephone pole, and you'd get a call in the middle of the night, or some other idiot would shoot somebody. Then there were drugs and wife beatings and petty stuff, once in a while an armed robbery. From then on, coffee and enthusiasm waged an uphill battle. Still, it was all small town garbage, not heaping landfills of crime like in the city.

Goddard lumbered out of bed, trying not to wake his wife. He admired Elmira. She could sleep through a tornado, sleep while wind hurled the bed halfway across the county. She wasn't much in the mornings, but she was quite a woman in the afternoon, after she picked up speed. He made his way to the bathroom, showered, shaved without cutting himself, basking in the heat of the water on his skin and fresh, soapy smell.

Before heading to the door, he put the final touches on his tan, starched uniform, strapped the heavy, black leather belt and holster in place, patted the black handle of the nine millimeter Glock, adjusted his collar and rambled out hatless.

At near seven o'clock, the sun peeked over the trees, casting sparkles where dew and raindrops lingered. A crunchy gravel road wound from his house to a two-lane black top. He let his mind seep around this Morgan thing and why it made such a difference. But he knew why. Morgan the outsider.

Cassavora's school system squatted dead center in the heart of this community, as in every other small county in America. And lately a polarization of opinions, wrapped around religion and change, had everyone jumpy. A new high school loomed and the football parents and the academic parents and the band parents were set to duke it out over how much money was spent for what and when. Plus, there had been only one high school, one united cheering section. All of a sudden lines appeared on the map, showing the community cleaved. He sighed.

Then the state's winning AAAA football coach, Wynn Gibbons, decided to sign on with a bigger school in another part of the state. Some said Cassavora could have kept him if the money had been right and if the old high school simply expanded to keep the football team's AAAA standing. Those kinds of issues led to angry whispers and flaming letters to the editor. Neighbors stopped talking to each other in the grocery store. A couple of Bible thumpers, one of whom served on the Board of Education, hadn't helped matters, raising issues about how the schools were run and what was taught. Now, Goddard's deputy plagued him in the middle of the night about Jake Morgan.

In the rear view mirror, Goddard usually saw eddies of red dust, but not this morning. Dust wouldn't come up again until the sun dried things off from last night's rain. That stretch of gravel usually took a toll on the sheriff's white car, but that's what prisoners were for.

Four minutes to the second after getting onto asphalt, he slowed and pulled into the drive-thru at the Golden Arches. His growling belly craved one of those bacon and egg biscuit concoctions. He fought the urge, reached down and patted his breast pocket for the package of those goddamned cholesterol pills. He also craved being twenty years younger and forty pounds lighter. Coffee or nothing.

The morning shone bright and cloudless. Millie smiled at him and extended a slim, white teenage arm to offer a steaming, Styrofoam cup.

"Morning, sheriff. Watch out now, this is hot."

"Morning, Millie. My word, you get cuter every day!"

Millie waved a dismissive hand. "So far you're the only one who thinks so." She brushed a strand of hair over her ear and smiled.

"I don't know. Your mother speaks very highly of you." Millie giggled and gave him a petulant pout.

"You're just starting to bloom. By the time you're my age, you'll have been married three times."

"I'll settle for once." She had a full, throaty, in-control voice.

"Right now you better settle for getting good grades and getting into college. Remember, alimony ain't gonna pay for everything!" She glared at him in mock anger. "But, my big question is, why are you here instead of in class?"

"They have me working in the morning before school. I've got girls' softball in the afternoons."

He pulled away from the window. All in all, this wasn't a bad county. With few exceptions, the young people were pretty nice, and there were enough jobs. But, the county was changing.

The poultry industry stood tall as the county's biggest business, and poultry workers included new arrivals who were more familiar with Spanish than English. Not too many native grown Americans yearned to stand at a table all day pulling chicken guts apart, at least not too many that Goddard knew, but folks from South and Central America thrived on the steady jobs and paychecks. Hola, America! Viva pollos!

When the wind shifted, you didn't want to be standing anywhere closer than ten miles to a chicken farm. Once you caught a whiff, you'd think twice before sinking your teeth into a chicken sandwich.

The sheriff smiled and took a sip. Most people hadn't been enlightened by a breath of chicken stench, so Americans still ate a lot of 'em. At some of the big chicken plants, they killed a quarter million birds a day. Good thing chickens are stupid, Goddard thought, or there'd be a chicken riot and a rooster on the school board. On second thought, the rooster still stood a chance.

Even with agriculture and poultry farming, the county grew taller and more urban with every rumble of a bulldozer. Urbanization roughed the edges of the county with petty crime.

In the end, county commissioners stewed over apartment construction and strip mall builders won more battles than they lost. Construction jobs brought in even more new people and meanwhile, the school system groaned with the influx, many of whom no hablan ingles.

Still, he'd been sheriff for going on ten years, and he had to say the constant tempo was still pretty gentle. Professionally, it lacked the sweaty palm action of the midnight shift in a metropolis. He could have stayed in the big city, as he'd done for twelve feverish years, working like mad, moving up.

Elmira wanted the country life, but then a small town girl doesn't thrive where bulldozers outnumber tractors. When it came to police work, what he loved, she hated. He'd lived for the rush, those blue lights flashing and rapid fire bursts from the radio. Armed robbery in progress! Report of gunshots! Not Elmira's cup of tea. The crush of the city itself didn't agree with her and being a cop's wife even less. It hadn't come to an ultimatum, but close. So, here he was, an elected sheriff, driving down a two-lane road in the breaking sunshine, trying not to spill anything on his khakis. Well, it wasn't so bad. He wasn't out on the mean streets anymore, but he liked being in charge. The only drawback was, come election time and sometimes in between, he had to shake hands and back slap as well as be the chief law enforcer. Also, he had to eat a little manure and salve the egos of the county politicos. But his race wouldn't be for another couple of years. Right now, he could enjoy the sunshine and the coffee.

The radio broke his reverie. "Sheriff, we've got a report of some vandalism over on Carlisle. I could send somebody, or maybe you want to take it? Over."

"Be there when I get there." Sam Goddard's voice drawled wearily, but not because of the lack of rest. Kids spinning their tires through somebody's lawn or smashing up trashcans, or using stop signs for target practice tried his patience. He hadn't seen a stop sign outside the city limits that didn't have a few bullet holes. It was a wonder somebody hadn't been hit. Beer cans and screw cap wine bottles dotted the roadsides, stuff that never even got your attention in the city.

Where in God's creation were the parents? Of course, the school system didn't step up either. There was a lot of drinking going on among the high schoolers, not to mention some weed. People in this county seemed firmly committed to the head in the sand approach.

Maybe he was getting himself worked up over nothing. Vandalism covered a bunch of territory. First rule of law enforcement, don't jump to conclusions. Maybe it was the second rule. Anyway, it was in the top ten.

4

Cassavora is blessed with a fine school system, led by an able superintendent, but lately it's been under siege by misguided and, in some cases, malicious parties. —Editorial in The Cassavora Advocate

Jake heard something of the commotion in the night, but didn't think of splitting pine fencing and the smash of a genuine hardwood baseball bat against light metal mailboxes. In a neighborhood so quiet a woodpecker's staccato echoed, a bat to a mailbox was an explosion. He'd rolled over and felt Cecilia next to him. Nothing came through clear enough to make him leap up and go running through the trees out to the street.

In the freshness of the early morning, with the smell of rain and rosemary and a background symphony of twittering songbirds, he plodded in shorts, tee shirt and clogs up his winding gravel driveway through the dogwoods and oaks.

Through the low-slung branches and over the split rail fence, he could see his mailbox hung by a couple of bent screws, the mouth twisted agape like road kill.

"Little bastards." His fists clenched automatically.

Down the street, amid the trees hung a few sad remains of other butchered mailboxes, some with the poles fractured and splintering. Jake leaned over, picked up his newspaper and was about to stroll back to the house, but stopped at the faint sound of an approaching car.
He ran a hand through his dark, gray flecked hair and readjusted his military style wire rimmed glasses.

The patrol car eased to a stop. "You live here?"

"Yes, officer, I do."

"The name's Goddard, Sam Goddard." Jake stuck out his hand. "I'm Jake Morgan."

"No shit!" The exclamation flew out of Goddard's mouth. "Sorry ... I mean I was just hearing that you're running for the Board of Education."

"News travels fast."

"Sure does."

"Unfortunately, it's the wrong news."

"You're not running?"

"I haven't decided. Still thinking about it."

"Mr. Morgan," the sheriff said, changing the subject abruptly. "You see anybody, anything unusual?" His arm swept down the street.

"Just got here myself." Jake flashed the newspaper.

"Like to get your hands on these heathens?" The sheriff shot him a smile.

"Yeah, my hands and their baseball bat."

"If you hear anything -" The sheriff pulled away with a parting wave.

From her kitchen window, Thelma saw the sheriff's car and the two men having a chat. It frustrated her not to be close enough to hear. By the time she'd made her way back down the driveway, the sheriff had pulled away.

"Morning, Mr. Morgan." She said it tight-lipped, condescending. No smile.

"Morning, Thelma." Jake nodded and took a deep breath. Thelma.

"I saw the sheriff out here." No attempt at soft, politeness.

Jake nodded again. Looked down at his newspaper, wanting the conversation over. Tough luck. Hints bounced off Thelma's thick hide like spent BBs.

"Did he want to ask you about anything in particular?" The last word hung in the air.

"Mailbox."

"Oh, I thought maybe it was something else." Jake signed. She must have seen Cecilia coming or going. Best just to let it ride.

"No, he was curious about the mailboxes. I see you had yours hammered, too."

Thelma turned her head towards the mutilated remnants, clearly disappointed there was no open scandal, no nefarious deeds reported, no justice dispensed.

"Tip top of the mornin' to you!" Jake walked toward his house.

Thelma blinked. Moments later, she was back in her kitchen a death grip on her phone. "And, he had the audacity to say something so vulgar." She let her friend try to pry it out of her, while she feigned not being able to repeat the words she was dying to repeat. "He said something about big tits in the morning!"

"Was he talking about you?"

"Who else could he have been talking about? Not that oriental woman who was sneaking out of his house!"

Jake tossed the newspaper on the counter and pulled another coffee cup from the bottom shelf.

Settled on a stool, he took a sip, spread open the paper and sighed. The usual. People complaining. Another proposed housing development was scheduled to go before the county commissioners.

Jake folded the paper and put it in the wastebasket.

The twisting, turning river of life, flying fast jets, ripping through places he couldn't pronounce, drinking strange fire waters with women he'd never remember, all that had suddenly dried up. Now all he had to think about was which little teenage prick smashed his mailbox, new housing developments and whether or not Thelma had a ten-power telescope.

A ringing phone spoiled the moment.

"Morgan residence." Jake still answered the way his parents had taught him. Even fighter pilots have parents.

"Jake, you asshole."

"Hi, Skeeter."

"You given any thought to what I said about running for the Board? You'd be perfect since you don't know nothin' 'bout no ed-ju-me-cation!"

"You found me out."

"So?"

"So, what?"

"So, whatta ya think? Give it a whirl? Just for the sheer shit of it?"

"Maybe. Might be fun, and I can't spend all my time writing best sellers."

"Well, the newspaper boys think you're running."

"You're assuming they can think."

"No, no, no. That's a piss poor political answer. You gotta learn to say you deny the allegations about running for office and your sister being a whore, and giving all those contracts to your best friends. I'd like to include myself in that number, by the way."

"You're hired. Press secretary."

"Maybe you're as crazy as ever."

"Suppose I stop out to the house and we plan our first news conference?"

"I don't charge for the beer, but if you want anything civilized you're going to have to bring your own bucket."

5

The devil is at work in the school system of Cassavora County. —*Caldwell Robbins*

By the time Goddard got to the low, red brick sheriff's office, two more people called him on his cellular to tell him the Morgan news. When he stalked through the glass doors and into air-conditioned comfort, another of his deputies, Don Hemsley, bright faced, short, roly-poly, servant of Jesus, poured out the same message. Hemsley's aura of newly discovered salvation suggested a detour clear around an airport rather than risking a chance meeting.

"Why in the hel .... dickens are you telling me? It's not like it's the end of the world. You're not saying he won the election. You're only telling me he's runnin'. So, what difference does it make?" It was difficult to keep from scowling at the deputy and still harder to cover the exasperation.

"Whenever a man inspired by the devil declares himself in opposition to a community of Godfearingchristians, I think the sheriff ought to know about it." Hemsley wore a weak smile on his cherubic face and stared intently, possibly waiting for the sheriff to speak in tongues.

"You think he's gonna win?" Hemsley was a good deputy, so Sam made the supreme effort of replying to this insanity.

"I think he's going to try to do the devil's work." Hemsley's lips tightened to white lines.

John Howard, the Chief Deputy, came over as Hemsley walked away. John was about the same age as the sheriff and tall enough to look him in the eye. His close-cropped hair, dark skin and piercing glance grabbed you and held on. Every inch of him the former Marine. No matter how hot or what time it was, Howard's uniform creases looked dangerous. "Don't worry about Hemsley, Sam. He just had to say something."

Sam deadpanned, "I know. He was just doing his Christian duty." He thought about telling Howard of his meeting with Morgan, but decided not to drag it out.

"Christian duty!" Goddard muttered, squatting his tall, hefty frame into the wooden office chair. Howard sat on the small couch opposite, looking at his boss, not saying anything. "These god-fearing Neanderthals going to war over this Morgan business? I must've got fifty phone calls already."

Howard allowed himself a small, white-toothed smile, watching his big, bull headed boss squirm uncomfortably in the tight chair. "I don't think anybody would step outside the law, if that's what you mean."

"Me neither, but I want you to let John Paul and Hemsley and the rest know I don't want to have to explain why Morgan and his kin suddenly get a fist full of speeding tickets. You know what I mean?"

Howard nodded solemnly, got up and moved toward the door. Sam watched him leave. Christianity in Cassavora County, Goddard thought, I could write a book.

Lately things boiled over. A member of the Board of Education ripped open issues about science and religion everyone pretty much figured had marched off the stage after the Scopes Monkey Trial. Caldwell Robbins, the wholesaler of building supplies, cotton farmer, and self-appointed defender of the righteous blurted out at a school board meeting that evolution was just a theory, being taught to naive youngsters as fact. It sounded like a sin against God the Father, God the Son, and God the Holy Ghost when he said it. He and his supporters wanted to have the book of Genesis taught as science in the local schools and they didn't call that one a theory.

A sense of collective nervousness trembled the community. For a while, no one spoke up in opposition, except for Jake Morgan. The majority strongly supported conventional education, but didn't want to be labeled anti-Christian, which they were not. Many attended church regularly, and in Cassavora County there were only Christian churches. Others just chalked it up to the rantings of a lunatic.

Goddard and Elmira jawed around the kitchen table about it. As Elmira said, "This is a case of religion and education twisted in the same rope." The sheriff saw the silence as a practical matter. The majority of this community wanted to get on with their lives without theological battles that could offend every one of their friends.

Even in a quiet spot like Cassavora, religion flowed wide and deep. Among some Baptists, any display of theological differences was as offensive as a belch in the front pew. That's why in a county of some twenty-five thousand souls, a dozen separate congregations of Baptists were scattered across the county. Willow Wood Baptist was very liberal, meaning they'd given up stoning and banishment as viable expressions of the common will, whereas Shimmering Light Baptist believed everything not native to the county was the work of the devil or aliens. They also made exceptions for some of the natives, like Jake Morgan. Jake Morgan, the sheriff was astonished to learn, technically qualified as a native, since he'd been born here. He'd moved to California with his parents, served in the Air Force and returned years later wearing a yarmulke to services on Friday night, although he had to go to a neighboring county to do it. To the faithful, it proved you should never let your children leave the county, let alone the country.

Cassavora had two faces, and the other one was cultured, educated and creative. Art and artists bloomed. Small galleries nestled between professional offices along Main Street. A community group provided live theater and several noted writers called Cassavora home, not the least of whom was Martha Bonner. Her national best seller, *The Polecat Tree*, was what in the music trade would be called a one hit wonder. An intriguing blend of the quaint and profound, it read as down home as a biscuit dragged through gravy. Goddard read it in high school, a staple of literature class. That was years ago, and Ms. Bonner's cup of fame had dribbled dry and cracked with age. But the literary mindset of the community remained embedded and people still pointed her out in the grocery store. Frail, white-haired, spectacled, she embodied the essence of a very senior citizen and a direct tie to the magic of yesteryear.

Aside from poultry farming, art and bedrooms were the rest of Cassavora's industries. All salved the yearnings of an ever-expanding population of consumers who needed homes close to the university and big city, paintings for the walls, pottery for fresh flowers and a new garage to park their SUVs. It was fair to say they also contented themselves with packaged chicken, rather than the older generation's tradition of wringing necks over the clothesline.

As far as the controversy over the school board race went, Goddard figured the rumor mill just needed something to grind. Life went on. Air conditioning would soon be humming and sweating pitchers of iced tea would dot the tables of local cafes. Revival meetings and Vacation Bible School ads would swamp the pages of *The Cassavora Advocate*, the weekly journal of Town

Council meetings, new building starts, and who died last week.

But, this was also an election year and Sam knew it wouldn't be long before people who knew less about politics than they did about cow piss, would rant and pound signs into other people's lawns.

The phone on his desk snapped the sheriff out of his revere. His thick fist enveloped the black receiver.

"Goddard." The deep, resonant baritone begged for a place in a choir, but he simply didn't have the time.

"This is County Commissioner Beaufort's office," said a female voice, high-pitched, Southern and very correct.

"Commissioner Beaufort will be on the line shortly." Sam Goddard cradled the phone in his neck, stared out the window, waited. There were Beauforts all over the county. Charles Junior, or C2 as he was known, came at you as a no-nonsense guy, hiding behind a warm smile and a handshake. He also ran the place as his own domain and Goddard dodged any showdowns, often balanced on a shaky tightrope between the right and the necessary.

C2 dressed plainly, always in a coat and tie, but his neck seemed to grow yearly, like a tree trunk adding another ring. His shirt collar stayed half a size behind and when he pulled at it, which he habitually did, it gave his eyes a squinting, porcine appearance. His daddy, the first Charlie Beaufort, was the county's premier realtor. For a while he was the only realtor. After he retired more than twenty years ago, the Superintendent of Schools' husband, Douglas Whitehall, took over. C2's younger brother, Mike, sat as the chief financial officer of the local bank, and two of his sisters taught school. The saying was you couldn't sneeze in this town without a Beaufort offering you a handkerchief.

None of the new folks would remember, but Charlie's moment of fame came in 1955, when Cassavora High School played Foster County for the AA State Football Championship. C2 played safety and from all accounts was a good one. On the final play of the game, with Cassavora leading, Charlie dove level with the ground to break up a pass in the end zone. Only trouble was, the ref didn't see the ball bounce on the ground and ruled it a catch and a touchdown. Foster County won the game. Some folks still chided C2 about it. He didn't take it well.

A city like Fletcher had a lightening rod for every significant bolt of information and it ran straight down through C2. The sheriff squatted near the bottom. What ever this phone call was about, Sam figured all five commissioners, the school superintendent, the mayor, the head of the Chamber of Commerce and all their kids already knew.

"I hear a former Baptist is running for the school board."

"He didn't sound too sure."

"You already talked to Morgan?" C2's voice clipped at the words and the pollen brought on a slight wheeze. His tone registered surprise. The sheriff had made a preemptive strike. C2 liked it better when people leaned a little off balance.

"The very same. Some of our kind and gentle children were on the warpath last night. Busted up some mailboxes and one belonged to Mr. Morgan. You ever meet him?"

"No, but he's probably a nice guy. Am I right?"

"He seemed nice enough. I tell you one thing, he's in good enough shape that I wouldn't want to be the one to bust his mailbox."

"But, he told you he hadn't decided yet?"

"That's what he said."

"I'm not sure a Jew on the Board of Education wouldn't be a good thing for the county. Although those newspaper letters of his have stirred people up."

"Changes in the wind," Goddard murmured, just to squeeze in a word.

"Anything that sounds like trouble?" Goddard picked up the whine in C2's voice. C2 could hear about somebody spilling iced tea and bubble with such saccharin concern that Goddard's stomach churned. In the end, C2 did what was best for C2. Sam harbored no illusions.

"You mean about Mr. Morgan or the busted mailboxes?"

"Morgan. I'm too busy to care about the postal system."

"I think our friendly little county will continue to prosper. Only been at work five minutes and I already heard about the news three times over. To tell the truth, I'm a little more tight jawed about last night's near fatal car collision and whether or not you're going to float me the money to rehab my jail."

"You're always worrying about your jail. I told you I'd take care of your budget. Don't I always?"

Don't I always get the job done? Goddard thought, but he kept his mouth closed. Things ought to be done because they needed to be done, not because of largess. And flying pigs might also be a good idea.

"You ought to sit in this chair for a while and try to juggle new neighborhoods and the water supply and a sewer system that's about to split wide open," C2 continued, "but, I need to know if there's trouble. Billy Reilly and his group been making any noises?" Billy and his cousins, high school dropouts and loud-mouthed underachievers, worked at Clifton Poultry.

"I haven't heard." Goddard's voice trailed off, as it always did when the pillars of the community suggested he should round up the usual suspects. Blessedly, the lecture ended.

"Sam, I hate to run, but I've got a meeting with two state senators in ten minutes." The line went dead. Sam put the receiver down and stared at it a moment. Charlie Beaufort wasn't a guy you wanted to confide in. With the suit and tie crowd around here, honesty was a lonely orphan and truth a chameleon.

He took another sip from the Styrofoam cup and picked up the carefully folded newspaper his secretary always left in the center of his desk. "Ten Candidates at the BOE Start" flashed the headline. He read on, "Ten potential candidates," Sam sniffed at the syntax, "signed up to run for the five seats on the board of education. Among them ..... " blah, blah, blah ... There it was, Jake Morgan's name. The article went on to say, "... as a former military officer and because he is a liberal in the area of religion, his running has caused a great deal of controversy." As usual, Wilbur Simon's newspaper got it wrong. The deadline for signing up to run was still awhile away. Half the names mentioned in the article probably had no intention of running.

"Liberal in the area of religion," Sam snorted. They didn't want to say he's a Jew and explain why they mentioned it.

Sam's mind floated over events of the past few weeks while he read. Nobody knew Jake Morgan was running until this morning's paper came out. The fact was, Morgan's letters to the editor lit a fire and pissed off people who thought they were governing by divine right. The paper rustled as he folded it less carefully than his secretary had.

Just then, the red phone on Sheriff Goddard's desk rang, the one connecting him directly to the rescue and emergency response team. Five seconds later, he slapped the receiver back in its cradle and headed for the door. Sheriff business was booming.

6

Education opens a child's mind and feeds his imagination. Unless we want to end up with a county of airheads and bureaucrats, we're going to have to put a lot more into public education than platitudes and promises. —Jake Morgan

Right after she came to work, Wilma Cook, Chief Postal Clerk, heard a shot, or something that sounded like a shot. It might have been a backfire. By the time she walked around the white, laminate counter, crossed the black and white linoleum floor and looked out the rain-splattered window, it was too late to tell what it was. She saw nothing except the usual parade of cars passing the United States Post Office, until a few minutes later when the EMT truck, complete with sirens and lights, pulled into the damp, asphalt parking lot.

While Wilma stood at the window, two men and a woman, dark blue pants and starched white shirts with red patches on the shoulders, jumped out of their modified white pickup, a cabin on the bed, and doubled timed over to the bushes outside her window. They knelt down and she could see their heads bobbing and arms moving, but all she could tell was they seemed to be in a hurry.

Bobby, the medic in charge, knew immediately he was looking at a body and not just an injury. The skin was cool to the touch, and the face had a flaccid, waxy appearance. A fly buzzed and landed on a corner of the left eye. A slight breeze played with the man's damp, sandy hair. He was a big man, probably in his late forties, early fifties, an athlete thirty pounds and almost that many years past his prime. The arms were still big, but the belly bulged, even lying down, even dead. His running shoes must have been size thirteen and he was wearing khakis and a white polo shirt. Something about him looked familiar.

Bobby waved his arms out, told his two assistants to cease work. "Leave it alone! Let's just back away from this one, folks. Try not to disturb anything else." Tanya had already unbuttoned the front of the soggy polo shirt, but she pulled her hands up and back like a free safety who'd just committed pass interference. Jimmy was unwrapping some equipment. He stopped what he was doing and stood, not sure what to do next.

The sheriff's white Ford Crown Victoria pulled in and Sheriff Goddard and one of his deputies jumped out. Traffic was already slowing down on the main road for the gawkers to get their fill. Goddard walked over to the kneeling medics. "Whatcha got?"

"The man's dead, sheriff." Bobby looked up.

"Any wounds? Cause of death?"

"We just got here ourselves." They were primed and ready to go to work, clear plastic hosing lying around, oxygen canister at the ready, but there was no point.

"If he's dead and you don't know why, what the hell are you doing stomping through a potential crime scene?"

"Sheriff," Bobby defended, "the call we got said there was a man on the ground who looked like he was either drunk or hurt."

"Who made the call?"

"Don't know. Came from a cell phone, maybe a passing car."

"We have a record of the call?"

"Sheriff, our equipment don't remember crap."

"Well, somewhere there's a record. Now, leave the body alone and go back to your truck." A group of well meaning medics, kicking up bits of grass and mud, moving the victim and otherwise destroying evidence was exactly what Sam didn't want. He paused a moment, looking over the death scene. It was pretty simple really, a dead man, fully clothed, lying flat on his back behind the decorative hedge next to the yellow brick wall of the Post Office. But the sheriff knew in police work, the simple is never, ever simple and last night's rain had probably already played hell with the evidence.

"You want us to put a sheet over it?"

"No. I don't want you to do anything, but back off." Goddard turned to his deputy. "Get two guys to tape off the area and guard the corpse. Tell them not to touch anything. And make sure Doc Moncrief is making his sorry way over here. Let's just seal off everything for now. Soon as possible, I want everyone out of this parking lot. We'll go over every inch."

"The parking lot or the building?" the deputy asked.

"Every damn thing!"

"Yes, sir ... okay." The sheriff glanced around to see if any representatives from *The Cassavora Advocate*, or a local radio station had come running. He didn't see anyone. Except for the ERT truck, the Sheriff's patrol car, and a deputy's white sedan, the Post Office parking lot was an empty, dark, shiny glow of wet asphalt. Employees must park around back, he thought. One or two cars on the road in front of the Post Office slow crawled, drivers trying to figure out what was going on. "Get over to the road and get that traffic moving," he shouted to one of the deputies.

The door to the United States Post Office was locked. Goddard rapped his knuckles on the glass. Wilma, her light, blue-gray uniform shirt bright and starched, dark blue slacks covering a middle-aged middle, walked over and gave him a pinch-faced stare through the thick pane. "Sheriff's Department, open the door please."

"I'm not allowed to open the door until eight thirty. We open at eight thirty." She said it as a closing statement.

A deputy came over at a half jog and stood behind Goddard. "The Doc's on his way, but he wasn't too pleased about it." Goddard let the remark pass.

"Ma'am, I'm conducting an investigation and I need to talk to you." The sheriff, like everyone else who has visited a post office, felt impatience creeping resolutely into his voice.

"This is federal property."

"I know what the hell it is," Goddard commented, "now open up." The deputy adjusted his wide brimmed hat and stared at his black, highly polished shoes.

"You'll have to wait until the Post Office is open," Wilma countered, obviously irritated. "These people all think they're special," she muttered and frowned. "This is a Post Office and we have regulations!" She said the last part out loud, then turned to walk away.

Goddard's face changed color. "If you don't open this door, right now, I'm going to book you as an accessory." Wilma kept on walking. She had things to finish and except for double-parking six years ago, she'd never done anything she could be arrested for. Anyway, it wasn't as if she could just turn the key and start the day. Wilma did things according to Postal Regulations. The clerks that worked for her did too. They'd better. She hadn't spent twenty-seven years working hard just so she could jump around at every customer's little whim. There was a procedure for everything and forms to sign and stamps and money that needed to be counted. The union rules made it clear she didn't have to jump just because somebody yelled grasshopper. "Why is it people are always so thoughtless and demanding?"

Goddard wanted to smash the door and slap cuffs on this irritating, jackass of a Postal worker, but instead he turned to his deputy. "Go back to the car. Call the Postmaster and tell him we found a body in his parking lot and one of his stupid, overpaid clerks.... did you get a look at her name tag?" He paused.

"Cook."

"Okay, Cook. Tell him Emperor-in-charge Cook is interfering with our investigation and saying it's on his orders."

Five minutes later, a peevish looking Wilma Cook opened the door and started answering questions. Other Postal clerks hovered in the background, going about their daily chores, all ears trained on Wilma, the sheriff, and the deputy.

Did she see anything? Only the usual. What time did she get to work? Seven thirty, like always. Was there anybody else in the Post Office when she heard the shot? Just her fellow clerks.

Anybody in the parking lot? Not that she saw. The questions came like a pack of angry yellow jackets, but she stuck to her story. Nobody was there. Everything was normal. She hadn't seen anybody else outside or inside. By now, however, she was sure she had heard a shot. As her interrogators walked out the door, she overheard the deputy ask the sheriff if a thirty-eight would make the same sound as a backfire.

Doctor Moncrief drove up in a dark gray, four-door sedan and stepped out onto the glistening asphalt with the confidence of a condemned man walking the last mile. His ferret eyes darted here and there, locking onto the sheriff maybe half a second, trying to eye-gobble the whole scene, but not knowing where to look. The plaid, blue and gold polyester slacks, red polo shirt, and white socks with black rubber flip flops told Goddard he was not looking at a guy who had gone to the office this morning with the rest of the grownups. Big surprise.

The socks bunched where the strap separated the doc's big toes from the rest. "I hope whatever it is, is pretty important," he said, his voice an off key chirp. He gave a nervous sniff, which pulled the narrow mustache on his upper lip into an inverted V. He scratched his stomach. The slight breeze caught a couple of strands of thinning brown hair.

"Well, good morning to you, Doc. Did I interrupt an interesting oral exam, or did you used to work for the Post Office?"

"Golf."

"Well, bless your heart."

The doctor stared; trying to read the remark on the sheriff's face, see if there was sarcasm. He didn't like sarcasm.

Deciding there hadn't been slights or slanders, but still suspicious, he asked, "What you got?"

"Why not go look for yourself?" Goddard pointed toward the two stoic deputies by the bushes. "You might find this interesting."

Dr. Moncrief peered across the parking lot at two khaki-clad legs barely sticking out from under a hedge. "Dead?"

"Good guess."

"Any marks on the body?"

"Don't know, but I'm betting your natural curiosity will eventually take over." Now that was sarcasm, but was it friendly sarcasm?

Doubts raged. He'd let this one slide. "Let me take a look." He didn't like being around dead bodies and the sheriff's tone was beginning to irritate. He exerted a little authority, pushed a deputy aside, got behind the hedge bush and called back, "White, middle-aged male."

"Anything else, in your professional opinion?"

Doctor Moncrief, DDS, crouched down and peered closer. Then, he leaned forward, reached out both hands and pried the mouth open.

One of the deputies wrinkled his nose and gave a what-the-shit look, not being all that familiar with the oral approach to cause of death.

Sam whispered, "Dentist. He always checks the teeth," like it was the most natural thing in the world.

The deputy shot a blank look. Dentist? Medical examiner? Sam put a finger up, and the deputy didn't say anything.

Dead people weren't Moncrief's main line of work, and he didn't know quite what to say. "Good teeth," was as close as he could come. He stared at the tongue, didn't see anything he recognized, his knowledge of forensics sharing the deep recesses of the brain normally reserved for hog research and words ending in the letter J.

Another deputy snickered. Goddard gave him a look to shut him up. He didn't need a political fight with the M.E., who hadn't gotten this job because he was top of his class in drilling and filling, or because somebody figured incisors held the key to the mysteries of life.

The dead man's eyes were shut, the mouth slightly ajar from where the M.E. had pulled the jaws apart. Pinkish blotches around the neck. No noticeable wounds. No blood on the ground. Fingers slightly bent. Goddard inched closer, reached out and lifted a hand. Cool skin. Underneath, the ground was dry.

The sheriff stretched his neck and looked back at the doc, who had moved to the safety of the pavement. "I know this guy."

"Who is he?"

"Football coach. Got any guess as to the time of death?"

The M.E. knew the pesky question was coming, but hadn't thought of a good way to swat it. Stuff like this wasn't in the plan when the Board of Commissioners honored him with the job.

"You going to do a body temperature?" The sheriff raised his eyebrows a little. "Just a suggestion."

"Well, I didn't bring my thermometer," the doc's voice trailed off into a kind of sour whine, pissed he hadn't thought of it.

"No matter," Goddard muttered, "you probably wouldn't know where to stick it."

"What was that?"

"I said these things can get kinda sticky." The sheriff was back in his office within the hour, having left his investigator, a guy named Collins, at the scene. Collins jumped on it like the first kid at an Easter egg hunt, happy to start Sherlocking instead of directing traffic.

Sam knew he could get the state investigators in here, if he wanted, which he did not. First of all, he couldn't ask for state help without the xenophobic commissioners going apoplectic. But, aside from that, there'd be an exponential increase in the paperwork. Also, he had to consider pride and morale. He'd give his man a solid shot. Collins didn't get to investigate much more than petty theft, it was true, but he had been well trained. Besides, as of now there was only a suspicious death, not a murder, which spun the pressure gauge down from aw shit! to sorry 'bout that.

Whatever it was, Sam needed to get on it, contact the school offices for next of kin notification, find out who made that first cell phone call, tie up the details and sort out the meat from the gristle. Everything needed to be done pronto. He could already hear the defense attorney asking those electrifying questions. "And, why did you delay in reporting this or investigating that?" Sam sometimes resented the perfection required of him. He understood it, but he resented it.

The biggest reason he didn't call for state investigative help right away was the politicos. Except for routine stuff, you didn't go outside the county without the county commissioners' okay. The system worked only as well as a whisk in a bucket of cement, but fortunately, most of the time it didn't have to.

He still had to deal with the body. Simple fact: Cassavora was bare-assed naked when it came to morgues. Fact two: Moncrief could bluff his way through a root canal, but not a full-blown autopsy. Sam would get the body transported to a nearby hospital, then charm another county's M.E. to consult. All that would take was money, and the state could stay out of it. It'd keep the commissioners happy and their favorite dentist on the payroll.

Back at the office, he dialed C2, hoping his secretary wasn't going to rush in and tell him someone from the newspaper had darkened the doorway. "Missy!" he yelled while the phone was ringing, "Get me a deputy!" He'd be damned if he was going to escort the body himself.

Improving our schools depends on asking the tough questions, then not scattering like rats when we hear the answers. —*Jake Morgan, letter to The Cassavora Advocate*

Lately, a sweet, seductive stream of convenience had flowed into Cassavora. Not only was there a rescue and emergency response team to run around finding dead bodies at the Post Office, but grocery stores stayed open on Sunday and you could finally buy a bottle of wine without crossing the county line. A family medical clinic and dental clinic and emergency clinic popped up overnight. Newcomers expected the same convenience they'd had in Atlanta and Houston, St Louis and Philadelphia, and all it took was the rustle of cash to drown out all the traditional objections and make it happen.

At first, people with money seeped in, educated people like Jake, although he didn't think of himself as affluent. Doctors and lawyers, professors and airline pilots demanded pricey homes, endless green lawns, custom stonework, and ice-blue swimming pools. As always, money followed money. The sound of it was the solid clunk of doors on European sedans and the ching-ching of cash registers ringing up crusty baguettes and gourmet cheeses. The smell floated on the scent of rich cologne in the supermarket aisles. Suddenly, money overgrew Old Cassavora like kudzu. A couple of rock stars bought two hundred-acre ranches and swapped guitars for cattle raising.

Still, the natives clung to the memory of the way it used to be, the memory they sold to carve out their share of prosperity. With money in such vast quantities you needed all your fingers just to count the zeros, loosened the hold of sentimentality on Granpappy's back forty.

Inspired by an instinctive faith in the past, old, familial clumps of power clung tenaciously to the roots of the county. But, more and more, maintaining the status quo became as fruitless as trying to raise fields of corn in a new subdivision. You could almost hear old Cassavora screeching, "I sold you land to build houses. I didn't sell you the right to push us out of the way and elect some son-of-a-bitch from Cleveland to the Board of Commissioners." As the newcomers were learning, living here didn't mean the same as being from here. To most of them, though, it didn't much matter. They drove to the airport, or the hospital, or did their lawyering in the city, then came home and let the county take care of itself. Most wealthy professionals didn't have the time or inclination to stoop to run for political office.

Population growth, the spearhead of natural conflicts, had an attack dog named commerce. When complaints arose about over-crowding and the demise of local farming, terms such as *tax base* and *net income* obscured the focus and led many residents to conclude Chicken Little had a point.

The school system, the soul of the community, soon became the skirmish line for fights over taxation, population growth, and general differences in opinion between old residents and new. Everybody paid for the school system, and most had kids there. Those who had no kids were not happy about paying for a school system they didn't use, and those who did had a gnawing in their guts that their kids were somehow being educationally cheated. Teachers thought they weren't being paid enough, and everybody else thought they were being paid too damn much.

On a Saturday morning in late March, with elections coming the following November. Percival Smith, sixty-seven years old, married for over thirty years, chairman of the Board of Education for the past fifteen, strolled to his car with a bag of groceries after a quick stop at Grand Foods. All of a sudden, he felt as if elephants were doing a war dance on his burley chest. The world blurred and pain ripped down his left arm. His lips moved, but no sound came out. He slumped to the warm pavement, his face even more florid than usual. Several people rushed to help. It was a small scene. By the time the ERT squad got there, the Board of Education needed a new chairman.

Meeting in emergency session, under the guidance of Superintendent Lucinda Whitehall, the board agreed prudence demanded the job be given to Tom Millage, a long-serving member and former farmer who knew a little less about modern education than he did about nuclear physics. Still, Tom's white hair and sun-wrinkled, avuncular face quieted the doubters, and everyone else followed suit, knowing they could count on a good night's sleep. Then the Board chose Caldwell Robbins to fill the gap left when Tom took over the chairmanship. The result was as though a large stone had been flung from a great height into a sewage treatment pond.

It was at that board meeting that Jake took his first look at the education situation. The room where the school board sat glowed with a dozen pairs of industrial neons. Members faced the audience over two banquet-sized fold up tables, draped in dark blue cloth. Fold-up chairs allowed the audience to face back. Air conditioning labored valiantly in the summer, but never fulfilled its promise. So, at any particular time, you could see hand fans fluttering in the audience.

As a rule, meetings usually ran with the quiet hum of wheedle and banter, but the first session that included Caldwell Robbins was a doozy. After the new chairman, Tom Millage asked everyone to stand for the invocation, Robbins launched into a prayer that would have made Cotton Mather dance and sing. He somehow got his bulk up on a folding chair and began, "Our heavenly father..." On occasion, the chair would creak, giving false hope to those who believed in a merciful God.

Robbins rattled on about the great responsibility of the board to set a moral example for the children, how Sodom and Gomorra had nothing on America when it came to sinning, and beseeched each citizen to reject the pleasures of the flesh. He ended up some fifteen minutes later, "in our beloved savior's name, Jesus Christ, amen." Coughs and sighs followed and several honest citizens collided as they broke for the bathroom.

Thus sanctified, the board bounded forward in the ardent pursuit of trivia. When the agenda finally trickled down to new business, Robbins mentioned that a parent had asked him about several questionable books in the high school library and wanted the superintendent to look into it.

Lucinda, who viewed any unscripted utterance as a threat to her throne, launched an irritating rustle of papers and replied that the screening subcommittee, part of the Library Committee, fell under the auspices of the High School Advisory Committee, a subset of the Professional Educators and Concerned Parents Association, but she would pass the word on. A tight-lipped look hinted she'd rather use her valuable time doing something more productive, such as pulling wings off of flies. Everyone seemed mollified by the answer except Robbins, who demonstrated his depth of feeling by rolling his eyes and shuffling his own papers.

Not yet ready to pronounce the horse dead, Superintendent Whitehall asked her assistant, Horace Gordan, if he'd like to lay on the odd lash or two.

"I just want to say the shared partnership, embracing all aspects of resolution, more than adequately defines our forward thrust in the continuance of this school system's pro-active stance."

Tom Millage nodded his head slowly, either adding his assent or catching a wink.

The board retired for discussions in Executive Council. Jake walked outside to catch the cooler air. Stars shone brightly in the dark heavens. Polaris, Aldebaran and a couple of friendly constellations winked at him. It hadn't been that long since he had been boring holes in that same sky, feeling the slap of the afterburners. All of a sudden, in a snap of the fingers, twenty odd years had passed, a retirement ceremony honored his service, and here he was, sitting in the audience of a school board meeting. The written agenda he clutched looked like an ode to the perpetually confused. Maybe that's what it was. Maybe he needed a fight, or at least a mission.

In a small office off the main meeting room, board members eased into chairs around an octagonal table; Superintendent Whitehall remained standing, handing out white fact sheets. "We may have a case of insubordination by one of our teachers." She paced, glancing at one board member and then another. "Harriet Hightower, the principal at Elgore Elementary, reported she has a potential disciplinary problem with one of her first grade teachers. Harriet said the woman, whom I will not name at this time, was, to put it frankly, insubordinate."

Tom Millage nodded, pursed his lips. "These teachers have got to know that it can't just be me, me, me all the time. We need team players." Millage, whose last team activity had been a hot game of let's check the prostate, had only one answer to everything, a shrill cry for more discipline. He'd eagerly have lemmings march in lock step over a cliff to show unity and rigor.

"We need to support our principals." Gloria Sweeney, former school teacher, age 68, slim, short, immaculately red-from-a-bottle hair, firmly believed each flotsam of change was a nasty little Trojan pony who needed its pee-pee soundly whacked. Cassavora schools had been good enough for her three daughters. Case closed, chained, and locked. Experience ruled as a ruthless dictator.

An astute back room politician in the Caligulan sense, she was too much the Southern lady to cross words with anyone in public. But, away from prying eyes, Gloria had no qualms about tarnishing reputations and destroying confidence with viper-like accuracy. On the night before the last election, unnamed Sweeney supporters telephoned voters to accuse her opponent of sending his kids to private schools, giving him no time to respond to this rape of the truth. Gloria won by five hundred votes.

"I'd like to hear more about the incident before I make any comments." Todd Ingles spoke softly. "What exactly do you mean by insubordinate?" A former high school swimmer, he managed the Fletcher branch of Hogmeyer's Grocery, also known as The Big Pig. Most times he stood alone, which the superintendent took as both interference and presumption.

"I'm really not at liberty to divulge the details at this juncture."

Todd gave her a look. Why did she even bring it up? But he didn't say anything. He'd fought before. Now, he was just tired.

Robbins and the fifth member of the board, Gordon Cuspid, sat watching the others. Cuspid looked the quintessential English professor, thinning hair slicked back, half framed glasses on the end of his nose. But English professors never shut up, and Cuspid never spoke up. He eased the tip of a forefinger to his left nostril and wriggled the tip so skillfully he attracted no more attention than a water buffalo in a bubble bath.

Lucinda, the soul of practicality, didn't care where he put his finger as long as he was under her thumb.

Moments later the board rejoined in open session. They raised their hands placidly for whatever the superintendent wanted. These stalwarts, who held the educational reins, asked no penetrating questions, made no memorable comments. It took an hour and a half to increase the price of school lunches by a nickel, get rid of an aged vehicle, and allocate money for board members to attend a conference in the city.

This was not the meeting of thoughtful sages, but the haphazard results of blatant billboards and vote-for-me cardboard signs hammered into peoples' lawns, the system Jake had defended on the outskirts of the empire for over twenty years. He tried not to think about it.

With the agenda fading weakly into the good night, it was time to drag out the soapbox and let citizens address the board.

Professor Wendel Hopper took the podium, wearing the professorial uniform of jacket, vest and bow tie. He spoke forthrightly. "My studies have shown conclusively the story of creation in Genesis is in fact perfectly aligned with science. The big bang, on the other hand, is nothing more than theory."

True believers gasped at the profundity.

Somebody yelled, "Is the moon Camembert or Brie?" The professor remained unfazed.

"But, I have not come here tonight to bore you with scientific facts."

"Science fiction," came from the back of the room.

"I have a sweeping proposal and one I hope for the good of education in Cassavora you will consider. I want to bring proven university educational techniques to our elementary and high schools." He paused. The expected applause scattered.

"I will address two specific areas. First, I propose to institute group learning. At the university, my classes often number in the hundreds of students. Using the same approach, one high school math teacher could teach the entire freshman class, thus saving money and insuring that every student gets the benefit of being taught to the same high standard.

Furthermore, schools should take advantage of economies of scale. By buying land now, around our existing schools, we could continually expand in the years to come. Five to ten thousand students, or even more, could attend one high school, instead of fracturing the community by sending our children to different, competing schools. Also, we could build dormitories and eliminate the expensive bus system."

Books are our passage to the far shores of knowledge. Burn a few of them, and you burn the boats you need to cross the wide, angry river of ignorance.
—Jake Morgan

Jake seldom mentioned his religion, but he didn't hide it. To some it was only a curiosity, but a few didn't want him talking to their children. Among the uneducated, Judaism, along with homosexuality shared a contagious reputation. Jake understood the dilemma, with Judaism the father religion and Christianity one of the offspring. It wasn't the first time fathers and sons disagreed.

On the other hand, he didn't squirm every time somebody mentioned history's most famous Jew. Around here, he'd look like a man with Saint Vitas dance. But, last night's board meeting left him strangely uneasy. Out of Robbins' mouth, Jesus Christ cut to the heart of everything Jake disagreed with.

It wasn't only Robbins. At one of Cassavora's biggest and more liberal Baptist churches, a friend of Jake's was told she was welcome, as long as she didn't bring her Jew fiancé. Infectious barbarism was just one of the many hazards of drawing breath. Part of the human condition. Interminable prayer in the school board meeting was only the latest infection.

Jake read an article that got him thinking about the chemistry and physiology of thought. How did the process work? Amino acids? Chemical shadows of what our parents taught us? Genetic or environmental? Were we all born with a full pallet of colors and some just decided to smear on the paint? Why did some crave truth and knowledge, while others sent money to TV preachers?

Jake blamed stray neurons for making him even consider running. The possibility hit him the morning after his first school board meeting, when he saw the front page of *The Cassavora Advocate*. "Caldwell Robbins Says 'Let's Get the Dirty Books Out of Our Schools'." Robbins' views apparently had plenty of support. Jake's neurons did back flips.

The Advocate reported Caldwell and some of his supporters were saying the dirty words in a couple of Steinbeck novels were the reason kids joined gangs and girls got pregnant. Jake knew they'd bring sex into it. "I think these boys really want to just play with their wieners and peek into everybody's bedroom."

"Careful, there's a lady present." Betsy peeked through a back door. "A lot of people in this county are behind him." There was a nervous hesitation. "Hope you don't mind me barging in."

"What's up Betts? Your mother send you over here begging again?"

"Do you have any butter?" She wrinkled her teenage nose and went all whiney, as though she were asking him to give up a kidney.

"Sure. Open the frig and take what you want. Leave the whiskey." Jake stuck his face back in the newspaper.

Betsy closed the refrigerator door, holding a paper-clad stick of butter between two slim fingers. "Remember what you always tell me. You can't believe everything you read in the papers."

"Did I tell you that? I meant everything you read about *me* in the papers."

"Mr. Caldwell came to biology class to talk about cotton farming," Betsy continued, "and he seemed really nice." Her soft voice took the edge off.

"Make you lay down your books and praise da Lawd?"

"No." Her mouth formed the edges of a smile. He put the newspaper on the counter, folded it.

"And, why aren't you in school?" He looked over the top of his reading glasses with a mock frown.

"Teacher work day. They're doing report cards. Well, see you later Mr. Morgan."

"Say 'hi' to your folks, Betts."

It was something to think about. Betsy's young, intuitive mind made a good foil for his fighter pilot's killer instincts.

Jake ambled to the desk and pulled open a drawer clogged with rejection slips. His next book ought to be on how to deal with rejection.

The second novel. Jake had scribbled at it for the best part of a year, while he queried editors, agents and other illiterates about the first.

He'd mellowed. The kill or be killed mentality of the jungle war had clung to him when he scribbled the first novel, his body once again young and hard, alive with fears and hates, while bullets in red, glowing arcs flew past his canopy. Sometimes when that old passion held him, he blinked away rivulets of sweat, his hands clinching and opening, yearning to grip a control stick. The memory of long ago G-forces wracked him through a steep turn, then released him as he rolled and squeezed the pill-sized bomb-release button.

Reliving the glory wasn't what drove the memories out of his mind and onto the page. Unlike the Hollywood versions, glory fades to nothing in the unrelenting face of combat. The sweat, the fear, the loyalties were real and still lived within him, parasites on his psyche. Some inner urge forced him to tell the stories of his war, the one true, uncompromised piece of his life. Writing burst open a magic time capsule and once again brought out the craving of beer for breakfast.

But, one thing not in his book was battle fatigue, battle trauma. Unlike the illiterati, who'd never been closer to Vietnam than the East Coast, Jake had never seen battle fatigue except in the movies. The men he knew fought and suffered until their duties released them, without quarter or parole. They did it for a bunch of reasons, most of which was a fierce loyalty to their brothers in arms.

In the meantime, until some bastard in a bow tie passed fair judgment on his novel, short stories and articles in local magazines brought in pocket money and allowed him to call himself a writer. But those little tidbits of success didn't make him feel like a writer.

Jake sat down and reread the opening paragraph of novel two. Beginnings were no problem, in war, peace, and marriage. Endings always danced in wisps of clouds, two chapters past his imagination. This morning, writing could wait.

Jogging cleared his head, leaving only the heave of his chest, the trickle of sweat and the constant thump of his running shoes. In the purity of exertion, priceless ideas fell before him like diamonds, and he gathered them like a beggar, hoping they didn't fall out of the pockets of his imagination before he made it back.

The smell of morning hung heavy in the air, fresh cut grass, dew mingled with road tar and pine needles. The swish of the leaves in the tall trees played a natural song. He trotted on the asphalt from his house, picking up speed, ignoring the tightness in his legs. Birds sang their short melodies, insects hissed and clicked. Springtime was a primo time to jog. By the time Cassavora languished in the stifling heat of summer, heart-pounding exercise would be shuffled like sin into the darkness of early mornings or late nights.

Instead of ideas for his book, his ex-wife Jill crept into Jake's mind. The parties, the passion, long-stored images of the electrical excitement of falling in love flickered and danced. Her blue eyes still haunted him. And in the midst of tender remembrance, the bitterness of her leaving flew at him like an angry hornet and stung him in all the old familiar places.

He replayed her leaving, a favorite video of the mind and ever changing. He peppered her with snappy replies or stood stoically and told her to pack her things and leave, cool as James Bond. Other times, he pleaded with her to think about the good times. But, the truth he'd buried under tons of self-analysis, until he never really remembered anymore what had happened and what he'd envisioned.

He made it her fault, then tried to make it his. Mostly, he just despised her. Acid rose in his throat. Nothing was going to change until he lost that spite, until his interest became disinterest. He tore up the last hill with a finishing kick that would put a smile on the faces of the gods.

9

Our community has been well served by our school system. We don't have gangs; we don't have drugs. —Dr. Lucinda Whitehall superintendent

Billy Reilly took a last drag on his cigarette and flicked the short, filtered butt onto the dusty gravel. It lay there, offering a thin curl of gray white smoke. He and his first cousin, Jerald Murphy, leaned against the corrugated siding of an out building of the Clifton Poultry Company, squinted, sweated, and shaded their eyes.

"Somebody's got to stop the son of a bitch." It seemed like the thing to say, and Jerald wasn't much for originality. He loosed a thin stream of brown tobacco juice.

"I got a plan." Billy always had a plan. He had a plan to get rich, he had one to get a degree from the community college, but his favorite, and the one he worked on the most, was the one to get into Betty Fowler's pants. The reality played out a little differently, so here he was, stuck at minimum wage, a high school dropout and Betty Fowler didn't speak to him for two weeks after the incident at the Dairy Queen. Still, a certain crude charm shone through his engaging half smile and dark brown eyes. And, a plan that didn't work was still half a mile farther down the road than cousin Jerald could get on his own.

"What kinda plan?" Jerald's version of trying to keep the conversation rolling.

"It's best if I keep this one to myself for a while." He snapped another cigarette out of the pack and lit up. Billy was cool, leaning against the building, one boot planted on the wall, draped in a blood-spattered apron, the cigarette dangling from full, pouting, James Dean lips. "But, I tell you what, Jer, this county still ain't ready for a freakin' Jew. And I don't think he's ready for this county, neither."

"What is a freakin' Jew?"

"You don't know what a Jew is?" Questions irritated Billy.

"Well, I was just askin'."

"Okay, I'll tell you." Billy set his jaw, glared at the dirt. "A Jew is somebody who don't believe in God and killed Christ."

"Holy shit! You believe this guy really ... ?"

"What?"

"You know ... killed him." Jerald's brow furrowed at the immensity of it.

"Not personally he didn't kill him."

"But, you figure he knows the guys who did it?" Jerald was hopeful.

"It's the Bible stuff ... you know." Jerald didn't know.

"It happened back a long time ago before people walked the earth. There was just the bad guys and Christ. Christ got killed, but he came back and that's why we have Christmas and Santa Claus and shit."

Billy and Jerald knew they were Christians, although the details were foggy. It was a basic tenet among the long-time residents of Cassavora County that everyone in the county was

Christian. Didn't matter if you didn't go to church. Christian was America and America was Christian. As a matter of fact, non-practicing Christianity was the most popular sect. Non-church-goers still marinated in the theology of whatever they remembered from vacation Bible school. But, on the very best Sundays, when the big Baptist churches popped at the seams, a lot more folks stayed home. It was Christianity with the default block checked.

Billy and his group resembled Jesus like Al Capone resembled the Pope. Still, Billy held that Christianity flowed in one river of faith, with no pollution, no branches, and it really didn't matter what you believed as long as you were a member and as long as you weren't Catholic, which everyone knew wasn't Christian. Jews were another matter. Fuck, everybody hated them.

With the influx of doctors, lawyers, professors, psychologists and national businesses flowing like rainwater into every corner of the county, Casavora's religious face also changed. Those for whom Sunday mornings meant hard church benches and Wednesday's meant pot luck suppers sat on one end of the religious seesaw while those who favored a Sunday round of golf sat on the other. The preachers were right, of course. Luxury is a seduction of the soul.

"So, what ya got planned?" Jerald began again.

"I don't want to talk about it here."

"Whoweeee! We're gonna have ourselves a piece of a Jew, ain't we Billy." He could have been a hungry man catching a whiff of oven-baked bread.

"I figure we ought to let him know he's not welcome."

"Now you're talkin'!"

"You guys taking a break or trolling for queers?" The foreman stuck his round, crew-cut head out the door and spat. "You come on back in here, or I'll fire your asses and hire some more Mesikins."

"Come by my house tonight." Billy pursed his lips, gave a crooked, Elvis smile. He curled his fingers and arced his cigarette into the air.

10

We need citizens, members of the community in law enforcement. A
voluntary S.W.A.T. team would be a good start. —County Commissioner
Rupert Barnes

"I think we need a S.W.A.T. team," C2 said. "The Board
of Commissioners decided on it last night."

"A S.W.A.T. team," the sheriff said, pressing the phone
against his ear, trying to find a middle ground between laughter
and incredulity. He wanted to ask why he wasn't invited to the
discussion, but he knew from experience that this was another
special employment opportunity, not law enforcement.

"We've got a volunteer fire department and some of the
commissioners would like to use the fire department as a model.
It'd give us more manpower when we need it to form a bridge
with the community. So, get one put together."

"A volunteer police department?" Sam couldn't believe
what he was hearing. He pictured deputizing whole
congregations and passing out double naught buckshot.

"Not a whole police department. A S.W.A.T. team."

"Who's funding it?"

"You are. You're the sheriff."

"So, what are we talking about as far as training and
weapons and uniforms and vehicles go? The training's going to
cost plenty."

"How much?"

"About fifty grand per man and that's at the state facility, if they have room for us. For a four-man team, you're looking at two-hundred thou."

C2 thought a second. "How 'bout we just buy some black uniforms and get Mike Mills to donate a black Chevy van from the dealership? Let 'em bring their own weapons. They're volunteers."

"Sure. And the training?"

"Sheriff, just get the thing done."

"S.W.A.T. team. Lots of flies around here in the summer." C2 let the sarcasm pass.

"Just make it look good. The commissioners are really hugging this idea of citizen police. All the big counties have 'em."

"Okay." Somebody had to pay the cost of the four new deputies. Goddard knew that much. Even if they were volunteers, any time they got a phone call they'd be on the clock.

A few days later, the sheriff and Chief Deputy John Howard strode around the black Chevy van parked in the Sheriff Department's parking lot. Big, magnetic white signs on each side read: Cassavora County S.W.E.A.T. team and under it, Save a Million at Mills Chevrolet.

"Sweat team?" Sam shook his head. "Get the sign changed."

"The dealership loaned us the vehicle and supplied the sign."

"Right. Sweat team. So there's a good possibility we could see men in black uniforms, with shotguns at the port arms, double- timing across the county because their vehicle got repossessed. I repeat, change the sign."

Howard nodded. "Who you putting on the team, sheriff?"

"I expect we'll be given a list of names to pick from, likely as not, none of them will know SWAT from SWEAT. The rest is up to you, but don't pick any of the traffic deputies to lead the team. They have important things to do."

Two days following, the sheriff was back out in front of the jail to review the troops. He found himself looking at four new, portly deputies, dressed in black combat boots, black leotards and black cowboy hats.

"What the hell is this?"

"The commissioner got the uniforms donated."

"By who? The Fairyland Ballet Ensemble?"

The Chief Deputy took a deep breath, pursed his lips and let the air out slowly. "Cassavora Players."

"Take some money out of the contingency fund and buy some black Levis or Dickies, whatever's cheap, and give each man one pair. I don't want to see men with shotguns doing pirouettes."

John Howard made a mental note."What else did the commissioner say? What about paying these ballerinas?"

"He said to just have them on call and pay them per hour whenever we call them up."

"Oh, shit," the sheriff said under his breath, as he turned and walked away. Over his shoulder he called out, "Make up a duty roster and then hide it."

Goddard couldn't let this insanity go without another phone call. Evidently, C2 was expecting it because he wasn't in. He'd left terse instructions with his secretary, and she wasn't about to get into another discussion. "The note just says, now that the team is formed, you are not to use it in tactical situations without approval from the Board of Commissioners."

C2 had done the usual politician's job of pleasing all the people all of the time. Goddard could go back to doing his job. Maybe he'd make a midnight call to each of the commissioners and test the recall system.

11

Caldwell Robbins is just a thin superstition away from reading chicken bones and squirrel droppings .But, I don't care what he believes, as long as he doesn't force it on our kids. —Jake Morgan, letter to The Cassavora Advocate

Days later, his anger over the newspaper article about the dirty books cooled and Jake wrote another letter, saying Caldwell Robbins should do the right thing and shoot himself.

The paper refused to print it.

Still, when Jake least expected it, beams of light popped out of the darkness and showed him a clean, dry path. But clean and dry didn't mean the path wasn't through a minefield.

Following Robbins' call for cleansing the library, over two- hundred people showed up at the next school board meeting, mostly new residents, but with a good sprinkling of irritated natives.

A sizable portion of the community had drawn a line in the sand. But, the question remained, where was the line, anyway? Who was counting the noses on either side of it? The next week's *Advocate* crowed that Robbins and Southmore had been stopped in their quest for a theocracy.

To Jake, the meeting was one evenly matched mob against another, slogan against slogan, with meaningful debate lost in the verbal gunfire.

Tom Millage's gavel rapped, silencing the unruly voices, but not the foot shuffling, the coughing, and the rumble of chairs.

Robbins sprang forth with a soliloquy on the need to protect the children, a grenade both sides tossed with alacrity.

The superintendent then wheedled on, "I've lived in this county a long time. I know this county and the good people who live here." Her eyes darted through the audience and lit on Adelle Witherspoon, a retired schoolteacher. "Adelle and I used to wander through the library in the old high school, didn't we Adelle?" Adelle's gray head nodded knowingly. "Cassavora is just a wonderful place to live, and I want you to know that no one wants more than I do what's best for the children. I resent the implication that this board, that this administration, is not performing a service to the community!" There was sustained applause, and no one but Jake seemed to wonder why a retired teacher would suddenly show up sitting in the front row at a school board meeting. Perhaps she was a concerned citizen like the other two-hundred who filled the room. Maybe not.

The chairman jumped into it with how much the superintendent had done to bring this school system to where it is today. More applause. More shuffling of feet. One woman bolted out the door to the ladies' room across the hall and the sound of violent retching floated into the room. The woman next to Jake murmured, "Bad potluck supper last night." Heads nodded.

Robbins proposed having a citizens' committee take another look at the books in the high school library. He failed to get a second and the motion died.

The whole meeting seemed as off kilter as a Dali painting. Questions went unattended; answers spoke boldly to nothing, emphasis banged around.

The Advocate blared: Robbins Attacks Superintendent. Board member Caldwell Robbins leveled a direct attack at Superintendent Whitehall, calling her actions detrimental to the good of the children. A spokesman for the superintendent said, 'Dr. Whitehall resents Mr. Robbins's personal attacks and feels the business of the Board of Education is to help the children of this county.'

Jake called his friend, Cleveland Amos, who mused, "Well, that certainly straightens everything out." Robbins hadn't been as strident as the newspaper suggested and Jake found it odd nobody had spoken in his defense. Not that he didn't loathe the man.

"Tom Millage is a close friend of the superintendent," Cleveland said, "and so is the editor of the paper. Did you notice the main players were members of the Cassavora Board of Realtors?"

So much to know, so much unknown. Like watching the surface of a lake and not being aware of the fish.

"I'm sure you know who Lucinda's husband is."

"Yeah, "Jake paused. "But I didn't see collusion, just mass confusion."

"This county's got more layers than a Vidalia onion, Jake."

"I know what you mean, but in this case I saw what was going on."

Cleveland laughed. "Convinced of that, are you? Hear any Robbins supporters last night."

"No, now that you mention it."

"Who was calling people to the podium? Tom Millage." Jake's new doubts rusted his memory. He'd heard Robbins talking about the books and the superintendent's disjointed reply. Maybe the newspaper screwed it up, or it could have been a reporter got some interviews behind the scenes. Or, the newspaper article might have fused an ongoing debate.

Jake thought about his barn burning letters to the editor. Had he got it wrong? He plopped down on the sofa to collect his thoughts. In the heat of the moment, there was clarity of sight, pureness of purpose. The facts and principles stood as tall as centurions. But now, the desultory meeting and spurious arguments brought everything back down to mortal size. Jake wasn't ashamed of what he'd written, but all of a sudden his arguments seemed a little tinny. If he was off the mark, then he'd helped obscure the real issues. Somehow he'd better separate himself from the buffoons and mudslingers and do it damn fast.

Jake's newspaper comments brought some unexpected and unwelcome notoriety. A circus of follow-up letters had sliced through their wake. Some said the county reeked from the stench of an outsider; others praised him for standing up and telling the truth. For a few days his phone rang with calls from strangers, some of whom called him an ignorant coward for abusing wonderful people.

Next board meeting, the paper reported Robbins was leaving the classics alone and going after "Atone in Silence," a locally authored coming of age novel about a teenage girl coping with her father's suicide.

The Advocate quoted Robbins. "How can we expect our young people to act with dignity and decency when our own high school library is the breeding ground of filth?"

Citizens of Cassavora leaped nimbly to one side and the other. Everyone was an expert. Battle flags rippled in the breeze. The Bible took a back seat to the framers of the Constitution. And, as Jake said, Robbins did have his bottom feeding followers.

Purcell Southmore avidly supported Robbins, a fellow member of the Cramp Hill Church of Holy Redemption. He and Jake had had a run-in over Jake's new driveway. "I paid you to put in a driveway and there's nothing but dirt out there where I park my car." Jake's knuckles went white on the telephone receiver. Liars always took him by surprise.

"Well," Southmore began in a drippy mockery of a Southern accent, "I done what I was paid to do."

"I paid you to put in a driveway. Gave you the money up front."

"I never take no money until the job is done." Point of honor. Jake could have called him a liar for all the good it would have done. Being a Southerner by birth, he was well acquainted with Southern honor and all its perversions. The first lesson, honor, is a man's game. Although men must protect the honor of women, men alone determined when honor needed protecting and need not consult the women. That wouldn't be honorable. Lesson two, others' wives and daughters were fair game. Protecting their honor was somebody else's business. Lesson three, ask me, don't tell me. No matter what lies the history books agreed to, that was the real reason for the Civil War. Lesson four, Southern honor does not encompass what you think it does. It was all right to lie and not be caught. Getting caught meant you must then lie indignantly. Southmore had mastered indignant lying, and there was also some talk about his familiarity with other people's wives and daughters.

12

Having this school board in charge of education is like having the Marx brothers direct a symphony. Hilarious, but never a source of pride. —Jake Morgan, letter to the editor

Jake oscillated, waking one morning in a lather to run like a racehorse and the next determined to forget the whole thing and wallow in comfortable obscurity. He decided the best thing to do was to have that chat he'd promised Skeeter Brooks. A cold one with Skeeter usually unsettled his mind, but settled his soul, which was what Jake figured he needed.

Skeeter lived just across the county line, out a thin, gravel farm road, bordered by rolling, green landscape, pastured and timbered on the edges. Behind the gingerbread home sat a separate pottery studio. Although Skeeter had gotten a little thick around the middle and a little thin on top, he still had piercing eyes and an intellect that could drive a nail through a flimsy argument.

"Hey!" Jake climbed out of the car amid a swirl of gravel dust. His friend stood on his cobblestone walkway, waved back. Daisies, irises, Sweet Williams and dwarf rose bushes danced up either side, leading to the front porch.

"Marcy's gone shopping for plants." Skeeter gave him a mock frown. "Look to you like we need a few dozen more?" His arm swept across the expansive flowerbed. "But, come on in. Let's grab a cool one and head back to the shed."

They sat on high swivel stools, sipping lager from sweating bottles, surrounded by various stages of pots, tubs of clay, legions of half-filled jars of glaze. Sunlight streamed in dusty rays through the flyspecked windows.

"So, what ya been up to, Jake?" Skeeter took a sip.

Jake sped through the litany of headlines and anguished letters to the editor and told him about the school board.

"You ought to do that school board shit. You're a natural born asshole, not to mention ignorant and obnoxious."

"Every fighter pilot's dream."

"Fits right into being a low-life politician."

"That's the part that bothers me."

"You know the difference between a reformer and an entrepreneur?" When Skeeter changed subjects, he didn't mess around.

"I know you're going to tell me."

"You want to get serious a minute?"

"Are ya out of beer already?"

Skeeter ignored him and launched in, "A reformer sees things that are obviously wrong and tries to make people who don't want to change do things his way. An entrepreneur sees the same wrongs and hopes they continue forever, because he knows he can make a ton of money selling solutions."

"I love it when you talk sexy! Can you say that in French?"

"Let me finish a couple of more beers and I'll give it a try."

Jake took a deep breath. "So what are you saying? I need to sell solutions?"

"I'm saying it'd be a tickle and a grin to get yourself a seat on the board, but you've got a serious streak that might spoil your fun, 'specially if you got all serious about actually doing something constructive."

"Know what you mean. Difference between Friday night fucking and marriage."

"Exactly, and forgive me, ole buddy, but you seem to be the marrying kind."

"Skeeter, let's not forget I'm not the one who's been with one woman for twenty-five years."

"Yeah, but that doesn't mean you don't wanna be." Jake frowned. Maybe he'd be just clumsy at politics.

"You're the guy who's always searching for perfection."

Skeeter gave Jake a glance. "You sound a little too angry to be doing this for fun. Anger ain't gonna win the war. Takes time and practice and a firm grip on your opponent's balls."

"I wonder if the war ever can be won, if we can ever reach perfection." Jake sat back, looked down, shook his head.

"Goddamnit, when I said serious I didn't mean maudlin. But getting back to the guts of it, if you're lucky you'll see a form of perfection eventually, but it won't be a startling revelation. Perfection is more a state of mind that things can get better. And I'd remember," Skeeter added, "Education is a grace, a path to learning. Personally, I'd have everyone throw a pot or two. When art leads the way, you end up with

Wedgewood. When technology and industry lead the way, you end up with Styrofoam. Then, when the government gets into it, you get Styrofoam that cost as much as Wedgwood."

"When did you get so philosophical? I only remember your dog's view of life ... eat it, fuck it, or piss on it."

"I think my orderly world started breaking down when my pants didn't go all the way around my waist anymore. Once you start questioning the eating part, you start to question everything."

"You must be getting old."

"We're all getting old. That's the treachery of life. Once you start to get comfortable with something, you're too old to do it anymore and have to move on to something else. The secret is to have something to move on to."

"So, how do you know what to move on to?"

"Like you, I have an inquiring mind." An inquiring mind. The finished pots in his house and along both walls of the studio were a testimony.

Skeeter had always been like that, a creature of discontent, pouring over dive angle and airspeed tables, following the curved lines, trying to figure a better way. Somehow it was old times, sitting on stools, sipping cool ones, solving problems.

"Tell me something, Skeeter."

"Anything."

"After living all over the world, how can you be happy living in this dusty little corner?"

"How can *you*?"

"I'm not sure I am. I think that's a big part of why this politics thing interests me."

"Gives you a new area to search, a new world to conquer?"

"I'm just out to have some fun, but I ask myself if I might be taking careful aim at my foot."

"Hey, you're retired. Your foot'll enjoy the attention."

"I ask myself if I ought to run and take on this whole thankless mess, or just turn my back on it."

Skeeter turned his head and looked at him. "Wading into it is the only to way to find out if there's any art left in the school system and if there's still the possibility of perfection."

"You're arguing both sides of the issue."

"Always my specialty."

"Anymore sage advice?"

"Never tell the truth. Voters resent it."

"I'm serious. Words of wisdom?"

"There's something else you're over-looking."

"What's that?"

"Some of these people are nasty mean."

"How mean could they be? I can hold my own in a 'who's the biggest asshole contest'."

"I'm not talking about assholes. Assholes only bother you when it's convenient for them. I'm talking about smearing your reputation and pressuring your friends. That county of yours is full of politicians like that, from what I see and hear and read."

Jake put his mind to the questions on his drive home. What was he doing? He'd never run for political office. Maybe at this time in his life, he needed to feel passion again, Cecilia excepted.

Could he become a politician? He hated politicians. No backbone. Values blowing in the wind. No guts. Retired and writing a novel and spending time pursuing the pleasures of life wasn't a bad way to live. Did he really want to mess around and complicate his world? Was it something else? Did his warrior's heart keep him from backing away from what he knew needed to be done?

Something else bothered him. What if he did get elected? What then? Let the kids read dirty books? What if the political game got so black and muddy he could never get clean? Skeeter was right. He had no experience with people who were mean to the bone, the kind of people who would go at him through his friends. He clenched his fists and shifted in his seat.

When he got home, Jake took a short, thick maduro cigar from the humidor and ambled through the trees and down to the lake, trying his best to think the thing through. It wasn't the same as a military operation with someone telling you the mission, feeding you reams of intelligence, then giving you a team of well-trained professionals to carry out the job.

He rolled the oily cigar between his fingers, watched the gray smoke curl.

He'd read about falling standardized test scores and kids who couldn't find the United States on a globe. It was just as bad here in Cassavora. But, could he explain it to the Cassavora voters? Would they believe him? Would they even consider the possibilities? Or would they just get pissed and blame him for running? This was sounding a lot less like fun.

Jake had spent his life either teaching or being taught. The military was like that; flying jets was like that. You had to be in a constant search for a better way or your opponents would find one first and kill you.

His mind stumbled on, oblivious to the cranial confusion. No one really knew what a board of education was supposed to do. The job description was banal tripe. He'd spent afternoons poring over the state constitution and local school policies. Didn't anyone else bother to look?

The board business was tripe except for the grandstanding of a few vitriolic Bible shouters. It could be so much more. Just needed a match. Who would torch the son of a bitch if he didn't?

He had to run. Jake Morgan never backed away from duty. Still, the prospect of a suicide mission didn't thrill him.

13

Administrators rebel at the word accountability, because they don't want anyone looking too closely at what they're doing. —Jake Morgan, letter to the editor

The day after Jake wrote his latest editorial comment, the superintendent called her husband and moments later Mr. Douglas Whitehall left his realty office and drove to Brice's Cafe. Mrs. Whitehall was waiting for him, sipping a Coke through a straw, chatting with Able Perkins, one of the county's biggest landowners and developers. Douglas and Able together was a common sight at Brice's, both of them being in the dirt business. Others sometimes joined them for breakfast, but this time it was just the three. Jeanie, the skinny, longtime waitress, poured steaming coffee into the men's heavy, white porcelain cups.

"Mr. Whitehall, Mr. Perkins, can I git y'all some biscuits and eggs?" Jeanie didn't ask Lucinda, who never ordered anything but Coke.

"No thanks, Jeanie," Perkins replied, looking up, "It's a little late for breakfast and a little early for lunch." He smiled. Jeanie nodded and drifted away, coffee pot in hand.

Able sat tall in the chair, white haired, sinewy, dressed in his customary light gray suit, white shirt, muted tie. His gravelly voice resonated with the quality of a radio announcer, inspiring confidence, radiating strength. "Douglas," he said, "Lucinda was just telling me this old war horse needs to mount up and lead another charge." He chuckled and shot an avuncular smile, showing even, white teeth. "I was beginning to think of living the life of a gentleman farmer." When Douglas called him and mentioned school issues, Able assumed he meant fundraising or another financial arrangement.

"Well, you know, Able, you've always been such a strong part of the community, we naturally thought of you. Lucinda and I and a couple of others are trying to address the question of the upcoming election and how we need to get the school system back on an even keel."

Perkins looked toward Lucinda, who didn't say anything and then back at Douglas. "What kinds of problems are we talking about? I've read a few bits and pieces in the paper ... the book flare up and whatnot."

Lucinda let the straw slip from her lips, leaving a smeared red mark on the white tube. She looked Able in the eye, leaned forward. The white, open necked blouse fell open to the crevice of her breasts. She smiled the barest of smiles as she saw his eyes drop. "It's not just Mr. Robbins that's a stray bullet, but also Todd Ingles, and now this Jake Morgan character. You've read his letters to the paper? Mr. Ingles is beginning to question some of the fundamental trusts and obligations that make this school system the tight, community controlled institution I've always thought it should be. I don't think the community wants people from the state house or other outsiders ... " she let 'outsiders' linger in the breeze, like the stench from a hog farm, "stepping in to do things that will absolutely ruin the fine community school system we have now."

Perkins wished she wouldn't lean over like that. It looked cheap, and he despised cheap, although he did like breasts. "Lucinda, Douglas, as you know, both of my sons and my daughter graduated from Cassavora High School. Now my grand kids are in these schools." He lost his train of thought.

"Schools," Douglas prompted.

"Yes, well ... the county and the school system are the basis of my life and my family's future." Even pronounced with the conviction his rich voice imparted, he and everyone else at the table knew it was only his version of the same mushy platitudes. But how much Perkins knew about Cassavora's school system didn't have anything to do with why they'd invited him for this little chat, and he knew it. He and Douglas, Sob Jenkins and a few investors from the city had built and financed every one of the schools that had gone up in the last ten years and business was booming and not only in Cassavora. The cost for a new high school alone ran to over twenty- million dollars. Just the mere thought of the sub-contracts activated his salivary glands. No matter whose name was on the contract, somehow the money flowed into many pockets.

"Lucinda tells me," Douglas began, elbows on the table, leaning forward, "the solid majority on the board of education is starting to erode." His lips puckered into a tight circle as he squeezed out the final ode. Douglas knew education itself wouldn't be the motivating factor for Able Perkins. And talking about grand kids wasn't going to get this buggy down the road.

"You know, we've only got five board members." Lucinda paused. "Right now I can only count on three votes."

"Well, three votes you can count on is a pretty solid majority." Able chuckled lightly. Lucinda smiled indulgently.

"We've got an election coming up." Douglas' tone faded. "Anything can happen in an election. You don't know what some of these people are like. They can turn against business leaders and farmers, the men and women who built Cassavora."

"And landowners," Lucinda inserted. "Men like Mr. Morgan have no permanent ties to Cassavora. They don't care if the taxes just keep building and building." Her voice trailed off.

Taxes were, by God, something Able Perkins understood. The federal government took a hell of a whack out of his nickel and lately the state had been upping the ante.

What if the county stepped in and the school board and both of them started raising taxes? He thought of his thousands of acres of pastured fields and woodlands. He thought of the homes his children had and of the grand kids romping on acres of lawn. He thought of trying to sit on development property and being taxed until he bled. His eyes refocused on Lucinda. "What I worry about are the small land owners who are being taxed off their land. People who have owned property in this county for years. Good people. Poor people having to sell their land to pay taxes."

"That's exactly what Douglas and I were talking about. " Lucinda leaned forward again and showed her most sincere look. Perkins chanced another glance down the front of the white blouse. He almost saw some pink and had to tear his eyes away.

"What would you like me to help you with? You want my recommendations for some good candidates?"

"We want you to run," Douglas said.

Perkins forgot momentarily about the low cut view, tried to keep the shock from showing. "Douglas, I don't mind helping, but I don't have time to run a campaign and end up running a school board. I've already been on the land commission, the transportation commission, and pulled a stint as a county commissioner. Besides, how's it gonna look?" He held out his hands, palms up.

"You wouldn't have to do that much," Lucinda said, "and the benefits would be substantial." She lingered on *substantial* long enough to make his heart skip a beat.

"That's right," Douglas continued, "Your name alone would get a wagon load of votes."

"And, you don't have to run for chairman." Lucinda smiled. "Tom Millage is doing a great job, and he's told me he's ready to run again."

"Tom's a team player and we need some other solid, team players," Douglas interjected.

"So, who do you want me to run against?" Perkins asked, as his mind tried to wrap itself around the concept. "I don't want to lock horns with Caldwell Robbins. I've been a Christian all my life and to tell the truth, a lot of the things he says, I agree with. Not that I would vote with him," he added hastily.

"We want you to run against Todd Ingles." Douglas stared at Perkins to note his reaction.

"Todd Ingles." Able slowly turned the name and possibilities over in his mind. Obviously, Douglas and Lucinda had already put a lot of thought into this.

"Your name ... and position carry a lot of weight in this county." Douglas continued eye contact like a good realtor, expecting an on-the-spot decision.

"And your expertise," Lucinda purred. "You know as well as I do this county is expanding. Good land is getting scarce. Schools will have to be built and someone has to sell us the land."

"We've put a lot of deals together, you and I," Lucinda's husband added. They had already cut deals so fat, the grease ran off their chins and pooled in their bank accounts, deals that had nothing to do with what a building contract said, or how much property really cost.

"How's it gonna look?" Perkins asked, peering at Douglas.

"How's what gonna look?"

"My running. You and I have done a lot of business. You're married to the superintendent. I'm not giving up buying and selling property to work on the school board."

"You wouldn't have to."

"This state requires complete financial disclosure."

"Nobody ever reads 'em," Douglas said, flatly. "And even if they do, who is going to complain? The law doesn't say you can't own land or a business or sell property. If it did, we'd only have the homeless running for public office. Besides, that's never stopped either one of us before. Look at all those other offices you've held."

Able mulled it over. "But this is the school board."

"So?"

"I never sold land to the Board of Commissioners." He started to salivate, swallowed. "How many new schools you figurin' on building?"

"Five in the next seven years, plus a new superintendent's office. The new high school will need lots of land for athletic fields and parking lots."

"There's something else to remember," Lucinda continued.

"What's that?"

"You'd be elected. The people will have an opportunity to say right out of the starting gate if they want you on the board or not. It's not like we'd be doing this behind a veil. You have to be elected." She leaned

back, crossing her arms over her chest, letting her skirt ride up to show a stockinged thigh.

Able's eyes shifted gently from husband to wife to stockings. "Well, well," he thought, "I guess I'm getting invited to the feast." The hint of a grin stole across his face. Sometimes business overrides personal concerns, he told himself. As an owner and dealer in county land, he had come to this meeting expecting to have to sell something. Instead, he was being sold. There was nothing wrong with doing business with Douglas Whitehall. Nothing at all. "Douglas, Lucinda," Able said, looking from one to the other, "I think this may offer an excellent opportunity for continued community service." He smiled. They smiled.

Afterwards, Douglas and Lucinda sat in her car in the parking lot, watching the lazy flow of patrons.

Douglas broke the silence. "We've done what we could."

"I don't worry about Todd Ingles." Her voice was smooth, unruffled, a poker player sure of a winning hand.

"Who then?"

"The other one. Mr. Morgan."

"Lucinda, nobody even knows him. He won't get five-hun'rd votes." She looked at her husband, so aware when it came to making fistfuls of money, so blind to people.

"He's stirring folks up. There's something about him. Something unreasonable."

Douglas shrugged. "I don't know. Anyway, I've got to get out of here and back to the office."

Yes, Douglas, she thought, without a shred of wistfulness, let's both go back to our offices. Sentimentality had its place, but a minor one, reserved for one's children and pets. Emotions took a distant second in the most important game on earth, the power game.

The feminists got it all wrong. It wasn't a man's world. The world belonged to the bold, determined people, who didn't back away from a fight and used everything they had to win. She could bat her eyes, if that's what it took and she could bust balls. And as far as her marriage went, it was a bland but useful vehicle. Her husband's position strengthened hers, a synergy of power that created wealth and position above the fray. If the love had withered long ago, so what? What was love anyway but an inconvenience to ambition? Lucinda kept the poker face on the drive back to her office, but she smiled on the inside, where it counted. Able Perkins was in the bag, and he'd win. His name and position alone would shoo him into office. Todd Ingles' interference would be a thing of the past. And if Mr. Morgan were foolish enough to stick his toe in the race, she'd cut it off.

There were other details she needed to clean up, but she had no doubt she was up to the job. She and C2 might not be buddies, but he was a realist. He knew his place, and he knew hers. The whole situation was very manageable.

14

Some people say grits are the soul of the South, but that ain't true. Peanuts ain't neither. It's biscuits, pure and simple. —Brice, owner of Brice's Cafe

Jake glanced at his watch, squinted and stepped into the blinding heat. He wore his usual khakis, faded polo shirt, brown loafers, aviator sunglasses. The sunglasses didn't cut the glare. Sweat trickled down the back of his shirt and chilled his spine while his face bore the brunt.

When Jake called, Cleveland suggested Brice's, the same place Lucinda and her husband had met Able Perkins earlier. Brice's was not only the benchmark of a good breakfast, but the site of more county business than either the courthouse or the fairway at the country club.

Brice's wasn't such an original name, but it was an improvement over Smith's, the name the cafe was born with in 1925. Just a block off the main square, it squatted unpretentiously on a corner, the brick building sporting white, un-shuttered window frames and a double front door that saw a new coat of paint every twenty years. The black and gold lettering may have flaked off the white, overhead sign, but it didn't matter. Everybody knew where to go for breakfast.

A framed poster of the Italian Alps provided a festive, cosmopolitan air to the ritual of the cramming in biscuits. It didn't take an expert to notice the poster was Bavarian, with Neuschwanstein Castle in the foreground. Evidently, Brice, tired of being contradicted, had scrawled "Italian Alps," in bold, black strokes.

Ten Formica-topped tables and rust-flecked chrome chairs, with abused Naugahyde seats, invited diners to sit awhile and add some plaque. During the week, people wandered in for breakfast and on Sundays for the buffet.

Jake stepped inside, inhaling decades of bacon grease and the toasty aroma of fresh biscuits. Cleveland sat, glasses on, brow furrowed, pencil in hand, working feverishly on the day's crossword. Except for the heavy, black-rimmed glasses, he looked like the black ink drawing above his newspaper byline.

"What's a three letter word for a bunch of bull?" He asked no one in particular as Jake sat down.

"Pit." Jeanie strolled up and sloshed black coffee into the heavy, white ceramic cups.

"Pit?" Cleveland asked, his forehead wrinkling all the way to the middle of his bald head.

"P-I-T," she said, "As in pit bull." She finished pouring and put the round glass pot on the table. "You want the special, or the big special?" Brice's had a menu, but if you ordered from it, everybody in the room turned around to see what came out of the kitchen. The special was two eggs over easy, a thick slice of locally cured ham, biscuits, coffee and grits with butter and red eye gravy. The Big Special, gave you three eggs. The story goes someone asked for scrambled eggs and Jeanie told him they didn't have any. Asking for just egg whites or an omelet might get you arrested.

Biscuits you got no matter what you ordered, like a pitcher of sweet tea in July. Jeanie disappeared and came back with a stacked plateful, steam rising in an ambrosial cloud. She plopped the thick, heavy platter in the middle of the table. They ordered.

"These are great biscuits." Jake crammed in a buttered mouthful between sips of scalding coffee. "I've had croissants in downtown Paris, but nothing compares to the flaky taste of southern biscuits. Of course, the coffee was better in Paris." He took another bite.

"Try some of the figs." Cleveland tapped a pint Mason jar clustered with all the southern staples, salt, pepper, Worcestershire, hot sauce and Catsup. Jake plopped on a scoop of preserves.

"Ummmm!" "You ever have figs?" Cleveland grinned.

"Sure. The Turks eat 'em with yogurt, but I like mine just like this." He smiled, licked a trace of sweetness off his lip. "Just like my mom always made 'em."

"Where's your family from?" In the South, this was a question that in bygone days would have been punctuated with the cocking of a six-shooter. Cleveland was surprised he'd never thought to ask.

"Right here."

"No!"

"Left when I was five and moved to California."

"What brought you back?"

"Culture and creativity." Cleveland laughed.

"I know about the culture. What's the creative part? Oh, yeah, you mean your writing. How's the great American 'N' coming along?"

"Just got my one-hundredth rejection letter. Time to celebrate. So kind of you to mention it."

"Ain't those a shot of shit! What's it say, we've got all the best sellers we need?"

"Nothing so encouraging."

"Hang tough. Next week some New Yorker who talks through his nose will be in a beggin', check writing mood." Jake cracked a half smile. "Name a decent author published on the first shot."

"James Michener."

"Doesn't count. He worked in publishing." The conversation stopped momentarily. Jeanie scooted full, white plates in front of them. The pungent aroma of smoked country ham, lightly-fried filled every nostril.

"Honor the pig for his noble sacrifice," Cleve said.

The place began filling up, but nothing compared to the after church crowd on Sunday mornings, when people waited in line at the door and the smell of pan fried chicken and catfish, greens with smoked ham, clouds of buttery mashed potatoes and puffy, yellow cornbread drifted across the county. It was an invitation straight from your grandmama's kitchen.

"So, what makes you want to run for high political office?" Cleve asked.

Jeanie poured refills.

"The honorable Mr. Robbins is a born again Neanderthal, and I want to have some fun."

Cleveland chuckled. "Nobody goes into politics for fun anymore than they go into hog farming for the smell."

"That's what a friend said."

"Your friend told you the truth."

"To tell the truth, the whole religion thing scalded my ass. In the military, we have Christians, Jews, Moslems, Sikhs, Hindus, you name it. Messing with somebody else's religion is off limits. Otherwise we'd all be at each other's guts. You gotta have a little respect."

"You're not in the military now. You're living right on the buckle of the Bible Belt." Cleveland dropped the grin. "The fiction is, is that we're all cut from the same cloth."

"That's bull."

Cleve shrugged. "Just like the Emperor's new clothes, who's going to speak up when everybody wants to believe?"

"I'd say it's gotten just a little inconvenient lately."

"People treasure lies one hell of a lot more than they treasure the truth."

"I'm beginning to notice." Jake drummed his fingers on the table. "I can't believe the fundamentalist crowd is so proud to be intolerant. You know what kind of crap they'd stuff down every kid's throat if they got their way."

"Just remember where you are and try not to alienate folks who can help you."

"Look, Cleve, I'm a fighter pilot, so keep it simple."

Cleveland broke into a warm smile. "We don't disagree on the intellectual ravages of stupidity. But, I've got friends on both sides of the line, and I like them all. You want tolerance, be tolerant. Around here, there're some slap-on-the-back regular folks I wouldn't trust to shovel horse manure and some fundamentalists I'd trust with my family and all my money. What I'm saying is, don't be quick to paste a moral label on your forehead or on theirs. Now, you want some advice from a long-time observer of the Cassavora scene?"

"I'll take all the advice I can get." Jake had a look that told you you were going to have to kill him to defeat him and he was looking at Cleveland just that way. It wasn't a mean look exactly, more like staring at determination itself.

Cleveland met him head on. "First of all, I'd speak to the issues and be very specific. The more specific the better. It defuses differences, if you catch my drift."

Jake nodded.

"You're going to be talking to people who don't wear uniforms to tell you which side they're on. I wouldn't toss around a lot of fundamentalist this and fundamentalist that. Even the evangelicals aren't all fundamentalists. Second, you're going to need some supporters. I'm talking money now. Someone to foot the bill for signs and fliers and whatnot. You're a newcomer with no name recognition. People aren't going to know anything about you. If they don't know what to think about you, they aren't going to vote for you."

"I've thought about that. I'm not taking anybody's money, and I don't plan to ask anyone to vote for me." Jake spoke slowly. "I'll go door to door and see where it gets me."

"Whew, Cassavora is pretty spread out. It'll be a job."

"One thing I've got is time."

"Well, that's the tough way to go. Let me give you a few names of people who can make you or break you." Jake scratched out the names Cleveland reeled off, touching every tentacle of power in the county.

Jeanie poured from a second pot.

"Now pay close attention to this," Cleve said, putting both elbows on the table and leaning close. "This is a mighty complicated county. The school board isn't about Robbins taking over, getting the dirty books out and Genesis back in. Matter of fact, I don't think he's won a single battle. It's another reason I'd glance around before I fired off anymore broadsides in what is probably the wrong direction."

"So, who do I point at when I pull the trigger?"

"A tricky question. Depends on how many bullets you got and who you're trying to kill. Board of Commissioners is a powerful crew. Board of Realtors exerts a whale of an influence, especially with all the development going on. Chamber of Commerce is big. Of course, there's some cross over."

"Is everything square?"

Cleveland smiled. "Anything ever square, except in geometry class?"

"How 'bout government? They still teach it?"

"Sure, in literature. The fiction part." They sat back, talked out, coffeed out. Jake started to fidget, edgy to get going.

He'd shoved back his chair, when he noticed a man across the room, sitting at a table by himself, working at a stack of papers.

"Who's that?" Jake nodded in the man's direction.

"Edgar Martin. Edgar's a special case. He's dead."

"Dead?"

"That's what the Social Security Administration says. Hey, Edgar," Cleveland called across the room, "Come meet a friend of mine."

Edgar ambled over, his frame as thin as a scarecrow. He stood medium height, with glasses and thinning brown hair and a perpetually irritated look on his sun-wrinkled face, like someone had just called him a bastard and he didn't know quite what to do about it.

"Pull up a chair and tell Jake Morgan here your story."

Edgar nodded, eased himself down and started talking like it was the most natural thing in the world to tell a complete stranger the details of his meager life. "I'm retired," he began, "living on a pension and social security. About six months ago, my social security check just stopped." He threw up his hands and then placed them on his knees. "No explanation. No nothing."

"Did you call Social Security?"

"Damn right I called. They said I was dead. The person I talked to said I needed to write a letter explaining that I was still alive. So, I did that. Dear dumb bunnies, I said, I am alive, so send me my check."

"What happened?"

"The letter came back, saying they couldn't find a record of my name on the active list. I guess when you're dead, they bury the stupid record with you. Then I got another letter asking for the name of my closest relative." Edgar's face was turning pink, working rapidly toward irate. "I called 'em again and told 'em not only was I alive, but their closest relatives dragged their hairy knuckles in the jungle. The idiot I spoke to told me to make an appointment to come in and speak to some other idiot in records and claims."

"What happened then?" Jake's brow furrowed and the fingers of his hands curled together. A slight smile played across his lips.

"Same damn thing. I called to make an appointment and they needed a letter. I sent a letter, and they had no record of me. Came back to me marked 'deceased.' I've written my congressman for help, which is pretty much like asking Stevie Wonder for directions, and I've sent a letter a week ever since. I'm dead and there's not a thing I can do about it."

Jake stopped playing with his fingers, pulled out a ballpoint and made notes on a white paper napkin. "I've got a friend who's a Regional Director," he said, not looking up. "Let me give him a call and in a week," he glanced up at Edgar, grinned and handed him the napkin, "Call this guy. If the problem isn't fixed, remind him that I can still fly circles around him, drink him under the table, and then kick his ass. "

Edgar stared at the napkin like it was manna. "Thanks." He really didn't know what to say and stumbled through the thanks.

Edgar left. Cleveland looked at Jake. "How do you end up knowing a Regional Director?"

"Air Force buddy," he said simply, leaving out all the good parts about dropping 500 lb bombs and watching them blossom into huge rosettes of orange flame and black smoke, about swilling bottles of icy San Miguel, right out of the freezer, while talking out every minor flaw in every mission, mining the secrets of life and death. He left out being with men who covered your ass without being asked to, and depended on you for their next breath. "When we retire, we fan out so we can stir up more trouble in more directions."

Jake could tell Cleveland was looking at him in a different light. "You may make a politician after all. If Edgar gets his monthly check, you just got yourself votes all over the county."

"I'll be damned if I'll be a politician and sell my soul for votes."

"You're sounding like one of those fundamentalist Christians." Cleve laughed.

The words stung. Jake tightened his jaw to stop a flash of anger. Cleve's offhand remark came too close, reminding him he walked a narrow alley between reasonableness and the zealousness he despised.

Cleveland also made him realize the call to arms was building in him like steam in a pressure cooker. He'd been out of action too long, been living quietly. Something in him needed to struggle, to right wrongs, to prove the fire wasn't out.

A couple of truly Southern things are biscuits and fruit preserves, and like so many comfort foods, neither is difficult. If you want to get the full effect of Breakfast at Brice's, you've got to make some of these.

Brice's Baking Powder Biscuits:

2 cups flour

1 teaspoon salt

2 tablespoons of baking powder

6 tablespoons butter

3/4 cup of milk

Mix the dry ingredients and cut in the butter. Add the milk and mix quickly. Turn the dough out on a floured surface and knead it for 30 seconds. Roll it out to a half-inch thick and cut it in rounds. Put the rounds a couple of inches apart on an ungreased baking sheet. Bake in a preheated 350o oven for 15 minutes, or until slightly browned. Makes about a dozen biscuits.

Brice's Fig Preserves:

2 lbs ripe figs (about 16 large ones)

2 lemons, sliced lengthwise in half, sliced very thinly on the diagonal

1 1/2 pounds sugar

1 cup water

Wash figs and remove stems, place in a steel pot, with sugar, water, and lemon slices. Bring to a boil, occasionally stirring figs off the bottom, and continue to cook until the pink color of the froth turns golden. Use a spoon to remove any surface scum. Put hot figs and syrup in sterilized jars and seal. Use any extra syrup over pancakes and waffles. Keep any unsealed preserves in the refrigerator.

15

Our principals have a lot of latitude. I don't make their decisions for them.
—Dr. Lucinda Whitehall superintendent

Goddard spoke to Doc Moncrief on the phone and got some preliminaries, but no startling surprises. After that, he drove to the high school for a chat with the principal, Bobby Miller. Miller didn't have much to add. Everybody liked the coach. The team was devastated to find out he was leaving for greener pastures, but they kind of understood, as much as teenagers whose whole lives revolved around the football field could.

Ask Mrs. Arston, the P.E. teacher and cheerleader coach, Miller suggested. She might know more about the coach's private life. Not that he was implying anything.

Roberta Arston had been a college cheerleader and still had vestiges of the body twenty years later. At least Sheriff Goddard didn't notice any major flaws when he knocked lightly on her half open door and peeked in to see her seated at her desk.

She was writing something on the monthly scheduling sheet, glanced up, motioned him in and went back to writing.

He sat down and waited.

She clicked her pen shut, put it down on the desk. "I take it this is about the coach."

"That's right."

Her cell phone rang and she quickly picked it up. The sheriff heard something about ordering new basketballs before she hung up.

"What do you want to know?" Mrs. Arston looked him right in the face. Her arms weren't crossed and neither were her long legs; none of the negative body postures he was used to seeing. Her eyes shone deep blue and her face didn't need much makeup.

"Have any idea where he might have been the night he died?"

"I understand they found him in front of the Post Office."

"Before that."

"No, why should I?"

"It wasn't an accusation."

She gave him a weak smile, crossed her legs. "Around here, every question is an accusation."

"Do you know who he might have been seeing?" Roberta studied him, wondering where this might be going, what she should say. "I don't know what you mean."

The sheriff gave her his policeman's tone, relentless and as cold as steel. "I need to know where the coach was that night, what he might have been doing, and who might have been with him." The question and the way it was asked were enough to put a crack in the dam. Mrs. Arston's eyes darted away as a hand came up to her mouth. He expected she was about to cry and she did, a little weepy cry with single tears down each cheek.

"I loved him." She choked a little when she said it.

"Yeah, he was a pretty popular guy." One thing he hated about police work was turning the screws. He could do it, but it made him feel better to offer a little dignity.

She nodded, kept tearing. Goddard snatched a tissue from the box on her desk and handed it to her. She took it, dabbed at her eyes. "You probably already know," she began, "so I'll just go ahead and say it. My husband and I are separated. We've lived apart for six months."

"I didn't know. So, you were seeing the coach is what you're telling me."

"Yes."

"Did you see him that night?"

"We had supper." Goddard's eyebrows went up.

"Where?"

"In the city, that big steak restaurant."

"Plenty of those." "I don't remember the name, but the waiters wore white shirts and black ties. Lots of dark paneling. A man's name, I think."

"Charlie Taylor's?"

"Yes...yes, I think so." Goddard made a note.

"What time did you leave and when did you see him last."

"He dropped me at home about nine or nine thirty."
"He didn't come in?"

"We had coffee."

"Any intimacies?" She looked at him, shocked he might expect an answer. "It's important to the investigation," he said.

She shook her head no. "We were both tired. I kissed him goodnight."

"Did you see him after that? Talk to him on the phone or anything?" She looked away from him. Shook her head. It wasn't the straightforward 'no' he was expecting. He waited a minute to see if she would add anything voluntarily. She didn't, and she didn't look at him as he got up and walked out.

Goddard thought about the revelations on his way back to the car. Miller hadn't known about two of his teachers? Pretty far fetched in Sam's opinion, especially in this tight little corner of the world.

Going across the parking lot, he waved to Millie, his favorite from the Golden Arches. She stopped and stared, then slowly waved back. Then she kept staring, making him wonder why. But, now was not the time or place.

Of course politics changes you. Everything you do changes you. You just have to make sure it doesn't warp you. —Charles Beaufort II, chairman, Cassavora Board of Commissioners

Jake fired off several more volleys to the newspaper. He wanted to say it wasn't Darwin who finally proved we descended from apes, but he bit his tongue and remembered his pledge to stick to ideas. His letters seemed bland, even to him. Return fire didn't materialize, except for one lady who wrote to say this was a Christian country and a Baptist county. Nice distinction.

So, Jake broadened his approach, calling for greater accountability and a more open system of hiring and firing. Those got explosive responses claiming Jake impugned the reputation of every teacher in the system and especially the superintendent. Sounded pretty much like he'd scored a direct hit.

Jake had no lack of ammunition. He read about the high school dropping an art teacher and scaling back the band program. So, he fired off another letter on the importance of art, the relationship between music and mathematics, how art in all its forms shaped our world. Three rapid responses appeared the next week, all of them accusing him of wanting to dilute the academic program, having no respect for the teachers and wanting to dictate everything that went on at the high school. They made the same points, using the same words.

Besides the newspaper blasts, Jake organized his campaign as methodically as planning a flying mission. He did skullduggery with Cleve and Skeeter, hammering out the necessities, including signing up at the Court House during declaration week and paying the fifty-dollar fee.

Cassavora County had five at-large posts. To run for chairman you signed up to run for Post One. The later you signed up, the more likely it was you could pick your opponent, but those fine points were lost on Jake. When he went to the courthouse, he saw some unknown was running for Post 2 and Purcell Southmore was running against Tom Millage for chairman.

Barbara Small, the county clerk handled the sign-ups and the fees. Her matronly gray-streaked hair and pleasant monotone were courthouse fixtures.

"I see Southmore is running for chairman," Jake mentioned, as subtle as a large Eskimo at an ice hole.

"Yes, he was in here earlier." No hints. No emotion.

Jake ran a finger down the white form, signed his name under Post 4. A furtive glance detected nothing lingering behind Barbara's pancake makeup and slightly pinched cheeks. The pale blue, impartial eyes simply followed the nose of his pen with bureaucratic correctness.

"Of course, he also has his detractors," Barbara ventured. Was that a sign she was on his side? A fellow soldier in the war against ignorance?

"I think the county has had about enough controversy." Jake threw the comment out, wishing for some indication of support.

"That's true." No smile. Not even a hint at the corners of the thinly lipped mouth. Could have been his own controversy she was referring to. Who knew?

"No one else has signed up to run for Post 4?"

"Nobody so far. But that's Todd Ingles' seat, so I expect to see him in here today."

"Wait a minute! I don't want to run against Todd Ingles! I thought no one was running for Post 4! I didn't see any names!"

"Well, you can't change it now." Her queen of the castle tone caught him caught him in the solar plexus. "Once you sign the document of public record, you can't change parties or positions. It's the law. Your only choices now are to run, drop out, or run for another office, like county commissioner, or something like that."

Jake slunk out of the courthouse. Uncertainty and uneasiness trailed him, like a patient who'd been told to call back in two weeks for the results of a biopsy. Last night, when he'd asked himself the tough question, he'd had no trouble with the answer. That was last night, in the privacy of his own home, with the fortitude of single malt.

With the dawn came details and the rules of the game. Not only had he bungled the sign up, but also his brief chat with the clerk bared Democracy's naked body politic. Every opinion counted for one vote. Sobered you up to realize a cretin and a genius homogenized into the average American voter. And, unlike the political theory of the classroom, every vote was suddenly a prize to be won or lost. Every move he made, every hand he shook, every word he uttered was a craps shoot for votes. The temptation to abandon all principles, promise all things to all people, slap every back, laugh at every joke, shake every proffered hand suddenly seemed as natural as grinning like a fool when someone shouted cheese. He thought about the clerk. How could he tell if she had secretly hated him and loved his opponent? Maybe she burned his letters to the editor and despised everything he stood for.

On the other hand, maybe she despised Purcell Southmore and treasured Jake's writings like bone slivers from dead saints. As much as he hated to admit it, he also wondered what church Barbara attended.

Robbins and Southmore's harangues started a religious brushfire, fueled by half-baked theology that put a match to flammable doubts. Before the furor, almost no one gave any thought to who went to which church. Now, whispers behind a small town's paper-thin walls fanned the flickering theological flames.

Maybe the clerk would have told Jake how to properly pick his opponent if she supported him. On the other hand, maybe he should have asked before signing his name. It was a ping-pong game with an invisible ball and no way to keep score.

It never occurred to neophyte politician, Jake Morgan, so astute in other ways, that the County Clerk was also an elected position and this day was the glorious beginning of a coming election for both of them. Barbara not only had a vote to give, but votes to collect and a vote was a vote, whether a person hated you or loved you. In the vote-getting war you picked your battles and your enemies with care and built alliances, which, if you did it right, would keep you from feeling naked, alone and out of office.

In his haste, Jake made the grievous error of running against the one member of the board he halfway supported. The error plagued him on the way home.

There was good change and bad change, and he knew what side he was on. All over the county, a lot of things were being torn down, plowed under — metaphorically and literally. "Seems like they could be a little more careful," Jake thought, driving past where the old Jefferson homestead once stood.

Just lately, the Jefferson place disappeared into the hungry jaws of metal machines. It wasn't much, having been deserted for several years, but it sat at a main intersection and was a part of the landscape. A few months ago, the short front yard and the white picket fence were touchstones to Jake's eyes. He could drive by and picture life here as it always had been, the idyllic life he thought he was getting when he moved back. The broad armed oak trees were probably in someone's fireplace now. The farm had symbolized his Cassavora County roots and now it was gone.

Older residents, whose families went back generations, complained about too much growth, but they were the ones who sold parts of their vast homesteads to the developers. And, the new people, like Jake, missed the sight of the old Jefferson place.

Grand Food Plaza sprang up where the farm used to be. Grand Foods, the grocery giant, dominated the old cornfield and there were restaurants and dry cleaners and record shops and shoe shops and even a tanning salon on the strip mall landscape. Maybe it was a sign Cassavora had moved into the consumer age. They should have at least left the old oaks. Jake sighed.

After supper, he picked up the telephone feeling like a guilty schoolboy. "Mr. Ingles, this is Jake Morgan. I just signed up to run for the school board."

"Congratulations."

"Thanks, but I made an error. I signed up to run for Post 4."

"It's okay with me. I've decided not to run again."

"Really!" Life was good. The sun shone. Sins of ignorance forgiven.

"Yep. I've had enough. Besides, my wife's parents are both getting older. That's going to take up more of my time."

"I'm feeling like the man who's watching his mother-in-law race off a cliff in his new Cadillac."

"I know what you mean, and I appreciate your support, but, as I say, four years is enough."

Jake was on a high until he checked his email and saw another pearl from Jill. This one was a little more specific, alleging that he had not fulfilled his obligations and her lawyer would contact him.

*****

Sheriff Goddard took a look at the morning paper and sipped his coffee, just as John Howard stepped through the door.

"What'd you find out at the school?"

"I found out we need to look closely at Mrs. Roberta Arston."

"Something going on with the coach?"

"Yep," Goddard looked up. "Both hanky and panky. She was with him the night he died. Says she didn't see him after nine-thirty, but who knows."

"That's it?"

"Don't look so disappointed. There's more churning around in my giant brain, but so far no print out."

17

Judging by what we pay our teachers, we don't want professionals; we want people who desperately need employment. It always amazes me we often get far better than we pay for. —Jake Morgan

Jake stood in the sunshine and ran his finger over a city map, the neighborhoods circled in blue magic marker, voting precincts outlined in yellow. Bold, black check marks let him keep score. Ahead and behind lay boiling days of tramping sprawling subdivisions, bothering complete strangers, sharing sweat with the universe.

He knocked on a solid oak door, the entrance to a huge, two-story white colonial from another era, squatting in the middle of downtown Fletcher. Old houses, some of them showing their age, lined both sides of the street. While he waited, he checked his map. He was smack in the middle of Church Pew, the largest voting precinct and some said the most cantankerous. Once again, he swiped perspiration with a white, soggy handkerchief and rolled his shoulders to let a little air between his skin and the dark blue polo shirt. The past few hours, he'd stood on blistering porches and chewed over the issues with dozens of people, most of whom treated him with a disinterested politeness. Some weren't so kind. One stout defender of the faith roared at him, told him to "Git off his land!" and somebody's cheery, Reubenesque wife offered him cool water and a seat on the porch swing while she prattled on, until he finally excused himself before his mind turned to mush. Every rare now and then Jake ran into someone with a real point.

"How much bang are we getting for the buck?" The guy stood robustly in a straining business suit. "I see public education out of control cost wise. Out of touch with the marketplace. I can't hire half the high school grads these days.

One young idiot measured wood for a shelf. I told him to make it a foot shorter and damn if he didn't reach for a pencil and paper to work it out. Stupid. Another guy told me he'd see if he could get to work by nine, but eight-thirty was definitely out. I ain't hirin' people for the feel good fun of it."

Jake knocked one last time on the door, turned to step off the porch and follow the narrow brick walkway to the white gate. One house more or less didn't matter. He turned back with the creaking of the door and saw a smile that erased everything he'd seen or heard all day. "Yes?" She spoke quizzically, melodiously, the soft tones floating in the humid air. Her smile just hung there.

Jake gave her the short and sweet of why he was hammering on her door in the middle of the afternoon. There were plenty of places for his eyes to play, but he did the impossible and locked on hers.

Brown eyes, shortish dark hair, pert nose, white, straight teeth fed his hungry heart. She opened the door wider, and he saw olive skin. Sunshine fell around her like a spotlight. He half expected a Spanish accent, but it didn't come. "Hi, I'm Maria McDuff." She held out her hand, the sleeveless sun dress a showcase for slim shoulders and smooth arms. The long, thin fingers ended in nails a wet red. Ferrari red. The tips of her fingers slid across his palm. "I'd ask you to come in, but the house is a mess." That smile again. "Mind if we talk on the porch? Wait a minute," she added quickly, "You must be thirsty. May I offer a glass of iced tea?"

And a bed for the night if it wouldn't be too much trouble. From sweaty cockpits to some sweet, Southern wife bringing him iced tea. Thoughts of her naked skin banished the shame. Generous in neither ass nor tit and yet beguiling.

Of course, his needs were simple, but definite. It didn't take much to satisfy them: dark hair, pretty feet, straight teeth, outgoing, but without the brashness of a hooker or the manners of a tart. No tattoos or piercings. No gum chewing. No open-mouthed yawning or confusion over the pronouns me and I. It would help if she knew the difference between Dom Pérignon and Alka Seltzer and could spell the former. His ex-wife had told him he was a secret snob. A secret from whom? The sky shone blue again. Running for office was the best idea since he discovered whiskey.

Big white pots of flowers dotted the porch, overflowing with blooms. Maria pushed the screen door with a hip and reappeared with a heavily engraved silver tray, probably as old as the house. The glass pitcher sweated. Two glasses stood tall and sparkled beside it.

Jake slouched back, she sat upright, in oversized, white wicker chairs, sipping the sweet, dark taste of summer, chatting, watching the parade of cars through downtown Fletcher. Baskets of ferns and impatiens hung from white beams, a profusion of cascading greens and reds and purples he hadn't noticed before.

"So, you're running for the school board?"

"Yes."

"And, you're retired from the military?"

"Yes." Retired. He'd been a fighter pilot. He still was a fighter pilot, wild and free and there was nothing anybody could do to change it, like being in a kick ass motorcycle gang only your mother was still proud of you.

"Lived all over the world, I suppose." Maria interrupted his self-congratulatory reverie.

He nodded. "Why?"

"Why, what?"

"This." She held the glass of tea precariously and spread her arms. "I'd have thought the school board in our little county would be too tame."

He shrugged. "I've spent all of my adult life either going to school or teaching." She'd shifted in her seat, crossing her legs, showing bare flesh up to mid-thigh. The skin was flawless, the muscles toned. Nicely shaped, sandaled feet, toenails the same racy red. He reined his mind back. It didn't come willingly. "What do you think about the school board controversies?"

"Interesting." The voice trailed off.

"In what way?"

She hesitated. "I believe in the separation of church and state, and I think the public is pretty ignorant about public education." A faintness of floral cologne floated past his nostrils.

"I'll drink to that." He prayed for a chuckle, a smile, a horselaugh. She was looking away, out at the road and seemed not to have heard him.

"Tell me about your name, McDuff. Scotch?" Aye, lassie, a full tumbler. Jake knew any Scots in this house came through marriage. Her cafe skin glowed, so unlike the pasty white flesh on the streets of Edinburgh.

"You've been reading too much Shakespeare." Now she laughed and it sounded like tiny silver bells. "Besides, it's spelled differently." She began to quote, lowering her voice an octave, creaking out the words. "Not in the legions of horrid hell can come a devil more damned in evils to top Macbeth."

"You know Shakespeare?" He'd just discovered a diamond in a gravel pit.

"I was in the county production of Macbeth last year. One of the witches."

"Must've taken a lot of makeup." She let the compliment pass, glanced away again. "Fletcher wasn't always this crowded." She pointed the lip of her glass toward the blacktopped thoroughfare. "When I was a girl we rode bikes up and down this street." Did he note an edge of sadness? Wistfulness?

"You've lived here all your life?"

"Pretty much. I went away to college, but only over to the University."

"So, tell me, what kind of salaries do the teachers get around here?" The question caught her off guard. She stared into her iced tea and then up at him.

"The pay is sufficient, I suppose. More money is always nice."

For some reason, maybe the hesitant tone, Jake pressed the point. "This is a pretty affluent community."

"I guess it's not bad, for the South." A slow, careful answer.

Jake wasn't certain what he detected, but this princess wasn't going to follow him home from the ball. Apprehension was there, no doubt. She obviously didn't want to talk about the school system. Perhaps her husband was connected.

"You really ought to come back when Mama is home." She changed the subject again, her face no longer relaxed. She moved to the front of her chair. Trying to hide a part of herself? Worried about disclosing too much to a stranger? Did she catch him glancing at her legs? He wondered if Cecilia would be jealous. Not likely.

The change in Maria's attitude was as clear as if she had pulled down her skirt to hide a knee, which she did not. "Mama knows this county in and out. She drove with Mark to Banberry's to get a prescription."

"Mark's your husband?"

"Son. He's a senior at the high school."

"Really?" He wanted to ask about the husband and the son, thought better of it. Let the fantasies grow, multiply, become one with his libido.

"Mama knows all the personalities around here, who's doing what and who's done what. I think you'd enjoy talking to her." She got up, smiled a tighter smile than before and said, "I know you've probably got more to do and I'm keeping you from it."

He wanted to say no, he'd stay a while longer, polish off the rest of the tea and race out for a six-pack. Instead he got to his feet. "Thanks for the tea and conversation."

Jake passed her the empty glass, hoping to touch her hand again, but her fingers avoided his. Intentional?

As he strode through the gate and onto the sun blanched sidewalk, he glanced back to see her going through the front door and caught a billow of sundress and a bare calf. An abrupt ending, almost as if she'd punched the clock the way she jumped up and got him out of there. Hubby coming home? Unlikely sitting on the front porch would disturb familial bliss. He knew he'd come back. After all, he had to talk to Mama.

And that night he dreamed, but not of Maria's well turned ankles and softly curved bust. Jill drifted back, beckoning him with full, flared hips, narrow waist, and the graceful curve of her neck. Her hands, warm and searching, slid up his arms to his chest; her full lips kissed his shoulder. She fit herself into him, molding the softness of her body against his strength. Her sigh drifted through him. The tickle of her breath, a hot, wet breeze, floated by his neck and across his chest. Then she morphed to Cecilia, then to a faceless nymph. His libido-powered remote changed channels on a whim. In the morning, everyone but his hard-on had vanished.

18

Our children are our future. We're committed to protecting the future. —
Bobby Miller, principal, Cassavora High School

Millie was the tip off. When the sheriff drove through
for his morning coffee, she hadn't been her cheery self, the same
impression he'd gotten when he'd seen her in the school parking
lot.

"I don't know if I should be telling you this." She
murmured conspiratorially, her arm reaching through the drive
through window to take the money.

Goddard took a quick sip of the coffee, winced at the
scalding heat, waited for what was coming.

"It's about the coach. I heard some things and once
after gym, I saw him kissing one of the girls in my class."

Millie was a good kid. It didn't take much prodding to
get a name and some less than savory circumstances.

*****

Dawn Heather Nelson was pretty in a nebulous sort of
way, dependent more on mere youth than real beauty. Rather
than picture her in her cheerleading uniform, showing off curves
and bare legs in front of a screaming crowd, Goddard searched
her face for the hidden part, the little girl. He wasn't looking for
innocence, but vulnerability and he wondered when the teddy
bears and Barbies got tossed aside in favor of lip-gloss and push
up bras. Happened younger and younger, girls with women's
bodies and teenage brains stepping into the grown-up world and
getting mud on their stockings.

"So, Dawn, is there anything you want to tell me?"

Dawn nodded, while she chewed her gum, clearly enjoying the attention. Her mother and father sat at her side in the sheriff's office, along with her attorney. The mother's hands churned in her lap, her dad was a marble statue. Dawn didn't seem to care about them one way or another.

Goddard already knew about the coach and could guess about the lust. He wanted to discuss the disappearance. He'd had words with the principal over not coming forward or even reporting one of his teachers having an affair with a student. The principal acted surprised, said he had reported it. Maybe he was telling the truth and Lucinda Whitehall was protecting her precious school system again. It was obvious a lot of people knew. Millie knew, and she didn't even hang with the wild crowd. Yet, apparently the coach hadn't even had his roaming hand slapped. Don't ask, don't tell? What a solid pillar of leadership.

At least now the coach was dead. That should keep things from getting too messy, unless of course the girl or her father or her boyfriend had something to do with it. Then the mess would reek like maggot-infested garbage.

"Well?" Goddard asked. A little prodding never hurt.

"What do you want to know?" The earthy tone told him she knew the score.

"We know you were involved with the coach."

Her lawyer whispered something to her, then spoke up. "I think we've been over this territory already."

"Please just have your client answer my question."

The lawyer hesitated, scanned the sheriff's face for a crack, a handhold. Finding none, he nodded to Dawn.

"I saw him a few times."

"You saw him." Sam played dumb.

Dawn rolled her eyes to the ceiling. "Okay, like we were an item for a while."

Goddard looked to the parents. "Could you leave us by ourselves a few minutes?"

The attorney and the parents whispered. When the parents left, the lawyer spoke to Goddard. "Are we sticking by our agreement?"

"Yep, I'm not involved unless she's got something to do with the coach's death."

Dawn had her cue. "The coach and I had an affair."

"How long?"

She looked down at her hands in her lap. "I don't know. A month? Two months?" A fuck-you tone hid beneath the answer.

"Were you still seeing him?"

"No." She blinked, looked away exasperated, the lie obvious.

"When did it end?"

"Last Spring." Another blink and she sucked at her bottom lip, smearing a bit of mauve lipstick on her teeth.

"You were a junior?"

"Yeah." The kind of sloppy answer with an attitude that made Sam want to back hand her across the room. He managed to control himself.

"Had you been with him lately?"

"I told you it was over." She glanced up at the ceiling, then gave a disinterested glance at the wall.

"Any other girls seeing him?"

She shrugged.

Goddard tightened his jaw and controlled the urge to shout. If this were his daughter... "This isn't cheerleading practice, Dawn. I'm investigating a suspicious death and right now you're up to your neck, so my advice is to cut the cutesy crap. Otherwise I'm going to take you into custody as a material witness."

"I wouldn't try that if I were you, sheriff." The lawyer stepped into the breach.

Sam looked him in the eye. "My advice to you counselor is for your client to drop the smartass attitude and answer my questions directly. That way we can all get to bed early. You can also tell her to stop lying to me."

Dawn's eyes shot up to Sam's. "My client is telling you what she knows."

"Then maybe your client can explain why two other students remember seeing her with the coach a few days before his death?"

"Okay, I saw him some after we broke up."

"So, you want to tell me if any other girls were seeing him?"

"Answer the question." The lawyer's voice sounded weary, like he didn't like this dirty skirt either, but a buck was a buck.

"He wasn't seeing any of the other girls. I would have known."

"Where does Mrs. Arston fit into all this?"

"She's such a bitch!"

"How about getting back to the question?"

"Well, she is! I won't even speak to her."

"She took him away?"

"She fucks half the guys in school. She's a slut!"

"Dawn..." The lawyer tried to soothe her.

"What do you know about the night he died?"

"Coach Gibbons?"

It was Goddard's turn to roll his eyes. What prompted a full-grown man, practically an idol of the community to flop in the dirt with a stupid, self-centered little tart? "Yes," he said patiently, "Coach Gibbons."

"I hadn't even seen him for like weeks, I mean except for a couple times. If anybody was with him that night it was Mrs. Arston. She doesn't care about anybody but herself. She probably, like, killed him."

19

Divorce is good practice for going into politics. You can't give too much of a shit about anything, but saving your ass. —Jake Morgan

Jill's lawyer hit him between the eyes with a one-paragraph letter threatening court action if he didn't immediately cough up twenty-five thousand dollars, her client's two-fisted share of the appreciation on the house.

His own lawyer brought home the fine points of separation and divorce. "See, Jake, you bought the house before the divorce was final."

"I know, but the separation agreement had the property settlement done. Finito."

"I haven't talked to her lawyer yet, but what she is probably referring to is the clause that allows for an amendment to the property settlement, prior to the final decree if there is a significant change in the amount of property. Usually it refers to stock splits or inheritance, or something more liquid than real estate."

"But, this is after the final goddamned decree."

The lawyer heaved a sigh. "I know. Look, I'm on your side. It's just that your former wife may argue she didn't know about your purchase of the property and its rise in value prior to the divorce. Now she thinks she's entitled to a chunk of change."

*****

John Howard had some news about the Arston woman. "She left the house after the coach left."

"You sure?"

"Neighbors saw her car pull out about half an hour later."

"How could they be certain?"

"A couple was sitting on the front porch. The time isn't exact, but they were between the news and their favorite TV show."

"Close enough. When did she come back?" Goddard's mind was whirling.

Howard shrugged. "Nobody I talked to had a fix on that."

"Suppose we check out the phone records, she if she called anybody from her house before she left."

"Based on what, sheriff?

"Based on the man she was dating showing up dead and it's likely she had a good idea he was cheating on her. And, how about asking her where she went." It didn't sound like a question and it wasn't.

"Already did. She got gas at the Flying K and bought some milk and bread at the Big Pig. Story checks out."

Goddard pursed his lips. "But nobody saw her come back, so exactly where she went and how long she was gone are still loose threads, right?"

"There's something else, unrelated." The sheriff waited, didn't say anything. "Rumors are flying about the Morgan guy."

"That's news?"

"The wags are saying women are leaving his house in the middle of the night."

"Lucky him. Mine won't go away." John Howard laughed.

"Don't you tell Elmira I said that!"

"Your secret's safe." "But, listen, John. Morgan is single right?"

"Divorced."

Goddard shrugged. "Not my job to see who's zipped up."

20

We pride ourselves on the way the school system works with local contractors in a community effort, for the benefit of the children. —Superintendent Lucinda Whitehall, quoted in The Advocate

You run this school system like a little dictatorship, giving contracts away to your friends. —Caldwell Robbins, outburst at a school board meeting.

Jake continued to prowl the neighborhoods, prying opinions from people who would rather be finishing housework or watching TV. They didn't make him feel unwanted; they made him feel unnecessary. He got back to Maria's street by circumstance more than design. The downtown roads tangled and his meanderings blundered him back to the big white house.

She'd eased into his thoughts so many times he'd begun to think of her as a flesh and blood personality, Maria, someone he'd really like to do some heavy breathing with. He ran into her once at Grand Foods. They'd spoken, exchanged polite smiles. There was something oddly attractive about her, but at the same time, an unknown element kept him from crossing the void. It sure wasn't the drop-dead perfect body or the beautiful face. But, there was something. He knew when a woman was holding back. Southern women were notably protective of themselves. Not shy, wary.

A look that usually got to him wasn't brassy, but brassy had worked in the distant past. Soft vulnerability. A slow smile, a happily guileless glance. Call it a lingering hint of corruptibility. That's what did it for him. Maria should fit, but didn't.

Cecilia was the only relationship since Jill left. Not quite true. He hadn't been celibate, but that wasn't the same thing. Something in Maria's wariness triggered introspection. Was she holding back because he seemed unapproachable? When she was unapproachable, he felt unapproachable. So which was it professor, la poule o l'oeuf?

The answer popped out at him. Married. He'd known it, but hadn't accepted it. Her husband. The nefarious bastard lurked somewhere in the shadows, spoiling Jake's fun, warding off the evil spirits of illicit passion. Still, for some reason, Jake kept thinking of her as single.

A lot he knew about women. You want me? Okay. That covered it. Diversions over the past few years were stray moments with old friends, not girlfriends exactly, but acquaintances who for reasons known only to God, suddenly turned friendship into ride-'em-cowboy.

Except for Cecilia. He loved her. No, he didn't. Why in the hell had that popped into his mind? With Maria, something seemed different, but familiar, like a face he couldn't quite place, a warm personality he might like to know better naked.

He puzzled over her in the days after their first meeting, then gave up and let his mind flit to other things, like mounting a reasonable campaign and avoiding the malodorous whiff of moral turpitude.

In the back of his mind, he'd wanted to return to the white house on Main Street and chat with Mama. It was a secret he kept from himself. Now here he was.

Older residents broadened his grasp of the county, with their snippets of history, personalities and scandal. Gradually the attitudes of the county, at first thin and hidden, flowed out, thickened and took on substance, like watery maple sap that bubbled down to thick, sweet syrup.

Maria's living room looked the way he'd expected. Women are naturally neater and care strongly about shit that doesn't matter. Take the little ceramic dogs and horses that stood playfully on the coffee table. He picked one up, marveled at the uselessness of a small ceramic dog, then put it back on the polished tabletop.

Waiting for Mama to make an appearance, he made small talk with Maria about how the campaign was going, how the weather had been. His eyes caught the books on the shelves and a clear glass vase with fresh cut tiger lilies.

Book-lined shelves gave any room warmth. Some books lay stacked, some opened. Soft armchairs caught the glow of the tall reading lamps behind them. The sofa was billowy enough to sleep on. No hint of a man here. Where was the smell of a good cigar, the well-worn Adidas by the door, something, anything out of place? She had a kid in high school. Where was he?

An older woman, rounded, fuller figured, gray hair, waddled into the room, pulling a shawl around her shoulders. She crinkled her nose to keep her glasses from falling off, used her arms to brace herself and plopped down heavily in an over-stuffed armchair.

"You must be Maria's mother." Jake rose.

"And you must be Jake Morgan." There was the barest hint of accent when she said *must*, as if she started to say *most* and changed her mind. She peered at him with dark eyes through thick lenses, smiled briefly, the way you'd pull back the curtains to let in a second of sunshine, then waved for him to sit back down. "Maria doesn't really care to talk about local politics. Kinda bores her, if you know what I mean, so she's *sicced* me on you. Now, why don't we just chat awhile?" No drippy touch of the South in that voice. The burnished silver hair had no doubt once been jet black and the letter *i* kept coming out of her mouth in a south of the border long *e*.

Jake sat opposite on a ladder back chair, leaning forward, hands on his knees. Maria curled herself quietly in another armchair.

"I understand from Maria, you're running for the Board of Education."

"That's right."

"Why?" Mama's voice rang strong and clear, barely controlled thunder. "What's your stake in it?"

"I bought a house a few years ago. I've lived here six months. I've been in and out of classrooms most of my life, between college and the military."

"A Johnny come lately."

"Seems this county could use a Johnny come anytime." He tossed it with more edge than he wanted, but anyway, there it was.

"No offense. Anybody who wasn't born here or married to someone who was born here is a Johnny come lately."

"You're from here?" he asked.

She looked to her daughter. "Maria, how about getting Mr. Morgan some of my pound cake and some tea?" Mama turned back to Jake. "You do take a cup of tea, do you not?" The accent wasn't going away anytime soon.

"Thank you."

They watched Maria disappear and Mama settled in, "It's a great little town, isn't it?" Her cheeks flushed to pink. She leaned forward and rasped, "It's a nest of greedy, undereducated know-nothins is what it is." Then she sat back, all debate on the subject settled.

"You asked if I was from here," she continued. "Yes and no. I married a boy from here and that makes me one of the clan. My maiden name is Martinez and back when I got to this county, you didn't want to have a name like Martinez."

"Times have changed," Jake said.

Her eyebrows shot up. "Well, anyway, here both of us are."

Jake didn't say anything.

"But you didn't come here to talk about me. Now you look at this poorly scribbled piece of tripe in *The Advocate*." Mama reached out with a folded newspaper. "Just read that bottom story and tell me what you think of the Pulitzer nominee who wrote it. The one about the real estate developer." Jake's eyes followed her pointed finger and scanned the column.

The county commissioners announced last night the real estate proposal by local developer Sob Jenkins to build a series of apartments for assisted-living, to be called Sob Jenkins Estates, would be tabled until a statewide, county-by-county study of water resources was released and studied by local authorities. Sob Jenkins wasn't the only one who put forth proposals, but Sob Jenkins was the only one named by the commissioners.

"I think it's an outrage," said Sob Jenkins, who added, "When has Sob Jenkins ever not done what was in the best interest of Cassavora County, which is where Sob Jenkins has lived for years. Sob Jenkins knows what he is doing."

"Sob Jenkins knows what he's doing!" Mama mimicked. "I can't even stand to read the newspaper anymore! Sob Jenkins this, Sob Jenkins that. I get sick of Sob Jenkins, just reading that one story. I was tired of Sob Jenkins years ago. He's a cretin, and the idiot who wrote that story is more than likely his twin brother. The only thing that newspaper is good for is lining bird cages."

"Mama, now don't you upset yourself," Maria cut in smoothly. She set a silver tray with a plate of sliced pound cake, a pot of tea and three cups and saucers on the coffee table. "The idea was to mention his name a few times, so people would remember him."

"They'll remember him all right! How could they forget the idiot whose name was mentioned twenty-five times by a reporter who's never heard of pronouns?" Anger flamed the accent.

"Sounds like you know the man," Jake interrupted.

"Know the man?" She moaned incredulously, drew a handkerchief from under the shawl and blew her nose with enough force to shred linen. "Wish I could say I didn't. I was his tenth grade social studies teacher. He was stupid as an armadillo chasing cars then, and I think he's lost a few brain cells since."

"Mama, maybe Mr. Morgan would like some cake and tea now."

"Yes, it wouldn't do to have him lose strength and faint dead away."

"Mama takes hot tea, even in the summer, Mr. Morgan." Maria once again poured oil on Mama's choppy waters.

"That's fine," he said, "It'll be a nice change."

He took his first bite and the buttery, lemon flavor put his taste buds forever in Mama's debt. "I've never tasted anything so light. It's moist as a cloud!"

"I thought you'd like it." Mama smiled, slurped some tea. "If there is one thing I can't abide, it's a man with no appetite."

"Then, I think you're gonna love me to pieces." Jake took another fork full.

"Mama's been making this pound cake since I was a little girl." Maria smiled. Jake smiled back.

"You were a teacher?" he asked Mama.

"For thirty-two years. Now my daughter is .... " Maria shot her mother a tense smile, and Mama let the end of the sentence fade.

"Maria is a teacher here in Cassavora?" He sipped his richly minted tea, trying to keep the surprise off his face. Why hadn't she mentioned it in their first conversation? Teaching was not something you would normally hide from a man running for the board of education. He remembered her hesitancy.

Mama didn't answer the question, evidently preferring to pop another at him. "Mr. Morgan, you been to any school board meetings?" Mama's booming voice snapped him straight back to the conversation.

"A few."

"Ever hear any of the teachers speak up? Voice opinions? Read anything in the newspaper any teacher's written?"

"Don't believe I have." "Mighty strange, no?" "I hadn't really thought about it." "Well, think about it." "Most of the teachers are very content." Maria had her own ideas. "I admit," Mama looked over the tops of her glasses. Jake felt like he was back in a classroom. "Teachers around here aren't used to standing on their hind legs, but even a contented dog barks once in a while."

"How 'bout you?" he said with a smile, "Are you ready to stand up and bark?"

"You haven't lived here long enough to understand," she continued, "Now, you'll have to excuse me. I have to go powder my nose." Mama un-wedged herself from the chair and carried her bulky, shawl draped self out of the room.

Jake understood all right. So far he hadn't seen anyone with the guts to swat a mosquito without a committee meeting. Everybody complained, though, and a lot of the time the complaints were about him.

The silence lingered. Maria smiled. Then she got up slowly, uncurling her legs, leaned close and took the dish from his hand, letting her fingers slide carelessly over his. This time, he was sure she did it on purpose. The top of the sundress fell open just a tad, and he glimpsed the white lace across the top of her bra.

His eyes followed as she placed the empty dish and fork on the table, but she didn't look back at him initially, only after she had sat back down, gained distance.

"So, do I get to meet your husband today?" The words were barely out of his mouth before he wanted to suck them back down his throat. Why in God's golden universe had he asked?

Maria's smile faded. "No, I don't believe so." She spoke quietly and looked back toward the distant sound of a toilet flushing. "You might as well know, I don't have a husband."

At least that settled it. Jake wanted to ask her some questions, get her to open up about herself, but she didn't look back at him. "So, how is your son doing? I haven't met him." Strategic retreat.

"Fine." She smiled briefly, then watched Mama shuffle back into the room.

"That really felt good!"

Maria's face rushed to crimson. "Mama has a touch of diabetes every now and then," she quickly explained.

"Every now and then? D' ya think Jack the Ripper had a touch of meanness every now and then? That's the first good, comfortable powder I've had in a week!"

"Mama!"

"Well, it is!" Mama settled back and looked at Jake. "So, you see the problems education has in this county?"

"I see a few of them."

"Well, there's enough to fill a bucket. Top of the list is ignorance, followed closely by development, which is another way of saying M-0-N-E-Y. They're carting it away in wheelbarrows, but you think they're giving much to the schools and the teachers? Building schools and selling land are cash cows. No money in buying books and paying teachers. That's the real crime with Sob Jenkins, not his ignorance. And, he's not the only one. A lot of other local trash are milking the school system for every dollar. Slapping each other on the back, padding each other's pockets. I'd bet you anything Sob Jenkins has the contract to build the new middle school in his hip pocket. He's built this and he's built that."

"I see what you mean, but I wouldn't put ignorance at the top of the list. Anyway, business is booming."

"Oh, it's booming all right. Douglas Whitehall is one of his partners." She paused for the name to sink in.

"Lucinda's husband?"

"And the school board paid a million and a half dollars for property that had been offered for eight-hundred thousand. Plus, the local bank handles all the financing."

"You suspect there's some dark deals." He wanted to ask how she came by all this back room knowledge, but prying, might break her stride. Other sources could help him with the homework.

"The color of midnight on a moonless night."

"So why doesn't somebody speak up?"

"Who? A retired, almost bedridden schoolteacher? Her daughter?"

As Jake was leaving, Mama looked him in the eye. "You've been going after the fundamentalists." Jake shrugged.

"Well, don't waste your time. At the most, they're pimples. You pop one and another one crops up. You want to do some good, go after the diseases that keep this county on educational welfare."

"You think it's Sob Jenkins?"

"Open your eyes, Mr. Morgan. Use your brain, unlike that dull collection on the school board right now. Don't just stand there and wait for some old school teacher to feed you the answers like she's fed you pound cake."

He'd have to wait even longer before somebody would just up and help. But, Mama made some good points. Was he tromping blindly through a minefield, swatting gnats?

"Maria, could you show our visitor to the door? I'm tired."

On the way out, Maria touched his bare arm, letting her hand linger. He said goodbye. She smiled a sad, wistful smile. Jake had no more idea what to think about her than when he'd walked in, but she sure had a talent for filling out a sundress.

Mama's Pound Cake

Oven: 325 °F, 1 hour 15 minutes Yield: one tube cake or two bread-pan cakes

2 sticks butter at room temp. 1/2 teaspoon baking powder 1/2 cup solid shortening, room temp. 1 cup milk 3 cups sugar 1 teaspoon vanilla extract 5 eggs 1 teaspoon grated lemon rind 3 cups all purpose flour

Cream butter and shortening. Add sugar, beating until well mixed. Beat in eggs, one at a time. Add lemon rind and vanilla. Mix flour and baking powder and add alternately with milk to creamed mixture. Whip batter until fluffy. Pour into a large tube pan, or divide between two bread-pans and bake in a 325 deg. oven for 1 hour 15 minutes, or until a knife inserted in the middle comes out clean.

Mama's Mint Tea

Four bags of black tea in a four-cup pot. A handful of fresh spearmint crushed and added to the pot. Half a cup of sugar. Add boiling water and let it steep five to ten minutes. Remove the bags; leave the mint.

21

Politics has very little to do with policy; in fact it has very little to do with anything besides getting elected. —*C2, off-the-cuff comment at a barbecue*

Cleve called Jake the next morning. "See the newspaper yet?"

"No. Should I?"

"I'd say it's worth a look. The name Colonel Humphrey McClary mean anything?"

"He was my squadron CO in Vietnam."

"Evidently, he doesn't remember you fondly."

"He doesn't remember anyone fondly." The Op Ed piece in *The Advocate* said Colonel McClary was retired in Texas. The Colonel was all too happy to report Jake had been insubordinate and a coward.

Local Hero's War Record Questioned

The article went on to claim, in the barest of language, Jake's cowboy attitude and reckless disregard for orders discredited the whole war effort, destroyed morale and brought consternation to his superiors. Tongues would wag, of course, but the specifics were fuzzy and vague enough to stave off litigation.

"Where in hell did this come from?"

"I'd say you've made some enemies."

"Good guess. Somebody went all the way to Texas."

"Hate to break the news to you, Jake, but your military service is a matter of public record. Anybody with time on their hands and a social security number ... you use it as the number on your driver's license?"

Jake's silence said it all.

"Well, there you go. I don't even have to leave my keyboard to find out your phone number and what you eat for breakfast."

Skeeter had been right. He was dealing with people who were mean to the bone. Clever and determined, too.

And, there was the crap he was hearing about women at his house, even though Cecilia was the only one. A taste of scandal oiled the wagging tongues.

22

There's Baptists and there's Baptists, if you know what I mean. They come in a lot of different flavors, all claiming to be the one true flavor. —
Cassavora resident

The Reverend Lester Monroe sat in his cramped, book-lined study at the Seminole Baptist Church and pondered the future. He clamped his eyes shut, carefully raised his glasses to his forehead and pinched the bridge of his nose. The Reverend was a well preserved fifty-five, with barely receding brown hair, a narrow face and a thin body hidden under loose slacks, white shirt, and blue patterned tie. His flock of faithful was over five-hundred strong and growing. It didn't make Seminole the largest congregation in the county, but it wasn't just a seedling either. Lester had been a pastor in six churches over the past thirty-five years, ranging from Delaware to Texas.

His wife of thirty years, his soul mate and confessor, passed away a year ago and that, along with seminary, marriage, and children were turning points in his life. Passed away. What a gentle euphemism for a body ripped and broken in an auto accident, until there was no hope and no life. What a perfect way to cover the shock, the hurt, the terror of loss.

Only in the past few months had he been able to think of Rebecca without excusing himself and stealing away. When she died, happiness turned suddenly to loneliness, with such a sudden chill that he lost his way for months on end. Dale Evers, the Assistant Pastor, had stepped in and shouldered the burden of all the dozens of tasks that fill a preacher's days and nights. Thank the Lord for Dale! God giveth and God taketh away in ways beyond measure, for reasons unknown.

At first, Rebecca spoke to him all day, all night. He would reach for her in his dreams and her warmth would be there beside him, until he awoke and his heart was pierced anew with the cold, merciless spear of unspeakable loss.

For a while, he thought he might never preach again. What would he have to say? Before his first sermon, Dale stopped by the office and looked in. "How's it coming?" Dale, the ever-hopeful twenty-five-year-old burning with new, untested faith. What would he know about loss, about shattered lives?

The Reverend remembered how his mind had drifted. "What of my son and daughter?" Married, moved, families of their own. His daughter's words echoed from the passionless telephone line. "Mom had a good life." A good life. Well, yes, if you counted following a country preacher, never knowing what job would come and depending on God to provide. The Reverend had tried to conjure the good times. Useless. They hid themselves in shame, unwilling to step out of the shadows and shine amid the gore of the accident. When he saw his young son's smiling face, he also saw the man the young son had become, no longer needing a father to cheer him at Little League games or show him how to ride a bike. He realized his life was passing before him, but in snippets.

And, what of the man he had become? His first sermon since the tragedy was to be on a Sunday set aside to honor marriage. Dale had asked him three times if he was up to it. Each time he'd said yes, not really knowing if he was, but unwilling to say no. It wasn't his pride, but a sure knowledge that defeat would make his whole life of faith a lie.

Preparing for that sermon, he had sat alone in his study, pen in hand, staring at the blank sheet of paper and wondering

how he could fill it with the trite words and phrases
salvaged from the ship wreck that had become his life. How
could he talk about God's mercies in the face of a loss that'd
crushed his will and his hope? Perhaps it was more than the loss
of his wife. He also cried when he thought of his boyhood dog.
Perhaps this deep sorrow was the sum of a lifetime of hurts,
magnified by tragedy.

It was at that very moment Rebecca had come back to
him, bathed in sunshine, her hair in golden glow, her sundress
billowing, an amused smile, barefoot in a field of daisies,
watching him. He loved her so. He couldn't lose her. Tears filled
his eyes and rolled shamelessly down his cheeks, choked him
until there was nothing left but sobs and descent into the deep,
velvet pit of pain that smothered his spirit. He wanted to reach
down and grab the white piece of paper lying like a white
hospital sheet on his desk, wad it up, and hurl it out of his life,
but he was too weak. Finally, he was too weak, too human to
preach, to live. He had not the strength left to write or even not
to write. And so he sat and wept and wanted her back and knew
he would never get her back, but somehow clung to a fleeting,
child-like hope that if he wished and wished he would have her
beside him again. She would come back to fill the hollow,
meaningless emptiness. He reached out for the pen that lay on
his desk, unsure of his grip. Still flooded with overpowering
sadness, unable to see the white sheet through his tears, he
scratched out a line. "Once I loved and was loved."

He felt her close to him. My God, she was so close. The
enveloping softness cradled his shoulders; her delicate hand was
over his. He wrote, "Love is the one true thing, timeless and
eternal." The words began to flow, even as the wetness dried on
his cheeks. He focused with the open-eyed intensity of a child.
Then the pain whirled inside him and out again, leaving him like
a breaking fever.

There was a small knock on the doorframe, not heavy-handed like Dale's. He turned to see a pair of green eyes staring at him. Small green eyes. Dark hair. A perplexed look on the face of a little girl, maybe six- or seven-years-old.

"Well, hello there, young lady. What can I do for you?" Out of little more than habit, he summoned his pastor's soothing voice.

"Would you boost me up to the water fountain?" A water fountain. What an odd thing to break into his dream of Rebecca. He thought of telling her he was too busy just now.

"Did somebody take away the stool?" he asked, getting out of his chair. The reply was a little nod. There was something in the child that engaged him, innocence, a lack of pain or the knowledge of pain. She felt so light as he lifted her up, her white sundress a white phantasm.

The cool water floated in a stream across her lips. He watched the little splashes and could hear her suck at the flow. And when he put her down, she looked up at him and said, "Go on with your life." It was Rebecca's voice.

He blinked. "What? What did you say?"

"I just said thanks ... for boosting me up." The child smiled quickly and ran down the hall.

When he returned to his desk, his cheeks flushed and like spring's first day, he was flooded with warmth that chased away the memory of winter's chill. The joy of his years with Rebecca sang in him. He wrote with passion and happiness he thought was forever lost with her passing.

When he had stepped into the pulpit, he was smiling with radiance only true love could bring. It was the smile you'd see on the face of a bride, or in the eye of a father watching his son walk for the first time, or the pure and sparkling bliss reflected in the face of a mother who saw her boy return from war. As he had written and thought and crafted what he was going to say, he renewed his faith in the Creator who could design such lasting memories. In those precious moments of reflection, he knew Rebecca and those joyous moments of fatherhood would never be gone from him!

How could anyone deny redemption in the face of such tragedy and such resounding solace? And it was all God's mysterious doing, through the eternally healing hand of faith.

Out of the fire, he had found strength. He wept once more as he spoke in front of his flock, but this time with the feeling of boundless joy.

That had been months ago and never since had he slowed. Never had that new strength failed him as he visited the sick and preached his sermons and led his flock through the problems of their lives. He chuckled now at the persistent rumors he had found a new love to drown his sorrows. He had found an old love, a true love. It was the love of God and the love of his wife. They both gripped his hand and led him through each new day. They loved him and he trusted their love.

But, this business about book burning and fundamentalism disturbed him. Concerned was probably a better word. The cornerstone of his theology was goodness, not mindless prohibition. Prohibition never worked well against a determined sinner who would find ever more inventive ways to sin. "I'm a Baptist preacher," he thought, "who doesn't believe in banning dirty books, or holding nonbelievers down with a heavy foot on their chest until they cry uncle."

"Reverend?" It was the delicate voice of Margaret Tillsmore, the widow Tillsmore who broke his reverie. "I saw something I'd like to talk to you about ... if you have a moment. I don't want to disturb."

"No, no, Mrs. Tillsmore, come right in." Reverend Monroe got up from his chair, and hastily shifted some books and papers off the faded seat of the dark blue armchair. "Won't you please sit down?"

"Thank you." She sank all 85 pounds of modest, high-necked sundress and wispy blue-gray hair onto the cushion.

She smoothed out her dress, then clasped her hands, then unclasped them. Something unusual here. He moved his chair in front of her so the two of them were nearly knees to knees, looked directly into her eyes and asked, "What is it I can help you with?"

"I don't know quite what to say." She looked at him. He smiled and patted her arm. "Late last night I saw something suspicious." She looked wistfully away. Then she turned back slowly, as if trying to regain the kernel of thought.

"Just take your time, Mrs. Tillsmore, and tell me all about it."

23

I don't make comments about an ongoing investigation, and you can't quote me on that. —Sheriff Sam Goddard to a reporter

"So, Mrs. Tillsmore, why don't you tell me just what you told Reverend Monroe?" Sheriff Goddard pulled out a gray metal chair and eased himself into it, directly in front of the woman. She sat on the brown and yellow tweed couch in his office, like a frail moth, twisting her hands in her lap, the skin looking thin enough to tear. The Reverend sat beside her, knees together, fingers intertwined, hands in his lap. Deputy John Howard stood nearby.

"Go ahead, Margaret," the Reverend gently urged.

"Well, it was dark and I couldn't see that much." The eyes behind the glasses had that watery look old people get, pools of cloudy blue.

"I understand." The sheriff nodded. "Just tell me what you saw." Goddard looked at her intently, knowing she might know something, but probably knew nothing and he was going to have to sort out which it was.

"Well, you know my house is just down the street from the Post Office?"

"Yes, ma'am."

"Two nights ago I was up late. I just couldn't sleep very well. I never have really, ever since my husband passed away. He was such a good man."

"Yes, ma'am." The sheriff's brow wrinkled slightly, but he willed himself to be patient. After more than twenty years, gathering bits of data still both thrilled and tired him. He hated the infernal sifting, although he knew it had to be done. Pecking through each lead was like trying to do a jigsaw puzzle, but having to dive into a full dumpster for the pieces. The worst thing he could do was to rush through and miss something.

"I got up to watch the teevee, but I got tired of seeing the same old news, over and over again. So, I walked to the window to see if the moon was out."

"Did you have the lights on?"

"Lights?" She looked blank, then anguished.

"The lights in your house, or the porch lights? That's all I meant."

"Why would I put the lights on? I wasn't expecting guests." A brief reflection on the depression generation. Mrs. Tillmore's lip moved lightly, pondering the importance of the question, the rest of her face frozen in concentration.

"I just wondered if you had the lights on is all," the sheriff said slowly. "It makes it harder to see the street if the lights are on."

"Well...no, I didn't have the lights on."

"So, you were standing at your living room window, lights off, looking out toward the street?"

"Yes, I was." "What time was that, Mrs. Tillsmore?"

"Heavens, I have no idea. I know it was late. It was very dark outside."

"Was there a moon?"

"Yes, it was very bright and the people I saw walked under a street light just down the street from me."

"How many people?"

"Three. Two men and a woman." Margaret Tillsmore said it definitely, as though her mental eye chart had suddenly popped into focus.

"You're sure it was two men and a woman? How could you tell?"

"Well, the woman was wearing a dress ... or a skirt. The men were wearing pants, and they were taller than she was, bigger. She was having trouble holding up the man in the middle."

"Okay, now just take your time and tell me what you saw. By the way, Mrs. Tillsmore, I'm recording this, if you don't mind." The sheriff was cursing himself for not telling her sooner. Recording was a touchy part of the interview process. Well, at least she hadn't said too much.

"Recording?" The confused look again crossed her face.

"Yes, ma'am. It makes it easier to go back and think about what you said, without having to bother you so much."

"Oh, all right. I don't need to get a lawyer, do I? Lawyers are so expensive."

"No, ma'am. You don't need a lawyer. You may be able to help us solve a puzzle, but that's all. We certainly don't suspect you of anything. We just appreciate your help."

"Well, okay, I guess it's all right.... " She looked at Reverend Monroe and got a nod. The tape recorder clicked on like the shot of a starter pistol. Margaret Tillsmore stared at the little black box a moment, listened for the faint hiss of the tape and then continued, "I saw three people. Two men and a woman. They were walking under the street light, but it didn't look right."

"What didn't look right?" Goddard hoped he was asking the right questions, but it was so hard to tell. You just had to get a feel for the witness and hope you didn't overlook something obvious or put words in her mouth.

"The man in the middle was dragging his feet, as if he were ... you know, inebriated or something."

"So, the other two were holding him up? Carrying him?"

"Yes, that's right. They all had their arms over each other's shoulders, but the man in the middle wasn't walking very well."

"You say he looked like he was drunk?"

"Yes, sir. He didn't look well."

"Did you notice anything else, maybe the color of their clothes? Where they went? Were they driving a car?"

"They weren't in a car when I saw them. They were walking. And, I couldn't tell what color their clothes were. It was dark. They were walking down the street away from my house."

"You said the moon was bright," John Howard injected.

Mrs. Tillsmore blinked, then continued as if she hadn't heard Sheriff Goddard ask, "Toward the Post Office?"

"Yes, away from my house ... down the street."

"How far away would you say they were?"

"Heavens, I don't know. They were a good ways away."

"Did you ever get a look at their faces? Did you recognize any of them?"

"No, I didn't ... " Mrs. Tillsmore spoke slowly, dragging out the words, trying to remember. "There was one thing .... "

"What was that?"

"The man in the middle, the one who was drunk?"

"Yes, ma'am .... "

"He was a great big man. He wasn't wearing a coat like the other two, and I think he had on khaki trousers."

When they were alone, Goddard and the Chief Deputy, John Howard, compared notes, the deputy's face devoid of motion. "Well, Sam, what do you think?"

"Sounds like we found a witness of sorts." Goddard looked off, out the window, his mind trying to picture himself standing beside Margaret Tillsmore in the black shadows, looking out her window, seeing what she saw.

"It's so fuzzy. She's an old lady. It was the dark of night."

Howard counted off the minuses on outstretched fingers. "And those glasses of hers must be an inch thick."

"Yeah," Sam cut in, "You can add, no positive ID. For all we know, it could really have been some drunks. Drinking is not exactly unknown in this county." His brow furrowed. "What we've got right now is maybe a woman and two men walking down the street, arm over arm. Would you call that a suspicious act, if we hadn't found the body in the bushes?"

"You want me to send someone over to Mrs. Tillsmore's house?" Howard was used to reading Sam's mind.

Their eyes met. "Why don't you find out what she can see from her window. Take a couple of deputies and talk to the neighbors. Somebody else may have seen something."

Howard nodded.

24

A little community like this, a body lying out in the open and still our pitiful police force can't find out who-done-it. I personally think it's somebody who didn't like the idea of our football coach leaving for greener pastures. —Parent of a football player

Sam Goddard sat behind his desk, leaning back in his chair, feet propped up on the corner of his desk. He held a cup of coffee idly in his hand and stared out through the dusty blinds, letting his mind wander over the day's activity. There'd been a two-car collision on the edge of town. One woman in the hospital with a broken wrist and a very confused senior citizen who still hadn't been able to figure out why his car slammed into hers. Last night a fight erupted outside the bowling alley and gave him two new residents for his jail, plus a mother of two who had been picked up for public drunkenness and found to possess half an ounce of marijuana. Then, there was still the puzzle of the football coach.

John Howard walked in and sat on the couch, not wanting to disturb the sheriff's reverie.

"Morning, John," Goddard said, not turning his head.

"Morning, sheriff."

"Have you seen the doc's report?" Sam had the only copy he knew about tucked in the drawer of his desk, but it never hurt to ask.

"No, sheriff, I haven't."

"Looks like a coronary, but there were some bruises on his back and buttocks."

"The doc said bruises?"

"There were both. Some bruises and some pooling of blood after death. The bruises wouldn't have been the cause of death."

"So, nobody killed him." Deputy Howard thought out loud.

"That's not quite what I said." There had been just a little bit of a hesitation in the doctor's report, coupled with the bruises being consistent with a less than gently applied whip. Doc Moncrief had improved on the coroner's report, adding bits and pieces about dental work and maybe taking out some of the original, possibly obscuring the real description. Time of death hadn't been fixed exactly, but that was often the case. They already knew the obvious, the coach died in the early morning, prior to the rain.

But, reading the report, Goddard also had the impression there was something else, the hint that the coach may not have died right away, that he may have lingered for who knows how long. A few minutes? An hour? Maybe nobody had killed him outright, but it didn't look like they raced him to the nearest hospital either. And those flogging marks on the coach's back and buttocks and privates got the coroner's attention. A dentist didn't usually get to see those things and keep his license.

There appeared to have been some swelling on the genitals. He wasn't going to get any more answers from his dentist turned medical examiner. Maybe he'd have to call the coroner, or get Doc Moncrief to do it.

Sam debated how much to share with his Chief Deputy. He put his feet down and rotated his chair to look Howard in the face, then gave him the whole pig, including the squeal.

"That means he either was driven in somebody's car or it happened real close to the Post Office." John's eyes widened slightly, the bright array of possibilities suddenly spread out before him. "And, the beating maybe gave him the coronary?"

"I think I know why nobody rushed him to the emergency room," Sam said.

"Another witness pop up?"

"Not yet, but there was something else of interest from the autopsy. Seems there was semen on the coach's underwear, on his belly, and the inside of his pants. His testicles were bruised as well as his penis."

"Did he try to fuck a grizzly?" John's eyebrows went up.

"No grizzlies around here, but, an angry husband could do a good imitation, I expect."

"Or maybe a little S and M right here in the middle of Good ole Cassavora."

"Better not say that too loud," Goddard chuckled, "Hemsley'll break out in a sweat and want to use his handcuffs on you."

"The thing of it is," Howard turned thoughtful, "We don't know whose hanky panky we're dealing with. Did the coach have a taste for a real cute tight end, or was he monkeying with somebody's wife and got himself caught?"

"Or somebody's husband?" Sam cut in. "That's police work. Nothing is open and shut." "Nothing ever has been open and shut, John. That's why they call it police work, not police play."

"Still, we're a ways down the road." John Howard's easy smile crept back.

"Yep," The sheriff began to tick things off, "a positive ID. A witness, such as she is. A car. And ... ," he paused for effect, "we've got the motive."

"You mean the car he was carried in?" Howard muttered, his mind racing to catch up.

"Well, that we don't know yet," the sheriff said. "We need to find the coach's car first. It wasn't at his house. Is it parked somewhere close? Are there any prints on it? Also, I want you to take the coach's clothes into the city and see if we can con one of our fellow law enforcement agencies into checking for fibers and anything else. I'll call my sometimes friend, Captain Giles, and see if I can grease the skids."

Howard rolled his eyes at the mention of the name. Giles had already loaned them his county coroner.

"I'd also like to go door to door and see if we can find some corroboration. A confused old lady, with piss poor eyesight, staring into the black of night is not my favorite kind of witness."

"How do you know it was black that night? Mrs. Tillsmore mentioned a full moon."

"I checked the Almanac and the radio station. There was only a sliver of a moon at best and a heavy overcast."

Howard nodded. "It's not like we're overrun with officers to put on this case," he muttered.

"Too true, John. Too true. If we stop writing traffic tickets, the mayor's going to complain. If we don't direct the flow of traffic around the schools, the parents are going to complain. If we strip the jail and let the low-lifes run free, everybody is going to complain. But, the bright spot is, this town's not too large. Mid-morning and again mid-afternoon, when the school buses are gone and the parents are content, take as many of our people as you can and send them up both sides of the street from Margaret Tillsmore's house. See if you can pick up any more witnesses. By the way, what did you see from Margaret's house?"

"Well, she's got a clear shot at the spot where she says she saw them. The streetlight is right there. I went out there last night. Bright. I'm surprised she couldn't see their freckles."

"Age," Sam said simply. "Also, she had no idea what she was seeing."

"How about them?" Howard asked.

"Them?"

"Yeah, the people who were under the street light. Why were they even there? I wouldn't have walked right under a street light if I were dragging a body."

"Amateurs. A touch of panic. We have to figure if the coach died of a heart attack, either before or after they dropped him off. They just wanted some space between him and them. They may even have been searching for medical help before he died and made them all piss in their pants. These people were not even considering a murder had been committed and they didn't have time to plan much. For their own reasons they just wanted to get rid of him. It's not like they were Mafia hit men. They were winging it. Might even have looked more suspicious if they'd gone out of their way to walk in the shadows, providing it even crossed their minds. So, if we ask the right questions of the right people and spend some time thinking about it, we should be able to come up with the who, especially since those semen stains give us a good idea of the why. First off, I want you to get over to Mrs. Tillsmore's and canvas that street. Also, send our cars through the neighborhoods and find the coach's car. Likely to be parked on a side street."

John Howard got up and walked out the door. The phone was ringing before it closed behind him.

"Goddard."

"Sheriff, this is Lucinda Whitehall." The superintendent paused to let the magical effect of her name bring glitter to Goddard's life.

"Why good morning, superintendent. I must say, this is a surprise." He hoped it wouldn't be about the investigation. The superintendent was known for her powerful friends, as well as for badgering people into submission. All Sam needed right now was a politico jumping on his backsides.

"Good morning to you, sheriff," came the purring voice. "I'm getting a lot of phone calls asking how the investigation is going. You know, the coach," she said it like that was his given name, "was very well respected. He had many wonderful friends." She said the word wonderful as though she were spreading the news.

"Tell 'em that the investigation is ongoing." He didn't talk to Lucinda often, but once was often enough.

"Have you found anything of substance?"

"No smoking gun, if that's what you mean, but we're edging that way."

"What exactly have you discovered?" The question hung in the air and he knew she expected an answer. She could hear Sam take a deep inhale.

He hesitated a moment, trying to let his rising irritation evaporate. He knew she couldn't care less about the coach, but the high school was her turf and she was protecting it. "Superintendent, I really can't say."

"I understand. I would appreciate hearing anything of note."

"Dr. Whitehall, although I can't tell you anything at present, the investigation is ongoing." He emphasized the *is*.

Ten minutes after he got off the phone to the Superintendent of Schools, the phone rang again. This time it was C2.

"Sheriff," he said in his characteristically clipped tones, "How's it going?"

"How's what going?"

"Sam, don't play games with me. You know exactly what I'm asking!"

"Oh, how's that going?" He feigned surprise. "I'm still investigating. It may or may not be murder, but the body was moved and we're trying to figure out why."

"I see. If it wasn't murder, what was it?"

"The doc says it was a heart attack. That's what I'm going to tell the newspapers. Let this thing settle a bit. Get the public off our backs."

"You sure you want to do that? Might that spoil any prosecution later?"

"You're the lawyer. What d'ya think?"

"Go ahead and release it. Also, I understand you spoke with the superintendent."

"She called me."

"What did you tell her?"

"Less than I told you."

"I suspected as much," C2 chuckled. "She sounded a little put out."

"Well, I can't help that."

"I don't want you to help it. Might do her good to figure out she's not queen of the world. I figure she'll blow a hole in her panty hose when she gets surprised by the press release."

When C2 hung up, Goddard pushed back in his chair and put his feet back on the edge of the desk. Why the Post Office? he was asking himself. Why not out on some backcountry road? Then it struck him. What's located near the Post Office? He decided to take a little drive.

*****

After Colonel McClary's allegations appeared, Able Perkins jumped on the bandwagon and wondered out loud and in print if the story had the ring of truth. The article ran in the same edition as the heart attack story. The city newspaper, not *The Advocate*, called to ask Jake's side of the new controversy. He began by telling the male voice on the other end of the phone that it was all a bunch of crap, but even as he said it, something inside told him this kind of grist in the political mill wasn't going to disappear on its own. Once again, he was out of his element and knew it. Vague shadows of old, long-discarded memories banged inside him. Now, he was going to have to explain to the public, to people who had never been to war, had no inkling of life under fire. In the end, he put the reporter off, then got Cleveland on the phone and Skeeter after that. They offered opposing tactics.

Cleveland viewed the episode pragmatically and intellectually, devoid of emotion, as one might view an opponent's chess move. Dangerous, but only as a part of the political game, digressions, feints. One man would be elected and the other went on to other things. Truth, honor, dignity weren't measurements on the sliding, colorless scale.

Everything registered as just another move and counter move. A lie told at the appropriate time trumped a truth nobody believed.

Skeeter, on the other hand, wanted to fly to Texas, shoot McClary and brag about it at the bar. Able Perkins would be next. "Everyone is entitled to his own opinion about that shithead McClary. Fucker is a disgrace. I went to war. I did my duty. So did you! McClary spent half his life at a rehab center trying to get over not making general."

Jake agreed with Skeeter, but followed Cleve's advice, for no other reasons other than he didn't own a gun and wanted to stay out of jail. "Just let the thing die," Cleve warned. "Anyway, nobody's interested in giving you a chance to explain the truth, so you might as well shut up."

Cleve turned out to be right. Nobody in Cassavora County would have known Colonel McClary if he'd marched up and pissed on the courthouse steps and within a week, nobody remembered his name either.

25

Don't keep guessing if the school board is finally going to flip the coin and have it come up heads. It's a two-sided coin and they're both tails. —Jake Morgan

Caldwell Robbins and Purcell Southmore had unusual names for any place other than the south. Southerners pride themselves on lineage, and stringing a few last names together twists together both sides of the family.

But, even if their names didn't raise any eyebrows, anyone had to wonder how either of them ever got a voice in school affairs. In a phrase, name recognition. For years the school system in Cassavora County languished in the solitude of complacency and benign neglect. According to a demographics professor at the University, the county got caught sleeping, as did dozens of other little pockets of change. No one drew a blueprint because for decades there wasn't any change to plan for. In twenty years, the school population hadn't even doubled. A few new teachers got hired now and then. A new school building sprang up every twenty or thirty years. Period. The citizenry dozed under the comfortable blanket of constancy. The previous superintendent had held office for more than twenty years without opposition.

Then a flash of new homes appeared, and this sleepy little caterpillar awoke as a bedroom community butterfly.

Jake was part of the metamorphosis. The old superintendent retired and moved out of state. Growth, that smiling bully, rode to town on a bulldozer, with a bulging wallet and a keen eye for steel and concrete.

Along with new homes and new neighborhoods, new grocery stores and new gas stations, a torrent of new children flooded the school system. Numbers didn't surge year by year, but five years of a steady tide will overwhelm classrooms and buses and lunchrooms. Cassavora never even saw it coming. Some, like Lucinda and Able Perkins, Sob Jenkins and Lucinda's husband Douglas grabbed for the brass ring. You didn't have to control growth; you only had to make sure the money flowed your way.

At first, the community smiled on the new prosperity, especially the older families. Not only did they make a killing, but most importantly, their gnarled fingers still gripped every position of power, elected and otherwise. They figured being in charge was the one steady rock in the swirling waters.

During the last election, some four years ago, they'd been right. In the turmoil of growth and change, a community naturally looks for something to cling to. A campaign flyer that read, "He's a native Cassavoran and graduated from Cassavora High School," trumped experience and education. Cassavora enjoyed that rare kind of transition election when new people were too new to stand for public office and long timers just blacked the little space next to a familiar name. The new race, Jake's election, promised to be altogether different. The worm had turned. Change became a flood that had people scared.

Sleepy school board meetings snapped awake to politics and suddenly religion produced tight-jawed debates. When Caldwell Robbins declared the power of prayer could overcome all obstacles, he referred to plunging standardized test scores and the inability of a third of the kids to read and write. *The Cassavora Advocate*'s headlines blared, "Prayer the Answer to Education's Problems," and went on to explain Robbins invited a lay preacher and deacon of Smittyville's First Baptist Church, to beseech the Almighty to help the children and teachers. Other members of the board, all church-going Christians, made no objection. So the preacher showed up and prayed for an end to wickedness, always a vain hope. Robbins didn't want to stop at the schoolhouse door, but wanted to hold revival meetings in all the schools and include a strong Christian on every staff. But, Jake was beginning to see that if Robbins didn't have the solutions, he was one of the few who would admit to a problem.

In private discussions, as well as those on the courthouse square, only the terminally ill and those who danced to the Bible thumping beat thought Robbins had good ideas.

"He's a fool."

"Hell no! He's a damn fool!"

"I'll call your damn fool and raise you one!"

But, discussions about Robbins' Biblical approach weren't the only educational things to cloud people's minds. Once someone holds up a microscope, there's no end to the discoveries.

On a subsequent Tuesday evening, the school board room lay nearly empty, except for the superintendent, who sat at the center of the table, with board members to either side. In front of them sat a reporter for *The Advocate*, a slew of principals, assistant principals, and other semi-interested school officials who knew they'd have to deal with Lucinda if they didn't show up.

Mumblings about nepotism had cranked up to a steady hum after four of the last ten hirings had some connection to the superintendent, through blood, marriage real estate.

"Regarding the issue of hiring two more teachers," Gloria Sweeney lowered her forehead, spoke over her glasses, "The state allows us to have up to thirty-five students in a classroom and I believe ... according to the figures the superintendent has supplied," she paused to smile, "we are well below that number."

The superintendent kept her voice neutral. Everyone knew she had a big hammer and their wee-wees were stretched across the table. "I can understand your concern, but I believe in this case, because of our increasing numbers in the sixth grade, another two teachers are warranted."

Cleve elbowed Jake. "One of those new teachers is her niece I don't know who the other woman is."

"How in the world do you know that?"

"Small town." Knowing she might face some opposition, the superintendent had taken the prudent approach of securing the necessary three-vote majority well before the meeting. It hadn't taken much. Board members also had close friends and relatives who wanted jobs.

"Any other comments?" asked Chairman Tom Millage. He paused briefly. "Hearing none, I will entertain a motion to approve two new sixth grade teaching positions." The motion passed unanimously. The superintendent, the only nonvoting member, didn't crack a smile.

Moments later, the board adjourned to Executive Council. As usual, the superintendent led. "First of all, I'm passing out a description of the candidates."

Todd Ingles stared at the sheet with only two names on it. There was no data, only a statement by the hiring principal that "This teacher is highly qualified and will be an asset to my school."

"I don't know about these choices, "Todd drawled.

"What don't you know, Mr. Ingles?" The hard edge in the superintendent's voice carved the question, made it bleed.

"For one thing, I don't know which grades these ladies have taught."

Superintendent Whitehall got up and stood behind Todd's chair, peering over his shoulder. "My secretary must have left that off," she said, making an effort to moderate her tone, "but I can assure you *both* are highly qualified."

"I've got some other questions," Ingles continued, pausing to shove his glasses up with a forefinger. "Do you have job histories and how well they did on their state teacher exams?"

The long awkward pause of silence around the table was like that which usually follows a grotesque belch. Finally, Caldwell Robbins spoke. "How many applicants did we have for these two positions?"

"Mr. Ingles and Mr. Robbins, you'll forgive me," said Lucinda Whitehall, her patience straining, "but I don't have the answers to those questions at my fingertips." She continued as if speaking to recalcitrant students. "As you should know, we delegate much of the hiring to our principals, because they are the ones who work with the teachers on a day to day basis and have a much better opportunity to access the needs of their particular schools. However, if these answers are important to you."

"Well," said Todd Ingles, "if it wouldn't be too much trouble."

"Lady and gentlemen," the superintendent said, glancing around the table, "how many of you need these answers before we decide whether or not to hire these two teachers? How many of you are willing to sacrifice our children's education to obtain test scores from years ago? I personally think it would send a negative message to our principals if I were to tell them their judgment was being questioned by the Board of Education."

Caldwell Robbins almost raised his hand, but thought better of it, eyes fixed on the center of the table. Todd Ingles raised his, but no one bothered to look in his direction.

Tom Millage scanned the table, but only after Ingles dropped his hand and slouched back in his chair. "I think we owe a great deal to this superintendent and ought to put aside any minor concerns and wholeheartedly support her recommendations. Everyone who is willing to approve this hiring, please raise your hand." Four hands went up and after a long sigh Todd Ingles raised his, too.

"The next topic of discussion is of a more delicate nature and should anyone in this room breach the confidentiality of what I'm about to discuss, one of our finest teachers might have her reputation tarnished forever, as well as the school system being opened to a law suit." Dr. Whitehall wore her seriously concerned face.

"A parent came to me privately to relate an incident that allegedly occurred in Peggy Windsome's third grade class." She paused for dramatic effect. "It is alleged that during an approved musical presentation, Ms. Windsome had her class singing 'Jimmy Cracked Corn.' As part of the refrain, she asked the black children in class to slap their knees and grin as the class sang the words, 'Ole Massa's Gone Away.'"

A couple of the board members shook their heads, evidently as dismayed as the superintendent that so trivial a matter should arouse the ire of parents.

Gloria smiled to herself before speaking, as though she alone could comprehend the stupidity of the matter. "I've known Peggy for years. She and I taught together, and I know she has the best interests of the children at heart. This sounds like a typical overreaction from the parents."

"Peggy Windsome is a member of my church, and I know her very well. I believe this to be just an isolated incident, and I think we should just let this thing be quietly forgotten," added Mr. Robbins.

"Well maybe we should look into it," ventured Mr. Ingles, "Something like this could blow up in our faces, not to mention how the kids must feel." Loudly breaking wind would have gotten a more positive response.

"I already have looked into it," said an exasperated Lucinda Whitehall. "Mr. Ingles, you may personally feel that I do not do my job, but I would hate for your personal feelings to be taken out on this fine teacher!"

"What did you find out?" Todd Ingles rejoined.

"I think Mr. Robbins' assessment is correct," she replied tersely and sighed deeply from the sheer fatigue of answering such ill-conceived questions. "And, if there are no further comments, I'd like to move into budgetary matters." There were no further comments.

"Here's a list of previously approved expenditures." The superintendent passed around another sheet of white paper. "You'll note our High School Improvement Committee has decided to postpone the purchase of band instruments, new middle school math books, and the building of the new science lab, so that we may complete the expansion of existing athletic facilities, put in a new phone system at the high school and buy two computers for each of the two elementary schools. I am also going to recommend Sob Jenkins Construction, Inc. be awarded the contract for the new middle school based on the time factors involved and on the close professional relationship the school system has enjoyed with that company in the past." Without pausing for the delay of discussion and debate, she asked, "How many members are with me on this?" Gloria Sweeney and Tom Millage's hands went up on cue. Then, Gordon Cuspid raised his.

Passed over without comment was the awarding of a middle school contract, worth upwards of fifteen-million dollars. Ingles wanted to say something. He cleared his throat a couple of times, looked around, but kept his mouth shut.

"Are we ready to go back into open session?" asked Chairman Millage. Nods all around and the sound of chairs being pushed back, when the superintendent spoke.

"There is one further item. A follow up on the insubordination issue I spoke of previously."

"You mean the insubordinate teacher?" Tom Millage asked.

"Yes, Mr. Millage. She has decided to resign."

"Was she under any pressure?" Todd Ingles asked evenly.

"Mr. Ingles, I resent the implication of your question! You seem to be determined to read more into this and every other situation!" The superintendent's voice raced up an octave.

"Not at all. I asked a fair question." Ingles locked on Lucinda Whitehall, her eyes like black, venomous points. She shifted her gaze to Tom Millage, who was looking down at the desk, collecting his papers.

"I am tired of my competency constantly being questioned! Did I force this woman to resign? No I did not!" She once again glared across the table at Mr. Ingles.

Gloria spoke. "It's probably a good thing she did resign. Many of the teachers have told me she's a troublemaker, and I hear there have been some parental complaints."

"What you don't understand, Mr. Ingles," the superintendent's voice had become more moderated, "is that this is a system. All of the individual parts must function within that system."

Todd Ingles smiled at the imperial tones. "If it wouldn't be too much trouble, superintendent, I would appreciate knowing the teacher's name, if I'm expected to vote on accepting her resignation."

"Mr. Ingles, her name is Stephanie Porcose." Lucinda Whitehall's voice backed off the anger. She had her three votes, plus one. Reptiles only bite when they're threatened.

Back in general session, in front of the meager audience, Superintendent Whitehall asked for a motion to finalize the hiring of the two teachers and the acceptance of the resignation of a third. A motion and second quickly followed. Tom Millage announced the middle school contract and Lucinda Whitehall moved quickly into the breach.

"Before we take a vote, Mr. Chairman," she interrupted, smiling broadly, "I'd just like to say that it is with deep regret we accept the resignation of Stephanie Porcose. Stephanie has been a real asset at Elgore Elementary, and we are sure sorry to see her go. We wish her the best in future endeavors." There was light applause, which was more than you'd get at an actual funeral.

Afterwards, a couple of reporters milled around, pens in hand, flinging out an anemic question or two. Nobody spoke to Todd Ingles. Board members quickly left. The crowd dissipated, but a good many clumped in ones and twos. Jake felt a touch at his elbow and turned to see a small woman, wearing glasses, her hair mannishly short. With her was an older woman, more severe looking, gray hair in a serious, skin stretching bun. The short woman held out her hand and Jake shook it. "I'm Cynthia Farnsworth, Mr. Morgan. I saw you standing here and thought I would introduce myself. This is Marcella Stokes," she glanced toward the woman beside her.

"I've read your articles in the paper. You're running for the board of education?" The soft voice, with an upturn lilt at the end made the statement sound like a question.

"Word races at the speed of heat around here."

"We'd just like you to know," Marcella intoned, "If you need us to do anything for you, help you campaign, or anything like that. We'd love to help out."

"Thank you, I'm really just romping through the neighborhoods. Either of you ladies ever do any research?"

"I'm a librarian in Foster County," Marcella said. "I've spent most of my life doing research."

"And, I've been a graduate assistant at the University for two years," Cynthia added. "I'm working on my doctorate."

"Both of us have kids in the Cassavora School System." Marcella smiled. "We'd really like to help." They handed Jake slips of torn notebook paper with names and phone numbers.

"Progress has been needed in this county for a long time," Cynthia said adamantly. "The school system isn't doing what it should and the parents aren't being consulted at all."

"Looks to me like parents are involved in everything."

"You mean the committees?" Marcella asked. She held her notebook up to her chest, crossed her arms. "For the most part, they're only a smokescreen to lull the parents to sleep. If it's an issue that doesn't affect how the school system is run, then fine, we're included, but everything else is out of our hands. I could talk to you all night about it."

Cynthia broke in. "I know you need to be on your way, but if there's anything we can do to help, please call. We'll be praying for you."

Todd Ingles bared his soul and secrets to his wife, who told half a dozen of her friends, condensing it to one of the superintendent's friends getting hired and an enemy getting fired. He never mentioned the school contract, partially because he felt like a coward for not speaking up.

The more Jake knocked on doors, the more his ears burned with details of the hirings and firings. Scandal blows a bitter wind.

26

I'd get to the bottom of this a lot faster if I knew how deep it was.

—Sheriff Goddard, asked about the investigation

"John, what do you think about Mrs. Tillsmore?" Goddard rocked back in his chair, cast an unfocused eye out the window.

John knew what he meant. Old people, people who wore glasses, eyewitnesses in general often talked a different story in court. A bulldog of a defense attorney could rip out the seams and turn a white shirt into a pile of dirty rags. In Mrs. Tillsmore's case, tatters would show as soon as she opened her mouth. More than one defense attorney prayed for an eyewitness he could flay in open court.

"We had to spoon-feed her the questions," Goddard continued, idly gazing through his window at the parking lot.

"Ain't that the truth."

Fragile, both the woman and her story. "What do you think of the preacher?"

"He's a good man from what I hear. Lost his wife a year ago."

"Seemed like a good man. Why don't we get him back here for a private chat?"

*****

The Reverend wondered about his second trip to the sheriff's office. He wasn't a witness himself and felt like he didn't have anything to add.

"Sit down, Reverend." Goddard motioned to the couch. "Thanks for coming. I know you're busy."

"Would you like some coffee, water, a soda?" John Howard stood ready to serve.

"No, thanks."

"What can you tell us about Mrs. Tillsmore?" The sheriff sat back in his chair, interlocked his fingers.

"What do you mean?" Monroe's forehead wrinkled. "She seemed a little hesitant."

"I'm sure she's not used to talking to the police."

"Anything else you can tell us about her state of mind?" The light came on. He thought a moment.

"She's been lucid all the times I've spoken with her."

"How often is that?"

"Not often." The Reverend's mind churned. A faint glimmer came on in the dark room of things seldom remembered. "About a year ago something interesting happened." He paused in thought.

"That was about the time." John Howard started the statement, but left it hanging, not wanting to reopen a sad chapter in the man's life.

"Yes ... yes." It was coming back to him. "It was about a month after my wife died."

The sheriff and his deputy exchanged glances, half expecting Monroe to break down. They were wrong. This was a strong man. The sheriff leaned forward, resting his elbows on the desktop.

"About six months ago Mrs. Tillsmore came to me. Said her son, James, was distraught over his job at Sob Jenkins Construction, but that wasn't the main part. She told me her husband, Sid, came back to comfort her. Told her everything would be ok."

Howard shook his head, took a deep breath.

Goddard's voice stayed even. "She's a widow, right?"

"Yes."

"So, she got a feeling of comfort?"

"Not exactly. She said Sid sat in the living room with her and held her hand."

"Anybody else see Sid?"

"No, she said it was late at night. Said she couldn't sleep."

After Reverend Monroe left, John Howard heaved a sigh. "That's all we need. I can hear the defense now. 'Aside from people walking down the street toward the Post Office, what else have you seen late at night? What's that you say? Your dead husband also came for a chat?"

Goddard ignored the comment. "Why don't you go see James Tillsmore? Go yourself. Don't wear your uniform and don't take any deputies with you." He didn't feel the need to say more. John was a smart man.

27

I don't know what to tell you. You think I'm stealing from myself? —Sob Jenkins.

John Howard pulled into the parking lot of a strip mall. A quick oil change business, dry cleaners and an insurance agency spanned the low building like crouched soldiers. On the far end, Sob Jenkins Construction looked no different than the rest. Evidently, a construction company didn't care for high architectural fees anymore than anybody else.

The receptionist doubled as secretary and clerk. Lose papers and manila folders covered most of three kitchen-sized tables, plus her desk. A long, low counter separated visitors from the work area.

Howard waited until she got off the phone.

"Kin I hep yew?" She adjusted her glasses and pulled a strand of bleached hair back over her ear.

"Yes, ma'am. I'm looking for James Tillsmore."

"Jist a sec." She turned in her swivel chair and bellowed, "James there's someone to see yew."

Moments later, Tillsmore ushered the Chief Deputy into his office. "Sorry about the clutter."

Howard nodded, found a chair next to Tillsmore's desk, moved a stack of papers to the floor and sat down.

"So, what can I help you with?" The son was possibly forty-five or fifty, thinning gray hair, blue eyes and thin build, like his mother.

Howard opened his wallet and showed off his badge. "Just a few questions about Mrs. Tillsmore."

"My wife?" Shock registered.

"No, your mother."

Tillsmore stiffened. "What do you want to know?"

"I just wondered if she's been feeling ok."

"Yes." He paused, alert as a deer. "Why do you ask? What's she done?"

"It wasn't what she's done."

Tillsmore shifted in his seat, mentally thumbing through the possibilities. "Well... what is it then?"

Howard wrestled with how to broach the subject. "Your mother came to us..." He let the words drift. He looked at Tillsmore and could see the wheels turning.

Tillsmores' eyes left him, flicked to one side of the desk, flicked back. "Came to see you, you say."

"Yes. She had a story to tell."

"It involves me? My work?" Tillsmore licked his dry lips.

Something wasn't right. The Chief Deputy could see it in Tillsmore's face and the way his grip tightened perceptibly on the wooden arms of his desk chair.

"What's your position here at Sob Jenkins?"

"I'm ... I'm the accountant." Tillsmore paused. "Only one of the accountants really." The words came in short breaths as he tried to picture an invisible jigsaw puzzle and match all the jagged pieces.

"Would you say your mother was an honest person? Open and honest?"

Tillsmore nodded.

"Is she prone to fantasies?"

"She told you."

"Told us what?"

"You know. What I told her about my job." Turn over a rock and who knows what you'll find.

Howard related the whole conversation to Sheriff Goddard. They stood outside the jail, next to the white Ford with *County Sheriff* emblazoned across both doors in red and black letters.

"This is one tangled ball of string." The sheriff shook his head.

"Well, at least we know she doesn't totally hallucinate. But, what kind of full grown man still cries on his mother's shoulder?"

"The kind that doesn't leave home, gets married, and buys a house down the block. Doesn't have kids of his own."

"Never cut the cord."

"That's it." Howard was curious.

"So, what do we do about the son?"

"How much do we really know?"

"We know he just about had a heart attack when I came within fifty feet of him." John Howard looked down, nudged a small stone with the sole of his spit shined shoe.

"And," Goddard added, "We know our witness sometimes gets together with her long dead husband 'round midnight."

Howard wanted to laugh, but instead let out a long breath. "He also told his mother a big chunk of Sob Jenkins Inc's money is missing, and he's afraid he'll be blamed. From where I'm standing it looks like either kickbacks or embezzlement."

"So says a man who thinks he's cornered. But he didn't tell you everything his mother told Reverend Monroe; he showed you no evidence and didn't speak in front of any witnesses."

"True, but, he did say there may be payments that aren't in the books."

"As for the Sheriff's Department," Goddard began, "I don't know anyone capable of doing a high powered accounting investigation, do you?"

Howard shook his head no. "Want to get the State Bureau in on the action?"

"Let's sit on this one awhile. I don't want the state boys tramping all over our ongoing."

"But, if we hold off, how are we going to explain it later?"

"We won't have to. All we got are bits and pieces. After we tidy up our investigation we'll give them the smoking gun and let them figure out who the shooter is."

"Ok." Howard hesitated. "Meanwhile, what about the widow? Ask her about her husband's nocturnal visits?"

"And spook her? No way. We've got what we got. I believe her about what she saw under the street light, don't you?"

"I do. But, if she gets on the stand..."

"If she gets on the stand, let some clever legal mind try to connect the dots. We just investigate, remember?"

28

Education is okay when you're young, but when you get old, it messes with yourmnatural prejudices and inclinations. —Overheard on the courthouse   square

Jake walked onto the square, toward the courthouse. The sky sang a happy blue song, in a mild 85 degrees. After a hard couple of days of campaigning and a good night's sleep, he was feeling good. The spring was back in his step and hope in his heart. He was having fun.

The center of a small Southern town comes in two varieties, those with a railroad station and buildings strung out along the tracks and those with a big courthouse in the middle of a square. Fletcher's courthouse housed both the city and county government offices, including C2's. Architecturally, it commanded the downtown and from any of its second or third floor offices you could see the businesses and houses trail off and soft green country begin.

Red brick dominated the courthouse, with hewn blocks of sandstone on the edges and around the doorway. A steep roof a couple of shades darker than the brick added to the massiveness of the structure and the feeling of the immense power of the law. Over the double-doored entrance chiseled letters read, Cassavora County Courthouse, 1887. Concentric sidewalks bordered both the courthouse and the two-story brick buildings facing it from the four sides of the street. The usual array of curved, iron benches and tall stone memorials to this war decorated the surrounding lawn. The largest was for the men of the 42nd Volunteer Militia who lost their lives serving the Confederacy. It wasn't unusual to see the graybeards sitting in groups of twos or threes, smoking pipes, or chewing tobacco, those that still had their teeth, and discussing all the things men discuss in the twilight of their eventful years.

It was on his stroll that Jake met Jimmy Joe Ellis. Jimmie Joe wasn't the smartest man, but neither was he the dumbest. His guileless, endearing smile split open as carelessly as a ripe cantaloupe. Jimmy Joe was neither short nor tall, neither thin nor fat and his brown hair lay naturally neat. Parted permanently with an axe, some said. Hard to tell what he was going to be wearing, but usually a uniform. Both county and city police, the volunteer fire department and the local Salvation Army had given him shirts and hats, complete with ranks and badges. His trousers swallowed him, with suspenders holding up the excess. His shirt sleeves rolled up to his skinny elbows and his cap toed brown shoes strutted.

In the mornings he hovered around Brice's Cafe, or the Confederate Monument and in the early evening around the jail, where he sometimes got the guards to let him chat with the inmates, unless the inmates could talk the guards out of it. Where he spent his noons and late evenings was a mystery, but not a deep one. He lived with his mother on Sheppard Street, so he might very well have been there when he wasn't in his usual spots or prowling the streets. Some nights he walked the square, gazed at the stars, traced with his finger the names engraved on the monuments.

Like most, Jimmy Joe never had an original thought. Radio and TV inspired his conversations. Every slogan, cliché, song title and other bit of doggerel that floated across the airways settled on his mind like intellectual dust. Sometimes he just repeated whatever was said to him. He wasn't trying to be rude; he just relied on worn phrases the way other people clung to a favorite pair of old pants. If you said anything resembling a line from a song, he could drive you nuts. See ya later would get you alligator every time.

His mouth occasionally got him into unplanned trouble, like the day he crossed paths at Grand Foods with one of Sheriff Goddard's former deputies, a man relieved of duty for lying on the stand about a car theft. Jimmy Joe called out happily, "You can trust your car to the man who wears the star!" The former lawman chased him out onto the sidewalk, swearing loudly, with Jimmy Joe squealing, "Here come tha judge, here come tha judge."

Other times, Jimmy Joe burst out with things neither he nor any of God's other creatures could place, like the record in his mind had a deep scratch. Whatever he said ran right into whatever else he planned on saying. "Winston tastes good before you leap," came out one morning at Brice's. Some people chuckled. Others slid their chairs back to give him some space.

But, Jimmy Joe's real fame came from something he did every four years, when he correctly predicted the winner of the Presidential election. His string dated back to the 1960 race between JFK and Nixon. A few hadn't been that difficult. Of course, like the Bible and the tax laws, everything Jimmy said could be interpreted. The last two election cycles, he tried his hand at the Governor's race and was two for two.

James Thadford Burton, better known as Bubba Burton, a four-term state representative from Porter County, in the southern part of the state, began his gubernatorial campaign by traveling to Fletcher to get Jimmy Joe's opinion on his chances. All the papers carried the short conversation.

"I understand you know politics," said a smiling Bubba Burton, while cameras clicked and flashes flashed.

"It ain't over 'til it's over." Jimmy Joe smiled back. They were on the courthouse steps with the humming, sweating crowd not more than ten feet away. One thing about Jimmie Joe, neither crowds nor being alone bothered him.

"You have a perfect record, I've been told." Bubba beamed for the reporters, thumbs hooked into the waistband of his trousers, rocking back on his heels as he spoke.

"That's the way the cookie crumbles."

"I know a little bit about politics myself," Bubba Burton puffed, grinning broadly, "And I know the people of this great state need a new governor. So, tell me, Jimmy Joe, are they going to get one?"

"All's well that ends as the crow flies," Jimmy said, still smiling.

"Did you hear that, people," Bubba cried out enthusiastically, "Jimmy Joe says it's going to end well! And you know what? I agree with him! When you have James T. Burton sitting in the governor's chair, I can guarantee you it's going to end well!"

That had been a few weeks ago, but people still talked about it and even though the election was months away, Jimmy Joe's uncanny ability for predictions spread from a wink and a chuckle to a truth of superstitious proportions. Local politicians made their way to Jimmy Joe like ancient Greeks to the oracle at Delphi. They didn't want his advice and didn't much care for his looks or his company, but they damn sure wanted to know if they were going to win. They'd slide up next to him on the bench outside the courthouse or buy him a cup of coffee at Brice's.

"How are you, Jimmy Joe? What's new Jimmy Joe? What do you think my chances are Jimmy Joe?" Most of the time they never got a straight answer and it was fairly apparent, even to Jimmy Joe that he was just being used. Still, he seemed to like the notoriety as well as the free coffee and donuts. And as the saying goes, nothing makes you famous like fame.

The Advocate ran a front-page piece with the headline, "Local Man Predicts Vice-Presidential Election," which brought a few chuckles around the county. Several citizens wrote in to correct the mistake, but Wilbur Simons, the owner and editor in chief, who was already about two miles past the retirement village, refused to revise or retract. "I stand by my sources," he said.

Then a state paper got hold of the story. It didn't make the front page, but it did get a full column in the political section. Three state representatives called for an investigation to see if Jimmy Joe were somehow getting inside information. They petitioned their United States Senators, but the senators were already too busy investigating the alleged price fixing of chicken wire. The controversy died and the trail to Jimmy Joe got so traveled it had ruts in it.

Potential school board member, Jake Morgan, strolled by the Cassavora courthouse on a sun bleached morning, when Jimmy Joe called out to him, "Sometimes you feel like a nut, sometimes you don't." Jake saw the man with the grin on his face, about fifteen yards away looking in his direction, but he wasn't sure what he'd heard.

He shaded his eyes and squinted. "You talking to me?" Jake didn't recognize the face.

"It's now or never!" The man in the baggy pants, police uniform shirt and red suspenders walked toward him, smiling like he'd just found out beer was a nickel a keg.

When the man got close enough, Jake stuck out his hand and Jimmy shook it, squinting into the morning sun, but still grinning. "I'm Jake Morgan and I'm running for the school board." It was the same delivery he'd made in neighborhoods throughout the county and the sound of it shot through him, as it always did, like a voltmeter that checked the circuits of his sincerity.

"Quality is job one," Jimmy Joe shot back.

"You're right about that and quality is what we need. How would you improve our school system?"

"Keep your options open. It's the early bird that gets the real coffee flavor." Jake could see he was dealing with a guy marching to the beat of a different trumpet. Yet, at the same time, there was something endearing, like the nice kid you knew at school who was too awkward to ever be picked when you chose kickball teams.

"You have kids in school?"

"You have kids in school?" The question ricocheted back at him.

"No, but there's plenty from my neighborhood. A friend's daughter is a junior at the high school."

"I'm Jimmy Joe," Jimmy said, maintaining eye contact and his ever bright smile.

"Glad to meet you, Jimmy Joe. I bet you know a lot of folks around here."

"You got that right."

"How'd you like to help me with my campaign?"

"Grrrrreat!" Jimmy Joe had a built in honesty detector and in the case of Jake Morgan he liked what he saw.

"Let me tell you what I'd like you to do." Jake leaned forward and spoke just above a whisper. "How about introducing me to those older gentlemen sitting on the bench?" He pointed toward the small cluster of men around the closest bench.

"Have it your way!" Jimmy said happily.

As they approached, Jake swung into his running for the board spiel. The men looked at him and nodded. Several of them took sips from the Styrofoam "Dixie Drive In, World's Best Barbecue" cups they were holding.

Jake introduced himself and shook hands.

"We got a fine school system." One of the seated men readjusted what appeared to be a permanently stiff leg.

"We sure do, but I think it can get better."

"You one of those money spending liberals?" Another of the men spit some brown juice into a cola can.

"Well, education costs money."

"Hell, it's already sucking up all the money in the county." A man named Fred took a sip of coffee. "You can't just throw money at it."

"I couldn't agree with you more. Money isn't a solution, but it can be a means to a solution."

"Waddaya mean?"

"When the school house roof leaks, it costs money to repair it. When the kids need books, it costs money to buy them."

"These damn kids got all the books they need. What they need is a good strappin'."

Jake braved it out in the face of irritating ignorance. "I spoke with a teacher who said she couldn't let the kids take their science books home because there weren't enough."

"Those teachers will say anything to get some more money."

Jake smiled, gave his one line spiel again and said good morning. Jimmie Joe trailed behind him. Jake's face burned. Aside from sex and religion, more people held more peculiar opinions about education than anything else. Everybody had been to school. Everybody was an expert. Fuck it. The steady diet of bullshit was making him retch and politics was already past the fun stage.

"Hey, young fella!" Jake turned to meet the voice behind him. One of the men waved at him. "Come on back! We was just funnin' ya!"

Jake came back, embarrassment clinging to him like road tar. Maybe he was losing his perspective and needed to chill.

A man in a red baseball cap, sporting a full gray and brown streaked beard, told him, "This whole town is crazy as a loon, so you gotta keep your sense of humor."

"Aw, hell." A sheepish grin crossed Jake's face. "I knew you weren't as dumb as you looked."

"Yeah, I'm afraid we are."

"You were in the Air Corps?" The guy with the bum leg looked up from the bench.

"Air Force," Jake corrected. "Twenty-five years."

"Fly did ya?"

"Every time I got the chance."

The old man chuckled. "I saw what that damn Colonel said about you. Never did like colonels myself and when I read that crap about you being insubordinate, well, I knew right away you were a guy who didn't take any crap. I was in the Army Air Corps. Dubya Dubya Two and before that the A.V.G. You ever hear of them."

"Yes, sir. American Volunteer Group. Chenault's Flying Tigers."

"That's right. Flew P-40s. Colonel C. Now he was a leader and believe me, there were a whole bunch of colonels and generals who couldn't stomach him. Got myself four nips.

Woulda had another, but the bastard spun through some clouds, and I lost sight of him."

"I'm impressed." The last person Jake expected to find here was another aviator and this one a bona fide fighter pilot, old school.

"Are ya? Ya shouldn't be. Just did my duty."

"Just did my duty!" One of the other men mimicked the first. "You fly boys had it easy. I was in the infantry myself."

"Whatever you was in, I bet you made a sorry mess of it."

"Scared myself to death. Damn near got killed, I'll tell ya that."

"Where were you?" Jake asked.

"Bastogne." And so it went. War stories from the best part of their lives.

Jake carried away a lead on where to find more votes.

*****

A cluster of modern, four-story apartments constituted Swaying Elms Retirement Community, or Sob Jenkins Retirement Home as it was often called. Woodlands surrounded the complex and offered a fine view overlooking the Cassavora River. The buildings bordered a black asphalt parking lot, dotted with young willows and elms. Around the edges, well-tilled beds held clumps of red carnations, black-eyed susans, tall, white lilies, and low blue asters, in the English style of careful abandon.

He drove into the lot and parked with no more trepidation than he felt in any of the other neighborhoods he'd visited. One person, one vote, old, young, or terminally stupid. Besides, the elderly didn't lack for opinions, especially on a topic as hot as school tax.

Jake spoke with those spryly getting their exercise in the sunshine of this beautiful day, then he stepped into the main foyer and exchanged pleasantries with a lady who waited patiently for her daughter to pick her up. The air conditioning hit him like a meat locker chill.

It was near noon, the dining room crowded and noisy. About half the fifty or so residents glanced in his direction. Several continued to stare, but most went back to pecking at their food and chatting.

Jake felt a tug at his sleeve and looked around to find a be-speckled older man looking at him. His brown eyes captured Jake and the bushy eyebrows bounced when he spoke. "You're running for the school board aren't you?"

"Yes, sir." Jake put out his hand and the man shook it.

"You know, my daughter is a school teacher."

"Oh, really? What grade does she teach?"

The man's eyes riddled with panic. "Holy shit and hell's fire! The bastards are tossing grenades!" The old guy crumpled to the floor. Jake grabbed him, but the guy was determined.

Two white-jacketed attendants ran over at double time and lead him away. One of the attendants told the man, "Don't worry Mr. Jenkins, we've got 'em on the run."

Jake felt another touch on his sleeve and looked down to see a silver haired woman seated at the table next to him. "Young man?" She gave Jake a mother's look and patted his arm. "That was Mr. Jenkins, Sob Jenkins is his son. He's the reason this community was built."

Jake only nodded, still recovering.

"He served in World War II. That was our war, dear," she said with a bit of pride. "The younger Mr. Jenkins is a nice boy, and if he and Mr. Whitehall hadn't built Swaying Elms, why we'd have had to move out of the county, away from all our friends."

"Mr. Whitehall?"

"Yes, he's the one that's married to the Superintendent of Schools, don't you know."

Cleve was right about this being a more complicated situation than simply dirty books in the schools.

*****

Across town, Sheriff Goddard sat at his desk and poured over a list of phone calls Mrs. Arston, the P.E. teacher, had made and received on the night in question. Only three, none of which were remarkable in any manner whatsoever. Still, there was that business of a cell phone call reporting the body and the couple who'd seen her leave her house. Maybe he should send John Howard out to chat with them again. Something that smelled like a lie had come from Mrs. Arston. He was almost sure of it and working with this tangled ball of string was beginning to annoy him. He either needed some answers or a dog to kick.

29

We have a wonderful school system, with wonderful parents, teachers, and pupils. And, as I've said many times, it's truly a community system. —Dr. Lucinda Whitehall, superintendent

Jake's battle ran straight uphill and he felt the strain every time he stepped onto a porch. He was a salesman with nothing but cold calls. When he rang a new doorbell, his heart beat a little faster, his tongue got a little dry. Likely as not the person on the other side of the door was hostile, or apathetic.

Doubts rattled like snare drums. Who were his real adversaries? Robbins or Southmore? Lucinda Whitehall? Her husband? Sob Jenkins? Was it communal inertia or conspiracy that kept the education cart from rolling down the road of progress? Self-doubt crept in. Who the hell was he to offer answers?

Was it the Emperor's New Clothes in the information age? A modern version where ethical surveyors defined naked as not always naked, if there was no intent to be naked? If the king follows his dream of the perfect cloth, who are we to object? Commentators staring blank faced and reporting government grants to find out the actual causes of nakedness, which hits the poor hardest of all. National Society for Nakedness supporters clashing with the Right to Dress contingent. The President of the Garment Workers Union declaring, "Working men and women have the right to make invisible cloth."

"Snap out of it, Jake," he told himself. Get on with business. Deal with what is and not with what you want. Oh, yeah, don't worry, be happy. Funny how the politics from the newspapers and TV seemed so simple. This wasn't fun. This was shit, and the water was rising.

He slouched over his kitchen table, pen in hand and willed himself back to reviewing his three-part action plan: canvass the county, door to door, visit influential individuals and pound his message home at the public forum right before the general elections. A map of the county lay on the table, slashes over the neighborhoods already covered. The list of names drifted through his mind. Selecting today's neighborhoods could wait a moment.

He ran his finger down the white scrap of paper. The list was fairly long. Clergy. Business leaders. Community leaders. School leaders. He had time to concentrate.

He made an appointment with the superintendent for later that day. Two other calls setup more interviews. Another glance at the map made his knees weak. The county didn't look this big before he started.

The superintendent's office nestled in a newly constructed administrative building in a copse of trees behind the high school. Cars and vans parked in front. Flowers lined the cement sidewalk leading to double doors and into air-conditioned comfort. Thick beige pile deadened his footsteps. He ambled over to the receptionist who punched a black intercom to the superintendent's secretary and motioned for him to have a seat. "Dr. Whitehall will be with you in a moment."

Jake thumbed a copy of Teachers' Magazine lying on the table, then noticed a bookcase of labeled notebooks. The spine of a thick volume read, Policies and Procedure, Part I. He'd glanced through it at school board meetings and picked up reading where he'd left off.

Fifteen minutes later Lucinda Whitehall strode in, coiffured, long eyelashes, immaculate gray business suit and a freshly pressed smile.

She held out a hand. Jake stood up. "Good afternoon, Mr. Morgan, I'm Lucinda Whitehall." Funny, Jake thought. She often referred to herself as Dr. Whitehall, but now evidently they were pals. Just Jake and Lucinda. She ushered him across the hallway into her office, pausing a moment for an aside to her secretary. "Mr. Morgan and I will be in conference for a few minutes. Hold my calls."

The secretary looked up from her computer screen, nodded. "Yes, ma'am."

He sat in an overstuffed armchair, she opposite, crossing her legs, hands on the prominent knee. Long legs were evidently one of her strong suits, and she didn't mind showing her hand. "I've been looking forward to meeting you, Mr. Morgan." A slight smile cascaded off the perfectly applied lipstick.

"And I've heard you've been having to thwart some book burning."

"Oh, yes." Little spidery wrinkles appeared at the corners of her eyes. "That sort of thing comes with the territory, you know."

"What kind of shape would you say the school system is in?" Jake asked, the master of subtly.

"I'd say we have a wonderful school system. Of course there are always things we need to do. At the moment, we're badly in need of some new science text books and a new science wing at the high school ... and the band is clambering for new instruments."

"No money?"

"Unfortunately not, but, that's what the Board of Education does. Sets priorities, makes policies and then I have to carry them out. The board is really in control, and I am powerless to act without their blessing."

"Would you say your relations with the board are strained?"

"No, not at all. Most of the board members are team players. Those that aren't make the papers."

"Would you characterize Mr. Robbins as not a team player?"

"Mr. Morgan, I try not to deal in personalities."

"How is our system doing on the standardized tests?" Lucinda stiffened slightly, decided maybe they weren't pals after all.

"Very well. In fact, on both the SAT and the Iowa standardized tests, we rank in the top ten percent of the schools in this part of the state who are most like us demographically."

Yes, Jake thought, modifiers and qualifiers can be an addiction. "So, how do we do compared to the national averages?"

"Well, that's difficult to say because all schools do not put an emphasis on the same standardized tests." An eel.

"I'm not sure I understand the answer, superintendent." He knew he was being too abrupt, but suddenly, he didn't like this woman.

Her eyes narrowed. "We do quite well, but as I said, scores are always open to interpretation and don't always reflect the full value of the educational experience. Plus, more of our students take the tests, so our average scores get skewed." Lucinda shifted slightly in her chair. He heard the rustle of her slip against the suit material. "Let me assure you, no one cares about this school system more than I do." She stared at him and her eyes reflected a cold, almost reptilian detachment, as if sizing up the threat, deciding whether he were worth a fang or two.

"What would you say reflects the full educational experience?" Jake marveled at the way she could take any question and turn it into a personal attack. Good defense. He should be more pleasant. He knew how to charm, but this woman was tough to deal with, one moment warm, the next a block of cement.

Glimpses of womanly vulnerability came and went like players on stage. Just when Jake was tempted to be caustic, she softened. At times a seemingly genuine smile flicked across her red lips. But often he saw only the stone look of a bureaucrat, defending her turf. She switched back and forth with alacrity. What was she trying to hide? Deep inferiority? A woman in a man's world?

He'd seen it in female officers, reflecting a normal social ease then offering leather toughness on duty, using regulations to slash friends as well as enemies.

"You see," she continued, without missing a breath, "we are a data driven school system. I have personally insured that we are." She paused. To let him reflect on her importance? To see if she were talking over his head? "When I first came to work in this office, this system was just beginning to grow." She held out her hand, palm up. "I could have written the names of most of the faculty right here. The superintendent picked up the mail and wrote out the checks longhand. Now, all that has changed. I have brought it about in an orderly and systematic fashion." She could easily have added, "And I will let nothing destroy what I have created."

She looked at him and saw a man just like so many others. This one might be quicker on the uptake, but he was no threat. He obviously didn't like her. So what? That could change if she wanted it to. Her game face concealed the contempt for an upstart stepping brashly into her lair. She had given heart and soul for this county. It was hers by right. Others served this school system at her pleasure and that included the pawns on the board.

She's not a bad looking woman, Jake thought, and intelligent, but there is something incongruous, like seeing apple pie and smelling sewage. She had the look of raw power sitting there, her eyes just barely on the polite side of a glare, clearly bothered by his pointed questions. Jake had sweated through a year of war and his determined finger had squeezed the button and released thundering bombs that ended lives in a flash of fire. He'd flown through swarms of exploding shells and wasn't about to back off now just because questions made this woman uncomfortable. Nor was he going to get into a shooting match right here in her office.

She had a right to be proud of how far the school system had come and her part in the journey. She could have been good company if she loosened up. Still he wasn't comfortable. In some ways this visit was an epiphany. Why was he suddenly the enemy? Tough questions? He never attacked her or the school system in his tantrums to the editor. His focus had been at first on the Bible shouters and then on planting educational seeds. The superintendent should have been an ally. Puzzling.

"How do you feel about the reading program?"

"The reading program, Mr. Morgan?" Her voice still had a bite.

"Yes, how do you approach reading and how do the results tally with your expectations?"

"That's a difficult question to answer, for the simple reason that our principals have a great deal of autonomy. They set the priorities for their schools."

"Well, what do the standardized tests show?"

"I think this is ground we've covered before. They show that we do very well as a system. We change the reading series every five years, and select a new one based on the recommendations of our Reading Committee."

"Besides the standardized tests, do you use any other measurements of output?"

"What do you mean?" Her brows knitted.

"I mean the reading books are input, the reading program, whatever the different schools use is input. What other ways do you measure output to see how well your programs work? Measure one school against another? Glean the best and then pass around the methods that work?"

"Mr. Morgan, we really don't think having some sort of reading competition is very healthy." She started to mention standardized testing, but stopped. Saw the can of worms before it spilled.

She missed the point, or she didn't have a good answer. Jake wasn't sure which. "How about the personnel system? How does it work?"

"What specifically are you asking?" She must have read his letter to the editor.

He wanted to know the specifics of hiring practices. His question hid a jagged edge. Wonder if the neighborhood wags were right about flagrant nepotism. Cleveland seemed to think so. Lucinda peeled off vague answers about being only the servant of the Board of Education. She only presented the members with selections the principals made.

He moved on. "What's the annual budget?"

"It varies, but it's all a matter of public record." Her response didn't shake him. He already knew the number. Soon she was looking at her watch. The welcome mat was threadbare. They shook hands and she thanked him for coming. Who was she kidding?

Education in Cassavora was rife with complications. He'd pictured only a classroom or two, with a couple of dozen little faces and a teacher, the only major problems being Robbins and Southmore. He'd thought wrong. Vast sums of money spilled across the educational landscape, in construction and maintenance, books and supplies. The budget ran to over twenty million dollars and that probably didn't count architecture fees, building contracts, and teacher pay, which mostly came from the state. Every budget he'd ever encountered had pockets of money stashed here and there. Still, the superintendent complained about not enough money and cast a cloud of doubt over every question put to her. A lot of tangles could be smoothed over with deep pile carpet.

When he got home Cynthia Farnsworth had left a message on the answering machine. He dialed her.

"You may not like the way they spend it, but the budget is clean." Mrs. Farnsworth sounded sure of herself, as if she'd spent a lot of time with numbers. "Believe me, we checked it line by line. Even complained about the lack of new band instruments. Lots of our friends have kids in the band." Cynthia's voice registered frustration. "They weren't too worried about us knowing. Maybe because the band parents are outnumbered."

"Who led you through the budget?" Jake asked.

"Mr. Gordan, Lucinda's assistant. He showed us every penny."

"And who did he say made the decisions about the instruments?"

"The board, of course."

"The superintendent only follows orders. I've heard it before."

After he hung up, Jake sat and pondered. Everything was a dead end. Of one thing he was certain. Numbers on a ledger never told the whole truth.

30

Criminals and honor go together like oil and water. —*Chief Deputy John Howard*

Jerald took a sip of beer from the chilled can and put his feet up on the Mustang's dash.

"Goddamnit! You're gonna ruin the car!" Billy slapped at the black boot and spilled some of his own beer down the front of his t-shirt.

"Sorry." Jerald really was sorry. He brought his foot down, watched Billy wipe at the damp spot on his chest.

"Now I'm gonna smell like beer when I pick Becky up."

"Ohhhh, she's hot ain't she!"

"Damn right." He kept dabbing with the hem of his shirt, blissfully unaware of the futility.

"So, Billy, what we gonna do to that Jew bastard?" Billy looked up. His eyes got that glazed look as he took another sip and pictured the perfect plan somewhere out on the horizon.

"First off, I think we might want to send the sumbitch a little note that tells him to back off." He looked over at Jerald.

"Don't look at me like that. I don't like to write."

"Just a little note. You wouldn't even have to write it."

"I can't type neither."

Billy popped him on the shoulder with the back of his hand. "Naw, you could cut the letters out of the newspaper or a magazine."

"Yeah and paste 'em on a postcard or somethin'." Billy's eyes gleamed with the possibilities.

"Not a damn post card. You want every fool in the county reading our note?" Billy realized he was not going to be able to totally delegate.

"How 'bout you get Becky to write it?"

"I can't ask her to do man's work."

"How 'bout Bonnie and Clyde? Or Hillary and Bill?"

"That's different. Becky's sensitive. I gotta protect her."

"I thought you wanted to screw her." Jerald's ignorance of the rules of honor didn't save him from another backhand, this one across the mouth. He drew away, dabbed his broken lip, stared down at the pink smear on his fingertips.

"Damn, Billy, that hurt!"

"Then watch your mouth." He hadn't meant to hit Jerald that hard, but it was too late now. He reached over, patted his shoulder, trying to ease the pain and the insult.

"Ya didn't have to hit me," Jerald whined.

"Okay. Okay. Now you gonna write the letter, or do I gotta find somebody else."

"What should I say?" Jerald looked puzzled. Then the clouds parted. "I know, I know! I'll tell him we're gonna kill him."

Jerald's enthusiasm wanted tempering. "Not to start with, we ain't. Maybe we can just scare him off."

"Castrolate him, uh, Castigate, uh ... Cut off his balls?" Billy shook his head no.

"Well, what should I say?"

"Just warn the bastard."

"About what? Say we gonna be watchin' him?"

"Not bad for a start." Billy the psychology major. " But, just give him a warning."

"Do you want me to cut the letters out?" "Yeah, that's fine."

"Well, do you want me to cut 'em out of the newspaper or a magazine?"

"I don't care." Exasperation was creeping in.

"I could go to the library and cut 'em out of magazines."

Billy pictured the complications, the gaps in front covers staring at everyone who walked through, the astonished looks from librarians when Jerald darkened their door. "Why not just write the damn thing?"

"I did the last one. Shouldn't you do this one? Maybe they'll find out."

"What last one?" A blank appeared where knowledge should be.

"You know, to the Quick Stop when they didn't sell us beer that time."

"Shit. How many more you written I didn't know about?"

"Just that one," Jerald lied.

"Then just write this one."

Jerald's mind was feverish with the prospect of his own inadequacies. Should he address it to Jew? Should he mail it, or just put it in Morgan's mailbox? Were the boxes even fixed yet? Damn, he and Billy had had some beer that night! What to say exactly? He'd ask his cousin Nick, to help him. Nick was great at thinkin' of rhymes and shit.

"And don't ask nobody else." Billy was a mind reader. Survival instincts. "Forget it," he added, "I'll write it myself."

The weight of the world floated away. There was joy in Mudville. "But, Billy ... "

"What?"

"What if he don't take the warnin'?"

Billy finished the last swallow, slowly crumpled the aluminum can and pitched it out the window. "Then, we'll just have to put him on the sidelines ourselves."

31

The schools are teaching evolution as fact. And, the fact is, that's wrong. It's only a theory. —Purcell Southmore

Religion was too controversial to be discussed in many Cassavora sanctuaries. In others, such as the Cramp Hill Church of Holy Redemption there was no need. The shepherd, Reverend Edward Jones Peabody, never skirted the issues, but came straight at his flock, with the unfiltered truth given him by Gawd. His heart told him every lamb in his field believed as he believed. They had seen the light, been washed in the blood, and dipped into deep pockets every Sunday. His passion was to help them turn their backs on Satan, in his many forms, many with which he was personally acquainted. Yes, he knew temptation. Yes, he had yielded a time or two, but with Gawd and Jesus at his side, he had the strength of ten.

Jake slid into a back pew on this hot and muggy Sunday morning. Rock of Ages already reverberated, binding the congregation in the full richness of musical praise. Having been raised Baptist, nothing in the service surprised him, but then he hadn't expected they'd be handling snakes.

News of Sunday school and picnics and other glad tidings followed the hymns. Then came the ushers to the front, anointed in prayer and afterwards fanning out to render Caesar unto God. Jake debated, fidgeted with his hand in his pocket. Propriety won out. He dropped ten dollars in the plate. Praise God from whom all blessings flow. That he agreed with. The flow part, not the commercial transaction.

At last, the Reverend Peabody arose and stepped toward the pulpit. Staring upward, he paused a moment for any last minute instructions from above, cleared his throat and settled into a sermon on the demise of the family and the ungodliness of those who disagreed. In vibrant tones echoing out to the street, he laid into his subject with verve and gusto, the organist punctuating the main points with deeply religious chords. The Reverend preached in a singsong of repetitions, as though having studied public speaking under Paul Harvey and James Brown. He also stuttered. "What we are seeing in today's world ... what we are seeing in today's world ... is not what our fathers and our grandfa-fa-fa-fathers saw in they .. they .. their world. Not in they .. they .. their w-w-w-world. Amen. What we are seeing in the w-w-w-world today is not the lighted holiness of Gawd's true p-p-p-path, but the black shadows, where the Prince of Darkness dwells. Can I get an A, an A, an A ... ?"

Jake wanted to shout. Somebody give the bastard an A! " .... an Amen!" the Rev finally blurted. He got one. More than one. "Let us think of our grandfathers and their grandfathers. They didn't have violence on television the-the-then! They didn't have girls getting pregnant the-the-then! They didn't have rap music!"

The bastard deserved another A. He got one.

Peabody kept rolling. "They picked cotton twelve hours a day in the backbreaking heat of the sun and paid for their bre-bre-bread with the sweat of their br-br-brow! Their hands were not idle and their minds were on pleasing the L...L...Lord. There was no talk of evil-lution, no perverting Gawd's ways."

Ladies weren't waving fans because the church was air-conditioned, something else they didn't have back in Gran' Pappy's glory days.

"A lot of things are done now that weren't done the-the-then. Young folks didn't do dru ... dru ... drugs. They didn't have insatiable lu ... lu ... lust!" The Reverend Peabody made exception for the marvel of modern pharmacology, by which he controlled his appetite, his cholesterol, his high blood pressure, his liver functions and his thyroid. The Rev had also forgotten his own mother's marriage at the ripe old age of fourteen to a man twenty years older. Sanctified lust. Gimme an A.

"Who among you would say the Bible ... I said The Bible ... was written so that Charles Darwin could interpret it for us?" The reverend paused to enjoy the satisfaction of a rustling in the pews and an undertone of disapproval for Charlie D. He smiled the barest of smiles. "Evil-lution is a theory and only a th ... th ... heory. The word of Gawd Almighty is a f ... f ... fact!" Amens burst as bubbles at a Lawrence Welk reunion.

Jake stayed quiet, hoping to remain anonymous. Then the reverend's scanning eyes locked onto him. "There are those among us who would gl-gl-gladly do Satan's b-b-b-bidding, who have turned their back on our Savior, Jay-sus Christ." There was more.

Having driven home his irrefutable points, the reverend launched into the duties of family members, compared them with the duties of deacons, wove intricate embellishments of what life was like outside a family and tied the package neatly together with a pronouncement on abortion. "Rap music and lust take place outside the d-d-door of the home and outside God's ch-ch-church. Those things are the plagues the evil-lutionists have foisted upon us. They are alien to everything your parents and your grandparents believed in."

Jake stood for the hymns, bowed his head for the prayers, watched the proceedings. Tried to keep his breakfast down.

The congregation mixed old and young and in between. He could pick out the ages based on the clothes. Every man over forty wore a suit, mostly dark, all off the rack. Saville Row wasn't sacred ground in this church. Men under forty managed ties, but no coats. Women followed the same route, but from dresses to skirts. In the younger crowd, the slim, lipsticked girls fared better than the lanky boys. Sun dresses predominated, with hose, high heels and push-em-up bras the badges of budding maturity.

Jake thought about approaching the preacher today, but didn't want a rushed, after service chat crammed between kids' socials and planning meetings. He settled for the greeting line with everyone else. When he shook hands with the Reverend, he mentioned he was running for the school board and would like to come back for a chat. The Reverend Peabody seemed distracted by two of the teenage girls prancing past and didn't look at Jake when he told him that would be fine. Jake expected more of a reaction. Was the eye contact during the sermon a coincidence? No.

Cramp Hill sat on the far side of the county, an area of farms and subdivisions, scattered like playing cards strewn across a green felt table. Lines of leafy green trees and high bushes divided the fields, except where black top thoroughfares split off into gravel roads. Here and there, clusters of homes perched on generous lots were set back from the street. Kitchen gardens overflowed with lush green tomato plants and long tendrils of squash. Occasionally a commercial nursery sprawled from the tree line into an open field, with bursts of blue and red and yellow and green, now fading into dark gray as twilight passed to evening.

The following Wednesday, Jake eased into the black topped parking lot, admiring the old, white, clapboard building, long stained-glass windows and massive white door. No telling the age, but the blush of youth was long gone. Cramp Hill wasn't the tiny church found in some parts of Cassavora. Five hundred worshipers would fill it to capacity on Christmas and Easter.

Reverend Peabody's office occupied a portion of the newer, low, white, Sunday school building that angled away from the sanctuary. It was smaller and plainer than Jake expected, with cluttered desk and old wooden furniture no corporate CEO would allow. Several framed certificates decorated the ivory colored walls and a poster, corners cracked and curled, featured a younger version of the preacher mingling with a group of holy land pilgrims.

The Rev shook Jake's hand and motioned him to a well-worn armchair. "C-c-coffee?" His voice wasn't harsh, but not overly friendly, like a corporate lawyer condemned to chat with an honest man.

The preacher pulled his chair to face Jake's, cup in hand. "What can I do for yew?" The voice lacked a heavy twang, but was vaguely Southern.

"You don't sound like you're from here," Jake said.

"Twenty-six years and before that over in Corburn County. My family came from Indiana, near the K-k-kentucky border."

"After twenty-six years, you must know the county pretty well. As I said, I'm running for the school board and wanted to get your perspective on a few things."

The preacher leaned back and brought his cup up close to his chest "I've heard of yew." He twisted "yew" like a maggot. "You're a Jew, aren't yew?" His right eyebrow rose, daring Jake to deny it.

"Yes."

"I have nothing against J-J-Jews." The reverend looked straight at Jake. His eyes were gray flint. "But, one thing you have to remember; this is a Christian county, and it values its school system."

Jake listened. Nothing against Jews? Nothing a few ovens couldn't fix.

The Reverend pressed on. "Christ has got to be a part of the school system of a Christian county. It's as simple as th-th-that." He blinked, flared his nostrils, blinked again.

The Rev seemed a little unhinged. A wounded cobra rearing up. Christian or un-Christian? America's system of governance and toleration was anything but simple. And obviously the Reverend Peabody's constricted view of righteousness conflicted.

"I noticed there's lots of Catholics here," Jake deadpanned. "Lots of Spanish speakers."

Peabody came close to a wince. "We don't consider the Cath-cath-catholics when we say Christian." The muscles in his jaw tightened.

"So, you're advocating separate schools?"

"Mr. Morgan, what's the real reason yew came here?"

"I want your opinions."

"Oh, yew do?" Sarcasm spilled out. "Our schools are full of filth. That's my opinion and Gawd's opinion."

"How do you tell the difference?"

"What's that?"

"How do you feel about evolution?"

"Personally? I think it's an interesting theory, but unsupported by any facts. I don't like to see it taught to impressionable youngsters."

"You believe in the Bible, as written."

"I do."

"And you want the Bible taught as fact?"

"I want the book of *Genesis* given the same cre ... cre ... credence as *The Origin of Sp ... species*. It's an ancient truth. As a Jew, you should know tha ... tha ... that."

"You think the earth was created in six days?"

"Yes." The Reverend took a sip, felt himself on solid theological soil.

"Do you allow the word *day* may mean a greater period of time than twenty-four hours?" Twenty-four hours was a pretty recent concept. He wondered if the preacher knew that.

"I do not."

"Then, how do you account for the scientific evidence of fossils and carbon dating?"

"I believe in a Gawd who can do-do-do all things." The preacher looked at Jake and spoke slowly, softly, a man straining to control his impatience.

"You mean God can make a 20 million year old fossil in one day?"

"Of course."

"Why would he want to?"

"Why would he not wa ... wa ... want to? We can't know the mind of the L-l-lord."

"So, you see empirical knowledge as irrelevant."

"I believe in Gawd's master plan, which we cannot know. Do you believe in Gawd, Mr. Morgan? It doesn't sound as if you do."

Jake paused. He wanted to say, I believe we have an active role in our own lives. God gave us brains to better our world and ourselves. But, he let the moment pass.

"If yew had accepted Christ, then you would realize our purpose is to know Gawd's will and to follow it through our Savior, Jay-sus Christ."

"But, you just said we couldn't know God's plan."

"We can't know the whole plan, but we get gl ... gl ... glimpss. Gawd told us plenty about f ... f ... following the ways of his only Son, but that's New Testament and yew may not be familiar."

"But what you want us to teach in school, alongside evolution is Genesis from the Old Testament?"

"I want the word of Gawd taught. Yew see, yew J-j-jews rejected The Christ and slew him. I forgive yew for it, just as He forgave yew." The Rev forced an icy smile.

Mighty kind of the two of you.

Back from his meeting with the preacher, he sat under the dark, whispering trees in his backyard. Cicadas filled the air with their chirping. Fireflies abounded. He watched them making their little, yellow Js, while he lit a cigar and lost himself in thought. The pungent smoke curled into the humid night air. What Peabody wanted was not to promote God, but to be God. He wondered whom he had in mind to play the Son and the Holy Ghost.

His thoughts turned to the larger question. The fundamentalist crowd made the papers, but the whole picture wasn't in focus. Love him or hate him, Caldwell Robbins didn't have any power. He was one vote out of five. He wasn't rich and only had a couple of issues on the table, the books in the high school library and evolution. Close-minded men such as the Reverend Peabody may have exerted some minor influence, but no power to enforce their views on a secular school board. Another of God's blessings.

Of course, both those guys had reasons to be nervous and angry with him. He'd blasted them and their views point blank with howitzers. Then, there was the superintendent. Still a puzzle. Where were the open arms welcoming him on the common ground of opposition to Bible thumping ignorance? The black cordless phone sitting in his lap let out a subdued, plastic buzz.

"Morgan."

A muffled male voice asked him, "Do you know what the issues are? Do you realize how big this thing is?"

"What do you mean?"

"Let's examine the whole school board election business a moment."

"I'm listening."

"Do you think it's about education or books in the library, or the Bible? " The low, male voice sounded somehow familiar and Jake tried in vain to place it. Black, white? "It's about money and political control. Tie that to the school system and you've got your answer."

"Any chance of getting a small hint?"

"You remember that first grade teacher that got fired for insubordination?"

"Vaguely." "It was a couple of board meetings ago." "I don't remember anyone saying anything about insubordination."

"It wasn't mentioned in open session. Her name is Stephanie Porcose. Her husband's name is Ed. Give her a call." The line went dead.

*****

The next day shone brightly. Jake took a cup of steaming coffee at eleven o'clock and hummed to himself as he ambled down his tree-lined driveway toward his new mailbox. His property wasn't in the country, but it wasn't the city either. His and most of the mailboxes had undergone repairs and restorations, but some still needed paint. The sounds of the forest opened up around him, wrens warbling, the clear, one note song of the cardinal, the buzzing of insects, the whispering of the oak and dogwood trees, the steady crunch of gravel under his feet.

His white, metal mailbox stood atop a four by four wooden post, also painted white. Betsy had helped him. Bright and straight once again, it glowed with a kind of country elegance. Around the base, a purple spray of Sweet Williams bobbed their little faces and a trumpet vine's orange blooms crawled up the post. The idea of flowers also sprang from Betsy.

Jake pulled the box open, extracted the contents and resting the coffee cup on top of the mailbox, began to shuffle through. Phone bill. Invitation to have siding put on his house. Sale at the local K Mart. A letter from a literary agent. He opened it carefully, hoping this answer wouldn't be like the others.

A form letter. "After careful consideration of your submission, see our reasons below." At the bottom of the page, someone had scrawled, "I do not approve of war. Also, in today's market, your main character should be a woman."

Among the bunch of mail, there was a letter with no return address.

He tore the envelope with a forefinger and extracted a one-sheet note with cut out letters. "You dirt Jew. I dont no why you are out to git the good people of Cassavora County. you dont have a clu people hear are nice and dont need nobody telling them what to do. I have lived hear back when there were not no new people movng in and no jews. I liked it better. why dont you just leave. you are stupid and dont no nothing about the schools. you have been warned."

Jake held a corner of the letter pinched between the forefinger and thumb, as though it oozed with infection. Leaving the coffee cup and remainder of the mail behind, he marched back to the house and put envelope and letter in a plastic sandwich bag.

"Jesus Christ!" He muttered to himself, "Anonymous phone calls, anonymous letters?"

32

Do you know a child only spends about ten percent of his time in School? That includes kindergarten through twelfth grade. Don't blame the schools for everything. —Nell Jackson, Second Grade teacher & parent

Everyone finally cleared out of the sheriff's office. Goddard slid back in his chair, thankful for a moment to be alone with his thoughts.

The intercom buzzed. "Sheriff, you have a visitor, a Mr. Morgan." The sheriff hesitated, glanced down at his calendar and saw the cramped list, tiny handwritten letters in black ink. It reminded him of barbed wire fencing him in. The last thing he needed right now was a visitor. Still, he was faintly curious to see the infamous Jake Morgan again and chat with this slayer of Christian dragons.

"Go ahead and show him in."

Dark hair, glasses, Morgan was even more imposing than the sheriff had remembered. He had a slight smile and piercing eyes when he whipped off the shades. He didn't look like the devil incarnate. Sam extended his hand.

He motioned Jake to take a seat, went back behind his desk, settled into the chair and crossed his hands over his belt buckle.

"What can I do for you, Mr. Morgan?" He tried to keep his voice a friendly neutral.

"I'm running for the board of education."

"I heard you finally made up your mind."

"Yeah, actually, I decided a while ago. Been pacing through the county, going house to house."

Sam Goddard nodded. "Evidently, you're making quite an impression."

"Good or bad?"

The sheriff laughed, rubbed his chin. "A little of both, I'm afraid."

Jake shrugged. "Actually this is a two part visit. First off, I want to feel out your views on education and the county in general. Second, I got this in my mailbox this morning." Jake passed the plastic bag.

Sam held it up to the light and peered through the transparent sides. "Looks like an envelope and a letter. I don't suppose it was signed or had a return address."

"Neither. No stamp either."

"Yeah, they usually don't. Does the letter threaten you?"

"Well, it says I've been warned."

"Warned about what, Mr. Morgan? Anything specific?"

"Not exactly. It just mentions I'm running for the school board and I've been warned."

"Miss Keys." The sheriff fingered a button on the plastic intercom box. "Deputy Howard, if you please ... if he hasn't left already."

Moments later, John Howard cracked the door tentatively, then stepped inside, closing it quietly behind him. "What's up, sheriff?"

"John, this is Mr. Morgan, the one who's running for the school board." Jake stood, offered his hand. Howard's face was familiar. School board meetings? "Mr. Morgan brought us a present. An anonymous letter he got this morning. Get our tech guys to compare it and see if the writing matches any of the others. Take it out of the county if you need to."

Howard wanted to ask, what tech guys? He refrained. Jake watched the deputy leave. "There are others?"

"Not exactly the same, but the same type, anonymous, threatening. Over the past year there have probably been two or three."

"And you'll be able to tell who sent it?"

"We can give it a shot, but I can't promise speed or success. We've got a couple of other cases we're working hard, and this Sheriff's Department doesn't have the facilities or the staff of a big city." Goddard already had a pretty good idea who sent the letter. The handwriting and lack of grammar set off bells. Anyway, this ought to make C2 happy. He could round up some of the usual suspects.

"But, can't you get fingerprints off a letter?" Jake asked.

"Oh, yeah and we can match them up with the prints everybody puts on their drivers' licenses, if we're lucky and the state computer isn't too busy to handle our request. Usually, we can find out in a week or so. The problem is, that envelope is going to have your prints on it, the sender's prints, and God only knows who else's. There may be something on the letter itself. Also, there's been no crime committed I can see, so I can't investigate, and I can't get the state boys to give me any kind of priority. But, I'm willing to try to match the handwriting. All the letters together might constitute a crime if the sender is routinely harassing people."

"I understand, sheriff, and I appreciate your time. Now, if you have a few more moments, tell me what you think of the school system."

The abruptness made the sheriff's eyebrows go up. He took a deep breath, then blew it out. "I've got a little time. Have a seat."

Jake plopped down on the same couch Mrs. Tillsmore had been on.

"You know, I don't have any kids, so I don't get intimately involved. Naturally we have an active drug prevention program all the elementary kids go through. Once, a couple of years back I had to break up a fight at a football game. From time to time there's a young speeder we ticket. As a county official, I go to the graduations and other public functions, but other than that I don't do much with the schools besides direct traffic."

"Drug problems?"

"A little weed, not much else."

"Have you hired anybody straight from the high school?"

"You mean a recent graduate?"

"Yeah."

"No. First of all, we're a small outfit. I've only got fifteen deputies total, including the ones that work full time in the jail. So, I have to hire people with some experience, although a sizable percentage was trained in house. Friends of friends. That sort of thing."

Friends of friends. Jake detected the odor of political favors, which seemed to run rampant in this county. Teach them to wave at traffic and other shitty little jobs. Keep the powers that be happy their nephews are employed.

"We're too small to have our own full-scale training program," the sheriff continued. "That means I have to send new folks to the state to train and that costs money. If there's no money." He shrugged. "It almost precludes me from using people fresh out of high school. Even if they're not trained, I need some age, some maturity." The sheriff was looking at Jake, trying to take the measure of him, deciding if this guy had an axe to grind.

Jake looked right back. "Do you have an opinion about any of the issues in the papers lately?"

"You're talking about the books?"

"Among other things."

"If it doesn't concern the law and law enforcement, I don't have an opinion, at least not while I'm sitting in this office with this uniform on."

"What about the situation with the football coach?" Jake maintained eye contact. "It was in the papers."

Goddard tried not to grimace as he remembered the headlines, Revered Football Coach Dies Between the hedges.

"That's an ongoing investigation, so naturally I would have no comment. It's true he is ... I mean was a member of the high school faculty, but as far as I know that's the only thing connecting this case to the school system. You saw the press release saying it was a heart attack that killed him?"

"Yeah." Jake shifted subjects. "What do you think of this community in general?"

The sheriff deadpanned. "In general, I think it's a great place to live. We have our share of fools, but so does every other place on the planet. Any special fools you want to talk about?"

"If you were running for the school board, are there any special fools you'd want to talk about?"

"No, but there are some I'd want to talk to. Have you spoken to the superintendent herself or C2? I'd hit on as many preachers as possible and every county commissioner and the President of the Chamber of Commerce. Not that I'm giving you advice, you understand. "

"Well, whatever it is, I'm listening."

"But, since you're here, Mr. Morgan, let me ask you a couple of questions."

"Shoot."

"Best not to say that to a sheriff." Jake laughed. "Are you running against or are you running for?"

"A friend of mine asked me that very thing."

"Let me put it this way, you got your finger on some positive changes or does Mr. Robbins just piss you off?"

"Me and half the county."

"Maybe more than that."

Jake leaned back on the couch and laid out his ideas on reading and meaningful classes in the high school and the whole school system as interlocking steps of education. In fact, Jake had spent a lot of time at thehigh school, sitting through classes, until one of the administrators questioned the frequent visits. Suddenly he'd become persona non grata and unknown to him, his activities were reported to the superintendent as interference. "But, most of all, I want openness, fairness, and to get the kids interested in learning."

"I don't want to be the one to stomp all over your enthusiasm, but you talked to any teenagers lately?"

Jake nodded his head in agreement with the spirit of the question. "I know they're a tough sell. Here's a question for you. You sit through any high school classes lately? A lot of 'em would make Hulk Hogan weep."

"Boring?"

"Worse. Stupid and boring."

"Things ain't changed much." This was getting way too deep. The sheriff got up. "Bottom line? I'd be mighty careful about hiring any of our high school graduates these days. But, I never said anything like that, did I?"

33

The schools have been integrated for a long time. We take pride in celebrating Black History Month and Martin Luther King's Birthday. Cassavora appreciates all its citizens, black and white. —Bruce "Big Boy" Claremont, Board of Commissioners

In Cassavora, the question of African Americans was more subtle than in other parts of the state. Blacks were less than five percent of the population, but aside from janitorial staff, the school system was practically barren.

Race seldom came up as Jake went door to door. On his list of people to see, only one African American name appeared. Mr. Albert Tubbs.

Cassavora born and bred, Tubbs left the county as a teenager, prospered in Chicago and returned in his late sixties, buying land and building a substantial house. Because he was black and successful, he'd become a touchstone for local politicians. If elections were baseball, he was one of the bases. His *de facto* title was Mydearfriend Mr. Albert Tubbs, although as far as anyone knew, no white politician ever befriended him in the usual social way. But they did call him on the phone and race up to his front door while the newspapers were printing and the cameras were rolling. A visit to Mr. Tubbs was an electoral inoculation against charges of not fully supporting diversity. So far, Tubbs didn't have a Hispanic counterpart.

Tubbs also caught Jake's interest because of his running complaint about the lack of black teachers and principals. Casualties of integration some said. Willful policy said others.

Jake and Mr. Tubbs met early in the campaign at a Little League baseball game, where Jake shook a few hands. They'd never had the chance for in-depth conversation. Tubbs seemed friendly enough, but still kept a polite distance between one more white guy running for office and a black man who had heard enough promises to last him a lifetime.

To prepare himself, Jake picked through some demographic data. The percentage of blacks in the county population had stayed the same for decades. But, more black professionals were moving in, drawn oddly enough by the school system, along with the proximity of the university and the big city only an hour away. Since 1965, when the schools were fully integrated, the number of black teachers dwindled from thirty-five, including three black administrators, to a total of three teachers today.

He and Mr. Tubbs met at the county park, at a picnic table, under the shade of a spreading live oak. There was no iced tea or barbecue, no cake, or punch and especially no beer. Tubbs was a teetotaler and let everybody know it. "Beer made Milwaukee famous, but never did anybody else any good," he was fond of saying.

He was a big man, in his early eighties, with white hair and a spry mind. Two younger black men and a black woman joined him. They seemed affable, although the conversation bordered on bluntness.

"Mr. Morgan, why is it you want to be on the board of education?" Tubbs asked and Jake gave the standard answer about wanting to improve the school system.

"You know, there's no affirmative action here in Cassavora." One of the other black men threw it out like a challenge.

"Let's not get into the affirmative action debate," the black woman interjected. "I want to hear what Mr. Jake plans for the school system."

"I don't mind talking affirmative action," Jake said. "I want affirmative action for everybody. Right now nobody can tell me what you have to do to get hired by the Cassavora School System. Black teachers figure they're not getting hired because they're black. Some white applicants aren't getting hired either and nobody outside the system can say why anybody is hired or not, black or white." A couple of heads nodded.

"We can say it, but we can't prove it," cut in one of the men.

"Well, that's right. We can just blame it on the system. Everybody else does," said the other black man.

"I have a friend who's an excellent teacher, with more than ten years experience, and they didn't hire her." The woman's eyes flashed.

"What I'm saying is," Jake continued, "there are white teachers in the same position who don't know why."

"The superintendent told us one of her staff was actively recruiting black teachers," Tubbs added, "but I can't see any results."

"Have you read the policy?" Jake asked. "You know, there's even a policy on recruiting black educators."

"I sure didn't know that." Tubbs and the others shook their heads.

"Here's all the policy says, after you get through the equal opportunity stuff." Jake read from his notebook. "The superintendent will establish procedures for ensuring equitable hiring practices and for recruiting minority applicants."

"What are the procedures, Mr. Morgan?" Tubbs looked straight at him.

"Well, that's the problem. As far as I know, there are no procedures for hiring anybody, white or black."

"And if they're actively recruiting minorities, I'd be real surprised."

The members of the group chatted among themselves a few moments, leaving Jake out of the conversation. He didn't know quite what to do, stay or leave, until Mr. Tubbs turned to him. "What are your recommendations, Mr. Morgan?"

"I know it's not popular to make a fuss around here. It never is, but I would go read the policy and from here on out, I'd be at every board meeting, standing up, asking pointed questions in some very specific directions. And, I'd keep on doing that until I got some answers and some satisfaction. But, here's the kicker. I wouldn't do it just from a black point of view. I'd form some alliances and make open hiring a community concern. You'd look a lot stronger."

"Mr. Morgan." The woman's soft voice cut in. "This is a nice county. We've lived here all our lives and speaking out at school board meetings is not what we're used to."

"Don't misunderstand me," Jake said, smoothly, "I'm not suggesting you cause a riot." There were soft chuckles. "I'm just saying make your presence felt and insist politely on some straight answers. You don't have to accuse. The newspapers will do that for you. All Cassavorans who are interested in education and in fairness should be speaking up, black, white, yellow, or brown."

Jake knew the complexities inside the questions. Not necessarily codes, but attitudes, outlooks, perhaps antagonisms he hadn't encountered in the white neighborhoods and couldn't fathom. For one thing, none of the blacks asked him how long he'd lived here. Rather, Tubbs and company wanted to opine on the very issues Jake championed. Perhaps he'd been caught in the skin color trap, set time and time again since the death of Martin Luther King, exhorted by the cult of civil rights and leaving the nation bound and immobile.

Mr. Tubbs and his friends were much more like him than those whites that tormented his every effort to promote change and improvement. Values were the thing. Those people he'd just spoken with had spoken his language. They didn't hide behind a spread of barbecue or a curtain of sociability. They were only interested in results. His kind of folks.

Eventually, Jake spoke with another African American, Rufus Johnson, a local businessman. Rufus sniffed when Jake told him he'd spoken with Mr. Tubbs.

"He likes to keep the pot stirred, pretend somebody in this county did something to him they didn't do to nobody else."

"That's a different point of view."

His voice took on the singsong lilt of a Negro spiritual. "He plays da role of da po ole darky. He feels sorry for hiss-self an his race. He keep his hand out." Then he got more articulate. "Every card in his damn deck is the race card."

"And you don't feel that way?"

"I made a good livin' in this county. I built a business. People don't eat my barbecue 'cause I'm black. My kids didn't graduate from college 'cause I'm black. Somebody in the State Legislature didn't introduce a bill to have twenty percent of the barbecue restaurants set aside for so-called minorities! Far as I'm concerned, the only minority is the lazy, feel sorry for yourself minority who want somebody else to make their livin' for 'em. The majority are the hard workers."

"Mr. Tubbs says there aren't enough African Americans teaching in Cassavora schools."

"And he plans to change that? How? By gettin' everybody to feel so sorry they hire the people who can't make it on their own?

Blamin' it on race ain't gonna change nothing. Who's he talking to? Huh? Tell me that! It's the slave mentality, 'axing ole massa to hep dem darkies. Da'll work.' There's plenty of black businessmen and doctors and college professors in this county. They live in the best neighborhoods, drive big cars, and send their kids to college. You don't see them flashing the race card. Those folks got business cards."

34

Schools are important, but we've already got good schools. We don't need to be taking more and more from the business community and throwing it at the school system. That's not the way the founding fathers intended it. —President of the Cassavora Beef Association

Cleveland Amos was exactly right. To win a local election, you had to sidle up to the movers and shakers to get your name spread around. That was a personal problem for Jake. He swallowed hard and tried to overcome his phobia about even giving the appearance of bending over and kissing ass. The mental picture cut sharply against the integrity grain. But it was necessary. As Cleve explained, people in prominent positions got asked two dozen times a day who to vote for. If the leadership wasn't in your camp or at least neutral, you might as well go sit back down on the couch and watch the news. Seeing your name on the ballot was only going to irritate the voters.

Jake rationalized by telling himself he was just getting to know people. A part of his brain still asked, why now? He was working his way down his list when he called on Paul Thaxley at the Bank of Greater Cassavora. The bank sat on a corner in downtown Fletcher, across from the Rotary Club and down the street from Miss Margaret Titwiler, owner of the oldest house within the town limits. Thaxley was not a native Cassavoran, but he married a native and moved here way back when Jake was flying jets on the other side of the earth.

Thaxley was big, heavy set, with thinning light brown hair, well into his forties. His immaculate grooming befit a banker, tasteful, but not elitist. The off-the-rack suit, a mid-gray with a lighter gray stripe, did its best to enhance a body a bit more rotund than the suit maker had planned on.

Thaxley spoke in a friendly way, looking through gold-rimmed spectacles. The even voice and trace of a smile almost never varied from friend to new acquaintance. Being the moneyman, he knew everybody, made loans and especially financed mortgages for practically everybody. With Fletcher and Cassavora growing the way they were, he had a lot to be cheerful about.

Jake and Thaxley shook hands over the broad expanse of a mahogany desk; then Thaxley settled into his high backed executive chair. "I'll be just a second." He lifted the black receiver on the telephone console. Three red lights blinked and one went steady when he picked up. "I've got a call to take. Just a second." He held out a chubby index finger punctuating his statement and stifling any retort. Thaxley leaned back in the luxury of the ox blood leather and swiveled to one side as a hint of privacy.

Jake glanced around the room, full of photographs with Paul Thaxley and everyone of note who had come within hand shaking distance over the past dozen years. The state's winningest high school football coach smiled back at him, his arm wrapped around Thaxley's ample waist; Nancy Reagan stared at the camera as if daring the lens to make her look bad and an award winning chef held up a thick lobster and a blue ribbon with Thaxley's hand on his shoulder. Sob Jenkins's picture was a close-up, just the two of them, Thaxley and Jenkins grinning, their heads together.

A smaller photo on the desk showed a round-faced woman with short hair and glasses. Jake picked it up, replaced it and sat back in his chair, just as Paul Thaxley hung up. Immediately, a benevolently smiling Thaxley leaned forward and moved the frame back into the exact corner of his desk, adjusting the angle.

Jake launched into his pitch. "I guess you've heard I'm running for the Board of Education, Mr. Thaxley."

"You have kids in Cassavora schools?"

"No, but one way and another, I've been in education all my life."

"Military," Thaxley replied cheerfully. Jake nodded. Thaxley continued, "You left the county for a while and then came back as I understand it. What made you decide to jump back in the middle of things and run for the Board of Education? I'd think you'd just want to settle in and enjoy the quiet life."

"To begin with, I'd like a little more emphasis on education. Seems we've gotten sidetracked in certain areas. With the county growing like it is, I want to add my voice and experience to our already excellent school system."

"I can understand that, Mr. Morgan. Going back to the basics is what we need to do. I have two kids, you know, one in school and one about to start." This was not news to Jake, whose house-to-house research also told him this was Thaxley's second marriage and the oldest child was from the first try.

"I know you must enjoy them."

"Oh, that I do," Thaxley enthused. "And, I do my best to try and teach them about life."

"Boys or girls?" Jake already knew the answer to that, too.

"I have two sons, aged ten and five."

"Being a banker, do you teach them about finances? That's always a tough thing to learn when you're a kid." Jake was getting better at small talk. He wanted to keep the conversation light, not knowing where Thaxley stood on the meat-and-potato issues, things like building new schools and keeping state and religion separate.

"I do teach them about money. How to keep it, how to use it, and most of all what a responsibility it is." Thaxley's eyes glazed with the thought.

"Sounds like you stay very involved in your sons' lives." Jake was ready to move on.

"Oh, I do. Let me give you just one example. Both get an allowance. The elder gets $5 a week and the younger, $2. But, I don't like to just give money away, even to my kids. I want them to earn it and to learn something about work and values along the way." Thaxley said *earn* as though Moses had made an unfortunate omission on the stone tablets. "My wife set up a list of duties, such as making your bed, picking up toys, doing homework, getting dressed and ready to go in the morning, things like that. If they don't do something, they get an X. Nothing happens until they get three X's. I realize no boy is perfect and everybody forgets or neglects something once in awhile. But, if they get three X's, then they start losing twenty-five cents for each X, including the first three."

Jake stifled a yawn, but Thaxley was on a roll. "The younger boy doesn't lose that much, because he gets much less to begin with. To teach them about values, I weighted all the tasks because obviously, forgetting to pick up your socks is not as important as getting ready for school, so there's a sliding scale. My wife pointed out we only listed the main tasks. I thought about that and added some sub tasks."

Jake looked at his watch, while Thaxley's eyes reflected the beauty of a perfect financial plan. "Making your bed, for example is important, but it's also important to do it right, so making your bed and leaving wrinkled sheets under the blanket counts off a proportionate amount. I didn't want one child to think that he could just pull up the covers and get full credit, while his brother slaved away to get things just right. So, I developed a formula to account for the weight of each task and sub-task." He paused to turn his attention to an invisible piece of lint on the left sleeve of his suit. Pinching it with a thumb and forefinger, he leaned to one side and dropped it into the polished chrome wastebasket. He stared into the basket a moment, then began again. "I realize thinking in the long-term is important, so I grade the kids the same as the school does, every six weeks. We can plot the task errors on our home computer and develop a graph to identify trends, even down to the sub areas. Then the child can be docked a greater proportion of his allowance if unsatisfactory trends develop over a long period."

"I'll bet your kids are breathless with anticipation at the end of each week." The cynicism was lost on the banker, whose cheery expression never changed.

"They are, except sometimes they are not getting, they are giving. You see, if a long-term trend projection identifies recurring problem areas, they may have been overpaid to begin with."

Jake pulled a wadded up piece of tissue from his pocket, blew his nose, balled it up and got two points for a rim shot. Thaxley looked at the basket a second or two, making a mental note to have his secretary scour it.

"Your boys are lucky to have a family willing to spend the time to instill some values." Jake hoped the banality would suffice as a closing statement. It didn't.

"I like to think of this county as I do one of my boys." Thaxley leaned back in his chair, put both hands on his stomach and interlocked the fingers. "This county needs to be unburdened of debt, the way it is now." The quick mental pirouette captured Jake's full attention. This was the meat of the conversation, coming as it mostly does, toward the end, when everyone is edgy from not knowing how and when to end it. "Education costs money and often it is wasted on frivolous, non-productive things. Lack of discipline can't be rectified with greater expense and students' self-esteem comes from the home. We've also got to be very prudent in the number of teachers we employ. In any business, payroll is your biggest expense." He paused to drop his hands, slowly shake his head and straighten the two solitary ballpoint pens on the desktop. "New books every year or two may not be fiscally responsible with public funds. People in this county will not be happy should a Board of Education dramatically raise the taxes. Education could bankrupt this county. Then where would we be? You have to use common sense. The men and women of this county work hard. The large farmers. The builders. The developers. The businessmen and women. They produce the wealth. I hope you understand all of those dynamics."

35

Police work is not as fast and colorful as they show on TV. Being a good cop is mostly just having an eye for detail and being too stubborn to quit. — Sheriff Sam Goddard

"So, here's what we've got." Sheriff Goddard scanned the room of deputies. "We have a victim, we have a motive, and we have an approximate time. What we're missing is the who. Who helped the coach to the Post Office? John?" he turned to his chief deputy. "Tell them what else we have." In a way, the sheriff was tired of talking about it. He wished he had a dozen men like himself or at least a dozen John Howards, so he could make this thing move along. As it was, he was stuck with what he had. Most of his deputies never probed anything more than a vehicle collision. They gave tickets. They picked up a shoplifter now and again, usually with the store manager pointing a finger at the kid and saying that's the one. They arrested troublemakers at football games and brought in some abusive spouses and gathered up a pot smoker or two. Now and then an armed robbery. That was about it.

The city was not going to spend the money to train his people to investigate murder or suspicious death and, to tell the truth, he wouldn't either. He was lucky he had one investigator and a couple of deputies who could take reliable fingerprints. In the case of the coach, how were his deputies going to know what questions to ask or what to pursue and what to discard? That took training and experience. He had a small town police force. That was all it was, and he felt impotent to realize he might have to cry uncle and ask the state investigators for help. He didn't want to do that. Not only would it hurt his pride, but it wouldn't make his troops feel all that great either. A body gets dropped off at the frigging Post frigging Office and he hadn't been able to figure out who did it. Still, the sheriff liked the men who worked for him and served the county. They were what they were and though they didn't make the papers very often, he loved the way they interacted with the community. He could count on Pearly Rogers and Dan Witcomb and any of the rest of them to be polite, to defuse an argument, to comment on how wonderful a young mother looked with her baby, to say *hi* to the folks at the two convenience stores and shout a greeting to people they knew at Grand Foods. Every now and again there was a bad apple, but Sam could generally sort it out before things got too interesting. Having a slew of big city cops in Cassavora would be big trouble in a hurry. Besides, city cops wouldn't work for what his deputies were being paid.

John Howard stood up in the front row and faced the group, hands on his hips. He didn't bother to slide behind the flimsy, aluminum podium. "The dead man's car was parked on Woodson Turnpike ... everybody know where that is? Dirt road behind the school bus storage barn, keys in the ignition. No prints on the steering wheel or keys and no prints other than his in the car. We're still checking. There were some fibers on his clothes consistent with automobile rug fibers, as well as several female hairs on his shirt."

"Probably his wife." A deputy shouted from the back of the room.

"He wasn't married." John Howard didn't crack a smile. "And he had at least a glass of wine and some steak on the night he died. Our best guess is he died in someone's house, probably a lady friend, had his heart attack, got helped into somebody's trunk or backseat, and dropped off at the Post Office. A woman couldn't haul a man that size around by herself, so she must have had some help. We have a witness who says she saw a man and a woman helping a drunken man down the street. Coulda been a dead man, or it coulda been a drunk."

Goddard listened along with everyone else. Heart attack was the cause, but some things still didn't add up. The time element bothered him. A body dropped off at the Post Office instead of being hauled to the hospital or dumped in the deep woods bothered him. He let the stream of doubts flow past him for now.

"As you know," he broke in, "We've combed both sides of the street where the witness lives, but no one else has spoken up. As nosy as this county is, I can't believe nobody else saw anything." There were some chuckles.

"What color were the fibers, sheriff?" Another deputy spoke up.

"Red. Looks like they come from a Ford."

"Well, that narrows it down to half the county."

"Yeah, unless the perps came from another county and parked the body here." The comment came from a hefty deputy seated in front.

"You may have misunderstood me," the sheriff continued, looking across his audience, his voice dropping an octave and slowing for emphasis. "I didn't bring you here to tell you the case was solved. We've got a lot to do, routine things like completing interviews with the coach's coworkers, his neighbors, anybody else that might know his habits and routines. Believe me, somebody out there knows something, but they may not even know they know it. Our job is to find it." He paused. "But to answer your question about the car, we've found five late model red Fords licensed in this county."

The meeting was over. Men and women shuffled out, the sheriff pulled his Chief Deputy aside and spoke in a low tone. "John, I'm going to drive out to the poultry company and give Billy Reilly a wake up call. And guess what?"

"What's that?"

"He drives a late model red Mustang. "

"Do tell."

"That's not all. His handwriting looks a lot like the handwriting on the note our favorite school board candidate gave us."

John Howard was too professional to give a yell. His mouth turned up in the barest of grins.

"Just give out the assignments and keep the investigation rolling. I'll be back as soon as I can."

"You don't need any help?" It was a plea to be able to come along, enjoy the look on Billy's face, share the excitement.

The sheriff gave him a crooked smile. "Hold down the fort and get everybody out working this thing."

It was hot and the sheriff wished he could do something about getting the air conditioning in the car fixed. Even his wife chided him about it. "You're the sheriff! Tell 'em to fix it." Goddard thought about that, but being sheriff was a big plate, and there wasn't nearly enough food to cover it. Looking out for his own comfort wasn't his first job, or his style. He pressed harder on the accelerator to move the hot air past him a little faster and crammed his Stetson down on his head to keep it from blowing away.

Down Main Street, past the courthouse he turned left, which brought him right past the Post Office. He gave it a glance as he breezed by, mentally marking off time and distance as he came abreast of Margaret Tillsmore's house. Yep, there was that streetlight. It was a shady street, at least at this end. Plenty of places to park in the shadows and even darker at night. He slowed up a little, then took a right on Hawthorne. Big old houses sat closer to the street than anybody with enough money to build them would want, but then they were built in the far away and long ago. He'd seen pictures of the turn of the century and these houses were here then, but the road was little more than a mule trail. Now it was three lanes and needed to be wider. Some of the older houses had been converted to offices. There were lawyers, a CPA, and at least one dentist and one doctor. How come lawyers always outnumbered everybody else?

As he headed out of town, the buildings disappeared and the trees and pastures started. He drove past Lenchmore Estates, with its trimmed hedges, stacked stone entrance and cascading fountain. A quick look down the street showed him a world of vast, rolling lawns, towering oaks, homes he couldn't afford if he worked and saved his whole life.

He rode down the two-way blacktop and thought about living in Lenchmore, or a place like it. What would it be like to have a maid bring you coffee in the morning, along with a crisp newspaper on a silver tray? Maybe he'd seen too many old movies. Most of the folks who lived there now wouldn't know what to do with a maid. Most of them were doctors, architects, builders. New Money. Sob Jenkins had the biggest house, a ten-thousand square-foot monster with a pool and a double tennis court out back. Sam could remember it being built a few years ago. Everybody just had to drive by and see it, watching the crane digging a pool the size of a basement, trucks bringing in full-grown trees to landscape the yard.

Who else lived there? A vice president of a city bank, the President of the Bank of the Greater Cassavora, Paul Thaxley and the Superintendent of Schools, but then her husband was in real estate, so it made sense. He wondered what all their houses looked like and made a mental note to drive through the neighborhood when he had the time.

Town was way behind him now. Pastures opened up into sprawling farmland, emerald green with spikes of sorghum and squat peanuts bushes. In some places black and white cows dotted the land. Sam took a deep breath, gathering in the cleansing air. It was freeing to be out of the town, away from the nagging ring of the phone and the constant blather of conversation. Gave a man time to think and there was plenty to think about. That a do nothing like Billy Reilly was mixed up in every evil deed just didn't make much sense. The note he could understand. And what did the note really say? I don't like you very much and I've warned you! About what? It didn't threaten anyone. Sounded more like a poor white trash's feeble attempt to wrestle into importance in the community and going about it in a sorry way.

As to the matter of being an accessory in the movement of the coach's body, Billy's having anything at all to do with it made even less sense. Just for starters, there was the presence of semen on the body. The coach and Billy Reilly? No way. Not in a millennium. As far as Sam knew, Billy had never met the coach. And if the eyewitness really was an eyewitness, the people she described didn't sound anything like Billy, who was only five-five or five-six. The one connection was the red Ford. That wasn't a crime or anything approaching reasonable suspicion. Anyway, he'd check it out.

Further down the road, where the city left off and the county started, the sheriff saw a red and blue sign with an arrow pointing the way to Clifton Poultry. The road was paved, but a thin cloud of red dust still kicked up behind him.

Sam pulled into the parking lot, got out, eased his Stetson up and wiped a forearm across his brow. There were only a smattering of cars, not more than thirty, some of them the old half dead Fords and Chevys the Latinos drove. He noted a red Mustang parked away from the others, like it didn't want to associate with the common folk. The sheriff was going to walk over to it, but figured he'd better go see Walter first and smooth the waters. Walter wasn't an unfriendly guy, but Sam knew how touchy these managers got when somebody started poking around without saying anything. The last thing he needed was a pissing contest.

Sam stepped into the front office and felt like he never wanted to leave. The icy air hung on him, and he liked the way it hung. He approached a gray haired receptionist, her hair in a bun, wearing those frameless spectacles that add twenty years. She had a wool sweater draped over her bony shoulders, did a half turn in her swivel chair and looked over her glasses and down her nose at him. "May I help you?" Her strained voice indicated she did not want to be disturbed, ever.

"Did you ever work at the Post Office?"

"I beg your pardon."

"Never mind. Forget it. Is Mr. Broomfield in?"

"Hey there, sheriff," came the raspy voice of Walter Broomfield, his bald pate shining under the glare of the neons. He was also wearing a sweater, a cardigan, but one that would never again completely enclose his magnificently developed belly.

"Morning Walter." Sam smiled. Seeing that she was off the hook, the receptionist went back to staring at her computer screen.

"What can I do for you sheriff?" Broomfield's curiosity was piqued. The sheriff normally didn't come all the way out here, but he didn't feel threatened, not like he would if it were a government team of poultry inspectors.

"I'd just like to look around your parking lot a little bit and then maybe talk to one of your employees."

"Which one?"

"Billy Reilly."

"Damn that boy! What's he done now?"

"Maybe nothing. I just need to speak with him a moment, but first I want to take a look at his car."

"Auto accident?"

"Something like that. Is that his red Mustang out front?"

Walter nodded. "Anything I can do to help?"

"No, I won't be a minute, but when I come back could you get him to come up here?"

"Sure, sheriff."

Sam walked back outside and was almost blinded before he got his sunglasses on. He missed the air conditioning already. The black asphalt didn't help. Even his shades didn't help all that much. He had to squint and cup a hand over his brow to try to block out the reflection off the Mustang's windshield. He was tempted to open the car door and pinch off a little fluff of carpet, but it wouldn't have been admissible anyway, and it would just be his luck for Walter or somebody else to be staring out the window at him. Sam walked around the car, slowly, looking for anything at all that shouldn't be there, a slight piece of string from the coach's clothes or anything else that might suggest something. He didn't see anything. He walked closer and peered through the driver's side window, glancing from the front to the back seat and decided he didn't need a pinch of carpet fiber.

Sam had just returned to the air-conditioned comfort of the office and asked to talk to Billy when he heard the squeal of tires. He turned, swung the front door open again and watched Billy's Mustang go racing off in the direction of the highway. His first impulse was to pursue, but he squelched that. He had no reason to stop Billy from going wherever he wanted to go. Leaving work early or quitting his job was not law enforcement's concern. A sudden exit was a mite suspicious. Still, Billy hadn't been accused of a crime. At this point, Sam wanted to talk to him, but that was it, the sum total. He walked back to his car and grabbed the radio mic. "This is Sam. I'm out at Clifton Poultry. Billy Reilly just left here in a rush." Sam paused a moment to consider what orders he could give that wouldn't send his deputies on a high speed chase. "Oh, hell, forget it."

The drive back up the highway gave Sam time to ponder. He'd have one of his deputies check out the other four Fords, while he had a private discussion with Billy about the nasty little notes. If only Reilly had been a little more forceful in his letters, a little more directly threatening, he could be charged with something more than illiteracy and failing to yield to good grammar.

36

A free press is the beating heart of democracy. —*Wilbur Simons, Editor, The Advocate*

"Mr. Morgan, I called to thank you."

"That's nice. What'd I do?"

"I'm Edgar Martin. The guy that Social Security thought was dead?"

"You alive now?"

"Yep. The idiots finally admitted it."

"No kidding. Have you gotten a check yet?"

"I got a letter saying my benefits were restored."

"That's good news."

"Yeah, just call me Lazarus." Next Thursday's *Advocate* devoted a quarter page to Edgar's plight and Jake's hand in solving it. It was an upbeat story heading into the last paragraph, when Jake got editorially sucker punched.

"It's typical," said Able Perkins, who is running against Mr. Morgan. "My opponent would like to take full credit for solving an administrative problem that would have solved itself over time. He's a publicity seeker and doesn't understand grandstanding won't work in this community. People around here appreciate a more quiet and sober approach."

"Goddamnit!" Jake put the paper down. The cup and saucer on the counter clattered, but the coffee didn't spill. In a continuous motion, he picked up the phone, dialed, hung up. His fire wasn't going to be quenched with a whining phone call.

The newspaper's low, tinned roof offices hid behind a new strip mall. When Jake strode in, the receptionist, protected by a narrow glass window with a speak hole cut in the center, was busying herself with a stack of yellow receipts.

"Is Mr. Simons here?" Jake tried not to sound angry. He failed.

She looked up and showed him a look designed to stop freight trains. "He's in a meeting."

"When will the meeting be over?" He guessed she might have been mildly interested if he were telling her dog had just been run over, but she wasn't a woman who would cry about it.

"Hard to say."

"I'll wait." He found a chair and a magazine. An hour later, another underling led him down the hallway into a small, but pleasant office. A couple of nondescript landscapes decorated the walls. A computer dominated the desk. Dozens of typed pages covered the rest.

"What can I do for you?"

Wilbur Simons was what Jake had expected, balding, glasses, slightly pudgy, striped shirt with the sleeves rolled up and loose tie.

"I've come about the so-called news article in today's edition. The one that turned into a libelous political forum for my opponent."

Simons didn't say anything.

Jake gave him only a second. "If you wanted comments, why didn't you ask me?"

"Mr. Morgan, I can see you're upset. But, you've got to understand time is critical in my business. We called you. You just weren't home."

"When did you call?"

"I didn't call, my reporter did."

"When? I was home all last night." Jake gave Simons a look that said he was about to come across the desk.

The Editor tried to hide the panic. "Hang on, now, let's ask him." He pushed the intercom, mumbled a few words. A thin, scruffy young man stuck his head in the door.

"Did you call Mr. Morgan for a comment about the Social Security screw-up?"

The reported adjusted his tie, stared at his shoes, brought a forefinger up to his nostril, thought better of it, dropped his hand.

"Well?"

"Sure, I called."

"When?" Jake cut in.

"I don't remember exactly. What's this about?"

"Fair and honest reporting," Jake shot back.

"Mr. Morgan, I resent your implication." The editor rushed to his reporter's defense.

"I don't doubt that."

*****

Cleveland had a half-smile, a little amused. It wasn't Brice's this time, but Le Donut Hot in the University Student Center. Students clustered at adjoining tables or scurried past. The din was constant, leaving the two men some privacy in a crowd. Jake took a sip of black coffee. A drip rolled down the side of the white mug. Cleve chuckled, reached across the table and wiped up a spot with a paper napkin. "Welcome to politics' muddy streets."

"Reporting is supposed to be truthful. That little snot-nosed shit was lying his ass off."

"So?"

"Cleve, you're a writer, a reporter ... "

"Not a reporter, a columnist. Reporters are lambs of God compared to us."

Jake wasn't in the mood. "Is there some way to get them to print a retraction, or at least give me space for a rebuttal?"

"You can write another of your letters to the editor."

Jake's letter appeared the following week, carefully explaining Edgar Martin's situation and his modest role in solving it.

In the column next to it, Able Perkins suggested Jake was trying to milk a simple misunderstanding and turn himself into a hero. "It's deplorable Mr. Morgan thrives on another person's misfortune."

Jake got a phone call the night after his letter appeared in the paper. Betsy had brought him a home cooked meal, compliments of her mother and in return for letting her borrow a couple of books from Jake's home library. She was in the back of the house collecting them when the phone rang.

"Oh, I'll bet you're hot." Cleveland's amusement bubbled over the phone line.

"Damn right."

"You asked me what you could do, not what you should do."

Jake didn't say anything, but Cleve could hear him breathing. "You see what happens when you fight fair?"

"But, Cleve, the bastards showed him my letter before it was even printed."

"Of course they did. But, if you say anything, Wilbur is going to claim when you call for fair reporting, you evidently don't want it to apply to you."

Cleveland started to say something else, but the words never got a chance. The bark of a bullet shattered the bay window in Jake's breakfast nook, catching him in a shower of glass, spraying it across the room. Jake dropped to the floor, frantically looking around for Betsy. He heard her scream down the hallway as a second shot smashed another window. He jumped up and raced toward her voice.

37

You don't have to be brilliant to be in law enforcement, but stupid doesn't help. —*Sheriff Sam Goddard*

Jake ran towards the sound of a body hitting the floor, rounded the corner to the hallway and found Betsy sprawled. Blood smeared her cheek.

"Betts!" He dropped to his knees, lifted her head, cradling her.

Betsy held on, her fingers clutching his shirtsleeve. Tears flowed. "I'm okay, I'm okay."

They waited, crouched together, inseparable. No more shots.

The girl began to weep, a sound just above a whimper at first. Then the dam broke and deep body-wracking sobs shook her. Jake held her tight, not knowing what else to do.

His fingers brushed across Betsy's cheek, and he peered down. The blood was a superficial scratch, probably from one of the shards of glass covering the floor and spreading out into the hall.

She might have more wounds. He patted her back, her sides. "Betts, you okay?"

"Yeah, they missed me." Sounded like a line from a B grade movie, but the words sounded sweet to Jake.

Betsy moved her hand to cover his, choked back the tears and gave a short, nervous laugh. Jake couldn't help it. He laughed too. Laughed that the shots hadn't hurt either of them, that life was still the same, unchanged by the terror of the shattered windows.

The laugher stopped as abruptly as it began. "Mister Morgan." The words lurched out of her. "This about you running for the school board?"

"I don't know." He held her, patted the top of her head. He never guessed politics would lead to anything like this. Did kids at school tease her, bother her about her neighbor's aspirations for office? How about the teachers? He'd ask later, not now. Not while they were both fragile.

Jake's mind kept churning. Was that what this shooting was about? Preventing his election was important enough to try to kill him?

A siren ripped the sudden silence. Jake pulled Betsy to her feet and walked toward the front door with his arm around her.

Out the living room windows, blue-flashing lights echoed off the dark trees. Before Jake and Betsy reached the front door, two deputies burst in. "Anybody hurt in here?"

*****

Goddard was at home having supper with Elmira when he got the call. Like a good sheriff's wife, she didn't pepper him with questions, just shooed him on his way.

He was halfway to Jake's, siren warbling, lights flashing, when the radio startled him. Sam turned down the volume a tad and listened. He recognized the deputy's voice, keyed the mic. "Shorty, I missed that last transmission, over."

"Roger, sheriff. John Paul and Hemsley are in hot pursuit. A couple of teenagers in a late model Mustang, over."

"Roger. Anybody else on the way?"

"Your Chief Deputy."

"Thank God." Goddard realized too late he still had the mic' keyed. John Paul couldn't find a leaf in a field of clover and Hemsley wasn't much help.

"Roger."

"Shit." This time his finger was off the trigger. He swung the patrol car into Jake's place, dodging trees up the curved, gravel driveway, leaving a billowing fog of powder.

Inside, deputies were already taking statements from Morgan and the girl. The girl looked a little pale, a little shaken. Understandable.

He moved through the hall, noticed a shattered window in a back bedroom, then walked slowly toward the kitchen, noting the spray of glass. More glass on the kitchen floor, the big bay window only a ragged opening with jagged edges. It took more than a BB gun or even a .22 to shatter a pane that big. The shooter must have been behind the house.

Sam stepped out the backdoor and gazed across the moonlit lake. Was the shooter in a boat? Was there more than one? He remembered Shorty saying John Paul and Hemsley were in pursuit of teenagers, plural.

He walked back into the kitchen, picked up the phone on the wall. "Sheriff's office."

"Shorty, I'm at the scene. You heard any more from John Paul or John Howard?"

"John Paul just called from a house across the street from the high school. Said his radio quit on him."

Goddard swore under his breath. "So, whatta we know?"

"Evidently, they saw the Mustang pull into the high school parking lot."

"Okay, nobody hurt here, so I'm headed that way."

"Roger, boss." Sam pulled into the high school. Two of his patrol cars sat by themselves, lights on.

Goddard walked over to John Howard. "What's the story?"

"John Paul tried to turn the volume down on his radio and turned the damn thing off. Couldn't understand why it didn't work."

"Gave up pursuit? Just like that?" The sheriff couldn't keep the amazement out of his voice.

Howard nodded. Sam tried twice to say something. Finally gave up. "It was a late model, too dark to tell the color." Howard licked his lips, felt the frustration, too.

Goddard let out a breath. "Teenagers normally drive for home. Scour the neighborhoods. Check the hood of every Mustang you see." Meanwhile, Sam figured he'd take another deputy and head out to Billy Reilly's abode, see if the boy was home and had anything to add to this tale.

Billy lived in a trailer park, the only one in Cassavora, out in the country near the city landfill. It took Goddard about fifteen minutes to get there. He had his deputy wait by the car, glanced down at the man's holstered 9 millimeter then back at his face. "Don't make it look obvious."

Billy's car was parked next to the singlewide trailer. Sam knocked, felt the door wobble and the siding shake a little. No answer. He sauntered to the Mustang, put his hand on the hood. Warm, but not hot.

The door of the trailer opened and Billy stuck his head out. He still had his shirt and jeans on, but was barefooted. "Sumpin' you need, sheriff?"

"Where were you tonight?"

"Movie."

"Anybody go with you?"

"Just me and Becky."

"Becky Fowler?" Billy nodded.

"When'd you get back?"

"I dunno. Maybe half hour ago."

"Is Becky here?"

A girl with, short brown hair appeared in the doorway.

"Your mama know where you are?" Goddard sounded more concerned than angry.

"Did they send you out here to look for me? They coulda just called. Billy's got a phone, you know." Since it was the sheriff, Becky was keeping a lid on the anger. Sam had a notion it would have been different if he'd been her Dad and she had an audience for her righteous indignation.

"I want to know when you got back."

"We ain't did nothin'," Billy volunteered.

"Becky, how old are you," the sheriff asked.

"Seventeen."

"That's too young, and besides, I'm conducting an investigation. Now you want us to give you a ride home or you want us to call your folks?" Too young for what? Goddard knew he hadn't a leg to stand on, legally speaking, but he'd bet anything the girl's folks didn't know she was out here and still messing around with Billy. But, she sure thought they did.

Becky stiffened up, evidently pondering the consequences. "Could you drop me off without going right up to my house?" Her voice sounded a little unsteady.

He nodded. "Get in the car. Now, Billy, I got some more questions for you. First off, anybody else see you two at the movies?"

"Yes ... sir. A whole bunch of kids." It pained Billy to use the "s" word, but he wanted this interview to be over.

"You mind if I check out your car?" Billy disappeared and came back with keys in hand. Sam's flashlight augmented the car's overhead light, the beam of light probing the dark corners.

Nothing. Front seat, back seat, trunk. Nothing under the seats or in the glove box.

He glanced over at Billy. "You own any guns?"

"I got a twenty-two and a four ten." Goddard checked the guns and Billy himself, even smelled his hands. Nothing. He asked him about any threatening letters he might have sent. Billy hemmed and hawed over that one, but said no. Sam warned him. Told him he knew otherwise and was keeping an eye on him. Billy didn't say anything. The kid looked pathetic standing there in the doorway of a white-trash trailer. He seemed even smaller than he was, slouched in the white light that bubbled out around him, leaving him as a dark silhouette.

It was late. Goddard was hungry, and he knew Elmira was keeping the food hot, as she always did. And here was this kid, bruised, tarnished.

Goddard couldn't help himself. "Come on over here, son."

"I'm not your son."

Sam didn't take offense at the harsh tone. The kid was scared and alone. He motioned for Billy to come closer. Billy stood up straight, not sure of the sheriff's intent. "You takin' me in? Fer what?"

"When's the last time you had a home-cooked meal?"

"I live here." The voice wasn't quite as strident or sure.

"The thing is ... I got called away from the table tonight, and my wife is keeping supper warm. Why don't you join us?" Billy still hesitated. "I'll bring you back later."

*****

The sheriff got his badge stolen for his trouble. "Still," Goddard said, "He may not be a bad boy."

John Howard nodded. "But, I don't think anyone would argue with stupid. So, anyway, what are you going to do about it?"

"I've ruled out death by bullet and a radical orchiectomy."

Howard raised an eyebrow. "Cutting his balls off." The Chief Deputy nodded.

"I think I'll just have him wear a sign around his neck that says never invite this boy to dinner. I got the badge back by the way."

38

I never said that everyone had to be Christian — I never said that. I never said a lot of things you said I said. —Caldwell Robbins to a reporter

Late autumn afternoons in Fletcher were like standing under Klieg lights. Jake pulled out his ever-present white handkerchief, wiped his brow and ran it across the back of his neck. There was no stopping the perspiration. It soaked the collar of his green polo shirt and crept down his back. He'd put on sun block, but sun block didn't stop you from sweating like a Baptist in a liquor store. He loitered a couple of dozen yards from the courthouse, near the street, waiting like everyone else for the Senator's entourage to arrive. Tubas and drums littered the grass where the high school band was setting up. Someone had added a wooden dais to the courthouse steps, topped it with a crude podium and slathered the raw wood with wrappings of blue and red and white. A Norman Rockwell painting, Jake thought, but now he knew the politics were never as clean and straight forward as the great illustrator had made them seem.

Jake was here to see the Senator, to take a closer look at the elected voice of the people and hear comforting words that would set his mind at rest about the future of the country he'd spent most of his life defending.

He wondered if Cecilia would be here. He hadn't seen her in weeks. She was probably off in some far-flung corner of the state, arranging a meeting, decorating somebody else's room. The thought was somehow less sour than he had imagined and therefore almost comforting. He wondered if this serenity was what trust felt like.

Across the street, Betsy stood under a tree, trying to stay cool, probably motivated more by the gaggle of other teenagers than by interest in the Senator. After the entertainment the other night, Jake wondered if she were still scared. Her dad had come over right after the shooting, put his arm around her and led her out the door, not saying anything to Jake. Jake understood. Somebody shoots at your kid and suddenly everything else becomes irrelevant. Already rumors were beginning to flit in the social wind. One of the deputies told a neighbor Jake had had his arm around her.

The sheriff was still non-committal about who had fired the shots and why. The uncertainly of it made Jake uneasy. The first few nights had been tough on sleep. Now the immediacy of danger was tapering off. Still, something so keenly endangering lingers and festers. The deputies had asked him who might be angry with him. Nobody. Maybe everybody.

A letter to the editor had publicly wondered why a young girl was at Mr. Morgan's house that time of night. Alone. Maybe the writer wasn't the only one. This time, Jake didn't write in to explain or complain.

Cleveland passed a little ways away and gave Jake a wave. A couple of folks Jake had spoken with on his neighborhood outings came over and shook his hand. Their names were forever lost, but the faces were vaguely familiar. He smiled, made small talk.

Then the oddest thing happened. Caldwell Robbins walked out of the crowd and shook his hand. "So, Mr. Morgan, how's the campaign coming?"

"Okay," Jake said, casting a cautious eye. Robbins was a little taller than he'd imagined. He'd seen him at the board meetings, but he was farther away then, now he had to look up. The stifling breeze played with Robbins' hair.

"And, I've read some of the things you sent to the paper about me." There was a flicker of a smile. Jake didn't know quite how to respond, so he waited.

"I have to say they upset me, but not for the reasons you'd think."

"How's that?"

"Well, Mr. Morgan, to tell the truth, if I only had the newspaper stories to judge me by, I'd be mad at me too. You only reacted to what you'd been told and what you took as fact. I really didn't mind what you said as much as I minded this gossipy, know-nothing newspaper of ours being able to print absolute trash about me and get clean away with it."

"What did they print that wasn't true?" Jake felt a sudden kinship, but didn't want a full-blown discussion in the middle of town, with five hundred people milling about. He fought feverishly to place exactly what he had read and what he had written. The sun and commotion and social chatter pounded like ocean waves on the sands of memory.

"Well, the whole blessed episode with the books .... " Robbins said, opening his hands palms up and trying to keep the exasperation out of his voice. "All it amounted to was a couple of parents complaining and me asking the superintendent to look into it."

Exactly what Jake had determined at the school board meeting. "That's not what I read."

"I know. I know."

A brain-splitting rattle of drums covered the crowd, followed by a crash of cymbals and the roar of people surging toward the street, splitting Jake and Robbins apart and filling every void. Horns honked. People were shoving forward and being pushed back to make way for the cavalcade of sedans that snaked in front of the court house and sliced the crowd in two. Jake made out a tight bundle of men in suits, clustered around a black Cadillac. One of the men stretched his arms upwards, his fingers giving the V sign.

Amid the whooping and hollering and band blasting, the small throng made its way to the podium. The Senator stepped forward, white shirt, tie, and suit, even on this blistering afternoon. His full head of gray hair was slicked back, his arms stretched upward, the starched white cuffs of his shirt showing. Not three feet away C2 smiled and awaited his moment with the man. Beside him the banker and the superintendent.

"Good people of Cassavora!" The voice blasted strong and metallic through the microphone and out the huge speakers. Then loud electronic squeals split the Senator's initial message of cheer. Two technicians raced to adjust the volume. "My fellow citizens of this great state," he continued, "you know every election is important! But do you understand why?" He paused, let the crowd noise settle. "They're all important because you are given the opportunity to exercise your right and duty as American citizens to vote! And when you do, vote for me! Together, we'll keep that rat pack in Washington off our hard working backs and keep this state moving forward!" Cheers broke out and the band, which had lapsed into uncharacteristic silence, punctuated the air with a chord or two. The Senator went on about how important   Cassavora was to him and how all his life he had admired the strong, hard-working people of Cassavora. Not only that, but he admired the first pioneers who had come here, and he admired their slaves who had pulled themselves out of slavery and Cassavora was a fine place to be. He was against taxes and for education. Help for the handicapped. A chicken in every pot. Join me in saving our great country! With that, he escaped to his limo and the whole entourage motored out of town at twice the speed it had come in, with musical strains of *It's a Grand Old Flag* chasing them down the road.

The Senator sat back in the soft leather seat and called out questions to his two attentive aides in white shirtsleeves, pencils poised. One was a young white man and the other a young black woman. "So how do you think it went?"

"Great! I think you really hit it off with the crowd," said the young man.

"Oh, Senator, you had them in the palm of your hand. I really liked that remark about the slaves," said the woman.

"Yes," echoed the man. "You acknowledged the debt of the early settlers and southern heritage."

"While not neglecting the advancement of African Americans," cut in the woman.

"Well, great," murmured the Senator. "Now what was the name of that place where we just stopped?" His brow wrinkled.

"That was Fletcher, in Cassavora County, Senator." It came out in a chorus.

"And, what's my next appointment?"

"We're on our way to meet with the Farmers' Select Council on State Agriculture, Senator."

"Yes. And, I want to be sure to make the point that I fully support agriculture in this state and agricultural workers." Both aides scribbled furiously. Twin Moses copying the voice from the mountain. "I think my voting record is pretty clear on this issue?"

"Yes." The young woman flipped to another page of her spiral notebook. "You have supported agricultural bills 97% of the time."

"Not 100%?" The Senator didn't try to mask his astonishment.

"No, sir," said the young man. "You voted against a bill that had a rider attached which gave pigs the right to vote."

"A stupid bill! I think it's fair to say my voting record is perfect on every *significant* piece of agricultural legislation."

"Unfortunately, that bill also contained agricultural subsidies."

"Well, in the end the farmers got their subsidies, didn't they? I clearly remember I voted for that! So, we pretty well covered the workers, the big farmers and the little farmers."

"Yes, sir."

"Yes, sir."

"Now did these farmers get their money or not?"

"Yes, sir, they did, or at least they should have." The young woman adjusted her glasses. "It was part of the Defense Authorization Bill, but the President .... "

"Where was I supposed to meet that loony who can predict elections?"

"That was in Fletcher, Senator, but you only said you might like to meet him and you sounded iffy, so I didn't set it up." Suddenly the young man's collar felt a little tight. But, he needn't have worried. The Senator's blazing intellect sprinted on.

"I just have one problem with that last stop." The Senator looked a little perplexed as he roared into a mental turn and his mind shifted gears. Two pairs of eyes locked on him, waiting for the secret of life to flow from his lips. "That shrimp they served for lunch was real crunchy. I'm used to tender shrimp. What do you think they did to it? Fry it too long?"

The two aides looked at one another, trying to decide who was going to be the sacrificial lamb. The young man spoke. "Senator, those were boiled shrimp. They needed to be peeled."

"Peeled?" The Senator was incredulous. "Who ever heard of peeling shrimp? The ones I've had have always been tender. Well, make a note. I want someone to step right in and peel those shrimp if they come at me again. Is there anything else that's going to need to be peeled?" No one gave the Senator an answer as the cavalcade sped on toward its destiny with democracy.

Cecilia never showed and she didn't call either. Jake started to miss her.

39

I don't think it would be proper for me to speak with you, Mr. Morgan.
I'm just a schoolteacher, and I need my job. —Teacher to Jake Morgan

Right after supper, the phone rang in Jake's house.

"Mr. Morgan, you don't know me, but I need to talk to you." The female voice sounded tired, bound with a thin string of emotion.

"Sure, talk away. What's it about?"

"You're running for the school board, aren't you?"

"Yes."

"Well, I'm a teacher. I just need to talk to you." The voice hesitated, quavered. "You spoke with me one Saturday afternoon. You came by my house. I live over in Foxberry Run."

"That's a pretty area."

"Thank you. I'm a single parent, and I have two kids in the schools." Jake flipped through his mental Rolodex, trying to place the voice and the house. He failed.

"Are the kids in trouble at school?"

"No. It's me."

"You sound a little too old for school." She tried to laugh, but couldn't.

"I'm a teacher and ..... "she began to cry. Not loudly. Just a little wet whimper, like a child whose puppy had died.

"Take your time. Just a couple of deep breaths."

She sniffed and then was quiet for a few beats. "I'm a teacher, and I am being forced to resign."

"What do you mean forced? How can anyone force you?"

"They told me if I didn't resign, they would fire me for cause, and the state would probably cancel my teacher certification. They said it would be better if I just resigned."

"What's your name?" Jake's voice became wary, and he suddenly smelled rotten apples.

"Stephanie Porcose."

"You just resigned at the last board meeting, if I'm not mistaken. I was supposed to call you."

"That's okay. Yes, I resigned, but I didn't want to."

Rather than continue on the phone, Jake preferred to look the woman in the eye, scope out the whole story and follow a trail to the truth.

Java Jive glowed from indirect lighting. Dark tables, book-lined walls and posters of Ché Guevara completed the cozy bookstore look. Jake didn't mind the posters. A warm glow of satisfaction came from knowing he was still alive and that commie bastard was dead.

Java Jive sat just off the university campus, between two buildings on the side of a sloping lot. Once a forgotten, slat-sided barn in the countryside, an entrepreneurial spirit had picked it up and trucked country to the city. The rusted roof and dark wooden walls looked only a good rainstorm away from collapse. Hidden steel reinforcements, slab concrete and various other expensive constructional sleights of hand kept the place safe.

Java Jive served European strength coffee at three and a half bucks a cup. Tonight, they were selling a lot of them. Beside the coffee bar, a refrigerated showcase of stacked chocolate pies and cream filled pastries promised to fortify even the most anorexic seekers of knowledge.

Stephanie was already at a corner table, perusing a leather bound volume in the dim light of a green-shaded banker's lamp. She looked up as Jake sat down.

"What're you reading?"

"Nothing special." She smiled, placing the book back on the shelf.

Unlike Brice's, there were probably half a dozen on the wait staff, young men and women, in white polo shirts, dark trousers, darting here and there. The noise level wasn't too high. You could actually carry on a conversation over the background of muted Mozart.

They ordered coffee. "So, what's this about being forced to resign?"

"Have you lived here long?"

Jake was tired of the question. "Six months." He spit out the answer the way you'd swat away a pesky fly. "But, tell me about your resignation."

"I told you. They said they were going to kill me, professionally speaking, if I didn't submit a resignation."

"They used those words? Kill you?"

"No, Mrs. Hightower just hinted strongly a fired teacher would have a difficult time finding a job, anywhere. She also said no one in the school system would recommend me, unless I resigned."

"I was at the board meeting when your resignation was approved. The superintendent praised you, as I remember. Now you're saying she set you up?"

"I don't know if the superintendent set me up. I only talked to Mrs. Hightower, but she inferred she had the superintendent's blessing. Appearances are deceiving around here, Mr. Morgan." Stephanie brushed back a lock of auburn hair. "I didn't play ball. They wanted me gone."

"Why did they want you gone?"

"Various reasons, but it's complicated."

"Are you going to tell me, or you just have a burning desire to see if I could afford the coffee?" Stephanie laughed, then put her hand to her mouth and glanced around to see if anyone was staring. No one was. She hesitated, got herself back into the seriousness of the question.

"About two months ago, near the start of the school year, there was an unpleasant incident with my principal."

"Your principal is a woman, right?" The thought of sexual harassment jumped out of the air and pounced on Jake's brain.

"Right. No, it wasn't anything like that." A mind reader.

"The principal tried to get the PTO to put all their money in her discretionary pot."

"She wanted to control the whole pile."

"That's right. It may not sound like much, but the PTO raises about $35,000 annually and spends it on the school, I might add." Jake nodded. "She asked for the money because the year before, that's the first year I was teaching there, evidently a squabble developed between Mrs. Hightower and the PTO. I don't know the details. So, after all the discussions about how things were going to be handled for the year, there was a vote and since I was the teacher representative I got to vote."

"Let me guess. You voted with the PTO against the principal."

"Well, I wasn't meaning to oppose her exactly, she just never explained why the money should be moved in a lump sum. I'm also a parent, don't forget, and a PTO member."

"Was there a specific reason she wanted to control the money?"

Stephanie paused a moment, reflected. "I don't think so. I mean, if you're asking if she was going to do something illegal with it, no. I just think it's part of her power play."

"And, now, months later you're getting fired for voting against her?"

"There's more to it than that." Jake fought to control his impatience. "The next time she did my evaluation, she noted some discrepancies."

"That happens." He'd dealt with evaluations every year of his Air Force life.

"It's not the discrepancies. They were minor. It was the timing of the evaluation. See, I'd just had an evaluation a month before, and I wasn't due another one for five months. The principal and her assistant each try to sit in on every classroom once a year. That was the other thing. Mrs. Hightower did my first evaluation also."

"How did the first one work out?"

"Fine. No discrepancies. There was a complimentary note on several of my classroom procedures."

Jake perked up. "Why did she say she was back to observe you so soon?"

"She said the paperwork on the first evaluation was lost."

"No copies, I suppose." Jake's eyebrows knitted.

"Oh, yes, I'd had the secretary make me a copy."

"Do you still have it?"

"No. I told Mrs. Hightower I had a copy when she came in the classroom. She asked me for it, and I gave it to her. Now she says she can't remember my having given it to her."

"Any other copies?" Jake's mind moved down the continuum.

"Not that I know of."

"So, besides the discrepancies on your evaluation, has there been anything else of note?"

"She called me into her office after a faculty meeting and said she had been distressed by my lack of attention."

"You weren't paying attention at a faculty meeting?"

"I thought I was. I mean I didn't do anything differently. Yes, I was paying attention."

"Anything else?"

"She gave me a letter saying I had been coming in late to school and my classroom preparation had suffered."

"And, had you been coming in late?"

"Only once. My car wouldn't start one morning and a neighbor had to help me jump it. I was about five minutes late."

"Did you call and tell anyone?"

"No. I know I should have, but I wasn't near a phone, and I thought I had enough time to make it."

"Cell phone?"

She frowned. "On a teacher's pay?"

"Do you think any of your fellow teachers will back you up?"

"Several have told me how sorry they are."

"Sorry doesn't do much for you."

"No," she said, "but I kind of expected it. Mrs. Hightower made an example of me and now everyone else is running scared." Stephanie took a breath and looked down into her coffee before looking back at him. "Mr. Morgan, I want my job back."

"Well, the thing is, they have all the aces. If you were going to fight this, you should have done it before you signed the letter of resignation."

"I know I should have, but I was scared."

"How about the teachers' union?"

"We don't have one."

"Have you spoken with any school board members?"

"I spoke with Mr. Millage, but he said it was out of his hands, and I should talk with the superintendent."

"Did you?"

"No. What's the point?" Jake didn't have a good answer. They sat in silence for several moments. The room seemed warmer and darker. Maybe it was the coffee.

"You may want to call Todd Ingles. I understand you might find a friendly ear. Also, can't believe I'm saying this, but you might want to talk to Caldwell Robbins. He and the superintendent aren't the best of friends. Make the calls first and let's see what gets stirred up. When does your resignation take effect?"

"Not until the end of the school year."

"This is just October."

"Yes."

"Isn't that unusual? Don't teachers normally resign at the end of the year?"

"Yes, but that was part of the deal they offered."

"You still seem a little hesitant."

"It's just that, well, I don't want to stir things up and make everything worse."

"I know how you feel. I don't want to talk you into anything, but you called me, right?" In fact, he hadn't a clue how she felt. This constant hesitancy to make any waves riled him. Everyone seemed to want a change, but nobody had the guts to speak up.

"Yes."

"This is going to be a long, uphill battle. What do you hope to get out of it?"

"My job."

"So, you'd like to go right back to working for the same principal who did this to you in the first place?"

She started to cry, softly. "I've got two kids, Mr. Morgan."

"I know what you mean." He reached across and patted her hand. "Listen, you're not helpless. You have a skill. There are other school systems around here. Good teachers are always scarce. Apply for jobs in neighboring counties and nail down an income for next year. That'll take care of the immediate problem. Then, if you decide you want to fight, get yourself some legal help. That's a lot easier than trying to get rid of a principal, possibly a superintendent and reforming an entire school system. Take care of you and yours first."

"I guess so." She sniffled.

"Could you do something for me? I need some information."

"Sure." She pinched her nose with a Kleenex, then put it back in her purse.

"Explain to me how the personnel system works."

"I don't know how it works."

"Okay, let's start at the beginning. Do you fill out an application?"

"Yes." She eyed him curiously as if he were any moment going to pop some complicated and unanswerable question, forcing her to say something traitorous that might be overheard.

"Tell me where you turn it in, how you find out about job openings, how you know if you've been hired. All those little things."

*****

Next morning, Jake called Mrs. Hightower. The secretary asked what it was about. Jake told her. The secretary came back on the line and gave him Mrs. Hightower's reply. She wouldn't talk to him about personnel issues. Board policy.

40

In an investigation, the important things are as plain as the nose on your face, except for those that aren't. —Sheriff Sam Goddard, asked by a reporter about any important clues

"I did it. I killed him." The voice was neutral, void of emotion. Man, woman? It definitely wasn't a kid.

"Who did you kill? Over."

The sheriff hit the stop button on the tape. "What's this 'over' crap? John Paul thinks he's on the radio?"

"God knows," Howard said.

"Amen." The tape picked back up.

"I tell you, I killed him."

"I don't know who you killed, over."

"The man at the Post Office. I slew him."

"God in heaven! What was his name? Over."

"I don't know his name. He was the football coach."

"Where do you live? Over."

"I tell you I killed a man!" Exasperation was setting in. This killer didn't suffer fools well.

"You expect me to believe you? Over."

"I whacked him."

"You say you slew him? Over."

"Not this time. This time I said I whacked him."

"Let me get this straight. Did you slay him or whack him? Over."

"You're an idiot." The voice sounded certain.

"Have you accepted Jesus as your savior? Over." The last thing on the tape was the metallic buzz of a disconnect.

Goddard shut off the machine.

"So, what do you think, sheriff?"

"I dunno. Sounds like a prank. But, I know one thing for certain."

"What's that?"

"John Paul made a bad career choice. We need to convince him to find another calling. I'm thinking hermit is what I'm thinking."

"Won't have to interact with humans."

"Bingo. Over." Goddard wanted to let it go, but couldn't. Everything had to be checked out. He sighed. Another worm on the plate. He'd *sic* one of the other deputies on it.

41

I have never felt more at home in a school system, and I've been teaching almost twenty years. —Cassavora County Teacher of the Year, Joann Hiller, addressing the Board of Education

Jake quickly found out you can't meet everyone door to door, no matter how many afternoons you spent tromping the neighborhoods in the hot sun. Some days were better than others. Saturday mornings were best. More people were at home. The rest of the time it was chaos theory. He figured he only got to speak to about a quarter of the residents. Even then, he either got to speak to the husband or the wife, seldom both. With the help of Cleve Amos and some of his other friends, Jake got himself invited to neighborhood meet-the-candidate parties. They were usually evening affairs. Fruit punch and cookies in somebody's living room. People would throw questions at him and let him speak his mind. He never ran into any hostility and figured it was because people who didn't like him just didn't waste an evening. The meetings let him show his face and tell his story. Getting votes was mostly like tipping dominoes. You tipped your message over and hoped enough folks would pass it on. If they didn't, you ended up congratulating the winner and going back to your day job.

One evening, Jake found himself at Brookhaven, a housing development a few miles outside of Fletcher. Lawns flowed, but not as far as they did in the upscale communities. The houses nestled closer together and cars in the driveways showed their age. Kids and forgotten bicycles sprinkled the landscape.

Jake sat on a couch between two women. A few others settled in nearby chairs or sat on the rug.

This was a teachers' group and they seemed happy, but a little nervous, as though meeting him were a seditious act requiring the anonymity of darkness. They dressed modestly, in slacks or sundresses, not overly made up. A couple of them wore glasses. They could have been housewives gathered for bridge.

Heather, a willowy blond and second grade teacher, spoke first. "Mr. Morgan .... "

"Call me Jake, please."

"Jake .... " She paused. A nervous twitter passed through the group. "You know all is not as it seems in our cheery little school system." Her low alto gave her a more forceful delivery than you would guess by her diminutive stature.

"It's not?" He didn't like to show his cards before all bets were down.

"How long have you lived here, Mr. Morgan?" The invariable opening gambit. Margie was heavier set, a dark haired fourth grade teacher. He saw suspicion in her round face, as if anything she said might be held against her. And not necessarily by him.

Jake gave them his background, as though it were a secret password for opening doors forever locked to outsiders. "Then, you've probably noticed a certain lack of *openness*, shall we say." Margie had a wry half smile and dark, knowing eyes.

Jake didn't say anything. Helen, a short, pudgy seventh-grade teacher cut in. "The teachers are intimidated," she said flatly.

Marsha, a high school arts teacher, sounded a little put out. "I don't know if you can really say that, Helen."

"Well, what would you call it, when all of these shenanigans are going on and the teachers are afraid to speak up?"

"I've spoken with Stephanie Porcose," Jake said. "Is that the kind of thing you're talking about?"

"That and a dozen other things." Heather looked at him intently.

"They railroaded Stephanie," Helen said. "All that talk from the superintendent about how they appreciated her contributions! That was bull!"

"You know, we're not really allowed to meet with you." Margie confessed her sin.

"Why?"

"They made it pretty clear," Heather said slowly. "The superintendent evidently told the principals, teachers were not to become involved in the politics of the county, including speaking with board members or candidates."

"She called it being disloyal to the school system." Helen again.

"Bet that's not in writing." Jake looked around and saw the nods.

"It's very difficult to attribute anything directly to the superintendent," Marie said. "She usually has her henchmen deliver the bad news."

"Or, she says something and then swears it's just a misunderstanding," Helen added.

"Any concrete examples?"

"Tell him about the reading series, Heather."

"I was part of a committee," Heather began, "to review possible replacements for the old series of reading books, a big group of teachers and principals and even some parents. We must have spent months hashing through more than ten series from several publishers. We settled on the reading books put out by Hargess Publishing. The superintendent reviewed our work; in fact she attended many of the meetings. Everybody assumed we'd get the books we wanted. In the fall we found out they'd gone with a different publisher. Executive decision they said."

Jake saw the flush of anger. "Who said?"

"Mr. Gordon."

"No, it was the principal," someone else added. "At first, we were told the publisher couldn't supply the books we wanted and they had to make a new choice. Two of us called the publisher and found out that wasn't true, the books were never ordered."

Helen said sarcastically, "We were irate!"

Margie picked up the thread. "When we told the Director of Curriculum, Mr. Gordon, he said the committee reconvened over the summer and took a new vote. Well, nobody I know who was on the committee was ever contacted over the summer!"

"What did the superintendent have to say?"

"Oh, she came down to visit us, wringing her hands and saying how sorry she was over this misunderstanding. She said it was out of her control because the books were already delivered and it would take too long to reorder."

"Then came the climax at the next school board meeting, when we were asked to attend and the superintendent thanked us for all our hard work on the committee. She also praised how we were all working for the good of the children." Marie's face was turning red.

"We were so stunned we didn't say anything. Everyone on the board and in the audience politely clapped and then we were ushered out." Heather almost spit out the words.

"So, all the teachers felt the same way?" Jake looked from Heather to Margie.

"Well, that's the thing," Margie began, "two of the teachers on the committee swear they were contacted over the summer and no one could get hold of the others."

"It was masterful," Heather said smoothly, "The superintendent and her toadies introduced doubt. One of the teachers on the side of the Curriculum Director was Teacher of the Year."

"Sounds like you were out-gunned." Jake took a quick sip of punch from the clear plastic cup and grimaced as he breathed in the tickle of carbonation. "So, why don't you speak up?"

"Stephanie Porcose spoke up." For Margie that settled the question.

"About this?" Jake asked.

"No, but she spoke up about other things."

"It's not as if this kind of thing goes on in just the elementary schools." Marsha nudged her glasses back up the bridge of her nose. "At the high school I can tell you plenty of teachers feel intimidated."

"Why do you let yourselves be intimidated?" Jake looked directly at her. He could see the flashes of anger with every revelation. Nobody was going to stand up and fight? The timidity churned his stomach.

"That's just the way things work around here." She looked away.

"It doesn't have to be that way." Jake hated to waste his breath repeating the obvious. "There are a hellofva lot more of you than there are of them. Speak up! Write to the newspapers, speak out in the school board meetings, sign petitions. There are a lot of ways to do it."

Heather looked at him, as if he were on the verge of madness. "We'd all lose our jobs."

"What kind of job is it when you go to work each day feeling helpless and intimidated?" Jake wanted to ask, but he bit his tongue.

"You haven't lived here very long, Mr. Morgan." Margie's voice took on the iron edge of a schoolteacher talking to a recalcitrant student.

"How long do you have to live here," he wanted to scream, "before you fight the people who are making you miserable?" But, again he didn't say anything, just forced a slight smile, ran a hand through his hair, readjusted his glasses. Cowardice and courage both took practice.

Helen blurted out, "They don't even treat us like professionals!"

He wanted to badger them, but knew his words wouldn't stick. Conversations like this one wearied him. He was used to relentlessly going after real solutions. These women only wanted to vent and indulge themselves in a bit of pseudo-action. They already had a standard solution, as inflexible as a novice's vow of silence.

Maybe Marsha could read the expression on his face. She spoke softly. "Try to understand where we're living and what our backgrounds are. We're just not used to speaking out. It's not only ourselves we have to consider. We live here. Our children go to school here. Some of our husbands own businesses here. It's not only impolite, but dangerous to step out."

It's only too bad those who seem to be running things don't feel the same way, Jake thought. He took another sip of punch.

42

Reading is the single most important subject in elementary school. You get the kids reading, and you can quickly make up for anything else they missed along the way. —Thelma Withers, Second Grade Teacher

Outside Fletcher, going south on a sun-blanched stretch of Highway 17, the countryside opens into farmland; then, there's a big weather beaten barn on the right. A little further on is a squat, concrete animal-control building. About three miles past town in a grove of oak trees, near a large, tilled field sits a vegetable and fruit stand. A mom and pop operation.

Jake mentally ticked off the landmarks, but his mind wasn't on where he was going. He stared out the windshield, thought about the shooting, the allegations, the injustice of it all. He brought his mind back to the road and where the hell he was going. Waist high white and orange signs advertised peaches, Vidalia onions, fried meat skins, cantaloupes, jellies, honey, and boiled peanuts, in sequence. The fruit stand was a well-promoted oasis.

This one gleamed a brilliant white, capped with a red tin roof and squatted in a well-used gravel parking apron, scarred with potholes. On the eaves, beneath the black letters that read 'Dan's Fruite Stande, bulging yellow braided sacks of thick, brown-skinned onions waited for hungry suburbanites. Pint baskets of red tomatoes sat in front on slanted, white shelves, beside jade green watermelons, rough skinned cantaloupes, yellow-orange peaches, mason jars of thick local honey, sunny glass jugs of cider and fat jars of jams and jellies. A butane flame licking the bottom of a big bruised aluminum pot. Steam drifted out of it like fog off a lake, soaking the near air with the salty fragrance of boiling peanuts.

Jake had a special reason for going to visit Dan the fruit stand man. Dan was born and raised in Cassavora, knew all the shakers and bakers and generally had his finger on the pulse. Cleveland had been adamant.

Jake got out of his car, waved to ward off the dust and walked over to the older lady fussing with stacks of little baskets, rearranging the fruit. She smiled showing off white teeth, brushed back a windy strand of

grayish hair and looked at him though thick, gold-framed glasses. "Good morning. May I hep you with something?"

"I really came here to talk with your husband, but those peanuts smell so good, I just can't resist."

She stooped a little, picked up a small, brown sandwich bag, walked over to where the peanuts were boiling and dipped a long handled, perforated ladle deep into the steamy pot. "I put these on yesterday mornin' and let 'em soak all night before I boiled 'em up again this mornin'." The ladle came up, brown liquid dribbling down the sides and back into the pot. Peanuts, wet and shiny, tumbled into the brown paper bag, leaving dark wet spots on the side of the bag.

Jake passed her a couple of crinkled dollar bills and took the sack from her outstretched hand.

The house sat about twenty yards behind the stand. "Dan, there's a man here to see you." Rose bushes, some with pink flowers, some with white, lined the tilled bed in front of the low porch. A wisteria vine wound its way up one white column and snaked across the roofline. Jake pictured it as it was in springtime, heavy with purple clumps of flowers.

The screen door creaked and a man stepped out in a faded blue polo shirt, equally faded jeans, point toed cowboy boots and a white, sweat stained baseball cap with a fancy, red script A on the front of it. Dark blue suspenders held the jeans up. "Hey, there!" he called to Jake, "What can I do fer ya?" Like his wife, he wore glasses and appeared to be in his late sixties. He had a kind of arthritic walk that was painful to watch, but he seemed cheerful enough.

"I came to talk politics." Jake grinned.

"Dan Persons." He shook Jake's hand. "I've been wanting to meet you. You're running for the school board. Right?"

"Yes, sir, I am."

"Heard some interesting things about you. Any of 'em true?"

"Only the one about me being a big enough fool to run for the school board."

"I figured." Dan shook his head slowly. "It's a hellofva job, I can tell you that. I was on the school board for the best part of fifteen years. For a while I was a commissioner and on the school board. That was back before they changed the law. You can't do that no more." He squinted at Jake, trying to take the measure of him.

"You've been busy."

"That I have, that I have. But, I'm not messing with politics nowadays. It's gotten too damn political!" He laughed at his joke. "These jackasses know how to get elected, but they don't have a clue what to do from there, but try to get reelected.

Could you imagine a doctor graduating from medical school and then starting medical school all over again? If somebody gave these yahoos the big picture, they wouldn't know what they were looking at. But, hell, you didn't come out here to listen to me rant and rave." He winked at Jake. "You know the difference?"

"The difference?"

"Between rant and rave. The difference between them."

Jake fancied himself a writer, a user of words, but the question came at him like a spitball and his brain stumbled. "Well, no."

Dan was still smiling. "That's 'cause there ain't no difference! We say rant and rave just because everybody says it, and the two sound good together. People expect it. S'pose I just said *rant*? It wouldn't have sounded right. If I'd just said *rave*, you would've expected me to be standing here with my hair on fire, what little I've got left." He tipped his baseball cap and scratched his head. "Now," he said, changing the subject abruptly, "you came out here to talk politics."

"Yes, sir, and to get your opinions."

"Fire away. Bet you wonder why we say fire away instead of just fire, but, what the hell, it don't matter. What's your question?"

"How about if I mention some names and you tell me what you think?"

"Shoot."

"Caldwell Robbins."

"Bright. Likable. Too hung up on religion. You might say his mind narrows like a laser at that point and everything else goes out of focus."

"Morgan Southmore."

"Makes the village idiot look like Einstein."

"Able Perkins."

"Oh, yeah, running for the school board. Is he your opponent?"

"Yes, sir."

"I served with Able on the Board of Commissioners. He's not a bad man, but he's always gonna do what's best for Able, if you know what I mean. I can tell you this, what he knows about education and teaching and so forth you could fit into a peanut shell and still have room for the peanut. To my mind, he's got too many fingers in too many pies. That might restrict the way he looks at educational needs for the county, if you catch my drift. But, I have to say, he's been around here long enough that he's going to get a lot of votes."

"What do you think of the superintendent?"

"Lucinda? Don't know her all that well. We rub elbows with her and her husband once or twice a year when I shuck these jeans and get into my tux. She seems to have done a lot for the school system. Overall, it seems to be in pretty good shape."

"Do you have any kids in school or relatives that work for the school system?"

"I've got grand kids there."

"No complaints or things you'd like to see done differently."

"No personal complaints. I wish they wouldn't spend so much of my money, but I understand the need."

"So, overall you're satisfied?"

"Hell no!"

"Why not?"

"Education has to be up with the times. It's like rant and rave. You always just stick with the expected and pretty soon the expected ain't good enough. Look, my grandkids are doing fine, but I don't know how much doing fine is doing for 'em. You been keeping track of the standardized scores?"

Jake gave a nod, waiting to hear the long and the short of it, without having to explain long and short.

"Well, go take a look. They're dropping like my Granny's bosom and they ought to be goin' in the other direction. About a third of the kids ain't readin' as well as they should. One out of three ain't good enough! That's what I mean about doing the expected. Long as there's no major pains, we just whiz along on cruise control. But, by the time the major pains start, it's too damn late and too damn expensive to do anything."

"Some say the standardized scores don't tell the story."

"Well, there's some truth to that and there's some lies. The folks that yell about using standardized scores are usually the ones that are going to be hurt if we look too close, like the teachers and principals and superintendents. And, I haven't heard anything else they plan on using instead, have you?"

"No."

"Make one of the younger kids read to you. Ask some older kid about the Pythagorean Theorem or where the hell Atlanta is on a map. Make 'em point out China on a globe. You'll know in five minutes if the school system is doing some good or is just a money hole."

"Here's something else for you to think about. Politicians ain't the ones who start the corruption. Hell, I was a politician, and I wasn't corrupted. Never took a penny or looked the other way when somebody else did. First you got to have a population that's willing to be corrupted. That's where it starts and that means you need a bunch of citizens who are ignorant, who think everything is too complicated for them to understand and don't demand any explanations about where the money comes from or where it goes. After that, corruption grows like mold in a damp cellar."

Jake smiled. "Yes, sir, but who said anything about corruption."

Dan gave him a look like there was any doubt. "And I'll tell you something else .... "

"What's that?"

"Having a third of the kids who can't read and write too well is a good start on having a group of citizens who don't think too well. Now let me change the subject." Dan didn't even take a breath. "Do you like pimento cheese sandwiches?"

"Yes, sir, I do."

"Well, I would hope so! You can't be a Southerner and not like pimento cheese. You are a Southerner ain't ya?"

"I am."

"You don't sound like it."

"It's a long story, but I was born here."

"That's good." They walked over to the stand. Dan leaned over the counter and pulled a plastic wrapped sandwich out of a plastic cooler.

"Sink your teeth into some Southern pâté."

"Delicious!" Jake took another bite. "You'll have to tell me what's in it."

"You married?"

"No, I'm not. Why?"

"I only give recipes out to family," Dan clucked, "So you'll have to marry my daughter."

"How old's your daughter?"

"She's forty-two, but she's married, so you'll have to wait for her husband to croak." He reached back over the counter and pulled out a copy of the recipe.

Dan the Fruit Stand Man's Real South Pimento Cheese 4 cups grated cheddar 3/4 cup mayonnaise 8 oz softened cream cheese

1 large red bell pepper, roasted, peeled and diced Generous 1/4 teaspoon cayenne pepper 1 teaspoon garlic salt

Mix everything together with a beater until well blended. Spread it on plain white bread or risk being called a Yankee.

43

*The band doesn't matter. We wouldn't even have a band if we didn't
have a football team, hell, we might not even have a high school.* —Football
parent

It didn't take police work to get the answer to the
shooting at Jake's house. The high school supplied the answers.
One kid talked to another in a chain reaction of unintentional
disclosure. Eventually the sheriff got a call from concerned
parents who bent over backwards to assure him it wasn't their
kids. When he tracked down the shooters, the big bore rifle was
still in the trunk of the Mustang.

A bright new morning, the sheriff thought, the start of a
bright new day. Sam let the two boys suffer through a night in
jail, just to warm up their memories. They'd been smart asses
when his deputies brought them in, but once in the cells they
deflated faster than balloons in a pin factory. Iron bars and grim
faces tended to have that effect on most people, especially
smart-assed kids. Right before breakfast, one of the boys spilled
the details of an adventure gone wrong.

Now another of the boys' fathers stood in Sam's office
pleading for leniency. Goddard listened, empathized, but didn't
budge. As far as he was concerned, endangering lives went
beyond a boyhood prank. Besides these were big guys, both of
them eighteen, seniors at the high school. They should know
better.

The problem was, the father explained, his son was the
starting quarterback and the game with Foster County was next
weekend.

"I agree it's a difficult situation." Goddard looked up at the man standing in front of his desk, pursed his lips.

"I know your loyalties lie with Cassavora." The father had the audacity to smile at him. His hoodlum son was the star quarterback, which was supposed to excuse a big tote sack full of dangerous foolishness. "You know as well as I do, that other boy and his old man," the father continued, "are only blaming everything on my boy 'cause they're jealous. Hell, they're just trying to get my son in trouble."

"It was your son's car and both their fingerprints are all over the weapon," Goddard said, flatly. "Looks to me like they took turns."

The father continued as if he hadn't heard. "You don't even know if that other kid is telling the truth." He paused. "Look, if Danny doesn't play ... " He paused again to gather all the good reasons, dropped one thought and moved on to another. "There are going to be scouts from four or five universities at that game." The father grabbed a straight back chair, pulled it close to the desk and sat down.

Now he was on the same level as Goddard and his tone changed as well, from pleading to the earnestness of a fellow conspirator. "My son has never been in trouble ... "

"Pot," Sam cut in. "Your boy was suspended ten days. I checked."

"That wasn't his fault. He was just holding it for a friend. Didn't even know what it was."

"Well, I've got a few choices," Goddard said, slowly. The man heard the words and looked hopeful. "I could charge them with malicious mischief, or I could charge them with

willful endangerment or destruction of county property."
He had another thought. "Or, I could charge them with all three."

The man's face fell at first and then the anger rose in him, as though Goddard was saying all these things just to spite him. "What does all that stuff mean?"

"It means Cassavora County is going to have to go with their backup quarterback on Saturday."

"It's that damn Morgan character, isn't it? He's the one making you turn your back on this county and the whole damn school system."

"I realize you're upset," Sam said slowly. "What you've got to adjust to is that nobody made your son pull the trigger."

"He was shooting at a goddamn stop sign Christsakes!"

"Apparently, he's shot at quite a few of them and the other night he damn near killed two people. We can both be glad his aim is as bad as his judgment."

"It's that Morgan character," the father said again, making up his mind. "Him and that girl having a good time together and now it's my son who's got to pay the price!"

"You can blame your son's actions on anyone you want, but you're lookin' at the guy who's filing the charges."

44

Cassavora SAT Scores Impressive —Headline in The Cassavora Advocate

The day of the open forum, *The Advocate* headlined "Cassavora High School Students Clobber Scholastic Aptitude Test." The timing of the report gave incumbents on the Board of Education a chance to puff their chests and take credit for everything good that had ever happened in the history of public schooling. Nobody mentioned the national averages, or Cassavora's scores being compared to only a small corner of the state. Few readers even knew what the S.A.T. measured, but they read "clobbered" and felt wrapped in a warm blanket of contentment. Jake called the headlines an award for the futilely fulsome, kudos for showing up.

In his eyes, board and education were no more connected than warts and watercress. Beating drums and blaring trumpets didn't change his opinion. He'd come to see the board as a rubber stamp.

*****

"Candidates to Discuss Issues," headed a column on page three of *The Advocate*, sandwiched between "Local Man Astonished at Two Headed Goat" and a list of arrests for the week. "Candidates aspiring for positions on the Cassavora Board of Education will share their views this evening at a forum to be held in Tibbins Memorial Civic Center at seven o'clock."

Jake pulled into a vast parking lot that the county athletic fields shared with the civic center. He saw only a smattering of cars and checked his watch. If this place were going to fill up, it would have to happen soon.

Inside was no different. The candidates and only about a dozen other people stood in little clumps. Either he was wasting his time, or the rest of the county was still on the road.

Hundreds of empty theater seats fanned out before a large dais. Cafeteria-style tables stretched across the stage, dotted with tall, perspiring pitchers of ice water and clear plastic cups. Microphones waited for the big event, their dark, twisting wires trailing across the state.

A local radio personality blathered his version of the rules of the game over a booming public address system.

More people trickled in, but still less than a hundred peppered the cavernous room. Two reporters chatted with the tech rep from the local radio station and watched him fuss with the microphones.

Able Perkins stood to one side, speaking with a man and a woman. When Jake walked by them he caught only a bit of a phrase, " ... a sense of community."

Butterflies flew lazy eights in the pit of his stomach, the same as before the start of a football game. Standing up and speaking held no terrors, but the raw tension gripped his belly. Jake rolled his shoulders, to relieve the tightness, flexed his fingers, stretched his neck.

So far, he and Able hadn't gone head to head, except for the garbage in the newspaper. But, that didn't mean it wasn't a dogfight.

Signs along the highways and spiked in neighborhood lawns blasted out Able Perkins For BOE. Ads in *The Advocate* promised Able was able. Jake didn't have signs, but now he wished he had. It might have taken the pressure off tonight, his shining moment in the media spotlight, his brilliant and only opportunity to be the educational Pied Piper.

Lights dimmed, conversation hushed. Chairman Tom Millage stepped forward, the stage lights giving the lines on his face the color and depth of eroded soil, his silver hair brushed, sprayed into place and shining. He spoke of his paternal love for Cassavora County, his appreciation of the superintendent and her efforts to bring out the very best in the children and his belief in the strength of the Cassavora School System. Polite applause followed.

Jake poured himself a glass of water.

The evening loped along in tedium of phrases and speakers, as if children had been given words at random and asked to recite endlessly. It didn't matter if it were Caldwell Robbins calling for a moral renewal and ending with "Our Lord Jesus Christ must be our guide as we struggle with the devil in all his forms," or Robbins' opponent, a pig farmer named Arthur Helburt saying, "I'm as much a Christian as the next person, but religion shouldn't be taught in the schools and we shouldn't teach arithmetic in church."

Jake's mind wandered. No arithmetic in church. Let's see, you have two fish, five loaves, and five thousand mouths. Your caterer doesn't show.

He entertained himself by scanning the thin crowd. Not many women. The superintendent stood in the far back, passing wisdom to her majordomo, Horace Gordon, his eyes darted back and forth from her to the speaker, like a dysfunctional metronome.

Jake knew Horace only from a couple of chance encounters, but there was something about him that stuck in his gut. Call it intuition. The man's eyes never quite looked at you and the thin mouth spoke silently of a lifetime of insincerity, his mind only a bureaucratic chalkboard on which to write the happy slogans of the day.

Not far from the superintendent, a group of expressionless men in business suits huddled loosely, saying little, feigning interest. Chamber of Commerce Jake guessed.

A volunteer clerk hustled up the aisles, collected slips of paper, hustled back to the commentator. Neither the businessmen, nor the superintendent contributed.

Jake listened to the litany of pithy banalities, long on opinions, short on practical ideas, devoid of hard data. He breathed in, breathed out.

Speech piled upon speech. Jake covered his mouth to stifle a yawn, scratched, drank water.

"Ladies and gentlemen," Able Perkins began, peeling back his coattails, putting his hands on his hips, "Most of you know me and know that I am, quite frankly, in love." He paused for effect, flashed an avuncular smile. "In love with this wonderful place we call Cassavora County. I have spent most of my life here, raised a family here, built a business and tried to fulfill my civic responsibilities by serving on various planning boards and the Board of Commissioners. It has been a privilege." He stepped from behind the long table and walked to the edge of the dais, elegantly thin, his white hair a badge of wisdom, his well cut gray suit, white shirt and tastefully red tie, symbols of a solid and successful citizen. "Except for my family and God, this county is number one in my heart. Best of all, I know all of you feel the same way." His eyes worked the darkened room; a slight smile crept across his face. This was his audience, and he instinctively sensed he owned their hearts. "There is something wonderfully satisfying about knowing ... " He paused again. "About knowing as citizens we can stand together, sure of our county and sure of the school system, which is the heart and soul of the county." Spontaneous applause followed him to his seat.

In the midst of applause the jitters hit Jake again. He'd spoken before important audiences, peopled by high rollers, military and civilian, who knew him well enough to call him by his first name. But that was when he wore a uniform, flew fast, was solid on everything he said and did. The uniform, the rank, the years of service assured him an instant place in that secure world. No longer.

Now what was he? Some old retired guy. Somebody who moved here six months ago and had a handful of friends. Somebody with credentials balanced precariously on a couple of degrees and some service to his county. The thin patina of credibility suddenly seemed as fragile as a robin's egg. And, he was running against a pillar, a rock, everybody's uncle.

His hastily chosen attire worried him. Instead of a suit, he wore khaki slacks, loafers, a white shirt, sleeves rolled to the elbows and a blue and red regimental striped tie. Should have worn a suit. Jake ran his hand through his hair, adjusted his glasses, mustered his best smile.

Self-doubt faded as soon as he stood up and the bright lights lit him up. Raw courage was no problem. He'd done it a thousand times, in tougher situations, with people shooting at him.

"Most of you know me because you read my articles in the newspaper, or you've chatted with me when I came by your house. You told me the school system needs improving. I heard you ask, can't it be better than it is? We agree that yes, it can." His voice boomed. "You came to me with positive solutions and now I come right back to you the same way. There are so many things to be positive about. We have involved parents, dedicated teachers and a school system among the best in the state.

But, you and I know that's not enough. If education were a mountain, this state wouldn't even be a foothill. All of us control what happens in the school system of Cassavora County, our school system. We can be the best, not just in our little corner of the state, but the best in the country. And how we do that..."

"Time!"

"It's up to you and me, working together." A smattering of applause greeted him as he took his seat. He didn't hear it. The pounding of his heart drowned out everything.

The moment passed, the Forum labored on, a plodding burro laden with moldy sacks of tired solutions. Questions from the audience came in scattered bursts, touching a nerve here, a nerve there. Caldwell Robbins locked onto the separation of church and state. "Praying in school doesn't mean the same thing as sponsoring religion."

Somebody blasted Gloria Sweeney about the absence of technology in the schools. She fired back that the board of education had done a good job of buying computers. Big deal, Jake thought. How about the electrical spark to set the students and hardware humming?

Out of the blue, Jake faced a charge of trying to establish an elitist high school catering to the rich kids who were headed to college.

He took another sip of water, pulled the microphone toward him. "Good education is for everyone. If a child is aiming for college, we ought to be giving him the best we've got. Same applies if he's going to tech school or joining the job market. Right now, we're not giving them all the tools they need."

"Look at the SAT scores!"

Jake couldn't see who yelled. "Our SAT scores have constantly declined for the past five years." A chorus of boos.

He shot back at them. "Anybody else out there with low scores?" A ripple of muffled laughter. "Using this state's record is like measuring with a toothpick and calling it a yardstick. Are we going to keep patting ourselves on the back, making excuses or are we going to do something about it?" More boos.

"Try to control your children," Jake fired off.

The commentator broke in to stifle the boos and maintain order. That brought a few more boos. Somebody in the back yelled out, "He just wants to get his hands on some more of those high school girls!" Jake'd heard some of the undertones asking what Betsy had been doing at his house, but he'd ignored them. This was out in the open. He stared at the audience, trying to see who'd yelled, but it really didn't matter. The comment hung in the air, like stench from an open sewer.

Able Perkins shoved back his chair and stood, ready in self-righteous rebuttal and pretending the comment had never been made. "My fellow Cassavorans, I disagree with my opponent. I don't think our schools are headed down the drain and to tell the truth, I resent him saying that about our kids, our parents and our whole great school system. Anybody can stand up here and throw stones as my opponent has done. He's free to make disparaging remarks about our long serving public officials. As for me, I have a great deal of confidence in the leadership, the teachers, and the students. Unlike my opponent, I think we are doing just fine." He sat down to lengthy applause.

Jake's final question was about reports of teachers being cajoled or pressured not to speak out. He saw Cleve Amos, figured the question came from him. "I've had some hints teachers are pressured. It's a travesty when people don't get a fair shake, when the small and powerless are simply cast aside. It offends my sense of fair play. I don't feel like I can say more at present. And can anybody at all tell me how teachers are hired and fired? Anybody want to give it a shot? I didn't think so." He looked toward the superintendent. She had her hand over her mouth, whispering something to Horace Gordon. Even from across the room, he could see her flushed face.

So many games. So little of it about education.

Afterwards, Jake and Skeeter met at a bar in the heart of the university city. Skeeter tried to be upbeat. The manufactured enthusiasm wasn't working.

"Look at it this way," Skeeter drawled between sips, "How many folks were there? Maybe fifty?"

Jake leaned forward, gazed into the golden ale, gave a nod.

"See, I'm telling ya, what happened tonight wasn't anything."

Jake wasn't sure about that.

"Except for that one stupid comment, did you hear anything you didn't expect?"

Jake looked up. "No, same tripe."

"So, how ya feeling, overall?"

"Gettin' elected is hard work."

"Fifty bucks a meeting? Hell yes! Why do ya think it pays so well?" Skeeter grinned.

"You know the one thing that got me?" Skeeter's eyebrows shot up. "I mean the other thing."

"What's that?"

"When my opponent said something about community. It sounded a hell of a lot more like a private club than a community."

"That seems to be the way it works around here."

Jake took a deep breath, let it out slowly. "The answer is to keep doing what I'm doing ... "

"And not worry so much," Skeeter cut in.

"I look at it this way. They're assholes, and I am pissing them off."

"Yeah, but who are *they?*"

Jake didn't have an answer. Not yet. But, he did have some clues. A few days later, Cynthia and Marcella came to him with court records, shadowy patterns of school building contracts, milk contracts, investments, large chunks of school money in the miscellaneous pile. He looked, and they explained, but there had been a lot more *ifs* than *sure things*. Finances and figures didn't perplex him, but he didn't have the eye for graft and corruption. He sent the women to see Sam Goddard.

45

Barbecuing is not a job for a man who's in a hurry. —*Rufus Johnson*

Neither is sheriffing. —*Sam Goddard*

The sheriff's stomach rumbled, reminding him of the grits and toast and sausage he hadn't had for breakfast. His face brightened. There was always The Dead Hog, a smoky little barbecue shack this side of town. Run by Rufus Johnson and his family since 1957, it enjoyed a reputation as the best smoked meat and ribs this side of heaven. Rufus retired from the business a few years back and his son, Washington, and Washington's son, Darjon, ran it now. Still, Rufus was often around, sipping a Pepsi and telling everyone who would listen the secret to a long life and a good barbecue. "You got to cook it real slow, like you making love to da meat. Eventually, it gonna git tender and juicy fer ya."

Sam almost missed the turnoff for Lenchmore Estates, tapped his brakes and heard tires of the car behind him squeal. "Sc'use me ma'am." He swung into the elaborate entrance and wondered why they didn't have a guard to go with the official looking stone gatehouse. Its green tile roof and half windows begged for a stout guy in a blue uniform, holding a clipboard. Maybe the rich were pinching pennies, but more than likely, they just didn't see the need, living as they did in the comforting bosom of Cassavora County.

Lenchmore opened a door to another world and he'd been meaning to feed his fantasies with a visit ever since his trip to Clifton Poultry. Hunger for some barbecue gave him his chance.

Some of the homes hid behind the rise of the lawns and a forest of spreading trees, the rooftops like ships in a sea of green. You could probably red line your Ferrari, or exchange gunfire and nobody would notice. A pecking order, stages of affluence, told Sam who was rich and who was richer. Some of the lawns stretched into green infinity. Many sported pretentious gateways with names like The Magnolias and Holly Farm. One or two offered whole fields edged in endless lines of white picket fence, punctuated with jewel like, private lakes, manicured to the edges in green velvet.

It had been awhile. Mostly the deputies did the routine patrolling. He did a double-take on one particular home, a big one, but not the biggest. A long, curl of driveway led to the front door. Near the top, a red Ford Aerostar van gleamed in the sun. He slowed to a stop, backed up, hesitated before pulling in. All of the red Fords registered in the county had been accounted for. What was this?

Parking right behind the van, he got out and threw a glance toward the front door. If he wasn't mistaken, Douglas and Lucinda Whitehall lived here. He thought about ringing the doorbell, but instead walked over to the van, cupped a hand over his brow and peered through a side window. On the floor was red carpet. It was also pretty spacious in back, certainly large enough to hold a big man comfortably.

Sam walked the brick sidewalk to the house, ambled up the stairs and pushed the brass buzzer. Pretty door, he thought, beveled glass and thin strips of copper. Shortly, a shadow approached and the door handle turned.

"Sheriff, good to see you." Douglas swung the front door open. "Come on in."

He smiled, waved a welcoming arm. If he had something to hide, he sure knew how to hide it. His business clothes smelled dry cleaner fresh, looked expensive, pleated slacks, white shirt, yellow patterned tie. "I was just grabbing a bite of lunch. Care to join me?" The sheriff said he wasn't coming in. Douglas kept one arm on the open door and moved out onto the porch, an indication this was going to be a temporary kind of conversation.

"Just passing through and admiring your red van."

"It's a beauty idden it?" Douglas was nonplused. "Only had it about six or eight months now. Lucinda drives it most of the time, but she's been taking my Cherokee lately. Says the van's too big for her."

"I can imagine it's a bit much for a woman to handle."

"No, not at all. Drives like a dream." If there was any uneasiness in his manner, the sheriff couldn't detect it. They were just two men stopping on the street to talk about cars. "Want to take it for a spin?"

He really thinks I just stopped by to look at his new toy? "I don't have time right now, but I wouldn't mind sittin' in it, if that's all right."

"Help yourself. Listen, if you'll forgive me, I'm going to go ahead and try to wolf down a sandwich. Kinda running short on time."

"By the way," Sam added, "the plate's from a different county."

"Yeah, licensed to my business." Douglas disappeared into the house, letting the heavy door close behind him.

Sam swung open the driver's door and slid into the smooth softness of leather. The seat was higher than his patrol car and a lot more comfortable. Even with his height and big frame, he didn't have to crouch down or keep his knees tucked under his chin.

He gave it enough time to make sure Douglas was gone for good, got out and walked back to his own car. The Aerostar's door closed with a solid clunk.

Time for barbecue. When he was within a mile, Sam could smell the aroma of smoked meat. He pulled into the dirt lot and disappeared into the slat sided shack.

When he got back to his office, he dropped a clear plastic bag on his desk, containing a little pinch of fuzz and a few long hairs. He'd finish his sandwich and have a cup of coffee before he gave Captain Giles another call, see if he could get the city cops to compare the fibers for him. It galled him to ask another favor and get treated like a poor cousin. With a small outfit like Cassavora's, it was tough to get any more Green Stamps.

The superintendent, he mused. Never even considered her, tried to picture her naked, doing the wild monkey with the coach. It wasn't a pleasant thought. Still it made a lot of sense, both of them being in the school system. Opportunity was there. Or it could be Douglas, some sort of man-to-man thing, as appealing to Sam as phlegm on the sidewalk. He shook his head slowly. No, unless Douglas was the finest actor in these parts, he was clean. He'd been too relaxed, too business as usual. Plus, in the coach's corner was the affair with the PE teacher, Mrs. Arston, and the hanky panky with the cheerleader. The coach hadn't led a quiet life. And these were just the women Sam knew about.

The van wasn't the end of the trail. In the real life sheriffing business, it just didn't pay to start leaping to all those TV cops' conclusions. He leaned back in the chair, took another bite of barbecue.

Smoked Meat from The Dead Hog The Meat: One 4-5 pound pork shoulder, or another cut of pork roast, sprinkled liberally with the rub (below). Smoke in a cool smoker, 200 degrees for 10-12 hours. Add water soaked wood chips to make smoke, but not too many or the meat will be bitter. AS AN ALTERNATE: smoke the meat for 2 hours, then wrap it in aluminum foil and bake it in a 250 degree oven for 2-3 hours.

The rub: salt, black pepper, red pepper, paprika, in equal proportions

The sauce: Collect meat drippings, chill in the refrigerator, skim off congealed fat. Add an equal amount catsup and then add whatever amount of beef bullion it takes to get to two cups. Add:

1 tablespoon onion powder 1/2 tablespoon garlic salt 1/8 cup vinegar Dash black pepper

Dash red pepper 1/2 teaspoon chili powder

1 teaspoon Tabasco 2 tablespoons honey

1 teaspoon dry mustard 1 tsp Worcestershire 46

46

I always suspected her. She's too friendly with the men, if you know what I mean and then she just stays in her office and never sits with us at lunch. —A teacher, who chose to remain anonymous

"You're kiddin' me!" Goddard sat back in his chair. "When did it happen?"

John Paul stood in front of the desk, twisting his hat in his hands, shifting his weight. "We don't know, sheriff. It was the night shift who noticed."

"The Coach's house," Goddard said simply, as though repeating the phrase would yield some startling revelation. "We don't even know it was a robbery, do we? Anything taken?"

John Paul gave a downhearted look, but didn't say anything.

Two hours later, the sheriff visited the site, followed by a swarm of deputies and his investigator. Nothing appeared to be missing. Most of the stuff had been tabulated earlier, when the department went over every inch.

One thing nobody had noticed in the initial investigation was a loose ceiling tile in the garage and a partially opened empty shoebox on the cement floor. Sam stuck his head up through the hole and peered around, following the pale yellow glow of the flashlight beam. "You get any prints out of this?"

Collins, the investigator was looking up. "Yes, sir. Looks like two people, although there don't appear to be full sets."

The sheriff grunted and climbed back down the ladder. "Well, don't be just standing around."

47

Football is the lifeblood of this high school! Test scores be damned! If we've got a winning football team, we've got a good high school. —Parent quoted in The Advocate

It was a warm fall evening and football crackled in the air. Jake wandered down to the high school stadium to catch the game and maybe schmooze a little bit with the parents. Campaigning was like that, attaching itself snugly to everything else he did.

Fans whooped and chatted and clapped in the packed stands, while the air carried whiffs of hot popcorn and roasted peanuts. Jake sidestepped some dark, sticky splotches on his way up the cement stairs.

It was billed as the Tri-County Championship, which explained the size of the turbulent crowd. A week before, Cassavora really laid it to Peterson County and Foster County had done the same about a month earlier. So this was it. Cassavora and Foster, the game fans pondered and dreaded and craved every season. Wild banners fluttered, bands blared from both sidelines. Betsy was in the crowd somewhere, but a quick scan didn't pinpoint her. It was just as well. Neither of her folks had spoken to him since the shooting.

The Cassavora-Foster rivalry stretched back a long, rocky way, haunted with ghosts. People still exchanged angry words over the 1955 Championship game. Foster's winning touchdown was, as one wag put it, "A gift that rivaled the second-coming of Jesus Christ." The night following that game, a group of Foster students returned to plow up the field and paint the final score on the new scoreboard. "More than a game" became the slogan that cut like a razor through the fabric of Cassavora football and the very honor of Cassavora County. It had become, through myth and memory, the focus of every season, the measurement of success or failure. Was it a good year for you? Hell, yes! We kicked Foster's butt!

High banks of stadium lights circled the stadium and tried their best, but managed only a glow in the fading, dust-tinged sunlight.

No sooner did Jake steal a place for himself on the end of a cement bleacher, next to a hefty and rabid Cassavora fan, than the two high school bands converged in the center of the field to do traditional justice to the Star Spangled Banner. On his feet, one among many, he stood at attention, his hand over his heart.

The National Anthem held a special place for him. Too many of his friends had paid a high price to defend that song and the ragged flag it sang about. A lump rose in his throat, his chest tightened and he had to hold back spontaneous tears. As the anthem played, out of the corner of his eye, he saw two teenage boys walk by the stands toward the chain link fence marking the edge of the playing field. Their voices carried, interlacing profanities, kicking at the dirt. A drum roll and crash of cymbals moved Francis Scott Key's composition to its conclusion. The boys kept talking, joking, hands in their jeans pockets.

With the dying notes, Jake walked quickly down the steps and crossed the ten feet separating him from the boys. They didn't pay any attention until his voice flashed at them. "Didn't you hear the National Anthem? How about showing a little respect for your country?" His eyes burned holes.

One of the kids just looked at him and then looked back at the field, the measure of his contempt. The other scanned him up and down, secure, confident. "It's none of your business, so fuck you!" Several people heard the challenge. Faces near the edge of the stands turned, waiting for the response, maybe hoping to see something more.

"I should have known I was dealing with trash." Jake said it quietly. It wasn't what he wanted to do. Anger boiled quickly like bitter bile. As an officer, no one ever spoke to him that way, but then the men and women he served with would never have been joking and kicking dirt during the National Anthem. These scraggly, openly defiant punks made him clench his fists. His face burned. He'd bluffed and lost and felt helpless he couldn't do anything more. What had he expected? A quick apology? A frantic, yes, sir?

Back in his seat, he talked himself back down. They weren't worth the frustration, the embarrassment, the loss of control. Why should embarrassment flood him, make him feel so alone? He'd done his duty, but not a soul had understood or stepped in to help. The little bastards! The need to hurt, to kill, to inflict pain turned his body to inflexible steel.

Names of the starting lineups crackled over the speakers and Jake allowed himself to relax, to reluctantly refocus on the playing field. He glanced again toward the wire fence. Where the boys had stood, there was now a blank spot, an embarrassed memory. They'd move on and so should he. Maybe he'd scared them off.

The whomp of the kickoff, the yell of the crowd, the kids on the field took over. Jake slid back into contented excitement.

Every now and again he'd look around, wondering if he should do some campaigning, but decided against it. One thing he'd learned about talking to voters was your mind had to be right and just now their minds were on their boys playing high school football. Football around here was a kind of physical religion. Besides, Jake had been at it all afternoon and the bone weariness of an endless task.

Cassavora lost by two points. Jake heard more than one wistful remark about how different it was to see a new coach on the sideline. He marveled how the whole business about the old coach had quieted down, as well as the Caldwell Robbins controversy about dirty books in the school library. Once in a while waves crashed and then the sea went placid. This was one of those times.

As he jostled through the crowd on the way back to his car, a tall, rotund man, with two days of beard, faded jeans, stained baseball cap and a XXL-sized tee shirt that asked, "What Would Jesus Do?" stepped in front of him. Jake side stepped, thinking it was just another confused fan, looking for his vehicle. What would Jesus do? "Go to Synagogue? Celebrate Passover? Give up pork barbecue?"

"Mister!" The man bellowed at him, startling him, blocking his path. The guy must have weighed three hundred pounds, although most of it was belly. "That was my kid you were yelling at!" His breath carried the fragrance of day old meat. What kid? What was he talking about? Then it hit him. The Anthem incident.

"I can see the resemblance." Jake stepped back, hoping he wasn't about to put on a parking lot performance with Hulk Hogan's cousin. His arms hung loose at his sides, one foot slightly forward.

"You think that's funny?" The man stared at Jake like a gunslinger in a B grade movie. Wisps of sweat soaked hairs curled out from under the greasy ball cap.

"I take the anthem seriously."

"Who do you think you are?" The man's eyes had a washed out, yellowish glow. The corners of his mouth curved down.

"He was showing disrespect." Jake's chin jutted slightly as he looked up. "Somebody should have taught him better." He wanted to back down and prevent serious bodily injury, but his cursed pride wouldn't let him.

"It's none of your business what my son does!" The man took another step forward. "Oh." A glimmer of recognition flashed across his face. "I know you!" There was a pause. "You're not even a Christian!" The immediate danger seemed to pass. The man took a step back. "You keep away from my boy, you understand me?"

"Believe me when I say I never want to see him again." By now Jake knew nothing was going to happen, with people meandering and cars pulling out.

The man gave him a parting shot. "You've got a smart mouth, but I'm warning you." He pointed a chubby finger at Jake's face. "Don't you go messin' with me or mine!" He stalked away, readjusting the baseball cap and glared back. He climbed into a faded green pickup truck, slammed the door. Tires crunched in the loose gravel as he drove off.

Hyenas can smell blood. Another man, smaller than the first, walked by Jake, muttering. "You're the one caused us to lose this game." He stalked off into the crowd.

Jake fumed on the way back to his car. He'd made that kid shoot a hole through his windows? These people didn't need better education, they needed education, period.

Jake knew how close he'd come to losing the election right there in the parking lot. People whose small lives had been ruined by two points in a football game probably hung with a lot of other small minds. A single blow, a single headline and his fragile campaign could collapse like a tent in a windstorm. Maybe that's what should happen. This was no fuckin' fun. He alternated between anger and relief. Getting into this race, he never figured on having to deal with cretins. He never even knew they existed.

What if the guy had hit him? What if the whole town was just sorry the quarterback didn't kill him outright?

A vague, but steady ache of conscience pulled at him, as though he had done something wildly wrong in either speaking up or backing off. It was the Star Spangled Banner for God's sake, and it was his house and his neighbor's daughter who'd been shot at. The incidents wound together. Around here everything seemed connected.

The next morning, he still wondered how many others in the community felt like those guys did last night. Quite a few, he imagined. Probably farmers and realtors and bankers and mechanics and plumbers who couldn't care less whether or not the county was providing matchless education to its children or just going through the motions, who figured high school was just a rite of passage and nothing more. He was never going to be able to explain the difference or get anyone to pay attention. What did they care if their kids spoke French or Spanish or read Shakespeare? They had no inkling of the changes in the world, or anything else outside this little county, where they lived and worked, slept and died. Maybe it had always been this way. Maybe his life in the Air Force was an anomaly, an isolated case of working toward a common purpose of trying to improve and learn. Maybe this whole campaign was farcical, with victory going to the one whose sights were set the lowest.

The phone brought Jake out of his reverie. He cradled the receiver between his neck and shoulder and closed the newspaper.

"Good morning, Mr. Morgan. Are you the one who's running for the school board?"

"Yes." He hesitated, hoping it wasn't another frontal assault by the Christian Coalition or an irate football fan.

"My name is Bobby Jones, Mr. Morgan. I was at the ball game last night, and I just wanted to tell you I admire you for standing up to those kids. They shouldn't have been stomping around during the anthem."

"Thank you, Mr. Jones. Not everybody agrees with you, but sometimes I just have to speak out." Even to himself he sounded as relieved as an armadillo at an underpass.

"We need more people like you. I didn't mean to bother you, but I wanted to let you know how I felt."

Maybe the world wasn't as skewed as it looked five minutes ago, Jake thought. Tweedledee and Tweedledum. Cursed and applauded. Maybe this campaign was worth the occasional close encounters of the scary kind. Maybe making a difference was the real issue, pulling back the curtains and letting a little light into the county, win or lose. So what if every now and then you found Earthquake Calhoun trying to yank the curtains closed again? Christ, why couldn't he make up his own mind?

Then Cecilia called and his world really brightened.

Martha Bonner is one of the finest writers this state or any other state has produced. The Polecat Tree is a true classic. —A Cassavora High School English teacher

Red and white Able Perkins signs stretched across people's lawns from one side of the county to the other. You couldn't miss them unless you stayed inside with the curtains drawn. God only knew how much money the man was putting in the campaign for a job that paid fifty bucks a meeting. But instead of intimidating him, the signs only egged Jake on. By late October, he was on his third tattered map of neighborhoods and voting districts. Phones calls and letters and getting stopped in Grand Foods was so much a part of his life, he felt neglected if someone didn't stop him to chat. More people than he'd imagined patted his back and gave him credit.

The election barreled ahead, a locomotive at full steam. You couldn't turn on the radio without hearing a fool making promises he couldn't keep to other fools he didn't know. Just a couple of more weeks, Jake kept telling himself as his feet ached and he plodded from house to house. At least it was getting cooler. He couldn't have lasted much longer. There were house things and novel writing things lying dormant, casualties of an election that ate ravenously at his time and energy.

Things had gotten considerably better with Cecilia. They'd shared many more nights of passion, many more evenings of reading and sharing.

He stepped onto the porch of a large and older home. White columns and great spreading trees that probably shaded Sherman on his march to the sea. The brass knocker clunked as subtly as a hammer on an anvil.

The door cracked open. Jake glimpsed a plain face, faded eyes framed by silver spectacles and a shock of billowy white hair. The soft voice of an elderly woman asked, "May I help you, young man?"

"Yes, ma'am," Jake began, but got no further.

"If you're from the police, I already talked to them." She paused, looked down. Her lips still moved, as if warming up to make a run at another statement. Jake waited.

"You see," she continued, once again looking up at him, "I didn't want those policemen to think I had anything to do with it." She sighed, using logic only the very young and very old understand. "I guess I was worried about getting someone in trouble, but now that I think about it, I know exactly who it was. It was the football coach. I've seen his face in the newspaper so often, I couldn't very well not recognize him. I spoke to my cousin, Florence, and she said I should speak up. Do you think I'm doing the right thing?"

The thrill of discovery ran up Jake's spine, like reaching down to pick up a wind blown piece of paper and coming up with a hundred dollar bill. Although the death of the coach had drifted to the back page, it was still very much a topic of fanciful speculation.

"The boosters in Rockford County had something to do with it," one man opined.

"No, it was losing the job at the high school that broke his heart."

"Well, you know, he had a drinking problem." And so it would go.

Now Jake felt like a man who had stumbled on stage with a play in progress. This lady obviously knew something, had seen something and if he played the part right, he was about to discover what.

"So, you were saying?"

"Would you like to come in and sit awhile?" The inside of the home was what you'd expect. A stuffy smell of ancient dust and uncompromising solitude hung in the air. He sat on a chintz loveseat, no softer than a plank bench. All the furnishings were dark wood, or beige, or tiny floral patterns. Every horizontal space held regiments of framed photographs, delicate plates, figurines.

"I don't see many visitors, except the other policemen." Utterly polite and soft-spoken, the woman was a patient watcher of the world, just tired of the race and waiting for the finish line. Jake studied her features, the slight body, sharp cheeks and nose. Suddenly, he knew he was talking to Miss Martha Bonner, author of the Southern classic, *The Polecat Tree*.

"Miss Bonner, why don't you just tell me what you were about to tell me on the porch?" Jake sat back, crossed a leg, tried to be as non-threatening as a torpid house cat.

"It was very dark ... " and then she proceeded to lay out what she had seen in the early morning hours, on the day of the coach's demise. But aside from the coach, she wouldn't name any names, preferring to talk directly to the sheriff. Jake didn't press her. When she finished her story, he said he'd send the sheriff down. She said that would be fine.

"I'm so tired of keeping secrets," she sighed. "I've been keeping secrets my whole life. Most of them are nothing." She paused to gaze through the gauzy beige curtains onto her side yard. Even in October, crowds of green hedge were topped with blazes of color.

"The most important secret was the one about the book."

"The book?"

"My book, or rather my sister's book."

"You mean The Polecat Tree?"

"Yes," she said slowly, dreamily. "It took my sister fifteen years to write that book. Then she died and I knew I had to get it published for her memory. But, everyone always assumed it was mine. They never really asked me. Not the publisher, not the editor, not any of the people from the radio or newspaper. They acted as if I were the author and God help me, I didn't deny it. Years later, they did ask when I was going to write another one. I didn't know what to tell them. Do you understand, young man?"

Jake said he did. "You loved your sister, didn't you, Miss Bonner."

"Oh, yes," she said, wistfully, "I loved her very much."

"Well, I think you did the right thing."

"You don't find my secret terrible?"

"No, ma'am. Your sister's memory was written in that book and you brought it to millions of people."

"But, it wasn't mine."

"No, but the memories were. Just think how much joy that book has brought to the world. If you had told them your sister wrote it, they wouldn't have asked you to be on radio. They wouldn't have written about you and the book in the newspapers and magazines. Your sister's work would have withered. Now it's one of the classics. I'm sure she loves you even more for what you did." He'd also been staring out the window at the flowers, blowing slightly in the breeze. When he looked back at her, Miss Martha Bonner was daintily dabbing at her eyes with a small linen handkerchief.

By the time he left, Martha had cheered up a little bit. Jake could tell the unburdening did her some good. Now he needed to take a little emotional weight off himself. It was a tossup as to whether he should drop in on the sheriff or give him a call. All the trails around here seemed to lead to Sam Goddard's office.

49

You could beat 'em with a whip, but it wouldn't do any good. Most crimes are crimes of the spirit, and most people don't even know when they're guilty. —Sheriff Sam Goddard

"Mrs. Arston, is there something you wanted to tell us?" Goddard spoke slowly. When the teacher didn't say anything he added, "We found the loose ceiling tile in the garage and your prints all over the place."

"So what? I used to help at his house all the time."

"The dust. The dust had been recently rearranged and the prints were fresh. Lots of oil. Now, you want to tell us?"

"Nothing to tell." Mrs. Arston flashed a quick, defensive smile, a weak rendition of you-can't-make-me-tell.

"Well, have it your way. You've been read your rights. Book her, John and throw her in a cell until her lawyer shows up."

She was halfway to the door, John Howard's strong hand on her elbow, when she turned around. "What are you going to charge me with?"

"Well, let's see," Goddard said. "There's breaking and entering, robbery, interfering with an investigation, concealing evidence, lying to police. You have a preference?"

"I ... I didn't kill him."

"Didn't say you did. But, you were there, weren't you." It wasn't a question. "The call reporting a body came from your cell phone. The people next door saw you leave in the middle of the night."

Roberta Arston didn't say anything, just shook her head no. "Go ahead. Put her in a cell for a while."

*****

The box contained a packet of photos. The first couple showed the coach standing behind Mrs. Arston, his arms wrapped around her, both of them clothed and smiling. Then it got interesting. She had larger breasts than Sam had imagined, the nipples dark and protruding.

"Looks like they tried to illustrate the Kama Sutra," Deputy Howard said.

"Yeah, she's pretty flexible."

"Flexible enough to drop her date off at the Post Office and trundle on home?"

"Why'd she wait so long to go pick up the goods?" Howard looked a mite puzzled.

"At first she had no choice. Then, she got bolder. She was pretty sure we hadn't found them or we would have said something by now. Eventually, she had to do something and figured it had been long enough. But, damn she was sloppy about it."

"Maybe the patrol car spooked her."

"Yeah, maybe, or maybe she hadn't found what she was looking for and planned on coming back."

"What could be worse than the Kama Sutra photos?"

"Yeah, what?"

"I got a feeling keeping her locked up ain't going to lead to answers."

"Okay. Turn her lose tomorrow morning."

"Giving her some rope?"

"Amen."

50

I never vote. If you vote you're liable for jury duty. Besides, all the candidates are about the same. —A neighborhood resident talking to Jake Morgan

Novembers were hard to predict in Cassavora, leap years even harder and Jake's election night was no exception. Evenings had cooled considerably from the flame-broiled summer, but still weren't cold, just smoother and more rounded as night drifted in. Women who gathered around the courthouse square wore cotton sweaters or folded their arms, anticipating a light chill. The men were still in polo shirts, except for some of the businessmen who had on coats and ties. The sun was down, but sundown was like turning off a stove. The glow lingered.

A low hum of conversation emanated from the scattered crowd, punctuated with nervous laughter. All of it was just election night preliminaries, the chance for people to gather and openly share opinions with their friends, or anyone else.

Jake knew about what to expect. That was before he bridged the great gulf and became a candidate himself. Overheard conversations tended to be outspoken and emotional, but only in generalities, with little specificity on either the issues, or the candidates themselves. It was nervous talk, born of a social need to say something knowledgeable, without the apprehension of offending.

"We have got to do something about taxes!"

"Well, now, Charlie, the gubmint has got to have some revenue."

"I'm not saying they don't need money."

"Well, that's what it sounded like you were sayin'." And so it went. Too polite or timid to come right out and name their favorites, the men communicated around a candidate's main points, debating the pros and cons. When they staked out their territory on one particular topic, like dogs marking bushes, they moved on to another. Women took part in these distractions with no less fortitude, but their minds turned more toward school safety, home issues and matters of integrity. Jake's name came up more than once, often connected with a collection of unsavory rumors. He had his defenders and detractors.

"The girl was there late at night."

"But, her mama told me she'd sent her over to borrow something."

"Still, it don't look right and I can tell you her dad wasn't too dadburned pleased."

"Bryan, you'd be pleased if somebody took a pot shot at your daughter?"

When the women's voices raised an octave, their husbands gently chided them, "Now Wilma don't upset yourself," or "I didn't know you felt so strongly." With the younger women, their voices could be a little more strident and their husbands grinned sheepishly and shrugged their shoulders.

The ritual of face-to-face political participation gave voice to verbally optimistic anxiety. Yet, there was something about standing around outside the courthouse Jake found very satisfying and very Southern. It was more than the soft, lilting cadence of speech and more than the heavy air. Maybe it was the sifting sound of the leaves in the live oaks or the tall specter of the old courthouse, shadowed out across the square. This was a gathering of democratic souls as they should be gathered on the second Tuesday in November. It brought comfort to his own restless spirit. One part of him would have been content just to wade through the crowd and walk back home, never knowing the outcome of the election. The other part of him hungered for the scores to be posted and the results known. The gathering was a pat on the back for all the time he'd spent on the edge of the sword, protecting the country and the multihued strands of people and opinions that bound it together.

Later on tallies would be scribed on big chalkboards, rolled into the main courtroom. Few people were in there yet, content to stand outside, rub elbows and chat. Few paused to think how rare this placid democracy was in a world swirling with tumultuous conflicts.

Betsy surprised Jake by stopping for a quick chat, reviewing some of the highlights of the election and wondering out loud what everyone's chances were. Two teenage boys dropped by to schmooze.

"Wish they could vote," Jake said, "That would give me four sure votes. Betsy," he quickly added, "you'd vote for your dear old neighbor who almost got you shot, wouldn't you?"

"Only out of pity."

"Seriously, Mr. Morgan." A man in an orange sweatshirt strolled up in time to hear Betsy's sarcasm. "You've got to figure your chances are pretty good." The rule about stepping around direct conversation didn't apply when you were face to face with one of the players. Then protocol required you tell him he was a good man, ran a wonderful campaign, and was about to win.

"Everyone I talked to in my neighborhood was impressed you came by personally." The middle-aged woman with him echoed his optimism.

"But you know," blathered one of the outside the courthouse philosophers, "you just never know what goes on inside that voting booth."

"This is my first time out, so I have no idea. They don't take polls to figure out who's going to win a school board election."

Cleveland stopped and spoke briefly, telling Jake to keep his chin up. Jake agreed he would. They parted with backslapping and handshaking, but Jake's mind really wasn't on what was going on around him. His thoughts were of that afternoon, when he went to cast his vote and saw the long lines of people. Most were complete strangers to him and they would shortly go in, give their name to the volunteer clerks, who would verify the particulars, pass out ballots and usher them into the booths. Strangers would see Jake's name printed in black and white and the whole county would get to tell him if he personally were good enough, if they had enough faith in him to put the fate of their children in his hands.

The ritual went on all over the county at voting locations with odd sounding names, like Whippoorwill Church, School, East Chancy, Mogel Creek, Lightning Round, Angel Corner, and half a dozen others. Most of the names didn't make sense unless you knew some county history. At Lightning Round, the voting was done at a civic center, but some seventy-five years earlier a huge bolt of lightening cleaved a tree and left a big round scorched spot in the earth. Names took on a life of their own in Cassavora.

Seeing those long lines also brought home to Jake how many people there were in the county and how many he had never met or spoken a word to? He had thin soles to prove how hard he'd tried, but even in a small county you just couldn't cover it all. He wondered if he should have put up some signs, or at least taken an ad out in *The Advocate*. But, it didn't pay to worry. His plan had always been to make this a personal campaign and he'd stuck with the plan. He never ran across any other candidates on his neighborhood walks. They, one and all, went with the signs and the ads. Funny, he thought, I'm supposed to be the radical, the outsider, the person who knows least about what's good for the county, but I'm the only politician, who did it the old fashioned way.

In the midst of his reverie, Jimmy Joe walked up, grinned, but didn't say anything. Under the pressures of the evening, Jake just couldn't resist, so he popped the ultimate question. "Hey there, Jimmy Joe, do things look good for me tonight?"

"Better late than never," Jimmy Joe shot back.

Whatever that meant. Maybe it was time to break out the tarot cards or call a psychic hot line. "Your grandmother was born a long time ago."

"My god, how could you possibly know that?"

Jimmy Joe was still grinning, so out of a total lack of things to talk about in a critical, nerve jarring time like the present, Jake asked him, "Whatcha been up to, Jimmy Joe?"

"Proud as a peacock!"

There was a message tucked in there somewhere. "Seen some fascinating things have you?"

Jimmy's grin faded. "Show me the way to go home."

"You want to go home?" Jimmy shook his head.

"Dead as a doornail."

"What are you talking about?"

Jimmy raised his arm and pointed down the street. "Over that way?" Jimmy nodded. "What's over that way?" Jake looked out past the crowd and didn't see anything except a few buildings, a tree- lined street and the dark shape of an American flag in the distance, by the Post Office.

"Nothing down there I can see, Jimmy." Then all of it hit him with the clarity of a snapshot. His brain churned. Jake took potshot glances around the crowd to see if the man he needed was close at hand. No luck. He patted Jimmy Joe on the back, told him he'd talk to him later. Jimmy's grin returned. "You may turn out to be the man of the hour, Jimmy Joe."

A man in Khakis and polo shirt stood on the courthouse steps and waved people inside. "If ya'll d'like to come on into the main courtroom, we're startin' to git the results."

People, still talking, strode up the steps, then hesitated, then stopped. Then they turned and starting running and scrambling, a wild stampede, trying to get back down the steps and as far away as possible.

"He's got a gun!"

Pandemonium. Men dragged their wives and sweethearts, pulled their arms, yelling. Women and some of the men screamed, surprised, and scared. Some didn't know why, but panic is its own reason.

Tangles of cars revved up and pulled away helter skelter from the both sides of the street. One car careened off another, the drivers ducked down so low they couldn't see what was in front of them. Two other cars banged their sides in a screech of torn metal, then sped off without stopping. A pickup truck backfired and more people yelled.

Jake crouched behind an oak tree and scanned the diminishing crowd for Betsy. He didn't see her.

At the courthouse, the front doors slammed shut, but the lights stayed on. Jake saw no shadows in the illuminated windows, heard no shots.

On raw impulse, he sprinted to the side of the building and pressed himself against the bricks. Half way down the wall he came to a window, about five feet over his head. Some of the bricks protruded, providing a shallow corner to brace his hand. Like a clumsy spider he eked his way high enough to reach up for the sill, then with both hands pulled up and looked in, his feet dangling below him.

A group of election officials cowered in one corner, some sitting on the floor, others hovered around them. Jake counted five. Three men, two women, none looked like they might move, short of being cattle prodded. A man paced in front of them, holding a shotgun across the crook of his arm. He wasn't wearing a mask. He turned toward the window and Jake recognized the wild-eyed face of the Reverend Edward Peabody. The Rev also recognized Jake.

*****

When the call came to the Sheriff's Department, Sam was at home. Deputy Howard was gone, too. John Paul took the call and fumbled around in the desk. He grabbed the checklist for emergency actions, but then something else caught his eye. S.W.A.T. procedures. Maybe he should call Sheriff Goddard, but how was that going to look? You get a situation, you deal with it. He was the man. This was his chance, his shining moment. He'd call the sheriff later.

*****

Jake dropped to the ground, felt a sharp pain as his ankle gave. He hobbled back toward the wide sycamore tree that had been his refuge and heard the window open behind him.

"Ye shall find Gawd's wrath a frightful sight!"

Jake expected a blast of buckshot, but he kept going toward the tree, gimpy, but not slow. He reached it. Still no shot. The window slammed, just prior to the scream of tires and screech of brakes announcing the arrival of Cassavora's masters of tactical operations. The S.W.A.T. team had arrived.

"Spread out! Keep low!" came the cry of a black clad avenger, his bullhorn to his lips. "Whoever you are, come on out with your hands up."

"It's the Reverend Peabody," Jake said loudly still crouched and rubbing his ankle.

"You don't look like the Reverend Peabody."

"Not me!" Jake pointed. "The guy inside the courthouse with the shotgun!"

"They're holding the Reverend hostage?"

"No, he's the one with the shotgun."

"Hold on, Reverend! We're coming to get you!" The S.W.A.T. team moved into what the untrained eye might assume was an assault formation, two members guarding the edges and two racing up the front steps. Before they got there, a shotgun blast shattered the glass and wiped out great chunks of the door frames. Heavyset men in black raced back down the concrete steps and scampered behind the S.W.A.T. truck.

"Prepare to open fire!"

"Hold it!" Jake yelled. "There's a bunch of people in there!" This time his words stopped the team in its tracks. They looked toward him, hearing the command tone in his voice and wondering if he was supposed to be giving them orders.

The head of the team raced over and stooped next to Jake. "So what's going on in there?"

"The Reverend Peabody has a shotgun and hostages."

"Peabody has the weapon?" The voice was incredulous. "What's he want?"

"He ain't saying." The guy in black seemed to ponder, hesitating. "Look," Jake continued. "There's only one of him. How about you engage him in conversation and send some guys in the back door?"

"How do you know there's only one?"

"I looked."

The S.W.A.T. leader thought a split second. "Hank, Tom, come here on the double!" Moments later, the leader chimed in on the bullhorn,

"Reverend, stop acting like a fool and come on out here. You don't want to hurt anybody!"

There was silence. "Reverend, you don't want to do this."

"Somebody has got to stop the evil in this county." The answer was yelled out the front door and echoed off the trees.

"Keep talking," Jake urged.

The two men who'd gone for the back entrance came back. "He's locked the door and looks like he's stacked some furniture. We ain't gettin' in there without a whole bunch of noise." They stood, staring, waiting for instructions.

Jake broke the ice. "Keep talking on the bull horn. You two guys go back and make all the noise you want. He's going to be distracted. I'll go in the front door."

"I can't let you do that. You're a civilian. Best to leave this to the professionals."

"Any of your guys have training?" Jake looked around. Nobody said anything. He looked the part, sounded the part. That was good enough for guys with no plan.

"Okay, then," the guy who seemed to be in charge said, "but, be careful." He sounded apprehensive, as any man would be, carrying a weapon in his first day on the job.

Jake nodded. In the city, any city, and even in most towns, the cops would have hustled him back behind a barrier and told him to shut his mouth and let them do their job. But, these guys had arrived at the party and didn't know how to dance. The guy next to Jake looked relieved. His eyes shifted to the building and back to the S.W.A.T. truck in worried little jumps.

At least Jake knew the person he was dealing with. That little chat with Peabody might have been irritating, but now the man knew his name.

Jake jogged toward the courthouse in a crouch, stepping lightly on his bad ankle, eyes glued on the yellow glare of light coming out the busted front door. He stopped by the stone steps, still in a crouch.

"Reverend Peabody! This is Jake Morgan. I wanna talk to you."

Silence reined, the moments creeping by. Jake listened for footsteps, some warning the Rev might be ready to let go another blast. There wasn't any noise behind him either. In fact, the whole area had drifted to silence except for the occasional chirp of an insect.

"Reverend?"

A shadow loomed near the door and Jake braced, ready to leap aside, but the shadow stayed steady. "I know who yew are."

"Reverend, what's this all about?"

"It's about the devil in this county!"

"Listen, Reverend, I know you're a good man, but this isn't going to help matters."

"You don't know anything! You're a Jew!"

"Why don't you come on out and let's talk about it."

"Godless county!"

"Things may not be as bad as you think. You don't want to hurt anyone, right? How about letting those people go?"

"Ye shall know the truth and the truth shall set you free."

"Good plan. Come on out."

Jake wondered if the cops were headed toward the back door. He glanced over his shoulder. Nobody had moved. What the hell were these cretins waiting for? He swung his arm, motioning them to circle the building. Still, nobody moved. He thought about going up the front steps, depending on Peabody not shooting. Brave, but stupid.

Maybe not so stupid. Peabody had only fired that one shot and evidently hadn't intended to kill or maim, otherwise he would have let the troopers get closer. Then again, maybe he hadn't known they were coming. He had to have known. It was the only shot he'd fired.

Two more shadows came to the door, then stepped out into the light. "I'm sending two people out. They're from my church and godfearingchristians." A man and a woman hustled down the steps and a black clad trooper led them into the shadows.

"Good man, Reverend. Think about this awhile and send the others out. It's not too late. We can settle this without anyone getting hurt."

The shadow that had been Peabody disappeared. Looked like the little chat was over for a while. Jake, still crouched, headed up the steps, but stopped when headlights caught him in their glare and he heard the squeal of brakes.

Goddard leapt out of his car and motioned for Jake to get his ass back to the car, even as he grabbed the bullhorn. "Peabody, get yourself out here. Now. And if you want to live, you'd better not be carrying a weapon!" Two more cars full of deputies pulled in behind him.

The sheriff glanced at his S.W.A.T. team and waved them to spread out, circle the building. This time the men in black didn't hesitate.

Goddard turned to Jake, who was standing beside him. "So, what we got?" Jake gave him the basics, noting the sheriff hadn't asked any members of the team. Sam listened, didn't say anything, felt a tug at his elbow.

"Sheriff, you mind if I talk to him?" The sheriff could barely make out Reverend Monroe's features in the shadows.

He thought a moment, then handed him the bullhorn. Monroe waved it away. "I'm going inside."

"Can't let you do that. Too dangerous." Ignoring the sheriff, Monroe stepped around the car and walked briskly toward the bottom of the courthouse steps. "Shit!" Goddard said under his breath.

"Want me to go get him, boss?" It was the head of the S.W.A.T. team. Goddard shook his head no.

Too late. "I just hope he doesn't get himself killed." He thought about sending a deputy to tackle him. Too little too late.

A scuffle might cause problems and shouting out something was even worse. He knew what he should have done. He should have cordoned off the whole front of the courthouse. This mess was what happened when you were working with amateur actors in a bad play and stepped onto the stage in the second act.

Reverend Monroe stopped at the bottom of the steps. "Edward!" he called. "Edward! This is Lester Monroe. I want to chat with you."

"What do you want?" The reply came from deep within the courthouse, distant, with a bit of a cavernous echo.

"I want to come inside and pray with you."

There was hesitation, but only slightly. "Okay, come on in, but this better not be a trick."

"I don't joke about praying, Edward."

Reverend Monroe stepped over the broken glass and into the light streaming out the front door. He went inside.

Outside, nobody heard anything. Even Goddard had to check his nerves. He thought about sending the team closer.

A slew of hostages came storming out of what was left of the front door, almost tumbling down the steps, fast enough not to catch everybody off guard and make the S.W.A.T. team raise their weapons. Goddard stepped forward and waved them down.

Regular deputies moved in and pulled the released hostages back behind the cover of the vehicles. Goddard and Jake waited. Then two more shadows appeared. Monroe had his arm about Peabody's shoulder. Neither man carried a weapon.

As the squad car drove away, carrying Peabody off to jail, Goddard turned to Reverend Monroe. "So, what did you tell him?"

Before he got an answer, a deputy dashed between them. "Sheriff, we got one of our cars crunched. The S.W.A.T. truck backed into it."

It was two more hours before the ballots were bundled off to the courthouse annex and the registrars and helpers calmed down enough to begin to tally the results. After having a shotgun shoved in their faces they'd wanted to call it a night.

Jake's adrenaline gradually sunk to a normal level and the election came back into focus. He had a mind that quickly compartmentalized complications and narrowed in on what was important at a particular time. It was a skill every fighter pilot needed if he sincerely wanted to live to fight another day.

It didn't do to be thinking about the argument you'd had with your wife when you were fifteen thousand feet in the air, hurling your body at the ground.

Apparently, there were a lot of other compartmental-izers in the county. Citizens straggled back in, a few at first, then more, until the crowd was almost up to its original size and noise level. People wanted to talk, to feel alive. "Could you believe that damn preacher?"

"I told you all along he had too much rum in his fruit cake!"

"Marvin, don't talk that way about a man of the cloth," a stout wife chimed in. "He's just misguided."

Corrected yet again, her husband rolled his eyes and snorted. "Did you hear what Monroe told him to get him to give himself up?"

"What?"

"He said Jesus didn't use a shotgun to clean out the temple."

"Well, we can be damn happy the son-of-a-bitch didn't offer the bastard a bull whip. Them preachers stick together."

"Marvin!"

Before long, everyone's attention was back on why they had come to the courthouse and the election results. Only now they were across the street, in a smaller room, more modern and brighter than the old courtroom. The noise calmed to whispers, the topics crept away from the shotgun-toting preacher and back to politics.

Jake felt the pulse of the crowd and knew this moment, standing in this courtroom, was the essence of every day he had spent in the military, every combat mission he'd flown, every brother-in-arms he'd lost. He'd never thought of it before. He and his buddies often joked about defending the skies that canopy free nations. But, this was it. This was the democracy they'd defended.

Moments dragged on and the numbers squeaked onto the dark board and the crowd alternately talked and sighed and dove back into the silence of anticipation. Jake pressed two fingers to his temple, felt the blood pounding.

The dangers that climbed into the cockpit with him, the cannons he'd faced, all came down to what was taking place at this moment.

Until now, he'd never distilled it into a simple election, a simple vote for county clerk and school board. Housewives and husbands, politicians and scoundrels in this packed little room didn't know what he knew and would never breathe a word of thanks, but Jake had guarded each of their destinies, more than any lawyer or doctor, more than any banker or salesman. Now it was their turn to decide his destiny. It wasn't the same as passing judgment on him personally. The very act of voting settled that once and for all. Their votes, for him or not, meant he had done his duty to his country and done it well. Without even knowing it, these people had trusted him to keep their homes and loved ones safe. Now they would simply tell him if they trusted him to serve on the Cassavora Board of Education.

51

If Mr. Morgan gets elected, this county will be draped in sin. He's a godless man. —Purcell Southmore

Names hastily scratched in white chalk covered two black boards in a corner of the annex, but Jake's vision tunneled to his own and that of Able Perkins. With two small precincts reporting, Able led him 251 votes to 198. People patted his back in passing, mumbled for him to hang in there. He had always hung in there. In a few more minutes, the numbers trickled in to put Perkins ahead 392 to 287. This wasn't CNN or Fox that could predict the outcome of a national election based on eleven percent of the vote.

Outside, night turned the world black, but inside, the room blazed with bare electric lights and expectation. Precinct after precinct reported. Men and women scurried out from a back room, looked down at hastily scrawled notes and changed the white numbers on the dark boards. The crowd ebbed and flowed, getting noisy and dense when new numbers appeared, then gradually thinning out.

Able beat Jake at Whippoorwill Church and he beat Able at School and East Chancy. Perkins took a heavy vote at Mogel Creek, only to lose big at Lightning Round. Going into the last precinct, the tally was Able Perkins 2687, Jake Morgan 2375. Angel Corner had over 600 registered voters and the turnout was averaging about forty percent. Jake did the math. With about 240 votes, he couldn't pull this thing out. Hope filled his heart, but reality loomed.

Defeat didn't have the bitter taste he thought it would. He'd run a great campaign, overcoming the long odds of Perkins' place in the community and his own lack of political backing or finesse. He'd roamed the county, listening to citizens just like himself who had hopes and dreams for their children and knew the value of education.

Next morning, *The Advocate* ran a special election edition. Chairman Tom Millage smiled broadly from the front page. Caldwell Robbins, Jake's initial aim point, had lost his seat. Gloria Sweeney and Gordon Cuspid won reelection. Jake's name lay buried halfway down one column, but he didn't bother to read the comments. Always looking ahead and never looking back had always served him well. He had his writing and his life. He had a backyard overlooking a lake and a chest full of cigars. Life bloomed just as sweetly as it had been the day before, maybe more sweetly. He'd done his duty once again, run a good, honest campaign and now he could relax.

Maria McDuff called to offer condolences. Jake said he didn't need any.

"I know," Maria said, "but I also know about loses and how they can make you stare inwardly until you burn a hole in yourself."

"Hey, I'm tough! I can stand a few inward stares," he said.

"But I read what Purcell said about you being immoral, and it just made me cringe."

"Purcell Southmore?"

"Yes." Her voice dropped, sounding thin and wispy.

"It sounds like you know the man."

"Oh, yes, Mr. Morgan, I know the man very well."

"Anything you'd care to talk about?"

"No." Her voice sounded strong again. "I just wanted to say how sorry I am. I really wanted you on the board. I thought you'd be a voice that might be able to open the county up, rearrange the way people look at education."

"I appreciate that." But, he didn't tell her what he was thinking. One man can't change things by himself and Jake was tired.

"You want to have a cup of coffee?" Her question caught him off guard.

"Uh, sure. When?"

"Now?"

They met at Java Jive and sat at a corner table. "There's a burning question." Maria said it with a laugh.

"Go ahead."

"Why did you become a Jew?"

"Just like that?" It was Jake's turn to smile. "When you said a burning question, I thought you wanted to know about my sex life and I was going to have to lie."

"Feeling a little less constricted now that you're no longer a candidate?"

"Something like that. By the way, how'd you know I was a Jew?"

"Have you forgotten where you're living? Everybody knows you're a Jew. They just don't know why."

"Really? Did I lose the election because I'm a man of mystery or because I'm a Jew?"

"You lost the election because you're too much of a free thinker. At least that's what Mama says."

"And what do you say?"

"I say," Maria hesitated, reached across the table and put her hand over his. "I say you're the most interesting man I've met in a long time, maybe ever." She withdrew her hand and took a sip. Dark eyes sparkled at him over the lip of the cup.

Jake smiled. "So tell me, why did you become a Jew?"

"Whew," he said, "let me catch my breath and scratch my brain. Why did you become a Christian?"

Maria laughed softly. "I asked first." Out of all the things she could have asked, this caught him most by surprise. He expected something about the election or education or what he was going to do next. "Are you in the mood for a serious theological chat or just trying to find out if you can lead me back to Jesus?"

"I'm interested."

"You're Catholic, right?"

"How'd you know?"

"Hispanic, right?"

"Ah, you heard my mom's accent. Actually, we're Dominican. Hispanic is kind of a generic word for a human who speaks Spanish."

"Well, you don't look Swedish."

The joke flew past her. "So, back to my original question."

"I remember going to vacation Bible school as a child. Did you go?"

"That and catechism and a million different religious celebrations. Name a day, we've got a saint and a celebration." He tried to picture her in a sundress, skinned knees, rosy cheeks. Why the hell was he even bothering to discuss this? "I couldn't buy into the Christian dogma, even then. I had questions and no answers."

"About what?"

"About the basics. Couldn't grasp the Trinity, still can't. Couldn't understand why a father would plan to sacrifice his son to take away sin, but there's still sin and the son isn't dead anymore and the father was really the son, too."

"How about Isaac? That's Old Testament."

"Yeah, but that's a parable, not the basis of a major religion and the father wasn't the son. Anyway, we believe what we believe and throw out the rest, so there's no rhyme, no reason and who gives a shit anyway?"

"So you couldn't fathom the father-son part of Christianity. What else?"

What else? That's pretty much the heart of it, isn't it? I could go on, but the coffee would get cold. Anyway," he continued, "I found my path back to Monotheism."

Jake hated getting into philosophical discussions with women. Chances of getting laid went down immeasurably, but the real reason was, he was uncomfortable laying his soul out on the table for public dissection. "So now I've got a question for you," he blurted out, trying to change the subject and catch her off guard. "What's between you and Purcell Southmore?"

"He's the father of my child."

Jake wanted to say, "You don't have a child." But, what would it accomplish to throw it in her face. The revelation hadn't taken in-depth research, no prowling through the records in the courthouse. Miscarriage, abortion, given up for adoption? He had no idea and had no inclination to pry. She didn't work for the school system either, although she had a degree in early childhood education, information compliments of one of his two researchers. Apparently, she had substituted from time to time. This county had so many open secrets. He just nodded, a commiserating shake of the head. "Look," he said, and it was his turn to reach out and touch her hand. She let him. "I know this is hard for you."

"You have no idea."

"But, I have to tell you. I'm seeing someone. It's serious."

She got quiet, her eyes either sad or resigned. He didn't know her well enough to tell, but he knew it wasn't anger he saw. Her shoulders stooped a little. Even in deep embarrassment, she avoided calling attention. He'd expected her to say something, to ask some questions, something. The conversation droned on a little bit, then Maria excused herself. Jake let her go. Christ, he should have handled it better. He'd been too abrupt, as if he'd pulled a gun and shot her in the face. He wanted to take it all back and massage it a little instead of being so straightforward and arrogant. Ah, well. So much for bravado. Despite his flaming libido, he was still a one-woman man after all. Whatever happened to just getting laid?

It wasn't the only surprise he got that night. Jill called. She'd decided to drop the lawsuit. "I'm getting married," she said happily.

Jake didn't say anything.

"Aren't you going to offer congratulations?"

"Yep. Congratulations. Who's the victim?"

"He's a lawyer, real handsome, and rich, and we're going to live on the West Coast. He works with some of the big names." Jill droned on. Jake said the polite things. He also made a mental note to have his lawyer contact hers. He didn't want another day in court when Jill's latest fantasy didn't work out the way she'd planned.

52

I serve the good people of Cassavora County to the best of my ability. I don't sell them real estate or try and tell them how to pray. I only serve. —C2, Chairman, county commissioners and Lawyer

Sam Goddard had it pretty well worked out. He and John Howard had put their heads together. Then, Sam chatted with C2 and here he was. Now they could deal with the superintendent.

Still, there were some loose ends that bothered him. For one, Roberta Arston. He and John Howard even uncovered the secret of the break-in at the coach's house. More photos. But not of him with Mrs. Arston. Teenagers. They hadn't been hidden in the garage after all, but under the carpet in the coach's car, in thin plastic bags. Must have been half a dozen girls, with gynecological evidence of each.

When he'd tossed them on the table in front of Roberta Arston, she'd broken down. Obviously, she'd known. Trying to protect the coach's memory, she said. He was really a good man and she'd loved him, she'd sobbed. Good man. Right. Well, that had been that. Mrs. Arston would no longer be working at Cassavora High School or any other school in the state. Sympathy for her eluded him.

Then he had to go through the sad, sad process of questioning the girls and their parents. Evidently, Mrs. Arston hadn't been directly involved in the photos, but she'd known and didn't say a blessed thing. The city attorneys didn't want to prosecute on scant evidence and, as usual, the city fathers didn't want to prosecute no matter what the evidence.

That was one piece of the pie, but another important question was why Roberta Arston happened to be driving in front of the Post Office at the precise time the coach's body lay cold on the ground. You didn't have to go by the Post Office to get to the high school, and it had been almost school time when the body was called in. Plus, the coach had been back from the road. Mrs. Arston's story was she'd been there to mail a letter. If that were true, why hadn't she gotten out of her car to take a look at what she'd reported as a man on the ground? Bobby from the EMT crew said the caller hadn't known if the man was hurt or drunk or what. Strange she was a PE teacher, probably trained in CPR and first aid, had been close enough to drop a letter in the box, but hadn't walked over.

*****

Close and angry summed up the atmosphere in C2's office. A small table and armchair had been shoved out into the hallway and a thin, spindle legged library table substituted. The space just didn't work, but it would have to do.

Lucinda Whitehall and her lawyer, Earle McCandles, the same McCandles who acted as attorney for the school board, sat alone on one side of the library table. On the other, C2 scratched out some last minute notes. A few manila folders lay scattered. Sheriff Goddard sat next to him and stared down at his hands, fingers intertwined and resting on his lap. Nobody was smiling and nobody was saying anything, leaving C2's pen as the loudest thing in the room.

Goddard looked at McCandles, tall, thin, white shirt, red, power tie and a nicely tailored gray, pinstripe suit. That suit probably cost as much as one of my deputies makes in a month, Sam thought. Look at his hair, dark, with gray at the temples, well trimmed, not a strand out of place. Didn't get that from a ten-dollar haircut.

Sam's mind drifted back to his earlier meeting with C2. The chairman had been adamant about what he wanted to do, although it flew in the face of Sam's instincts, not to mention the police view of law enforcement. The whole thing left Sam a little galled. He didn't relish having to belly up to deals as the lawyers and judges seemed prone to do. Call it professional pride, but Sam and his inexperienced task force had done a good job of seeing this thing through. They lined up three witnesses, which was not to say the best witnesses, but they also had evidence Sam would be proud to take to court. He knew the *whys* and *wherefores*. He knew the *what* and the *who*. What else could a county sheriff hope for? He looked over at C2, scratching away, and saw a politician in the best and worst sense. C2 had a good legal mind and more insight into the workings of the county than any other ten people. And, given the notorious fickleness of juries, with a public trial the whole thing could end up as just another bad memory. The only hard labor might be what he and his deputies put in to get the case to court.

There was something else, something Sam couldn't quite put into words, but it felt heavy in his gut. This story wasn't yet being told in its entirety. There were those loose ends. The pieces kept filtering through his mind. It was a cop thing, an honest man thing.

C2 glanced up, pulled at the neck of his shirt once again. His voice was firm. "I think it's about time we get on with this procedure. As everyone knows, Mrs. Whitehall has taken some actions that in my opinion disqualify her for the office she holds." Sam almost chuckled out loud at C2 addressing Lucinda as Mrs., in light of her noted preference for Doctor, or superintendent.

"Mr. Chairman, I have some remarks I wish to make on behalf of my client."

C2 held up his hand and stared hard at the lawyer. "Counselor, you'll have all the time you want to make your pronouncements, but please let me finish. This isn't a court of law." He left his hand in the air a moment and kept eye contact until he saw McCandles sit back in his chair. "Now, I have a proposal I think will satisfy the delicate needs of this special situation."

"Just a minute." McCandles interrupted again, his voice rising. "It has never been proven that my client committed any malfeasance whatsoever in the performance of her duties. For anyone to suggest we should move through anything more than an exploratory phase is absolutely absurd."

C2 looked at him again and pursed his lips. "Mr. McCandles, the whole point of this exercise is to come to grips with a solution that is palatable to the whole community. We have no wish to drag this county through a public mudslinging affair ... excuse the choice of words." He'd facetiously accented affair. "It wouldn't do us or your client any good." C2 strained to keep his annoyance below the surface. "But, we are willing to take judicial action if that becomes necessary. Protest all you want, but you know we have proof of malfeasance, not to mention morally objectionable acts. We've sent you the particulars. But, if you want a quick review ... and to outline everything clearly for the benefit of those in this room ... your client was having an affair with Coach Gibbons."

"You can't prove that." McCandles' eyes burned into C2's; the muscles on his tanned face tightened.

C2 ignored him and continued. "When he had his heart attack, she panicked and with some help from her assistants, loaded the body in the back of her red Ford Aerostar and dumped it .... "

"Please!" Lucinda burst out. "Stop! I don't want to hear it!"

C2 was merciless. " ... Dumped the body at the Post Office." His voice echoed his exasperation. "You two get your drama together! I'll give you time to practice, if you want. I can either tell the tale or not, one way or another, we're going to get ourselves through this! Now which is it?"

McCandles leaned over and whispered something to Lucinda, who seemed to quiet a little. She reached into her handbag and took out a Kleenex, dabbed around her eyes without disturbing the tears. She sniffed twice and waited.

To the sheriff, Lucinda acted more like a TV preacher caught on videotape than a Superintendent of Schools. He could imagine how much pity she would show if this were one of her teachers.

"Mr. Chairman, please go on." McCandles glared, but at the same time reached up to pat his slicked back hair, as though he were in the middle of a courtroom and couldn't afford to have the camera catch him disheveled.

"As I was saying, she loaded the body in her van and dropped it off at the Post Office."

"How do you know it was her van, Mr. Chairman?"

"Sheriff, would you like to answer that?" C2 glanced at Goddard.

"The fibers on the body matched the fibers from the back of her van."

"How do you know? I'd like to see the lab report!"

"I can show you the report, Mr. McCandles," the sheriff continued, "in a court of law if necessary, but the fibers on the body are consistent with a late model red Ford."

"There must be dozens in this county alone!" McCandles seemed to have forgotten there was no jury for him to play to.

"Actually, there are only five cars in Cassavora County that could have matched up with the fibers in question." Sam's voice was even.

"You see." McCandles was exuberant. "There you go! Five that match up and you picked my client because it just happened to be convenient."

"I picked your client," Goddard said, "Because none of the other Fords in this county had red carpet. There were three blacks and a tan and a cream, as I recall. By the way, your client's van is registered in Morse County."

"That doesn't prove anything. The vehicle could have come from any number of counties."

"There were also three of Mrs. Whitehall's hairs on the Coach's shirt."

"Where did you get a hair sample?" He flung up his hands in a gesture of exasperation. "My client hasn't submitted a hair sample, and I won't permit her to do so without a court order. Furthermore, I would like to know how you obtained the carpet fibers!"

C2 didn't want to have to say the hair samples came from the front seat of Dr. Whitehall's van, but he didn't squirm. "Nobody is asking your client to do anything. You seem to forget, counselor, the reason we're here is to keep the courts out of it." C2 had had enough of the histrionics. "What I'm telling you is, you want to go to court, we'll damn sure go to court!"

C2 turned to Sheriff Goddard. "Sam, tell our legal friend what else you have and let's put this thing to bed. Sorry, Lucinda."

"We have three witnesses who saw the body being carried and we know the name of the worthy assistant who helped her."

"Now." C2 continued, looking straight into Mr. McCandles' eyes. "I'm trying to protect your client and this county and come to an equitable solution that's good for everybody, but you're making it hard to do when you keep fighting me every step of the way. So, I'll answer a few more of your questions, put all my cards on the table and tell you what I want in return. To start with, her helper, Horace Gordon, has not agreed to cooperate with us, but I have the distinct feeling a short look at the consequences and a trip to the witness stand may change his mind." He paused and when no one said anything, he continued. "I'm offering your client a good deal. She doesn't have to admit anything, or make a plea. All she has to do is sign this resignation saying she has served this county long and well and has decided to pursue other options." He tapped the paper in front of him with a forefinger. "She has enough time in to retire and we would not interfere with her normal retirement or pension in any way."

"Why would my client drop a body off at the Post Office, assuming she had anything at all to do with this sordid matter?"

"Good question. Sheriff?" C2 once again turned toward Sam Goddard.

"She wasn't taking the body to the Post Office. She was taking a live man, who had had a heart attack to Doctor Perry's office, which is about a hundred yards further down the road. Perry's her cousin, by the way, not to mention a silent partner with Sob Jenkins' Contractors. Turns out he was out of town, so the superintendent never did get a hold of him. While you're considering the situation, you may also want to consider the coach did not die at Mrs. Whitehall's house. Lab reports show the heart attack was not initially fatal. That makes the superintendent's actions clearly criminal."

"What exactly are you saying, Mr. Chairman?" McCandles leaned forward, no doubt gearing up for a rebuttal.

"I'm saying if your client had taken better care of her lover, if she had called an ambulance or our rescue and recovery team and gotten him to a hospital instead of wringing her hands and wasting time trying to guard her own backsides, the man might still be alive today."

"That's preposterous! The medical report said Mr. Gibbons was dead at the scene."

"He was declared dead at the scene." This was thin ice and the commissioner wanted to move on. C2 paused and then continued, "My guess is she parked where she did to avoid anyone seeing her car. She and her assistant probably planned to stay off the road, in the shadows. She didn't do a very good job with that, by the way. One of my witnesses saw all of them under a streetlight. But, on the way to the doctor's office," he continued, "your client and her helper figured out the coach had already died or was going to. Failing to raise the good doctor by cell phone, they panicked and dropped him off near some bushes, which happened to be near the Post Office. They were running out of time and darkness and they knew it. The trouble is, the coach wasn't dead yet. But, he was getting there."

"You can't prove any of that."

"Try me. Just say the word and we'll go to court. I had to talk to the sheriff here for a good hour to get him to agree to this arrangement. He's chomping at the bit to go to court. He may have even more to say about the school system and building contracts and Lucinda, her husband, and our friend Sob Jenkins." C2's voice had none of the awkward tones of a man under pressure. It made Sam know for sure he wouldn't want to play poker with him.

McCandles stared hard at the chairman of the Board of Commissioners. "What exactly are you asking for?"

"I thought I made that pretty clear. I want her to sign this resignation ... today ... right now, before we walk out of this room."

"Resignations are normally submitted to the Board of Education," McCandles countered.

"This one will be also, but I want it signed right now. The other thing you can do, since we are operating in a democracy, is to insist we prove our case. Now, I'm just guessing, but I think when this thing blasts into the open, two things are going to happen regardless of the outcome of the trial. First, we are going to have a very surprised husband, because my hunch is Mr. Whitehall is ignorant of the situation between his wife and the coach. The second thing is the State Professional Ethics and Practices Committee is going to look very hard at Mrs. Whitehall's conduct and her moral qualifications to hold the office of superintendent. That could just about finish her in educational circles, as well as put her pension in jeopardy. But, you know all this already. You knew it before you stepped into this room, so why don't you quit the foot dragging and let's get on with it. Just tell me if she's going to sign or we're taking this thing to court." C2 had the weary look of a triumphant gladiator standing over his prostrate opponent, waiting only for a thumbs up or a thumbs down. Without waiting for further comments from McCandles, C2 added. "We're looking at involuntary manslaughter, at the very least."

"You wouldn't dare charge my client with manslaughter, voluntary or otherwise."

"You know, Mr. McCandles," C2 said evenly, "you've spent most of your time practicing school law."

"I assure you I am qualified to take this case as far as you wish to take it."

"I'm sure you are. In addition to our little school system, you also handle a number of systems in the city and in some other nearby counties." He didn't wait for an answer. "One thing you ought to realize is in the big city a case like this might be neglected or plea bargained, but in Cassavora, if we do go to trial, we'll go after your client, hard. Manslaughter might be just a note on the blotter in the big city, but it is sure a big deal here. If you go to court, you can kiss off your free time until this case is over. How are your other clients going to feel about that?"

Lucinda Whitehall was clearly shaken. She turned slightly, looked at her attorney, mouth agape. Then she did a very uncharacteristic thing. She began to cry, not in the TV tears many public figures have mastered, but in deep, gasping sobs. Goddard wondered if she were finally feeling pain, or if this were still just a continuation of self-pity. No one moved to put an arm around her or offer comfort. He suddenly realized he had come to loathe this woman altogether, the imperial tones she used on the telephone, the haughty way she conducted her school board meetings, the constant lies and infuriatingly false smiles. Something deep in his guts pulled at him, had him hoping she would turn down this deal so he could see her quiver and whine in court, watch her toppled with all the refinement and modesty of a whore being thrown out of a tavern.

But, as a deep acid rage came over him, his professional attitude surged, rinsing the personal dislike from the walls of his mind. This was just a case like any other. There was no complete justice and there never had been. In this instance, he had done his job, tracked down the culprit. Now, he could go back to thinking about those important parts of his life, like Elmira, and getting coffee from Millie at the Arches and being sheriff for a few more years. He let his mind drift and the rancor seemed to float away.

McCandles looked at Lucinda and then back at C2. "Mr. Chairman, may I have a short consultation with my client?"

"Certainly. Just step out in the hall, if you don't mind."

When the superintendent and her lawyer left the room, neither C2 nor the sheriff spoke. Silence was a leaden cloak no one had the strength to lift. Presently Lucinda and Mr. McCandles came back in and sat down. Lucinda wasn't looking too cheerful and her eyes avoided the sheriff's and the chairman's. She didn't say anything. McCandles did the talking.

"We've decided to accept your offer, but we have one condition."

"We didn't come here to negotiate with your client."

"I understand, Mr. Chairman, but we must agree my client will not be further charged with anything associated with her duties as superintendent."

"I can't promise that." C2 sounded outraged. "For all I know she embezzled money or killed somebody else. I haven't followed her around. I don't know everything she's done or hasn't done. No, sir! This deal is for what we all know about and agree to. And believe me, counselor, believe me, I'm doing this only because I think it's for the good of the county. If this little episode weren't going to bring disgrace on the whole school system and make us look like the Peyton Place of the state, we wouldn't be sitting here at all. Furthermore, if this episode were a higher order crime, we'd settle it elsewhere. We have peculiar circumstances here. The coach died a natural death, not counting Lucinda's playing hide and seek with him. He has no family to complain about how his body was treated. And, somehow a lid has been kept on the details. Now, take it or leave it. I'm not even signing any sort of an agreement. Because if this gets out ... breaks out in the open ... the first thing I'm going to do counselor is sacrifice your client." C2 knew if the word ever got out, the superintendent wouldn't be the only one on the political altar. He pulled at his collar once again, the only chink in his air of confidence.

When Dr. Whitehall and her lawyer left, C2 spoke with the sheriff. "Sam, do you think you're going to be able to keep things quiet?"

"Now's a fine time to ask me! Only three people have put the whole thing together, you, my chief deputy and me. You know John Howard?"

"Sure I do."

"I told him this is just one of those times he's going to have to bite his lip and realize the punishment is for the superintendent to resign. That's money out of her pocket, loss of a job and the county gets to keep its face out of the mud. A trial probably wouldn't do much more than that, anyway. He and I talked awhile and he's okay with it. As far as law enforcement is concerned, it's just another man who died of a heart attack. It's not murder, rape, or robbery, so I think it'll just fade."

"We could lie a little and tie up the loose ends."

Goddard shook his head no. "Saying nothing is better than lying."

"Good. But, I have news for you, the three of us are not the only people who have the whole picture. Other people in this county realize what it would do to business and especially the real estate business if we had corruption and moral turpitude plastered on every front page across the state."

The sheriff looked at C2, expecting more of an answer.

C2 reached up, put a hand on Goddard's shoulder. "I don't run this county by myself, you know. This solution didn't come to me in a dream. I had some help from ... as I said, people who think Lucinda might be bad for business."

"What about her assistant?" Sam asked.

"He's got five years to go to retirement and a kid in college. He'd be a fool to open his mouth and if he does we can charge him as an accessory. And, it wouldn't surprise me if Lucinda had a thing going in that direction, too."

"My, but the lady does get around."

"The witnesses?"

"We know Margaret Tillsmore has no idea exactly what she saw and I defy anyone to make sense of anything Jimmy Joe says. As for Martha Bonner, I suspect she has her own secrets to keep."

"How about Mr. Jake Morgan?"

"He brought us two of the witnesses," the sheriff said, "and he's turned up some interesting details about Sob Jenkins Inc., but that's about as far as it goes. I'd be surprised if he knows any details."

"Well, talk to him and make sure."

"I will, Mr. Chairman."

"I guess that's the end of it then." C2 let out a sigh.

"I certainly hope so, for all our sakes. Now, I just have two more questions Mr. Chairman." C2 waited.

"Why did McCandles cave so easily?"

"Simple. We gave his client a super deal. Besides, he makes money either way and this way uses less of his time. Then there's the little matter of something he and a few of his associates want to build. I told him we might be able to help. What's the second question?"

"Wait a minute. So this little back room charade was a slam-dunk from the beginning? This whole thing sounds a little personal. Do you know McCandles from somewhere?"

"Yeah, I know him. He was the quarterback on the 1955 Foster County team. Now I've got a question for you. What about the phone confession you got?"

"Disgruntled football fan from another county. The sheriff over there is handling it."

"Any other loose ends?"

The sheriff slapped C2 on the back and smiled without saying anything. Loose ends? Probably a million of those little beggars. Who was C2 kidding? All of the commissioner's laundry wasn't spotless either. It could have been him sitting there, shaking and crying.

The school system is the county and the county is the school system. You can't separate them. —Dr. Lucinda Whitehall superintendent, remarks prior to her resignation

But, it wasn't the end of it. At the next school board meeting, the superintendent gave her heartfelt reasons for stepping down after six years of what she called, "the very marrow of my life," in order to accept a position as educational consultant with Todd, Limonson, & Jackson, an educational consulting firm in the city, not so far away that she would have to move her residence.

If she were ill at ease, it didn't show in her face or her voice. She actually smiled as she said, "My life and my husband's life are interwoven in this community." She even left the door open for further community service, which made Sam Goddard, standing at the rear of the room, wince.

Chairman Tom Millage got to his feet, something he never did during a meeting, and regretfully accepted what he called a bittersweet surprise. Sweet because he knew Dr. Whitehall would go on to even greater things and bitter because her resignation was a pill the community would have to reluctantly swallow. He asked her twice during the meeting if she were absolutely sure of her decision and each time, much to Sam's relief, she said she was.

The board voted unanimously to accept the superintendent's resignation and declared by a show of hands the search for a new superintendent would begin immediately.

The search began, some two weeks later, with few surprises. Tom Millage assumed the role of chairman of the search committee. The superintendent's assistant, Horace Gordon, was a member, as was Harriett Hightower, the principal at Elgore Elementary. Two parents represented the community.

The committee decided, due to the current superintendent's imminent departure, a nationwide search was out of the question. Cost became another salient consideration. A nationwide search by a specialized firm went for as much as twenty thousand dollars, whereas the firm of Todd, Limonson, & Jackson, the superintendent's new employer, agreed to aid the committee for a consulting fee of a mere five-thousand dollars. One of the parents on the committee resigned in protest of what she said was, "The most blatant case of back scratching, brother-in-law-ism I've ever heard of." She was replaced by the Teacher of the Year.

For the next month, the committee issued periodic updates through the board, until at last, some forty-five days later, they announced they had selected a man who had done so much for the community in a variety of positions, a man whose loyalty to the School System and the children of the county could never be questioned, Mr. Able Perkins. Although Mr. Perkins did not hold advanced degrees, his thriving business, his grandchildren attending Cassavora's schools and his previous services to the county made him the perfect selection. The board then proceeded to begin the selection for a new board member to replace Mr. Perkins.

When Tom Millage got home, C2 called him. "Tom, I understand you've picked a new superintendent."

"Yes, we picked Able Perkins. I think you know him."

"Of course I know him. We were commissioners together, for God's sake!" C2 didn't know which he liked least, the man's ignorance or his tone of voice.

"He'll have to resign as a board member."

"When?"

"We accepted his resignation this evening. Now we're all set to work on picking a new board member."

"That's already been done for you."

"What do you mean, done for us?" It was Tom's turn to sound a little hostile, as if the commissioner were usurping the Board of Education's powers. "The law says the board will pick someone to serve the remainder of the term. That's what we did last year when Percival Smith died. We picked Caldwell Robbins, not that that was such a good choice."

"This is a different situation." C2 sounded every inch the lawyer who knew the law and was going to quote it for you.

"What difference?" Millage sounded off balance, trying vainly to conjure up the punch line.

"I mean the state dictates if, for whatever reason, death, resignation, whatever, the elected member in a county election is not willing or able to serve within sixty days following an election, the candidate with the next highest vote total shall be declared to have been elected. Unless there was a tie and then you need to have a run off."

The wheels spun in Able Perkins' head and finally found some traction. "So, you're telling me in January, when the new board assumes office, that Morgan fella, who lost the election, is going to be a board member?" Consternation reigned, as Mr. Millage scrambled for something to tell his fellow board members, other than he had screwed up and gotten caught short by not knowing the rules. "There must be a way around this thing."

"I'm telling you that's what the law says."

*****

Millage called Jake directly. Caught him at home, at night. "So, that's the story. If you want the job, Mr. Morgan, it's yours." His voice reflected no bitterness. That's the way the game was played. When you got your ass kicked, you wore the imprint of the shoes without complaint and waited your turn.

Jake said he'd get back to him and suddenly felt like the dog who'd chased a car and caught it. He'd worked his tail off, but now had a quivering feeling it wasn't what he wanted. Law or no law, he also wrestled with the element of fairness. Voters might be stuck with him, but they hadn't chosen him. He knew that wasn't the normal reaction. Politicians lived to be elected. Period.

Cecilia called to offer congratulations. Jake offered them right back. Her Senator had won another term. In the back of his mind, he wondered how she found out about his turn of fortune so fast.

"We need to celebrate."

"Sure," he said, "Your bed or mine?"

"I was thinking more on the order of making you dress up, plying you with ten dollar martinis and feeding you a slab of Kobe beef."

"Think you can afford that?"

"No way. It's on the Senator's account."

"Tempting," he said, but his voice wasn't as positive as he wanted it to be.

"What's the matter, being a politician starting to get on your nerves already?"

"I'm not sure I'm cut out for the job."

"You need a martini worse than I thought." She drove him to a teppanyaki restaurant so exclusive it didn't have a sign out front. The valet took the keys and spoke to her by name.

"Where'd you find this place?"

"Don't try to come here on your own," she laughed.

"I couldn't afford it anyway." Lobster with wasabi cream sauce was heavenly, the wine superb. Dessert at Jake's house was even better.

*****

The sheriff and John Howard hovered over another taped phone call. At least one of the voices was all too familiar. Goddard took a deep breath, then pushed rewind and started the tape again.

"He's having women over to his house in the middle of the night."

"What's he doing with them?" Leave it to John Paul to lend the benefit of the doubt.

Thelma Norton, the village wag sounded indignant as a wronged wife. "What do you think he's doing with them?"

"Excuse me ma'am. What do I think he's doing with them?" There was a pause, no doubt to allow time for John Paul to rack his brain. "Well, I don't rightly know."

"They come and go in the middle of the night." Slam-dunk logic from Thelma.

"So there's nothing wrong with them. Is that right?"

"He's not killing them, if that's what you mean."

"Do they appear to be afraid?"

"Mercy, boy, but you are thick."

"I've been trying to lose weight."

Goddard pressed the stop button on the recorder. "I've changed my mind about John Paul. Found a new use for him. Complaints."

"Yeah," John Howard said, "He rates his own office."

"And his own phone."

"Put a sign on the door, Irrational Complaint Dept."

"Think we could get him on the next ballot for commissioner?"

"Or make him Superintendent of Fools."

"Let's hire Thelma to be his secretary."

*****

The decision wasn't quick. The tough ones never are. But, Jake knew which direction his mind pointed. He hunkered down in his house for most of a day, disconnected the phone, stayed the hell off the Internet, took a jog, rearranged his closet, pretended not to hear the doorbell.

The next night he met Skeeter for a beer, right across the county line, a ripped t-shirt and jeans, gravel parking lot, tin roof place. The stools creaked, the lighting hummed and a little bit more beer slopped on the floor didn't change anything. The jukebox twanged on and on about broken hearts and pickup trucks.

"You didn't call me down here to give me celebratory news."

"Perceptive, Skeeter."

"So, I'm right? You're not taking the job?"

"Fraid so."

Skeeter took a sip, wiped the back of his hand across his lips. "What the fuck was all this about? Running all over the county, sweating like an Eskimo in Miami."

"This was a close up look at what we've been fightin' for."

"Shit. We weren't fightin' to make the world safe for new apartment complexes or get assholes elected."

"What were we fightin' for, Skeeter?"

"Me? I was in it for the pussy."

"That's why you've been a safely married man a few decades."

"You sayin' I'm not getting any good stuff at home?"

"Spare me the details."

"Jake, you really need to think about what you're gaining and what the hell you're throwing away. What does your politico girlfriend think?"

"Might as well discuss vegetables with a shark. Politics is her lifeblood. She thinks I'm nuts."

"That assessment gets my vote."

"Maybe. But, I've had my fill of shoveling shit in a sewer."

Skeeter took another sip. "A bit harsh. Lots of good people supported you. Far as I know, they still do."

"Too few."

"You thought the movers who run Cassavora were just going to cave? You walked in looking for a fight."

Jake shrugged. "I underestimated the raw power of ignorance. This battle could take a lifetime. I don't plan to devote the rest of mine."

"Problem is, you stirred up the hornets, promised to wipe out the nest, but now you're walking away."

"The hornets will go back to their hive and I've got a feeling nobody else is going to pick up a stick and start whacking. Maybe someday they will, but not now."

"I never, ever thought I'd see you walk away from a fight. And how about the kids?"

"They got parents who ought to give a shit. Besides, I'm not walking away, I'm disengaging. When you're out of ammo and outnumbered, nothing wrong with that, right?"

The real surprise was that Cecilia had been okay with it. She said they'd manage, which sounded to Jake a lot like commitment.

*****

Tom Millage told Jake there was a week until the next school board meeting. He used every minute of it, even brought Cecilia into it again. She understood. She came over to the house, and they had another sweet night. It had him thinking this might be something after all. He told her he wanted to sell the house, move somewhere, anywhere. True to form, she suggested he rent it. More money, especially with depreciation, etc. She cleverly suggested he could move in with her until they found a place they both liked. He asked if he could bring his own curtains.

He also called his closest supporters and on the advice of Sam Goddard, he spoke with C2. The commissioner didn't seem fazed. For the most part, politicians deal with what is, not with what they want things to be.

Jake attended the school board meeting, thanked his supporters and said how sorry he was he would have to decline the honor. The dead silence ranked higher than applause. Even

Millage and Perkins didn't say a word or break a smile. Cleveland sat in the back of the room, along with Skeeter, Maria, and a bunch of others Jake had spoken with along the way. Maria was a surprise. Probably Mama told her not to worry. Jake had a feeling that's the way things generally played out in that household.

Cynthia Farnsworth and Marcella Stokes brought arms full of notebooks, just in case.

When Tom Millage had announced Jake's name at the start, a scattering of applause had broken out, followed by a pounding of the gavel and Tom's stern instructions to "Please delay these outbursts to a more appropriate time," whenever that was supposed to be.

Jake offered a few remarks anyway about freedom of speech and democracy. He squeezed in a kicker. "This board is also going to have to address the important issue of buying land and building schools."

Millage, beet red, gave his gavel another workout, silencing everyone, including Jake. In the far corner, Stephanie Porcose shot Jake a thumbs up. She'd told him she was withdrawing her resignation.

The next week's *Advocate* brayed about Jake Morgan and how he incited the crowd. Editor Wilbur Simons wondered if Mr. Morgan would continue to disrupt the Board of Education's attempt to be a positive factor in the lives of Cassavora's children.

*****

Ten days later the city newspaper ran an article about a case being looked into by the State Bureau of Investigation.

Allegations surfaced of a major construction firm giving kickbacks to various county officials in return for preferential treatment in the letting of construction projects. Evidently, some realtors were also involved. The investigations were on going and no names had been released, but arrests were expected shortly. A grand jury was being convened.

The Cassavora Advocate was mute on the subject.

54

My novels plot themselves. They don't need any help from you or me. —
Jake Morgan

Jake met Mr. Wilbur Walkins and Ms. Gwendolyn Price-
Shuberry at a nondescript, but expensive restaurant, off one of
the main, traffic-clogged arteries in the city. He'd received an
invitation, under an exquisite Wicked Willow Press letterhead,
expressing great interest in his romance novel, or at least saying
they liked the first three chapters, which was three more than
anyone else had admitted liking. Jake was excited, eager,
unexpectedly happy, and swept up in other such unreasonable
emotions.

Cecilia had set everything in motion. She hadn't said as
much, but publishers don't just call unknown authors and offer
to meet them for cocktails and dinner. She'd let a couple of
hints drop about the Senator publishing his own book on the
state of world affairs and how one hand washes the other. As far
as Jake was concerned, the cliché didn't work for politics. But,
here he was, of his own volition, but with creeping reservations.
If he'd learned anything at all about life outside the military, it
was the power of hidden agendas, sliding under society like
tectonic plates. What would this seismic shift in opportunities
mean? A favor owed, an offer made, a book published? Or, was
the offer enough. He certainly cared and he was pretty sure of
Cecilia, but how about the Senator? Anyway, here he was, white
shirted, tied, coated.

Mr. Walkins looked to be about forty-years-old, thinning
hair, glasses, wearing khaki slacks, a sport coat and bow tie. With
red hair shining kinky and bright, only rapidly advancing age
prevented Ms. Price-Shuberry from being a stand-in for Annie.

She ordered a large bottle of Perrier and a dish of lime wedges, smiling indulgently, as if it were an iffy prospect in this tiny corner of the world and the waiter might scratch his crotch and say something Southern, like, "I'll send da help out back to da creek." Instead, he just nodded and looked to Mr. Walkins.

Noting his colleague's success, Mr. Walkins also ordered Perrier. Jake asked the waiter for a beer, no glass.

"We both were very impressed with your novel," Ms. Price-Shuberry began, showing a Cheshire cat smile and a flutter of white napkin that billowed to her lap.

"Very impressed," echoed Mr. Walkins, his voice perhaps only an octave lower than a wounded eunuch's.

"We'd like to discuss the possibilities for your property," Ms. Price-Shuberry said. She looked to Mr. Walkins to continue the glad tidings.

"We have just a few things we'd like you to consider."

"To give the novel a more, how shall I say it?" pondered Ms. Price-Shuberry. She didn't have to ponder long.

"A more today look," offered Mr. Walkins.

"Exactly! As it stands, your work is more yesterday."

"That's because it's a *historical* romance," Jake said.

"Still, there are some things." Ms. Price-Shuberry continued.

Jake looked from one to the other. "Go ahead." Mr. Walkins smiled, showing large, white, beaver-like teeth.

"It's nothing really. Just cosmetic. We see a shift to the Western milieu coming for the romance genre. A more westerly wind, shall we say," he smiled again, pleased with his own nuance, "Your story takes place in Scotland."

"It's in Scotland all right." Jake tipped the bottle and took a gulp.

"That is easily remedied," Ms. Price-Shuberry explained patiently. "We thought you might consider placing it in Amarillo."

"Amarillo? As in Texas? How 'bout the pirates? Want 'em to ride steers?"

Mr. Walkins ignored the comment. "You see, the desert could be a metaphor for the high seas." No, Jake did not see. "You could use some thoroughly unsavory galoots in place of pirates." Walkins was nothing if not helpful.

"Galoots," Jake repeated, rolling the word off his tongue as a dung beetle would his favorite meal.

"Nothing much grows in either place," said Ms. Price-Shuberry, the budding botanist.

"How about the quest for ancestral lands?" Jake inquired hesitantly, his mind spinning with the range of answers.

"We'd like you to consider Alamogordo."

"New Mexico." He said it flatly, without emotion, as one would attempt to pacify the incurably insane.

"Just as a starting point," said Mr. Walkins. "That used to be in Mexico you know. Mexico has the flavor of romance."

"I'm reminded with every nacho," Jake murmured, but they ignored him.

"Yes, after that, the sky's the limit," said Ms. Price-Shuberry jubilantly, "You could throw in Taos or even Santa Fe."

"Not Santa Fe." Mr. Walkins wrinkled his nose. "Too clichéd. Then there's the matter of your heroine."

"What about her? Too short? Wanna make her a volleyball player? A canasta card shark?"

"Not mainstream enough," Mr. Walkins continued, as though the discussion were progressing nicely. "We thought she might be an Indian maiden. I don't mean Indian. I mean Native American." He shot Ms. Price-Shuberry a glance for guidance.

She shook her head to indicate even this did not appease her keenly sensitive self. "I prefer the term *Americano Nativo*. After all, it was Hispanics who settled the American west."

"Not Hispanics," Jake corrected, "Spaniards. A fearsome race. When it came to dispatching *los Americanos Nativos*, the Seventh Calvary were choirboys compared to *los conquistadores*. They did some hardcore *cajone* collecting."

She blinked, evidently not comfortable with harsh or even differing opinions. Then, her cell phone rang, and she dropped out of one conversation and into another, whispering loud enough to keep all but the deaf from eavesdropping.

"How about the sex and violence?" Jake asked brightly. "Everybody okay with knuckles and nooky?"

Mr. Walkins locked eyes with Ms. Price-Shuberry, who nodded, while continuing her scintillating cell phone conversation. "Well, there is just one thing."

"I'd be thrilled to hear."

"Your hero might be more *au current* if he were gay."

"I don't know anything about gay."

Ms. Price-Shuberry smiled obsequiously. "We have consultants on how to best portrait the gay life-style." Jake looked at Mr. Walkins and gave him a wink.

"No!" Walkins stammered. "Not me! I mean I..." Jake didn't let him finish.

"How 'bout bestiality, too? Does he have to strain his hemorrhoids with old Paint's fire hose?"

After dinner, Jake called Cecilia, who wanted to know how it went. He told her and she was silent for a moment.

"Doesn't sound good."

"That'd be my guess."

"But, not hopeless. I'm going to make a few calls."

"Cecilia, wait. I don't want you to make this happen."

"My romantic, darling Jake. You want it to happen because you've written a good romance, which you have. You want politics and publishing and everything else to rise to the moral level of duty and love of country." She said with a soothing lilt.

"I wouldn't say that exactly."

"I know you wouldn't. Look, you wrote a good book. It deserves to be published and Wicked Willow Press isn't the only publishing house."

"I don't know."

"But, I do. Look, I don't blame you for walking out on that Cassavora circus. I never wanted you to get involved with that crowd to begin with." She said it with a voice silky smooth enough to cut through the political grit and make him smile. "But, this is different. This first book shows your talents and will make money for anyone smart enough to publish it. I'll tell you what you always tell me, suck it up and keep it up. Cassavora was the time to cut and run. No question. This isn't. This is your life. We're going to get your novels published, all of them." Cecilia smiled. "You're going to be my famous lover." The last notes trickled out and her eyes met his.

Jake had to laugh. He'd chosen well. This woman was tougher than he was. He didn't stand a freaking chance.

This is a wonderful little county. It's almost like an extended village. People speak to each other, say good morning. It's the quiet politeness I like. — New resident from Ohio, quoted in the 'Man on the Street' section of The Advocate

Goddard had one more loose end, and he didn't like loose ends. He pulled into Roberta Arston's driveway. The house was half empty, open boxes and rolled rugs lying about. She stood in front of a suitcase, packing clothes as though disgusted with everything she touched. Another open suitcase lay nearby. "Where?" he asked and she smiled a faintly brittle smile.

"Anywhere."

She mentioned her husband wanted reconciliation. She hadn't made up her mind. The woman was definitely walking on a narrow pier over shark-infested waters.

"So, Mrs. Arston, I need to ask you again why you happened to be in front of the Post Office?"

Her voice was tired, resigned. "We've been over this before. I told you everything I'm going to tell you. If you keep asking, you'll get the same answers."

"You know what I think?"

"I don't give a damn what you think!" The tired voice was suddenly alive, angry. "You've ruined my life! You and this nasty little town!"

Sam wanted to slam her up against a wall and beat the answer out of her, but as usual, he restrained himself. It wasn't difficult. These days he'd had a lot of practice. "Well, I'm going to tell you what I think."

She shrugged.

"You followed him. You saw where he went and when he got dropped off at the Post Office in the middle of the night, you waited until everybody else left and went over to have a chat. You'd seen who he'd been with. You were angry, but also concerned. He was your lover and he'd betrayed you. You didn't know if he was hurt or drunk. Betrayal shouldn't have been a shock. I'm sure you knew by then he did that every time he got half a chance."

Tears welled up in her eyes.

"He wasn't dead when you saw him. He was lying on the ground, helpless. So, why didn't you call for help?"

Her face was in her hands, her body shaking. "Why, Mrs. Arston?"

Between sobs she choked out an answer. "What do you want from me?" The voice got higher, more distraught. "My life is destroyed! Isn't that enough? I'm ... I'm not going to say anything more to you, or to anybody."

"What happened? He died right there when you were staring at him?" The anger burned through.

She shook her head still crying. "I'm not going to s ... say ... say anything."

"This was the man you loved? Jesus damn Christ!"

Sam walked out of the house, letting the door slam behind him. What a nasty bunch of worthless little shits this county held! He took a deep breath, walked to his car, opened the door and got in. Another deep breathe.

Things to do. He needed to focus. He rubbed his eyes, took the dark glasses out of his breast pocket and put them on. John Paul needed to find another job, that was for sure. It was past time to disband the clownish S.W.A.T. team. Nothing but promises of more trouble there.

Maybe he needed to swing through the arches and get a cup of coffee from Millie. That would cheer him up. Wonder what Elmira was fixing for supper?